ACCORDS

Artorian's Archives Book Eleven

DENNIS VANDERKERKEN
DAKOTA KROUT

MOUNTAINDALE
PRESS

ACKNOWLEDGMENTS

From Dennis:

There are many people who have made this book possible. First is Dakota himself, for without whom this entire series would never have come about. In addition to letting me write in his universe, he has taken it upon himself to be the most glorious senior editor and keep straight all the madness for which I am responsible, with resulting hilarity therein.

An eternal thank you to my late grandfather, after whom a significant chunk of Artorian's personality is indebted. He was a man of mighty strides, and is missed dearly.

A special thank you to my parents, for being ever supportive in my odd endeavors, Mountaindale Press for being a fantastic publisher, and all the fans of Artorian's Archives, Divine Dungeon, and Completionist Chronicles who are responsible for the popularity allowing this to come to pass. May your affinity channels be strong and plentiful!

Last of all, thank you. Thank you for picking this up and giving it a read. Accords is the continuation of a multi-book series, and I dearly hope you will enjoy them as the story keeps progressing. Artorian's Archives may start before Divine Dungeon, but don't worry! It's going all the way past the end of Completionist Chronicles! So if you liked this, keep an eye out for more things from Mountaindale Press!

Please consider giving us five stars on Amazon, Audible, and anywhere else you'd like to spread the word!

CHAPTER ONE

Cal's pilgrimage drove him through endless labyrinths, only for him to end up lost in a dreamlike space.

Wandering across the great clockwork arms of the intricate machinations that comprised the **Time** layer, Cal soldiered on. His exhausted feet dragged him across a messy, yet seamlessly interwoven network of might and metal as the ineffable construct languished and click-ticked along at exactly the pace it was supposed to. Like a wizard who claimed to always arrive exactly when they meant, and then actually did.

Cal was spent. Worn. Shorn, even! Though that came with the territory of living through the life of a double-S ranker. Not just any, either! *A-leven*, a baffling name for a profoundly intellectual wooly mammoth type creature—with a deep cultural heritage carved right into his tusks—that strode dauntlessly onwards to an unseen end goal.

An end goal that must have been out of reach for Cal as the dungeon knew, *he knew*, that he was there. The barrier was at his claw-tips. The finish line to the double-S ranks seemingly already passed. The journey was surely over! So why…?

Why couldn't… *He. Wake. Up?*

This dreamlike state was endless! Pulling back from climbing this stairway and returning to his soul space had been entirely fruitless on all accounts. He was doing all he could to remain himself. To not be sucked into the solitary solace and pensive depth that A-leven—or Levin for short—adored getting lost in. The double-S ranker freely allowed the sands of time to ebb away during silent, blissful meditation. Patiently spent in a state of nothingness.

"Those years of unmoving silence were awful." Cal mumbled in his usual dungeon voice, unable to stand that exact kind of nothingness and boredom. Cal heard his own words, regardless of a significantly larger mouth moving to speak. He and A-leven were not the same person, after all. At this deep stage of climbing the stairway for ascension towards a higher incarnate rank, it was important to create 'markers' for distinction between oneself and the life followed, or the lives would bleed together. Causing the S-ranker climbing the steps to *lose* that distinction. If they did, they would be lost.

His gait faltered at the thought that this would cause him to be lost forever.

Cal croaked, complaining to find strength. "No! Better to... walk. Celestials, I'm tired. I'm not even awake and I'm tired. I haven't made a pun to anyone in eons, and it's not like you're magically going to respond to me is it, Levin?"

Silence was his only reply, prompting Cal to fill the gap. "No? Shame."

Struggling across an Escher-inspired glass beam several kilometers long but only a few meters wide, he wrestled control of an arm away from the predecessor whose steps he was retracing purely to rub his face for some comfort. Even if the sensations were not human-equivalent. Running claws through Levin's thick fur was divinity itself, the barest tips brushing over the thick spiritual hide underneath a downright blissful affair.

The difference brought a refreshed spark to his eyes when the trundling resumed, though in no time flat did Cal resume reminiscing and talking to himself. He couldn't stand the silence. Which was likely what had saved him from being swallowed up more than anything else. "You know what I miss, Levin? *Books.*"

His voice dropped to a reverent murmur. "The unique smell, the crisp crack of a cover, the rustling of pages both fresh and ancient, even that strange sting up the nose when there's too much glue in the binding."

He could swear the scent was actually there when he thought

of it. "I wonder how many books my early life would have been. Six? Nah, *five*. Definitely five. A nice, smooth number. I was born, had a bit of madness, a small calamity, a wee bit of desolation, and then there was just this eternity. That doesn't make for a good pun. Eternium? I did meet the guy. That sounds better. I'd call it the Divine Dungeon series! It's about me, after all."

Puttering along, he kept on topic. "There should be at least one book on Essence. Like a collection of short stories. Maybe two? Though the second one should be an actual book about Essence, like an explanation guide. I'm sure Sunny would do it if I asked."

Rubbing his mammoth chin, Cal wondered while counting on his borrowed claws. "How many books would Mr. Pillow-lounging pot of wisdom-tea get?"

His eyes narrowed. "Why do I feel it's more than me?"

With a small tinge of jealousy, Cal counted. "I bet... easily ten books by this point alone, and if I call this roughly halfway then we're looking at twenty-one books. Either by conclusion, or by meeting a minimum threshold. The man is *wordy*."

Mulling that over, he clucked his tongue. "Unacceptable, I need to have more books! When I wake up, and get my affairs in order, I'm going to make sure we get some kind of second series going where I'm important."

Cal chuckled. "I'm always important. I'm the only one able to directly and freely remove corruption from anything and everything without needing to put it into something else."

Proud for a moment, he schemed. "What was it the old man said?"

Chuckling to himself, Cal replayed the scene of a fresh-minted Administrator fumbling about his Soul Space. Near the beginning of his own **Acme** journey, Artorian had crashed into the tiny soot-ball that was Hel. As the dust settled, the man laid prone on his back and groaned loudly. With the crashing settled at the bottom of a crater, Artorian the Administrator had coughed out his first pained complaint. "Cal! We need to turn you into a completionist! You can't just outline large sections and then ignore them! Your world has holes in it, and we are going to fix them!"

The words his favored Administrator spoke still felt like a jab to the ribs, but after all these years he'd learned to take such a gentle ribbing as more of a loud and affable outcry of assistance. Those holes in his world really hadn't been intentional, no matter what he might have said at the beginning of book five.

The look on Sunny's face had been so worth it!

He was also glad the whole 'Cale' thing was over. That had started during that exact time as well, hadn't it? "It's Cal! Just call me Cal. Short, simple, sweet, a Divine Dungeon."

He giggled at his own half-joked accolades, then sighed. "Heavens, it's lonely. Distractions! *Completionist*. What a good word! Artorian has his Archives... Those letters match, so these should too. Something with a C. Contemplations? No! *No*. That's Levin sneaking his way into my thinky-space. Not allowed!"

Passing over a particularly noisy clock gear that intersected with his current one, he jumped ship from the current clockwork piece, landing on another before continuing the pilgrimage. He really wished he knew where Levin was going, but according to the mammoth, that was part of the journey. He repeated the mammoth's statement to himself in his slow and humming voice rather often, like a mantra. "Be good and thoroughly lost, before one can find themselves."

Cal shook himself from those musings.

"Correlations? That... means nothing. Conundrums? No, I work through those. Capitalists?" Cal needed to squint, a wave of dread washing over him. "Big no no. I don't know what's up with that one, but it seems like it would upset a whole lot of people. Not doing it."

Ignoring the temperature change as he wormed his way through the freshly made openings of two clicking gears the size of small moons, he thought he had it. "A log of my deeds. My great works. My successes... and my failures. My mistakes. My regrets. My *chronicles*."

"Completionist Chronicles!" he declared loudly, all proud of himself. "Also at least twenty-one books! I can't let longbeard one-up me. I'm sure I can do something to fill the empty void between the covers. Not like I wasn't *always busy* back in my Soul Space. Or I could take a peculiar interest in a few exceptional troublemakers. Follow them around. There's always *some*. Who *wouldn't* want the system to pay lots of attention to them? It's not like I get snarky. Or bored."

He felt a sudden need to shut himself up. The feeling of bristles rose along the back of his neck along with an image playing across his eyes of a grandmother rubbing a thumb over a brand new slipper. That just did something to quench the flame. That, or perhaps it was the sudden addition of a piano playing the funeral march reaching Levin's floppy ears.

"Chopin? That can't be good." Cal had barely uttered the words when the layer went dark. All save for a simple staircase, which formed in front of him out of shards of raw, glimmering existence. The building path provided the only illumination when the eternal gears quieted. Their constant clicking continued unhampered, but was no longer audible to Cal's ears.

A minor detail.

The act that actually frightened Cal was that Levin took a step upwards, and he did not. Forcibly separating from this Incarnate's journey that had reached its end, Cal found himself entirely unable to follow. The journey of a step ended when the person whose life you lived stopped at the end of their rank, and moved on to the next. A point Cal had correctly surmised that they'd arrived at.

Or, at least, the point Levin had arrived at.

For Cal was stuck, and unable to wake from what had quickly become a nightmare. If he could not wake, he would be swallowed up by the journey. Lost forever in the sea of half-life. This dream-like existence of being and non-being. With human hands, he clawed at the staircase that slipped through his fingers like it wasn't there. His voice, becoming more Dale-like, knew only panic. "No, no, no, *no!*"

"Not like this!" He whimpered as the shards of existence fragmented upwards, leaving his grasp entirely, careless of his inability to interact with the staircase. Cal keened in distress as he watched, the eerie wail heard by none. Levin ascended to a higher level of Incarnation and stepped ever further out of his reach, while the place he left sunk into deeper darkness, the visible world fraying at the edges.

Cal's hands sunk into his hair, a copy of Dale's that was slowly but surely manifesting as more and more of Levin's influences left him. Pacing in a circle, Cal's vision began to resemble a tunnel, as no matter where he looked, the options dwindled. Every pathway steadily darkened as empirical information fled from his senses. The plane of **Time** ticked ever onwards, expanding ever outwards, yet he could not hear that telltale sound anymore.

He felt abandoned. Alone. Had he struggled for nothing all this time? Weak in the knees, the strength of puns and cheap jokes that he used to keep himself upright failed him. Cal collapsed to his hands and knees as his wide eyes shot from one patch of growing darkness to the next. He could no longer see where the pathways led, the movements of the clock, or where it was safe to tread. Any movement of the arms could crush him. Any gear could come from nowhere and bisect him.

Levin had a knack for this. The mammoth had been able to traverse the plane with a confidence Cal currently did not share. Like he'd always trusted the pattern, given himself to it, and walked the path without regard to himself. Trusting in luck and fate to see him through. For Levin, that had worked. For Cal, who was so enamored with control over himself and his surroundings, the plane of **Time** closed itself to him.

Thoroughly devastated as thoughts of the end kept hitting him across the mind to smother any others that arose, he pressed his forehead down on the only remaining visible ground.

Then, he surrendered as it all became too much. He could not do this alone. He could not walk the path in solitude. He could not do everything, no matter how badly he wanted to.

He thought he'd learned this lesson with his Liminal tasks, his Soul Space, and his dungeon, but no. The feeling had never truly left him. He'd always believed, like a kernel of **Pride**, that with enough time, he really could do it all. He who never tired. He with the most powerful work ethic. He who loved the nitty gritty details. He who got lost in the fugue of millennia of work, only to secretly be delighted when something broke so he could make it better.

A solution more perfect for the job. More 'correct' for the task. He, tinkerer eternal, could rule over all variables and unknowns! If he only… If he only…

He exhaled his delusions away. "No."

The domain of **Acme**… was not his. That was a concept that did not fit the crafter and creator he was. He was the inventor of the new. The Core with eyes full of stars. The designer. The programmer. The maker. He was no ruler, and could not rule **Acme**.

Nobody could rule perfection.

One could not rule that which did not exist.

He was Calcite. The divine dungeon. The curator!

He was no ruler.

"Please," he whispered to nobody. Nobody but his own soul, as he didn't know who to address when none were here to listen. His voice cracked, breaking as the tears rolled down his cheeks. "*Please, help me.*"

He grit his teeth at the oppressive silence. Nobody was coming.

He had pushed everyone away on his personal quest to build a new world, and this was the price. Keeping his supervisors at arm's length. Keeping the wisdom of an administrator barely near his fingertips. Accepting only the proximity of his direct loved ones, believing it would always be enough so long as he had Dani and Grace. Would they even be there if he woke?

Cal's head lifted only to fall to the ground again. His hiccupping was almost no longer audible to himself as even that began to fade. His fingers squeezed the smooth crystal floor, the vibrations of movement still barely felt. "I'm sorry. I'm so, *so sorry.*"

He closed his eyes, and prepared for it all to quiet as his tears stained his cheeks.

Instead, his fingers felt the vibration in the clockwork hand. A click, the movement of a wheel, the turn of a gear. All methodical. All flawless. All intentional and determined. Then, underneath it all, the brush of an ocean crashing against a shore. Then far, far beneath that…

The plink of a kalimba, reaching out for him as hard as it could.

A hand to all who were lost, when there was nowhere to go, and no one to lean on.

With it, weak as the faintest whisper, the voice of a grandfather.

"*I am here.*"

CHAPTER TWO

Cal's eyes snapped open, he could feel his heart suddenly beat so loud that it rang in his ears. Squeezing his eyes closed to refocus, he grit his teeth and grimaced. Throwing all his attention on that minute, tiny, whisper of a sensation.

He poured himself into the detail, feeling a gut-wrenching pull similar to ranks of Mana being siphoned away as he expended the energy on a technique. Weakened further, he refused to stop. He was wrong! He wasn't alone. Someone was reaching for him. He wanted to question why, but dismissed the notion out of hand. "Gift horse. Mouth. Don't do it."

The smell of sweet honey reached his nose first. Then the tang of seawater as his maddening expenditures of energy paid off. More whispers bled through as he clung to the grandfatherly words for dear life, even as those words too, sounded resigned to some terrible fate. A sympathy experience bound them together. "The path to victory is the path you're on. It becomes a path to victory the moment you decide it does. Step one. Place one's hopes in dreams. Step two. Forward unto dawn. Three. Run the clock."

Then Cal had it! A feeling of something in his grip. Like the end of a fishing line that lacked a hook. With his teeth still clenched, he dared open his eyes to see what he was holding, only to repress deep emotion and another bout of tears. The faint, pulsing, thinnest line of pink light he'd ever seen was coiled between his fingers. Through it, more words reached his ears. A message, meant only for him.

"Sweet dreams are made of these. Hold to hope and reach your seas. The lighthouse shines, and the buoy is down. One foot in front of the other, let your heart resound. Step hard, and listen with your feet to the ground. From one-one-seven, to one, the timer is wound."

Inhaling with force, Cal cried out a powerful yell as he pushed himself to his feet before instantly stumbling forwards as one foot fell in front of the other.

His legs felt like lead, his muscles made of Iridium bricks, and his breathing labored beyond belief. The exhaustion of this climb was catching up to him, and fast. Failure once again tried to claw its way into his thoughts, demanding to be the only thing he could consider.

Cal bit those away too, actually taking advice right away for once as his voice turned breathy instead of emotional. He had to hold on to the things he could do something about, not the things he could not. Nobody went this out of their way to get him data if it wasn't critically useful. "One-one-seven. Numbers. Countdowns. That's... almost two minutes? Or do I count in minutes?"

Answers clicked into his mind like gifts pushed into his hands. "No. *For me*, it's seconds, for the other end of the line, it's minutes."

The number slapped the intrusive thoughts away as he forcibly kept the count in mind. Each second, he subtracted one. The count had begun! He was on a timer now. Intrinsically, he knew that was the maximum length of time he was going to be able to hold on to this lifeline as he wrapped it around his wrist before gripping the pink line again.

Determination and resignation once again bled through the connection. Cal could feel it. As concerning as the latter was, the sensation of determination was a breath of fresh air. He relished the gift. To know the feeling. To be reminded of those pathways. It gave him purpose, and he spoke with newfound vigor. "I... I need to move."

Yet where?

Where did he need to move to? The lifeline did not give him direction, only a connection. He considered the words again, mouthing them sotto voce. "Lighthouse... Shines? What... What did he do at the top of the iceberg to kick me the first time?"

Looking up properly with that thought in mind, a buoy blazed into being in the farthest reaches of the distance. The luminous dot rebuked the darkness, pulsing from on high. Like... like a lighthouse! Cal's eyes widened as he listened to more of the guidance, fumbling one foot in front of the other only to fall and scramble right back up. Only to fall again and repeat the motion. "I must... I must go. One foot... one foot in front of the other. I can do this."

Cal nearly slid from the edge of the clock hand as he stumbled to the right, catching onto the platform before he could roll and fall off. Pulling himself back to flat ground with the strength left in his arms, he laid there with his hand out-stretched to the blip of light, groaning from the exertion.

It was so far away. So, so far away.

He screamed at his inept state, slamming his fist down. The impact resounded with a thud, and he felt the vibration. Breathing loud for a few seconds, he then frowned and hit the ground again, creating another *brrr* that moved as vibration beneath him. He could feel the waves, steady and strong until they petered out. The motion gave him an idea. "Let... Let my heart resound, and listen to the ground?"

Focusing inwards since he was prone anyway, the beat of his heart kept on going, the sound filling his ears. He began by tapping out the rhythm with his palm. *Pat pat. Pat pat. Pat pat.*

Each time he hit the ground, a small vibration ran through the clock arm. With each hit, he could then feel, roughly, where the ground was. Inspiration struck him like the sudden addition of gravity. He could feel where the ground was! Plus edges!

Cal pressed to his feet, no longer trusting his eyes as he dropped his foot to the ground hard with each heartbeat, letting his weight carry him forwards as he focused on matching the pattern. How was his heart so steady and calm when the rest of him felt like he was eating himself alive? "I can't think about that right now!"

He pulled himself forwards like a sack of bricks, moving with a dexterity about equivalent to one. A wave of raw tiredness washed over him three steps in, the fatigue threatening to close his eyes. He couldn't! He wouldn't open them again if he fell to that feeling. "Focus! Fifty-four!"

He'd eaten through over half his time already, but was

nowhere closer to his goal. Cal felt a pang of guilt, and let go of more of himself. "Need... more help. *Help*."

Each request gutted him. The very act of saying the words pulled something core to his being out of him, only to leave a void in its place. He gasped and clutched at his sternum when it happened a second time, far more potent and demanding. The line in his hand began to burn, the marks searing into his wrist. He felt boiling pain, but could not cry out. Instead, the mote of a tiny bee floating by him stole the entire breadth of his attention.

His eyes followed the mote as it floated over his shoulder and passed him. Turning his head, the bee snuffed like a candle, and with that loss of light, his heart fell. But only for exactly the moment of time it took for him to look in front of him again, finding an open, outstretched hand belonging to the Incarnation of the **Sun** as it reached for him.

"D..." His voice failed him when he tried to speak, but his open hand was gripped tight and saved him the trouble. With a heave, Cal's whole being was pulled from the ground like a fancy paperweight. His arm was hauled around Amaterasu's neck, who looked far more yellow in the details than Cal remembered. Her form shifted between the lithe elven woman he knew, and someone sturdier that flickered in and out as the reds and oranges occasionally washed across her frame. He didn't understand the dichotomy of what was happening, but forgot all about asking as the line in his hand pulsed one last time. Grandfatherly words provided their last spoken guidance.

"Run, boy, run."

His feet moved before his mind did. Expecting to fall, he reached out with a hand to brace himself for impact. An impact that did not come as his feet found the ground, then found purchase again, and again, and again. Faster, then faster still as with his arm around Ammy's neck, he could keep pace. The weight of his own being wasn't dragging him down, carried by her silent, burning strength. When he tried to speak again, he was hushed when he'd barely gotten his mouth open.

The voice was Dawn's. "*Shush*! I'm not happy. He *needs* me, but you need me more. I already know that he would have told me to rush for you had it ever come up as a question, but still, he needs me."

She grit her teeth, furious. "And I am *not there*."

Cal felt chastised from her gaze when she turned her head to meet his eyes. That raging, ice-cold fire of a woman scorned by circumstance roiling inside her. Her supernova irises might have been yellow, but they contained all the rage, wrath, and pain of a war being lost when she drilled her glare into him.

His mind told him he should freeze. His body instead was spurred to run faster. To run from this heat he had no chance of fleeing from. A small portion of his mind whispered to him that the fire being lit under his behind was intentional. That no words of support would make him move any faster. Disappointment in him, on the other hand? His heart couldn't abide it. He despised the feeling. His legs found new strength in response as they moved ever faster, straight in the direction of a mote of light with barely twenty seconds left on the timer.

Cal, supported by a silent Amaterasu, broke through the outer edge of **Time**'s current confines with a step that made him feel as though he'd ended up... Not elsewhere in terms of space, but elsewhere in terms of... concept?

"This is as far as I can take you." When Cal glanced at Ammy, there was no sign of the Incarnate he knew. He hadn't noticed at all that she'd dwindled backwards in forms, because he was looking at an ancient silver grandmother of an elf. One with long gray hair, Iridium eyes that had seen too much, and had lived too long without purpose. "I can't go where there's no **Time**."

"Where...?" was all Cal managed to get out before Ember began to disintegrate, her manifested form unable to remain where she was. She cut him off with a quick answer, as she also knew that she'd run her clock dry.

"**Possibility**. Now *run!*" With a final heave of effort, a hand on his back pushed and spurred him onwards before the heat retained by the lifeline faltered entirely. The line around Cal's wrist was no longer hot, nor burning. He had scars on his soul from where they'd cut deep, but he had no time for that.

Stumbling forwards under his own power, the world felt like it would drag him to the ground again when he fell once more. Like a foal, his feet found the ground, but they lacked the stable pattern needed for him to not trip over his own toes. By some miracle, he did not fall.

Cal looked behind him, hoping for a moment Ember was actually still there, and about to catch up. She wasn't.

Instead, he saw the exterior of the clock of **Time**. An unfathomable construct of absolute certainty and deterministic truths. He could see the details again now, no longer confined by the darkness within that told him he was so very unwelcome. The ineffable construct was growing. Expanding. Reaching outwards with the *tick-tock* of another second being claimed. His head snapped around, finding only an empty void, and the single visible pulse of the lighthouse higher in the distance.

He should not look down. He should definitely *not* look down.

Cal looked down, and found neither ground or path to speak of. When his perception caught up to his brain, his interpretation of reality shook its head at him in disapproval. He felt like a stone beginning to crash through the ocean waves, sinking as his own adherence to the concept of gravity tethered him to that truth. A reality he was forced to abide by, as possibility gave way to establishment.

As he fell, he could see the edges of **Time** encroach second by second towards him, large hands clicking outwards in upward swings to form the bracing and skeleton for more gears and detail to shape upon. He flailed with his hands, hoping for any handhold. Any at all as he tumbled into the void. A void that was starting to emanate a feeling of... *hunger*. The identical kind of hunger that he had for *moss*, back in his earliest dungeon days.

That was what he was here, he realized.

Moss.

He felt small and insignificant in the face of it all. The lighthouse felt like it crept ever farther away from him, and a sick feeling crawled up the inside of his throat. An avid consumer himself, he was certain he was falling into an open mouth of some kind. One he couldn't see, or even begin to understand. His thoughts whirled to the only thing they could hold on to. The guidance. The instructions. If they could be called that.

He had been forwarded Dawn. A vessel to drag him out of one endless space, only for him to fall right into another. Wait. No! He was missing one! There was an instruction he hadn't followed yet. Drawing breath, he howled out the words. "Run the clock!"

Instantly, with the idea so strongly in his mind, the arm of a clock appeared beneath his feet in an upwards swing. Cal slammed into the new floor with a groan, then felt the vibration below him as the arm clicked upwards. Inching closer in the direction of the lighthouse as the timer flared to the forefront of his mind. "Six."

Six? How was he *ever* going to make that?

The arm moved again when the count became five, the angle of the hand having inched even closer to the dot of light. Cal badly wanted to look behind him. To gain control of the knowledge and understand what the back of the hand was connected to. Where it had come from. Why a single hand was so far out and away from the rest of the clock.

He surrendered that part of himself, and howled with force as he rose. Cal put one foot in front of the other and ran forwards on legs that felt like they were made of fire. Another void wrenched from his gut as he spoke the words a third time. They came easier, even if the feeling of what it did to his pride was like a rending tear that shredded him like tissue paper. "Help!"

The line around his wrist lost all color. Instead, it began drawing light in, the fishing line visible only by the outline of what wasn't there, as he could no longer see what was. He pulled his mind from it, and reached out a hand. He put all his hopes into the dream that this would work.

The arm of time clicked upwards. Four seconds left.

Cal closed his hand, and found hope had not failed him. From the void itself, Occultatum formed in a blur of motion, then grabbed him wrist to wrist before hurling him onwards. Occy spoke, but the words were not for him as he was sent flying at blinding speeds towards the dwindling mote of pink light. "Tim! *Catch!*"

CHAPTER THREE

Cal had never been so happy to slam into the chest of a portly man. Eternium's silhouette filled his vision when he approached at speed. One he didn't know how to calculate. Instead of that concern, Tim stood implacably in his trajectory. The man was even checking a stopwatch, which he snapped closed with his fingers before sliding the object into his chest pocket.

With his arms wide, Tim spoke jovially as he caught his friend with an *oomph*! "Got ya! Right on schedule! Look at you, sticking to **Order**."

"No, we need to go! It... *Three*!" Cal panicked at the stop, the count in his mind blinding him to his new surroundings.

His panic subsided slowly but surely when the burning weariness in him evaporated. Something had changed. The rules of reality he now experienced were different. He was no longer in **Possibility**, as the void was gone. As was the clock, and his sense of urgency.

His head swiveled for information, and where there had been only potential, there was now an established pattern. A floor! Or many small squares that formed a floor. He knew this design from somewhere? His tone turned flat and his face fell as he saw the carved game pieces littered across the landscape, a match currently in motion. A glass opalite pawn had just taken a rusted off-green copper queen, after which the opalite pieces began to be mopped from the board in a flurry of unforgiving movements. Cal's throat croaked out his question. "Why are we on a gameboard of Kings and Castles?"

"Welcome to **Order**," Tim said with a good modicum of pride. A sensation that currently hurt Cal immensely on the inside when it washed over him. He squeezed a hand to his chest and winced, but the pain faded as quickly as it had come. Tim seemed to understand, and spoke. "There's a mandated sequence to this, and there's something you have to do before you can keep running. Consider **Time** paused. You'll have those three seconds when it resumes."

Cal blinked wordlessly. His mouth gaped like he meant to say something, but the words failed to come. Instead he motioned around, clueless about what was going on.

Tim chuckled ruefully, then shook his head. "Come now, pal. Don't go thinking you're on top of the world now. You might be of a higher Tower Tier, but that's all you've got on me. Did you forget how to ask questions? You asked for help, didn't you?"

"How…?" Cal began. "How did *you* know I asked for help?"

"Because Incarnates can hear people crying out for assistance when they're stuck on other planes. I'm guessing you weren't around when Amaterasu told Dani. Though she was Dawn at the time." Tim slapped Cal on the back of the shoulder, then made a 'come along' motion. "Walk with me. You'll find it's easy while you're here."

Feeling that the number three in his head was thoroughly stuck in place with the countdown halted, Cal held his own arms and shuffled behind Eternium as he tried to get a grip on events, himself, and what those three gaping holes in his stomach were. Just what had he given up in order to get this far?

Eternium answered as if he could read Cal's thoughts. "Finding you was the easy part. *Getting to you*, not so much. Keeping you bridged is a *costly* affair. You're still walking the path in **Possibility**, and stuck in the half-life. That doesn't mean you're not still tethered to the planes of concept, but it does mean that you're sort of… *out of sync*. Like you're on a different wavelength, as I am at the moment."

Eternium paused for a longer breath while watching another opalite piece bite the dust, shattering to shards. "Or rather, I am on this wavelength specifically because I was supposed to encounter you here."

The triple-S ranked dungeon made a broad motion to the whole space.

"*Here* being your Incarnation-path to the double-S ranks. Your stairway isn't done." Tim clarified, then added some more with a smirk at the eye-bulging look Cal was giving him. "Yes, bud. Your thoughts are loud here. You might as well have been shouting."

Another percussive glass-shattering impact in the distance made him wince. "Staying on this altered wavelength has caused terrible, terrible problems in both of our Soul Spaces and all the connections therein. Once Barry was handled, I had little choice. In order to get this extra time we're both enjoying right now? I had to pre-pay and freeze my own. The choice had to be quick, so not many people got out of Eternia's Alpha Version."

"Wait, so you and your Soul Space have been stuck, because you've been waiting on me?" Cal surmised.

A dark expression crossed the older dungeon's face. "I had to pause the entire game world in my own Soul Space with a *serious* stasis lock. Letting it run was so against my **Order** that I just... couldn't. Nothing we can't mend, but it's going to take time and effort once we get you out of here. Exceptionally perilous fixes are going to require sending people back in when we're both on the same prior wavelength again. We must extract some dangerous 'gifts' left behind that *need* to be gone before I can safely wipe the place and start a new iteration. Enough of that. Any questions?"

"What are the holes I feel in my stomach?" Cal asked, direct and to the point as he was glad to get back to him being the focus. The lead weight and pain might have been gone for now, but he was still feeling tension and strain.

"Bits of your soul missing." Tim didn't miss a beat. "Like I said, *getting to you* was costly, and took payment from both ends. That's *with* the guideline to help us find you."

Cal's panic resurfaced like a fish who needed to complain at the sky for being too blue. "That sounds really, really bad, Tim!"

"It would be." Eternium mused, before pausing a step to let Cal catch up. Tim settled an arm over Cal's shoulders before falling into step with him. "If you didn't have some really good friends who knew what to do about that. That is, unless you want to run to the end of the line with those chunks still missing?"

Cal choked on air. "No, I'm good! I would love those chunks back. Even if I had no idea what they were."

Tim patted his shoulder, aiding in the temporary relief of Cal's fatigue. "Bits of your values and personality, and parts of the pattern relating to how you see and interact with the world. Your pattern and your soul are the same thing, after all."

Cal made a truly inhuman sound that crossed between a wheeze and a silent scream. Tim understood the distress, his patting upgrading to a backrub while they both stood still. Cal needed to cope, both his hands pressed over his mouth as wide eyes bored into the square pattern of the floor. He felt momentarily drunk, and saw all the squares make a circle.

A hidden truth in the world that he didn't have time for right now.

Shaking himself out of that half-trance, he blinked and turned to look up at Tim, who had all the patience of a saint as the portly man waited on him. "Am... am I going to be okay?"

"I think you will be," the older dungeon replied. "If you want to be."

Cal squeezed his hands over one another, frowning as his eyes looked for something to hold on to as the board was becoming devoid of pieces. They found Eternium's face when he looked up, and that would do. "If I want to be?"

"You only find help when you look for help, where you would find none if you didn't want it, regardless of it being there." Tim nudged him along, the walking resuming. "You will also only recover if you want to recover. If you want to blaze a path ahead and ignore the consequences, you can. Though, you will not recover what you have lost. Those fractures will be filled entirely by new glue, new experiences, and new outlooks. That's how it is for all non-curators. We? We have a choice few others do. We can recover a viewpoint once lost, and re-integrate it into ourselves. Other Incarnates can only heal, and be made anew. The views they lost are lost for good. They will become someone else over time, depending on what they lost, and what new memories they gain."

That was a bit too much for Cal, who needed to hold his forehead. "Why... why are you all going so far to help me? This is starting to sound like a costly affair hurting all parties who *try*. Ember... did not look okay. Tatum looked like he could only appear and hold on for the miniscule moment he was there. I didn't see him vanish but I know his clock had no time on it."

Tim stopped at a gazebo, the shattering sounds paused as a copper king piece looked to be taking its time savoring an impending victory over a mostly broken opalite castle piece. Cal had not noticed the gazebo sneak up on them, nor the chair that he was helped into. A field of flowers began to sprawl out from the edges of the open building once he sat, more of Eternium's influence settling in as Cal felt an uncanny solidity in his surroundings. He felt a need to grip the table, and did so with a squeeze.

"I assure you it's real." Tim chuckled, amused. "The hard part, honestly, is over. The only real question was whether you could reach me or not. Since you did, that means I can help properly. As to why… Well. Do you consider me a friend, Calcite? Do you consider me a *peer*? Or am I just some little dungeon you picked up from the north pole and made a deal with because the world was ending?"

Cal clamped his mouth shut. He blinked into the distance as the field of flowers spread. They were beautiful. Well ordered. Soothing to be around as the smells reached his nose. Warmth crept into his skin, and the pillow under his seat became more comfortable.

"I… I've been selfish, Tim." He bit his lip. "I feel that… like with most topics I should have paid more attention to, grandpa long-beard has smacked this one over my head as well."

Tim smiled, then nodded after some thought as he sat in a chair himself, fingers lacing while his palms rested on his heavy stomach. "Could I put some music on?"

"Sure?" Cal felt like that came out of left field, like a stray hare who had a sudden need to bite him in the shin and run off. "Music would be nice."

Tim clearly appreciated it, a soft melody falling from above. "This is Nuvole Bianche. I find it calming to the heart." With a motion of his hand, a musical staff appeared on the ceiling of the gazebo. Then a few more along with it as more than one instrument began to play. "I consider *you* a peer, Cal. Even if we differ, and our methods couldn't be more apart. You're a dungeon. You're on the tower top with me. We're working towards the same goals. We're even working together on many projects."

He drummed his fingers on his stomach to the tune of the

evocative piano, his feelings exposed. "I did not realize how pleasant it would be to not work on everything alone. For so much of my life, I was the best at everything, you see. That shapes how the eyes see things. How I approached life. A problem I'm sure you've come to appreciate."

Cal listened to Tim, a little dumbfounded by the direct honesty. The older dungeon, snug as a bun in his chair, looked at Cal with an expression the younger dungeon didn't know what to do with. Tim just smiled wider, already knowing the answer Cal had reached. "Isn't it nice to have a peer?"

Cal didn't understand why he was crying. His face scrunched up, his hands squeezed his chest, and where there had been three gaping holes, there were now but two. He tried to say something, but no sound left his throat as a wave of emotion slammed through him. The wave knocked him right over, and when he could get back his mental stability, he stammered out his speech. "Is… is this what it feels like?"

Cal didn't equate the feeling to pain or sadness.

There was a somber freedom to the thought. To the combination of knowledge and prickling sensation that he did not stand alone on the mountaintop. He did not watch the sun rise and set alone, and thought that instead of there not being anyone there with him… He had never truly bothered to ask the questions, or look.

Tim's expression changed from empathetic, to sympathetic, to understanding. "Yeah. That's what it feels like. First is getting knocked off the horse. Second is getting back up and realizing that no matter how high you've climbed, it's barely out of the frog's pond. No matter the scale. Last is actually looking, and seeing everyone else who stands with you."

Cal slumped in his chair, a hand pressing over his face as a thought hit him, and he weakly bubbled out a pained laugh. "To be thoroughly lost, before one can find themselves."

Tim raised an eyebrow. "That's some harsh, profound wisdom, found through pain."

Cal inhaled firmly, his hands covering the two internal wounds he considered holes. He lost himself to the piano for a moment, but Tim was once more patiently waiting on him when he pulled back. Other songs by the same artist melodiously fell from the gazebo's ceiling, and Cal could not help but find them consoling. No matter how sad some of the melodies were, there was a happiness hidden away in them. A life, nested between the notes.

"Levin was wise. Cal began. "He had this... serenity to him. Even having lived his life, I can't put myself in the equivalent of his shoes. He went through horror and hardship, and walked out proud of his scars, unafraid of life."

Tim grasped his meaning. "The same boiling water that softens the potato hardens the egg. It's about what you're made of, not the circumstances."

Cal felt calmer. No longer tense, like his heart was going to jump out of his chest. A new comfort rested in his sternum, and he didn't know what to do with it. "That... sounds right."

"How are you feeling, bud?" Eternium interjected. That saintly expression soft and gentle as it laid on his face, like it was home there.

"Different, and... exactly the same." Cal tried to place his own state of being. "I'm aware of the holes, but they're bothering me less and less as I sit here. Just... *being*. I don't even know what I gave up. Can you tell me?"

Eternium scooted a tea saucer his way, the cup and contents forming on it as he did so. "'Course, bud. Your first 'help' cost you a chunk of your solitary nature. Your second request cost you some of your resilience against the opinions and feelings of others. The third? A bit of pride. Every time you asked, it cut closer and closer to the source of what prevented you from asking in the first place. Change as an Incarnate is a dangerous affair, even with all your convenient bonuses in malleability."

Cal observed the cup, needing a minute to come to the realization it was actually there before he took and sipped it. The flavor was akin to freshly squeezed foot, except in hot leaf water format. He winced, and made something up on the spot. "Strawberry."

His friend sipped his own, then swirled the contents. "Mine's peaches, it seems."

A moment of silence hung between them before they broke and cracked smiles from the absurdity of comparing tea flavor lies. Cal put his cup down, and stared at it. "I feel so exhausted. So raw. Like a rag that was twisted to get all the water out, and then someone didn't get the memo to stop."

"Well, you *did* slam through your second step all in one go."

Tim chastised, putting his own cup down before arching a brow to prod at his peer. "That's generally not how you do it."

"Me and mine have a history of doing things the wrong way." Cal chuckled. "We're obstinate like that."

"Including other people in a self-evaluation are we? Progress!" Tim clearly approved of Cal thinking on lines that had him including other people, but was waiting for Cal to speak more. As if it was his turn, and there was an order.

"What bit of me was healed just now?" Cal inquired, his mind falling on the topic.

Tim once again stabbed right into the heart of the matter. "You blazed the path and replaced the missing bit instead of restoring it, but that would be the chunk of considering other people's viewpoints. Except that instead of picking the 'obstinate' part of your nature back up, you replaced it with open-minded-ness. Good music can do wonders."

Cal thought about it, his head cocked at an angle. "Hey, Tim?"

"Yes, bud?" the older dungeon replied.

Cal's smile filled with genuine warmth as his head rose. "It's nice to have a peer."

Eternium matched the comforting expression, the warmth shining through in his voice instead. "Feeling's mutual, friend. The feeling is mutual."

CHAPTER FOUR

"Health of the spirit, once you're at this table, is just as paramount as the health of the mind." Eternium motioned at the flowers, pointing out some tulips in particular. "Building your environment helps build towards that goal. I found that one cannot simply drown themselves in work, tasks, and the act of doing without pause. It's poison to the soul. We have to allow the rest of life to wash over us, until we are all that remain. Who we are after that… is up to us."

"The potato and the egg." Cal started to see the threads and pattern. "How does one normally heal their spirit, or regain what they've lost?"

The older dungeon leaned back in his seat, fingers resuming their laced spot on his stomach. "You know how you live the life of others as an Incarnate? Same process… except it's your own. Your memories and experiences shaped you in the first place, so to shape them again, you must relive them. Allow yourself to be shaped by them once more. This is also the process normal cultivators need to go through in order to patch themselves up once they're in a soul form. Just slapping in Mana or Spirit doesn't cut the mustard."

"Is that why it takes so long?" Cal surmised. "Or, it seemed so when I heard Occultatum reference 'centuries to millennia.' He strongly appeared to mean it."

Tim nodded firmly. "You need to relive all the crucial points that made you become a certain way, and you can't skip one or fast forward. So, the longer you've been alive, the longer it will take to find the first marker that begins a certain transition. Then from that point you have to hit all the markers, accept them, and then you become 'whole' again. Which is how you heal a Spirit body. Unless you're a curator though, it's *only* the body. Pattern restoration is not clear cut. I even did extensive testing, and... may have used our favorite longbeard as a test subject."

"You did *what?*" Cal leaned forward, exuding a mixture of insulted '*Excuse me?*' and curious 'How did it go?' that he wasn't certain how to articulate.

"Most interesting!" Tim lauded, his huge smile hiding all the details held within as he'd clearly discovered much more than he was letting on. "That talk will need to be for later. Time to pick. Recovery, or blazing it?"

Cal melted in his chair, eyes on the dancing ceiling of the gazebo. His answer came surprisingly easy. "Recovery. Though, I may not accept some of the changes. It depends? I'll go through the replay of my early life, but the way I was, and the way I want to be, don't line up anymore. What use do I have for ingrained values that I don't believe in?"

"That's up to you, bud." Tim eased from his chair, standing and motioning that it was walk time. "I'm just here to help. I may not have a speck of this 'humanity,' but I do have a sense of decency and decorum. You deserve help. You deserve friends. Your attempt at a daily life was admirable when you tried, but you fell back into old ways before you realized it. Perhaps this time, you will find you have more people standing in your corner to trade those ideas with?"

Cal chuckled as he got up, falling into step with Tim as the portly man mumbled something about wine vintages to himself.

Eternium coughed and returned to the topic after noticing Cal smirk. "At any rate. I'm ready when you are."

The younger dungeon pressed his hands to his hips. "How do I start?"

Tim exhaled firmly, and helped get him going with a memetic trigger. "It's a beautiful day to die."

Cal's smirk vanished from his face, his perspective no longer occupying a body that stood next to Tim. Instead, his viewpoint hovered over the oldest scene he could remember. His death. Well, his birth as a dungeon Core. The wibbly-wobbly, timey-wimey mess that needed Heavenlies to *personally* get the broom in order for that to get sorted out.

Unexpectedly, the sequence of events flashed across his eyes, rather than be some deep delve that Cal needed to spend elaborate swaths of time in. Meeting Kantor and Dani. The Silverwood sapling. His first kill. The Adventurers Guild investigation. Being saved just because the sapling grew above his Core. The distortion cat incident. Dale 2.0, the dungeon born. The loss of Dani to the Collective. Xenocide stealing his **Madness** whispers. The Mage ranks. Flying Mountaindale. Rescuing Dani. Him and Dale being two sides of the same coin. Meeting Barry. Getting swatted out of the air by Xenocide. The Northmen's realm and meeting other dungeons. Going to the source of Wisps. Opening his Soul Space for the rescue effort. Merging with Dale when his Core was shattered. Eons of Soul Space tinkering…

The flashes felt like they left when they'd barely arrived, but the speed of their passing made sense to him when the experience reel ended. He'd accepted none of the old memories or ways of being. He thought he would, but in practice… He'd skipped by each and every marker without a second thought. With his own life's reel having no reason to slow down, it zipped along out of principle before tucking itself into a waistcoat pocket, crossing its metaphorical arms to be pouty about having been called for no reason.

Cal glanced at his friend as Tim sipped from a brand new cup of tea. The older dungeon peered at it with a sour expression, disappointed and uncertain. "Going to call this one… mango."

"More squeezed foot?" Cal poked with amusement. "Sorry, *fruit?*"

"Burnt toast mixed with the pit of a fruit, and nutshell shavings." Tim put the cup down and swatted in its direction, dismissing the entire set. "This happens when **Order** isn't adhered to. Small mistakes. Little holes in the world. Distortions. Déjà vu cats."

"I don't want to talk about *holes in the world*." Cal made a face, an expression that cleared and altered to panic when the hand of a clock very loudly rang through the entire space. A second that threatened to tick by. "That is *equally* as unpleasant."

"I'm afraid that's all the **Time** I'm able to buy you." Tim rose from his seat, the music dulling to nothing as the scene of the gazebo frayed at the edges. The flower field wilted into a brown haze, and the sweet smells and warm air went with it.

When Cal got to his feet, feeling the lead burn in the bottom of his feet return, he bounced on his toes to mitigate the spread. "No, this has been far more than I deserve already. Without all this help, I wouldn't have survived. This would have been a most unsatisfying ending for everyone involved."

He stopped bouncing, face rueful. "So... Thanks, Tim."

Eternium chuckled, making the 'come along' motion as he walked out onto the game board, inspecting the pieces with an impending sense of dread. "Thank me when we all get out of this with gleaming Cores and shining smiles, after it's all said and done. Right now you're looking at the longest three-second walk of your life, and by the time you make it... we might be short an Administrator."

Cal's gaze hardened, his eyes flicking to the game pieces that suddenly took on a whole new meaning. "*Ah. No. We won't be.*"

Tim's eyebrows climbed up with interest. "Oh? Where's this sudden confidence from? You've still got two holes in your soul, and it's not like you drew anything from your reel."

Cal squeezed his hands, shaking his head. New purpose flared in his eyes. "Naw. I think I get it now. I've been... 'me, me, me.' But that doesn't work anymore. I've found the limits of my greed, my drives, and my passions. I have crawled to the finish line and found that complete silence at the end of what should have been a roaring victory is... the worst. All I found at the end of that finish line was a cold mountaintop. With nobody to see the sights with, or share in the shiny new trinket I hold in my hands. Of... whatever little madness I was working on."

The younger dungeon motioned at the broken castle piece. Broken, but standing. "There is more joy to be found in sharing tea with a beggar than there is in hollow success, no matter how great. I'm not going to make that last stretch for *me*, Tim. I'm going to make it for *them*. Three seconds...? Three seconds might as well be an **Eternity**."

Cal lurched as **Time** caught up with him, the culmination of that clock hand resounding. All he heard before being forcibly pulled out of the **Order** layer—his feet hitting the angled clock hand that pointed at a fading lighthouse beacon—were Tim's parting words. "That's the spirit!"

Feet on the ground in the realm of **Possibility**, Cal booked it. Right from the starting block, he exploded up the ramp as the deafening click of the clock thrummed beneath his feet. Keeping the number in mind, his heart gripped his determination. "Two!"

He made it a respectable distance before two became one. When it did, the angle at the tip of the click-clock hand raised above his goal, obscuring the light behind it with a muddled bloom that outlined the rising machination. When one became none, Cal wasn't having it. He refused, and boomed his defiance to the heavens. "Again!"

Eternity was three seconds. Mid-stride, he found himself back where he began, the number 'three' solidly held at the front of his mind. Just running with physical legs wasn't good enough. He needed more. He needed to be faster! Couldn't he do more to attain a case of the '*nyooms*'?

Epiphany struck him. He needed the *concept* of faster! The very power of '*wheee*'!

The fishing line around his wrist burst with celestine illumination. He was finally asking questions. Now all there was left to see was if he found the *right* questions.

"I am **Speed**!"

Racing up the clock hand with an additional zero or two at the end of his zoom-formula, Cal noticed that the edges of his vision were neither tunneled nor blurred. The realm didn't change either, like it wasn't fazed by his paltry changes. He made it so much closer before the tip of the hand crested over the light, and right as his timer hit zero, he decreed his continued defiance. "Again!"

How many seconds in **Eternity**? Was it actually three? Cal's stride continued from where the journey began. From where it always began, again, and again. He called on more **Laws** with each loop. Higher concepts. More potent ideas. Devious and clever measures.

Instant-transmission tricks merely reset him, so **Teleportation** and its kin were out. As were the more roundabout ways of getting from point A to B. There was nothing to fight, so aggressive **Laws** held no potency. The emotive **Laws** kept silent; the contemplative ones held a tiny flag in support, and by the time he reached the highest tiers, he had a thousand hands on his back. Pressing him ever onwards.

He was not alone.

He was never alone.

Not if he didn't want to be.

Not if he didn't choose to be.

Yet there wasn't a single **Law** able to help him make it all the way. Up and up he went through the Tower, coming up *just barely short* each time. Something was missing. An aspect was lacking. He was traversing so fast across the clock hand that he was an almost constant line of light beaming directly towards his goal. Only to never make it, like he was trapped in some cruel twist of fate named non-Euclidean geometry.

Not even **Space** and **Movement** from floor seven hundred and nineteen got him to the buoy. Cal arrived within a finger's distance, but that last inch felt immeasurable.

When he stepped on the highest Tower floor, **Order** felt faint, already expended. **Time** was currently not his friend, not when he was playing around with **Eternity** the way he was. Opposite to them, there was a different story. **Discord**, **Entropy**, and **Chaos** all wore matching shirts that said NasCal with a crossed-out picture of some strange, hot-rod-red, four-wheeled construct. They also wore matching headgear—truly baffling hats with a duck-like brim in the front—and oversized foam fingers with the number one proudly emblazoned on the side.

Matter did the equivalent of shooting him with crossbow fingers, but was of no help here. **Madness** was here too, leaning forwards in its makeshift recliner while shoving handful after handful of butter-coated popped-corn into his mouth. Was he going to help? Not even a little. Was it amusing? Kinda, yeah. Specifically because it was **Creation** cranking out all the popped corn and merchandise like an obsessed, shrieking, delighted-as-could-be loot goblin.

While there were more, Cal couldn't see them as his heart dropped into his stomach, eyes turning to **Love**. The rest of the floor and all its contents bled away faster than the red lines spilling from the edges of an old man's mouth.

Artorian replied with a gaze of steel as Cal's reach for him turned hesitant. Bleeding Mana, battered, and missing some legs, he raised his trembling arm. The hand on it formed a fist, as if in defiance of halting a journey before it was over. To another, the fist was clearly part of a martial pose to indicate combat readiness. To Cal, the silent message in Artorian's eyes was simple and clean. Even laying on his side on the ground, Artorian was the picture of the last strand of hope, tightly squeezed.

He wasn't done. He wasn't going to quit.

Neither should Cal.

The fishing line on Cal's wrist shattered, its light expended. **Love** had been helping this entire time. Right from the start, all the way to now. Cal had been a fool. He felt like one anyway, as the determination in his heart loudly beat in the face of that which was unyielding.

How many seconds in **Eternity**? The spirit of the old man before him answered, fading into shards along with the connection of the fishing line. "One."

'One' became true when **Time** was no longer buffeted by some of the other **Laws** on its tier. With **Love** and **Order** now too weak to interfere, **Eternity** ended by **Time**'s decree. A **law** that wanted a permanent end to these seconds three.

Noximillius, the Heavenly of **Time**, wound the clock.

Cal found himself on the clock hand once more, though he supposed he'd never actually left it during that little peek into the Tower. A different question crossed his thoughts as he returned. Not one of means to an end, but one of *being* with purpose. Finding himself right at the start of the track as he asked the *right* question, the puzzle piece clicked. His first step cost him half a second, but that basic and simple motion brought him all the way to the mote of dying light.

"I am... Cal," he whispered, his mind exposed to a flood of knowledge that Dale had not been able to handle during his ascension into Magehood. "But that is just *one* of my names, is it not? I am more than merely *me*. I am... **Acme**."

CHAPTER FIVE

Cal's hand closed around the mote of fading light as if it had never been more than barely out of arm's reach. He felt one last hand on his shoulder. A silent motion, spoken with loud action as his own **Law** conferred a measured modicum of... *pride*.

There was no special transition. Cal was in his Soul Space, the journey complete. That second 'S' fell into place like the wheel of a slot machine clicking in its second spin, and Cal knew he was home. Home, and alive.

Speaking of living! He really should make sure that he kept his promises. Whisking the closest available body he could find out of storage—if that ransacked hall could be given that name—he tapped into a joke Tatum must have made since the words sprung to the front of his thoughts like a whisper from the void.

Instantly locking down all the energy of the offender he was going to need to have words with, he happily and verbally finished the countdown timer for his own sanity. He couldn't resist the instant quip. It had been far too long.

"*Zero*. Somebody called for a Cal Ex Machina?"

Broken words replied from below as his palm caught and stopped the full motion of Odin's fist to make sure he was preventing any and all harm. Just in case. "Scholar D. Kota?"

Cal was pleased as punch to hear the old longbeard speak. "Hey, buddy. Miss me?"

Artorian's choice of words, on the other hand, made him quickly glance at the body he'd run off with. The person looked to be someone Artorian knew, so it was best to clear that misunderstanding up. Couldn't get the credit for good puns if they thought he was someone else! "No, not him. It's Cal! I do like the look though. This model was the quickest thing I could ease into to get here faster."

Odin blinked, his eyes glued on his failed attack as the man appeared to have utterly forgotten that Cal, as owner of the Soul Space, had complete control of all the energy in it. Including who got to *play* with said energy.

"Who d—" Odin barely got out his words before they, too, were denied to him.

As Cal's Soul Space bled back into his stream of empirical information like it was another sense—just like touch or smell—he realized just how much of 'home' was… in a poor state.

Cal turned, giving Odin a cold look as of all the things he realized that needed attention, an uppity supervisor was dropping ever lower on the priority list. "I woke up to a busted Soul Space, pure anarchy, and my worst supervisor beating up my best Administrator. I'm not in a good mood, Jaspy. Why don't you go spend some time in your seed Core?"

Before the man could even think of a retort, Cal fractured him like dusty plywood.

"Much better!" Cal mused, clapping his hands together as his eyes followed the soul returning to the Silverwood. On the branches of which Cal saw a real, honest to the heavens, full-on Celestial. Waving frantically, he couldn't hide his sudden good mood in the slightest. He knew that face! "Hello there! I've been so looking forward to meeting you!"

"Cal…" Artorian wheezed. "A *tiny* bit of help? Please?"

"*Hmmm?*" Cal looked down, and realized that the simulacrum of Artorian which he'd seen during his climb was not an exaggeration. If he didn't act now, his own hubris would walk all over him a second time. Or was it third? Best not to count, Dani kept receipts. "Oh, wowza! You're in terrible shape. I'll fix the basics but I am sorely needed everywhere else."

Mending Artorian was an easy task in comparison to the literal flood of entries populating his to-do and repair list. The Mana in the air normally didn't give him any trouble, but it was exceptionally friendly and helpful with this current task. He didn't quite have the extra time to put the legs back, as there had in fact been some serious Eternium-fingerprint tampering with the body Artorian was housed in, but doubted there wasn't going to be a fix sooner or later. "There you go, buddy. Now, excuse me for a moment. I'll thank you for helping me wake up later, Mr. Lighthouse."

Noticing Adam had come to him instead of him needing to make a trip up to the tree, Cal shot his arms to the air. He halfway noticed two of his Incarnate friends enter the scene, but could already feel that they needed to beeline towards the others.

He heard Dawn and Artorian softly share some quick words, but clapped as the heavens brightened, his attention devoted to welcoming the new arrival with wide arms. There was an order to these things. He had more of a sense of it now. Before he could move on to other projects, this *needed* to happen. "Hi! What did you think of my Cal Ex Machina, *hmmm?*"

Fluff rained from above, only to vanish as it touched the ground while Adam descended from the sky, matching Cal's pose. With a serene smile, the celestial spoke, like welcoming someone home. "Hello there, my dear old friend. Very well timed indeed, but just a touch *inexact*. Can I interest you in the good word of Acyrologia?"

Knowledge of the word filled Cal, and the dungeon broke down laughing. He needed to name book ten of Artorian's life after that absurdity. It was happening. Cal clapped his hands, turned the page on the next iteration, and got to work on his world. All according to plan.

———

Artorian remembered falling asleep in Ammy's arms.

He also recalled that waking up to familiar ceilings was usually better than the alternative. What felt uncanny this time around were the warm beams of sunlight streaming in through the window while he laid half-swaddled on a pillow-laden cot. A really good cot, mind you, but a cot nonetheless.

"Look who the C'towl dragged in." Lunella's hands were busy knitting socks while she lounged in a rocking chair. One leg laid over the other as she kept within reach of a table stacked so full of supplies that only a seasoned brick-stacking professional could retrieve anything from the pile without the entire mountain of... probably very useful junk... toppling over and causing an avalanche that would bury the entire town.

Alright, maybe his thoughts were exaggerating. Slightly. *Half* the town. Artorian sounded drowsy. "I don't know if I want five more minutes or to ask what year it is this time."

Lun picked up one of her knitted crafts, then fit the plush beanie over his bald head to keep his noggin warm. The whole 'Mage' thing either went over her head, or didn't matter to the matron. Mothers were going to mother. "You've been asleep for a couple of days. Which were so hectic that I envy you having napped through it all. That is to say, if you had meddled even a little bit, I would be chasing you with Titania's spoon. Yvessa had *quite* the bonfire stories for us."

Artorian suddenly doubted the legitimacy of this 'couple of days' measurement, but wasn't going to press it. Life was good. If Lunella was here instead of hen-pecking the village to behave, then things were certainly going well.

Tibbins picked that moment to poke his head in through the window, a bowl of divine-scented fowl in his hands. Artorian could smell that the amount of garlic added was equivalent to Tibbins having let his spiritual ancestors decide when enough was enough. Which must have been around the time his arm got tired from shelling them. "Lu—*Oh, hey*! Look who's up! Bowl of fili-fili-fowl?"

Artorian had no qualms accepting the bowl. Handed the spoon, he didn't catch a word of the conversation between the Fringe natives as he inhaled the masterclass of culinary delight. There was an art to *taste*, and he spoke with his mouth full. "Mn... Tibs! Thish ish sho gewd!"

"Courtesy of Madame Chandra's lessons." He grinned, his pose adopting a 'yes, praise me more' stance. "If we can drum up a couple more chefs, I want to start a competition. Just to win it, of course. We need to settle once and for all who makes the better pastries."

The fire in his gaze when he turned towards Lunella made metaphorical electricity crackle between their eyes. Lunella *mhm'd* him hard. "In your dreams, son."

Artorian chose not to poke this hornet's nest, and held up the bowl. "Seconds? Preferably out of a slightly bigger bowl? Say, I don't know, the pot it was cooked in?"

Lunella chided him for the greedy comment. "Grandfather, you leave some for the rest of us!"

A fit of giggles bursting from the longbeard made the village elder prune her lips at him, an expression that made Tibbins run for the hills. His voice trailed off behind him. "Good luu~u~u~ck!"

"If you are going to *misbehave*." Lunella's change of tone stopped Artorian's giggling cold. "Then you don't get *gossip*."

Artorian pressed his hand to his chest like that was the single most hurtful thing she could say, his gasp deep and incredulous. "My most *precious* gossip? You wouldn't!"

Lunella took his surprisingly spotless spoon and pressed the end of it into the tip of his nose. "*I* am the village elder here. Do you want to press your luck, or put on this sweater I made for you?"

Clearing his throat, Artorian stuck his arms straight up. "I'll take the sweater."

When Lunella moved to dig it out of the precarious pile, Artorian unfurled himself from the shell of snugness. Throwing open the last comforter, he pushed himself to sit on the side of the bed. Which was the point where he realized something was wrong. Looking down, he noted that while he could feel his toes wiggle when he thought he performed the action, there was a distinct lack of actual toes. "*Ah.*"

Lunella looked over her shoulder to see her grandfather staring longingly at his knees. At least he still had those? His expressions turned complicated, like he was trying to move a limb that wasn't there. "Grandpa, you okay?"

Artorian raised his gaze to see Lunella had found a... Well, it was a horrendous sweater. Truly ugly. A monster in clothing form. "I thought I was, but what's the wild animal in your hands supposed to be?"

She slapped him on the shoulder with a gasp of mock insult. "I worked hard on this!"

"And I'll wear it." Artorian retorted, his face adopting a leisurely smirk before his head dipped to look back at his very permanent injury. "I'm... I'm not sure. I definitely feel... the spirit? Of what's supposed to be there. My body is busted, but I know how to mend patterns thanks to Tim, so I should be able to whip this back into shape."

The mere act of tapping into a technique made bursts of agony and searing pain explode up his thighs, chest, and culminate in a booming instant headache that forced him to bend over and squeeze his head with a brutal groan. Lunella was next to him on the cot right away, her old man suffering from labored breathing and a sudden case of the sweats. "Crackers... and... Y'know what, that's not enough here. *Waffles and syrup*! Auw!"

"Grandfather, what happened?" Lunella's concern oozed from her voice, her hand turning white from the hard squeeze on his shoulder.

"Can't use my magic juju." He let out another groan as a delayed pang of headache clapped him across the back of the skull. "In technical terms? I need my entire Mage body in order to form any and all details of the techniques and runes that I know."

He swirled a finger at his chest. "I form them internally, and the act of performing the task is dependent on the path the energy takes. I am missing both legs, and thus massive swaths of 'path.'"

Lunella... did her best to pretend she understood, rubbing at the back of his neck for comfort with her thumb. The motion calmed her more than him, until she was provided his hand to hold and squeeze. "I'll be alright in time, this just means I need... alternatives. I can feel I'm locked out of Cal's pylon system? That's a strange feeling. Though, they left the metaphorical window open."

Lunella pulled back, both her hands wringing his grip. "Those words I have heard before? There was more commentary along those lines a while back. Something about 'complete overhaul'? I didn't follow the explanation from the balls of light while they got into an argument-fight with the tiny people. The... Gnomes? Yes, Gnomes. Mostly they had shouting matches and threw out the words 'metric' and 'imperial' at one another a lot."

Artorian blinked at her. "Oh joy. Definitely more than 'a couple of days' then, *huh*?"

"Shush!" Lunella commanded. She swiped the sweater and held it up. "I said it was a few days, and we are all going to act and keep pretending it was a few days. You will not ask anyone how many times those 'few days' have needed to repeat already, and you will not go meddle. I need you *here* for now. You hear me?"

Artorian surmised that maybe not all was right in New-Fringe land, but given the act of walking, hovering, flying, or most other forms of locomotion were out until he thought of something else that would allow him to become someone else's problem, he wasn't going anywhere. "Of course, dear. I have also done 'loops' before. I can't say I like them. I was hoping to spare you from that fate, but I will assume that Cal is hard at work making the world work. You did mention Titania and a host of other pleasant company. Any chance I could meet them one or two at a time? You know how I get when I have nothing to do."

Sighing in extreme relief, she nodded and helped the amicable grandfather into the new sweater, replacing his temporary medical-patient shirt with the... artistically creative item.

Why was there a fern with little shiny balls and streamers on it? Never mind. Lunella needed happiness, so Artorian would wear it and hush. At least he was still in cozy pants! Well, shorts. His fate on that topic was sealed when she revealed the rest of the matching set. All equally abominable. "We can... we can do that. I'll organize something. I'm glad you're with us, grandpa."

Her words ended with a hug as she was pulled in. Lunella melted into the squeeze, and refused to let go for a whole hour. Artorian held her like a small sproutling from the Fringe, lightly rocking with better support than that chair next to him ever could. "I'm here, dear. I'm *home*."

CHAPTER SIX

Not long after Lunella left, Wux squeezed himself through the front door. The fatherly, well-rounded man grunted when he finally made his way inside. Though navigating between all the piles of stuff was clearly difficult as he wrestled with a massive pot of stew.

Wu sported an unbuttoned, lapis spider-silk vest with a recognizable insignia, simple pants, and a light sprinkling of mill-dust. He must have picked the color to match Lunella. Or rather, Lunella must have picked the color and Wu didn't fight her on it.

"Mornin' Pa!" Being the quintessential dad, he opened with a bright smile and poor joke. "I swear these homes get smaller every week."

"Pa? Oh, *Grand-Pa*. I see." Artorian smirked at the antics. "Surely it has nothing to do with your ever increasing fullness? Your fatherly figure indicates a life of plenty, and thorough enjoyment of rich food."

"Hey now!" Wuxius whined out as he set the large ceramic pot on the floor, his towel-wrapped hands pressing to his quality-meal-appreciating curves. Newly grown with the possible addition of some very rich mead that he found surprisingly fresh, light, and airy to drink. "I need a lot of energy to be a miller! Did you see my arms? Look at these logs!"

Flexing for his grandfather as he sat next to the cot, Artorian gave the tree-trunk of muscle that had become Wux's arm some affectionate prodding. He threw in some *oohs and ahhs*, nodding while making high pitched noises of approval. "Sturdy as a double packed sack of flour!"

Tuning some essence sight, Artorian felt a pang of fear as he'd immediately forgotten that trying a technique had whacked him just now. To his vast relief, just changing his modes of sight received a pass! He would need to delve into why this worked, but his techniques didn't, later.

Giving his son a thorough once over with his scan, Artorian found his grown up sproutling to be in frankly amazing health. All that extra girth really wasn't a detriment, aside from his complaints about tiny doors. His heart was great, the liver was a little fatty—but nowhere near problematic as would be assumed—his lungs were crystal clear, and his stomach was an iron cauldron. A person could refine *pills* in that thing. "Well, you are healthy, regardless of your newly discovered voluptuousness. I knew you'd been leaning into your 'dad' figure, but the change from last time I saw you is a bit drastic."

Wux grinned, stood, and performed a wiggle. "I finally feel like I can throw my weight around! Also, Dad-pillow is my kids' favorite. Now they have more to nap on! I see this as an absolute win! Don't tell Lunella that group of dastardly deeds is responsible for sneaking me casket after casket of the good stuff back home in the old Fringe. We had a good deal goin'."

Artorian laced his fingers, listening with clear bemusement.

Fatherly pride beamed over Wu's face. "Lu is always the stick, so this father figured, I like carrots. I like them in a stew. I like them in a brew. I like keeping a spare few in my vest. I like sneaking them to my animals when they've been put to the test."

Wu grinned like a scheming father as he rubbed his hands together, a new idea for something to teach his young'uns springing to mind. "It turns out that with just a *wee bit* of encouragement—and a devious idea of something Mom clearly doesn't want them to do—my fluffle of rabbits perk up their ears and flock to Dad for a tiny hand-cupped whisper. Then their smiles stretch from ear to ear, and like a horde of sugar-fueled squirrels, they zip off in a wave of rabid giggling."

He thumbed his large nose, a teensy touch red from his mead proclivities. Artorian's sight adjusted to see the 'normal' again, then noticed his boy had freckles! Also stretch marks when the health-check did another pass, but he wanted to focus on the freckles. Wux pulled a stool closer since he didn't trust the rocking chair to hold his width and keep its armrests. "Seeing my kids fail hurts, but seeing them learn from it is... It's something special."

His hands fell with a contented sigh, resting on his stomach in a way that made Artorian's mind think of Tim. They had that same leisurely, lazy lean to the way they sat. "Anywho! Hungry? Lu slapped me on the ass on her way to the house and told me to, let me quote: 'get you some grub.' Then she mumbled something about 'upsetting the whole pot,' so of course I had to misunderstand on purpose and bring the whole thing!"

The old man made excited grabby hands for the ceramic pot that could fit half of Wu's stomach. His boy chuckled good naturedly and got the hot pot into his grandfather's eager hands. Who—unlike him who needed the thick cloth to hold the handles —wasn't fazed by a little heat as the old man drank the delicacy down into the bottomless void of his stomach.

Wuxius couldn't help but gawk as his grandfather drained the whole thing in one slow, sustained set of gulps without his waistline budging an inch. He chuckled when Artorian handed the much lighter pot back. "Where did you put it all?"

Tapping his chest twice and clearing his throat, Artorian wondered if Aura was still on the table. A quick Essence-wipe of his face, and intense relief once again washed over him. He'd retained Essence sight and Aura! That hopefully meant he still had Presence in his pocket too. "Same place you did, just pretend Mage anatomy is bigger on the inside."

Wuxius's eyes widened, the thought making sense. He raised his left hand, pointing at his digits with his right. "Like the rings the traders show up with!"

A nod from Artorian had the man grinning like a fool. Wux was so excited to have figured that out. Temporarily losing himself to the pleasant thoughts, his grandfather gleaned a look out of the window and took stock of the updated village. Was that a bit of snow falling? Navigating would be difficult. First on the docket, roads! Lots of roads. No foul smell was a good sign. He swore he heard running water somewhere out of view, and Lunella was pitching a fit in the longhouse. Nice to see that place still standing!

Keeping his eyes trained on the view, he asked his boy more

pertinent questions. "So what did I miss? I thought the plan was for a circular design? All those snow-indented walk-patterns make squares."

"Ah, but enough squares make a circle!" Wu replied with a quick finger in the air. Artorian wasn't awake enough to get the joke. Though he didn't know about Wu's jovial drunken benders that ended up with him staring at floors for hours on end.

Wu pouted, but cheered up right away. "No? Nothing? Wait 'til one of the late night bonfire gatherings, it'll be clear, nice and quick!"

Artorian momentarily lifted the blanket and pointed at his distinct lack of walking units. "Someone is going to have to come and carry me out there, then. Unless you want to see me do a lot of hand stands or power-crawling."

Wux paled a little in discomfort, and tucked his grandfather back in. "Listen, Pa, there's a bit of a raging debate on what to do about that. You didn't hear this from me…"

Artorian leaned towards his boy.

Wux swallowed and twiddled his thumbs. "I *hear* that 'fixing things' is supposed to be easy here, but that you're three whole cake layers of 'special,' according to the people I see as the biggest shakers and movers. There was talk about a body replacement, which… don't ask me details, I know nothing. That wasn't going to work because none of the 'forms' had 'two hearts,' and mending your current one would need Tim and Cal's combined attention. A luxury neither of them have, according to the very stoic lady occasionally made of fire."

"Which, wow, Gramps. I thought *I* liked them hot, but I see I didn't fall too far from the tree." He didn't quite land his joke. Wux was clearly trying his best trying to explain a topic he knew little to nothing about, with terms he'd heard maybe once with how much he strained trying to pronounce them correctly. "Does any of that mean anything to you?"

Artorian nodded with a sigh, and eased back onto his cot. "Of course it couldn't be easy. That's what I get for being an outlier. It's fine, my boy. I'll find a way. I've got a nose and knack for these things! Can't say it's not good to hear that Ammy is glaring holes into dungeon Cores either. Or that's who I think she's getting angry at. She's a spark, alright!"

A sharp wink and tap on the side of his equally big nose put

Wu at ease. Wux nodded, then squeezed his digits around his massive thighs made entirely of corded muscle, and lifted himself from the stool. "We know how it goes, Pa. If there's anyone who can find a roundabout way of getting through this, it's the master architect himself. I shouldn't have worried, huh?"

Artorian patted his embarrassed son on the hip, since that was the only portion of him in reach. He smiled up at the man shyly rubbing the back of his short hair, and nodded before making a sharp nose-motion for him to get going. "Tell the next person to sneak in that I'd like to hear how the village is going. As is, I just heard Lunella confront Tibs in the kitchen, and she's very interested why her breakfast is missing. You best hustle! If it's any consolation, the stew was tasty! Give Tibs my regards and tell him to sneak me some more goods, like the old days!"

Wuxius had that pot in hand and his fat-rolls lodged between the doorframe in no time flat. "Why didn't you tell me sooner! I'll be back later!"

With a *pop*, Wu worked himself through the now-buckled door frame as it gave way with a hurried crack; whisking himself away with an abundance of short, tiny strides that made his legs turn into a circular sonic blur.

Artorian wheezed out weak, inhaled giggles as he watched his son scurry, only to bark out with hooting laughter as he heard Lu smack Wu on the ass all the way from his cot. He slapped the windowsill and made an accidental hand imprint, then wiped the feeling of tears away as the feeling ebbed.

A ball of purple light whisked into the open frame when he got a hold of himself, Genevieve boring her vision right into the marred wood. She sounded like a barmaid in the middle of her shift who had just been given more to do. "Excuse you, I have been fixing frames everywhere that *Santa* over there goes. If it gets any worse, I'm going to design a chute and chimney system purely to eject him from the premises with force. Don't be adding more tasks to my handywoman to-do list!"

Given that, regardless of her outburst, Artorian could tell she was speaking with fervor in jest, he settled into his pillows and laced his fingers, both hands resting on his sternum. "I'm definitely going to whittle this 'Santa' title out of Wu, during the next bonfire meet that I'm able to attend."

If he found some time with Wu. There was a big cast to check on!

He was sure it was all juicy gossip, and a bright case of furious cheek-burning embarrassment for the perpetrator. He could taste the gifts of joy already, but turned his attention to the Wisp. "Good to see you too, newlight. How's the brightness business?"

CHAPTER SEVEN

Genevieve huffed and turned away from him. The sight didn't alter her glowing ball any, but given she was turned, Artorian attempted to poke her through the Forum as an amusement. An effort that failed with an unexpected result, as one of the Pylons fired up to slap a prompt directly into his face. *Smack*!

He even felt the impact before it moved away from him in order to be legible. The error message read:

The Pylons are busy at this time. Please try again later. (Error 37.)

"How diabolic! Calling Pylons 'busy.'" Artorian rubbed his nose, his voice tingling with amusement as he meddled a second time, expectantly smacked by another notice. "Ha! How many error notices exist for me to get to *that* number?"

There was an error with your Pylon account. (Error 3006.)

Genevieve partially turned when Artorian puffed his cheeks, shooting him a half-glare over the shoulder as she'd seen the notices appear and smack the old man before she interfered to dismiss them. "What are you doing?"

His face deflated.

"Oh, nothin'. Since you were being a pouty butt, I was going to poke you through the Forum, as you're *juuuust* out of reach for the ticklemaster nine-thousand." He wiggled his fingers and eyebrows at the same time, like no tickle spots anywhere were safe. "I'm not sure if I want to gamble trying to Forum without the Pylons right now. Migraine spikes to the noggin' are undesirable, and it's no simple technique."

Genevieve understandably backed up a little, defensive of her rib-equivalents since she was horribly ticklish. "The only thing with a rating of nine-thousand around here is my *concern*. Put those away!"

With a guffaw, Artorian put his hands down and shook his head from left to right. He was stuck in bed again, so he was going to need to make his own entertainment. "Oh, you were safe all along! I only deploy that most devious trickery against uppity children who don't realize they should be laughing. Which I expect we will be seeing shortly?"

A raised eyebrow added weight to his question, prompting Genevieve to snap right into assistance mode. Like a flip being switched, the bubbly nature of her voice returned like some kind of magical customer service skill. "Sure will! With Cal back at the wheel, the timetable for mass decanting got shoved a~a~a~all the way to the front. I was actually going to bring it up shortly, but I wasn't going to get in between you and the Task Manager."

"The who?" Artorian queried. "Do I know the person behind this title?"

"I don't think so!" She replied all chipper. "T.M. is a very... erm... 'Winter Court' type of Wisp. Don't expect to get along. I expect if you prod him again, he's going to get feisty with you right away."

Artorian, of course, immediately pushed that button. With another small *blarp*, an error message appeared over the old one. "Even the error sounds are broken? Must be bad up there."

PEBVAC has been noted, closing access to the Pylon system. (Error ID10T.) Please RTFM.

The old man crossed his arms, cocking his head as he tried to unscramble those ciphers. "Well you certainly weren't wrong, but I don't know what this means."

Genevieve gave the message incredible side-eye, partially in disgust. Her customer service voice was nowhere to be found in favor of: 'displeased associate manager.' "That first bit is short for: 'Problem exists between viewscreen and chair.' Closing access means that if you try to access the Pylons, they just won't respond. The error... *err.* The error is calling you not smart. The last bit demands you read the manual, but only Wisps have access to the Catch Twenty Two storage shelves where those are kept."

The longbeard blinked at the message. Then a widening, scheming, most pleased grin slowly spread across his face and cheeks as he drummed his digits together pyramid style. "Oh *really?* And here I was worried about entertainment."

Genevieve glowed a welcoming light blue, the chipper tone back where it belonged. "You don't like him either? Wonderful. This has been a most productive day already! Would you like that decanting breakdown?"

"Sure would!" Breaking from the prior topic, Artorian sat up in his cot. "I actually expected it all to be done already. I remember something about decanting being a 'must' before Cal woke up. I notice we didn't get struck by heavenly bolts from the great **Oath**-man. Did Cal pull some more wiggle-room out of his back pocket?"

"If you already knew, why did you ask me?" The Wisp pouted, properly this time as her light dimmed to a soft orange. "Cal and the Incarnates are going through the lists, getting everyone out of their Cores. Unfortunately that does mean *everyone*, demons included. Which... well, that's having all sorts of interesting side-effects. Your wall is on the docket, but it's going to be a few days before they will get to you. If you want to go forward with it yourself, of course, I'm here to facilitate."

Artorian nodded, pensive as he descended into thoughtfulness. "*Mm.* Can you show me my lists of who was left? Or is that locked out too? I could likely pull it up myself if I really wanted to tick the T.M. off, but I want to save that for when it's relevant."

"Sure can, sugar!" Genevieve stole some words from her favorite people, and made the list appear. "Here you go!"

Category: Bardic College
Decanting complete.
Category: Mountaindale

Amber, Ian, Exem, Snookem Bookem, Emilia Nerys, Father Richard Demonbane, Raile, Snowball.
Category: Skyspear
Alexandria.
Category: Fringe
Ra, Bastet, Hathor, Osiris, Set, Anubis, Ptah, Isis, Ma'at.
Category: Other
Alhambra, Wo'ah.

Holding his beard as he settled into the pillow pile, he tried putting one leg over the other before remembering that was futile. Though, it didn't really bother him? No legs really should be hitting him harder, but the loss just wasn't registering. Eyes turning back to the screens, he tapped his chin. "When I was getting my face remodeled during that last fight, I could swear I saw a blip of the Skyspear. I don't know where, because I was getting slapped around a little hard, but does it actually exist? I know my Chosen have made several copies, or moved it, or whatnot."

Sitting on the windowsill, Genevieve began to do some digging. "I'm not sure if…"

"I can find it." Titania appeared, her green light landing on the open spot next to Genevieve. "You focus on decanting."

The purple Wisp froze, flickered a sharp violet, and stuttered over some words that sounded like a royal greeting. One ended prematurely as Titania put a green tendril of light on her head. "No formalities for me, precious. Keep those decanting screens steady, our old man is already trying to grab at their edges. They're fraying."

"Good to see you, Yv—I mean, Titania." Artorian had both arms wrapped around one of the screens to try and prevent it from fleeing. He needed those! When their stability returned, he let go, noting the purple Wisp was now vehemently holding to her original colors.

Titania's green hue kept equally steady. More of those Wisp rules? Titania changed the topic for him. "Sunny, remember that you have carte blanche from basically everyone to use the older names? Yvessa is fine. Which is not something I can say for that *atrocity* you are wearing."

Her soothing affirmation and camaraderie pertaining to his attire calmed him, his fingers lacing as he settled down into the bed again. Nodding, he looked out the window at the hectic, busy village while it fought with the weather. The Fringe and 'cold' did not go together. "Feels like old times now. All those years spent in that bed, and look at me now! Right back in it."

"A blessing of convenience for the rest of us, you brat." Titania's voice carried her grin without her light ever needing to show it. "Who knows what you'll be up to in no time. I heard you were awake, so I zipped right over. I'm resuming caretaker duties."

She paused to regard his living conditions. "I see that people have been trying to 'care' for you, but whoever thought that this pile of junk was anything but obtrusive has my spoon coming for them. I'm going to clean this up. Please continue your conversation."

Releasing a Wisp-barian warcry, the green blob of light smashed herself face first into the largest pile of wayward goods to commence the great cleansing. Genevieve and Artorian watched her for a moment before sharing a look, as the event played out like a training montage. The old man shrugged, pointing at the screens. "Back to it then?"

The purple Wisp bobbed to nod as Artorian gave her notes to take. "If Skyspear is conveniently real, everyone left in these lists will be going there. Plus some of the crew that are already in the New Fringe."

He pulled the Fringe screen close, moving his finger to whoever he was speaking of. "All these kids are Lu and Wu's. They need a combination of schooling, and not to be underfoot while an entire region is getting one celestial rumbling of an overhaul. Ian and Exem are counted as part of the kid-group. Alexandria needs a library, and I believe the 'Spear had one. If not, I will need to set one up, because this is a great time to spend an extraordinary amount of time doing some scribing and studying. I have a backlog burning a hole in my pocket and a host of ideas that need to see paper."

That cleared up the Bardic College, Fringe, and Skyspear lists. "Now the hard part. Alhambra, Wo'ah, Amber, Snookem Bookem, Emilia Nerys, Father Richard Demonbane, Raile, and Snowball."

"*Hmm.*" Pressing his hands together, he leaned his fingers over his mouth. "Raile and Snowball are those original Dungeon monsters? I think? I really don't know what to do with them. No humanizations either, they're *originals*. Gonna have to leave those to Cal. Scratch them from my list and hand them over to the bigshot."

Genevieve did so, the names vanishing from his list as the Cores were transferred. He gave a nod, and got back to work. "I'm stuck on Alha. Everyone else would be an easy Skyspear fit. I can ask Amber to make some portals. Wo'ah is going to love the tower-top isolation back in the place he had statues. Snook we need as a teacher. Nerys too, though I want a chat with her. As for Richard... well. We've got a whole society of demons with short moustaches for him to go after. I doubt there will be a lot of push back."

Drumming his fingers, he had to resign himself. "Alha needs his own spot. He's a society builder. Best to let him practice at the 'Spear and see what comes from it before we can find him a place. No idea how to get him people, though..."

"Found it!" Titania yelled from under a pile. She shot above it, shaking herself free from knitted creations. "Found the Skyspear building, I mean. But, it's far too big, and nowhere nearby. Somehow a copy of 'Mayev's Spire' ended up meshed into the base of that Menhir mountain. Currently it's in the middle of a desert, stuck in a comparatively tiny oasis. Ah, that *used* to be a massive lake. Lake's gone now. The underground floors of the spire are completely flooded, so at least we know where it went."

Artorian grumbled. "Amber's value just went up. I can't make platforms at the moment, so we'll have to rely on her for a gateway system. I doubt Grace is free. I'm sure we can find suitable bribes. On the plus side, I have the feeling Alha knows his ways around sand. Either way, I'm going to put a pin in this. Genevieve? Please decant Amber at the next bonfire meeting. Yvessa, can you let people know? We're going to need a host of volunteers to check the location out after the gates are down on both ends. Once they are, I'm afraid Lu is going to have her children back in tow."

The purple Wisp made her notes, performed a tiny pseudopod salute, and zipped out.

Titania hovered to the window to watch her go, her light dimming. "I wish they weren't so full of nerves around me."

"Do they have a reason to be?" Artorian wondered out loud. "She's a sweetums, and even learned how to return a good ribbing."

The green ball wobbled from left to right. "Sort of? Wisp society is a right mess, like ten C'towl all tangled in the same ball of yarn. I've got a lot of pull and sway, but the reason I have it is a bother. All I did was be myself and chase Obi around. It's not like I'm as powerful as Tot or Turnie either."

Artorian felt like his brain just encountered a runtime error. "I'm sorry, who?"

"Tatum and Eternium?" Titania clarified. "Those second-wave Chosen hanging around Occultatum that are obsessed with cooking. The soup for the soup god duo? They found out that 'Tater Tot Tatum' loves baked potatoes, while Eternium has this immense weakness for turnips. So, Tot and Turnie."

The old man's heart melted like a stick of butter in a hot pan from how precious that was. His mouth gaped as he held his cheeks with both hands, expression excited. "Now *that* is the kind of gossip I am *here for*! Tell me everything."

CHAPTER EIGHT

By the time Titania finished spilling the tea, whole napkins were stained and several pots sat empty. Artorian needed to fan himself at some of the delicious gossip. He'd learned so many juicy little tidbits nobody would want him to know! *Perfect.*

During the chat, he'd received several more visitors that only came to say hello or pop their heads in. The bards got handshakes and well-wishes, with a request for calmer music. Some orchestral goodies, or perhaps a bit of choir. Lu and Wu had gotten used to those calming tones, and that music lacked presence here entirely.

The troupe had been... *experimenting...* with something they picked up from a roaming Otter crew called 'Rock.' Meg had faltered after the others had left, then backpedaled to stick her head back into the open window, leaving some details about layering vibration effects on daggers in order to increase their cutting potential. Little discovered secrets she didn't want the others to know about yet.

Jin and Tibbins had come purely to poke fun, but were shooed away by an overprotective Blanket, who chittered at them before chasing the troublesome duo all the way around the palisade. Jiivra took their place, bringing the news that Artorian had asked of Wu.

Crossing her arms, Jiivra counted on her fingers while leaning her hip against the window sill. The flaps of her long spider silk dress fluttered in the light breeze. Unlike the excited duo of trouble who'd been chased away, the current city planner's demeanor was the picture of calm. "We've focused on several unexpected aspects due to some scarcities we didn't expect to run up against."

Settling in his pillows, Artorian paid attention. Before Jiivra could start, Keeper Irene saddled up next to her at the window, a silver Wisp sitting snug on the Keeper's left shoulder. Since standing and leaning against that hard frame was not Artorian's idea of comfort, he offered both a pillow. Unfortunately, a pillow on the ground was far too low for a proper chat, so Titania moved some chairs from within the house to facilitate. There was too much clutter in the home for her liking anyway! Placing them on the opposite side of the window in the midst of her continued cleaning efforts, Titania hovered next to the silver Wisp for a moment as the newlight gave her a salute, then got back to assigned tasks.

"Is Tarrean coming as well?" Artorian inquired when the girls customized their seating arrangement.

Irene shook her head as she sat, wearing a matching outfit that made her and Jiivra look official and important. Prominent lapis hues denoted being part of the township's council, even if Lunella had final say. "He's enamored by his bees, and the little yellow monsters seem to adore him. He doesn't go anywhere unless I drag him away from the hives. Currently he's pacing back and forth around the apiary, worrying his little head off about the cold. The bees aren't bothered, but he's worried anyway. He even asked Lunella about tiny bee-sweaters."

Artorian nodded, then moved his head to the other Mage.

Jiivra still had her thumb extended, and continued from before. "Scarcity. So we were in serious danger of running out of trees. We've sorted that out by implementing sustainable forestry. We didn't have a name for it until Cal came by to see what we were up to, suffered from a thousand yard stare, and then called it 'Daisu-gi.' A forestry technique where cedar trees are pruned heavily to produce 'shoots' that grow perfectly uniform, creating straight and completely knot free lumber."

More nodding made her raise a second finger. Artorian didn't feel like pressing the mysterious wood shortage, they had it in hand. Jiivra spoke. "We had to abandon the circular town design. As we did math on the amount of people we're likely to host in the region, we can't uphold the circular pattern for more than the part of the town you heard about last time. That wooden palisade with the Wisp trees in each cardinal direction? That's boxed into a square now. So while this square has some nice circles to it, the others might not. We needed an easier way to get our urban planning done."

A third digit went up. "Thanks to the Wisps, terraforming is easy. If we need a few acres smooth and flat for a field? Done. If we need some natural hills against the wind? No biggie. If we need water streams? Like eating a peach. The downside of that convenience is that we need to include all of those options into our planning, and we aren't exactly suited for the job. We sadly don't know anyone better. Cal *tried* to comfort us by saying, 'Don't worry, it might not survive an iteration wipe.' In truth, that demoralized us straight into the dumps."

Artorian reached to pat her on the back of the hand. "I'll talk to him, see if I can't find someone with an eye for city-growing. You do the best you can until then. Please continue."

Jii nodded, and up came the next finger. "Access to easy macro-projects was a problem we didn't expect to account for. The Wisps get bored, and the more there are, the stranger some of the... *surprise* changes are. So we've had to come up with macro-projects for them to do, and we've needed to figure out where to put them. The latter of which, surprisingly, has been a massive pain. Because we need to build the *rest* of the town around those hulking monstrosities."

The old man took his beard, trying for a braid while they talked. "Are they against smaller projects?"

"Oh no, not at all." Jiivra mentioned while sarcasm oozed from her tone. "They just finish so quickly that suddenly they're back in my office when I'm trying to get other work done, and they will not, *will not*, go away until I have something new for them."

Artorian paused his braiding. "I see how that might be disruptive. What kind of big projects have you slammed them against so far?"

Jiivra tiredly looked over at Irene, the Keeper smoothly flipping open some well-bound vellum that devoured Artorian's attention. Stuff to write on!

Her voice surprised him, as he'd forgotten she'd used that Morovian Revivification technique to patch herself up. Rather than Grandma-Irene, she now had that youthfulness back in her words. "In order; an underground sewer network that spans a square league. Part of why we needed to transition to squares for planning."

She paused for a quick clarification when the silver Wisp began making motions of concern. "A league mostly matches our old measurement for the word, with a slight change. Now a 'league' is intended to represent, roughly, the distance a normal person—non-cultivating—could walk in an hour. Depending on if you ask a Gnome or Wisp, you'll get told that's either five kilometers, or three point one miles."

The silver Wisp calmed, and got patted on the head before Irene continued the list. "Other megaprojects include: A public bath that benefits from a direct stream connection, while not connected to the water lines that we draw from in order to cook, or gather clean drinking water. Flat-stone roads connecting every part of the square league, public sanitation stations, a natural granite wall so big and thick some people wanted to live in it, a frankly obscene defensive tower on each of the four corners, and an upgrade to Genevieve's initial Odeum."

Artorian drew the map in the air, releasing a bit of Mana since he wasn't going to accomplish anything internally. He scratched at his chin when trying to fit the details. "So are the Wisp cardinal trees at these towers located at the corner points of the square league?"

Irene leaned in and pointed at the middle of the wall, near the center point between two of the towers. "No, they thought it would be fun to keep their trees near the main gates. Even though we have four main gates with this current set-up. My comfort is down the drain with how poorly designed these defenses are, but I'm working on it. I'm considering adding a star-shaped fort outside the current layout for the next Wisp project. Halcyon gave me some blueprints. We'll see how it pans out."

The old man dismissed his drawing. "Understood. Jii, anything else?"

Perking up, she pointed at the bonfire over her shoulder. "Well, I heard the Skyspear was found, and I want to go. Problem being that I can't conveniently hand off my tasks. Ali and Razor are also craving to return, and many of the local cultivators have heard the stories and are 'hype' about exploring and clearing the place of any and all monsters. They had a great time hunting through the sewers and slinging their Essence techniques around with wild abandon."

She crossed her arms to shake her head. "All the spare Essence here is both maddening and marvelous. It's so *easy* to practice. Familiarity that would have taken me years is accomplished here in weeks. Everyone is skipping whole cultivation requirements that used to be mandatory for us. They're of course *sloppy* as all abyss because there's barely any self-reflection occurring, while for us old-guard that script was flipped. So we're rather harsh on them."

Irene scowled. "Rather harsh words than a need for another *redo* because some people couldn't..."

A touch on the arm from Jiivra ended her sentence. She inhaled deeply, then exhaled firmly. "Things are much better now. Yes, I know. Astrea, Ty, and Grim learned their lessons. Though I *know* Craig was involved somehow. Even if I can't prove it."

Sagely nodding signaled wordless agreement.

Artorian just chalked it down as something to ask the monk later. If he had the chance. "Hmm. So where does that put me currently? I somewhat assumed the role earlier, but is delegating people where you want me? Most of them will know where they want to go. We need only to make the spot."

Jiivra stuck her finger in the air. "About that. Lu has been very vocal about this, because of an eventuality. See, people *will* flock to you. It's going to happen. We've already prepared for this by sticking you in an inner-circle building with a direct view of the bonfire, instead of in the housing circle where it would be the norm. We would rather people congregate in the open space and come sit at your window than creep about trying to get a word in."

Artorian *hmm'd* and resumed playing with his beard. "I want to say that I'm surprised, but I'm not. Can I safely assume that my presence is both boon and bane?"

All three women in his vicinity nodded in flawless unison.

"Right." He sighed. "Enough about the village for a bit, then. I think I'll be able to see how the rest of the developments are going just by staying snug as a bug. What's the bit I need to avoid doing?"

Irene flipped a single page in her ledger, prepared for every-thing. "People are going to come ask for your opinion and prefer-ences, but since we don't have the luxury of time to sit here all-day every-day and keep you primed on larger town plans... we were hoping you'd just direct people to whoever is doing that job. There's going to be some tasks only you can do, but the rest of us don't want to start feeling incredibly useless because so many want to guide their information flows through you. You are *ridiculously* well loved."

Artorian was both a bit proud, and yet made an apologetic shrugging gesture with the edge of his lip curled up in a tiny smile. "I'm not sorry for caring about people."

Irene hung her head. "I know, I know... I'm not complaining about that part. It's just come up before, and it was a massive problem last go around."

Artorian frowned. "Can I ask what happened?"

Jiivra and Irene both bloated their cheeks as they exhaled a fat breath, looking skywards while crossing their arms. Titania, able to skip that move, slid in with answers. "Last 'redo' was when Cal and Eternium fixed their synchronization. A whole lot of Pylons went up in flame, and Tim hurriedly spilled any soul that didn't grow up in his Soul Space out of it. Jormungandr dropped right on the borders of our village and flattened half the region. Then he caught your scent and we lost another third, as nobody could stop him from getting to you and pressing his nose up against your window to sniff-smell and see if you were alright."

Jiivra kneaded her brows. "Getting some of the more 'normal' crowds away from your window was doable. Dev, Brianna, Henry, and the like? We could reason with them. You needed space, rest, and time. Some of the others, though... not feasible. You try telling a landmass-sized super-wyrm that he can't be somewhere. Surtur had to come get him, and we didn't have a village left afterwards. Just a big serpentine ditch."

Exasperated, she sunk deep into her chair and hid her face with her hands, releasing a groan. "Irene, please take over. I'm running on fumes and need sleep."

Irene moved her hands up before dropping them. "Same boat, I'm afraid, and unlike you I'm no Mage. My hair might not be turning gray, but I feel seventy on the inside. I have completely forgotten my actual age."

Titania hummed a comforting green. "You get to restart the counter once you ascend, I hear. So try not to make it a burden. You'll be able to bypass the entire matter soon enough!"

Irene waggled her hand. "With *help*, maybe. I'm a body cultivator through and through. This Aura nonsense is *abyss*."

She then counted on her fingers. "Craig did what he could, Jii's method of ascending doesn't work for anyone else and neither do the methods. The other visiting Mages haven't been able to stay—plus I really *don't* want lessons from Henry or Marie, given they flatten anything they're near—and none of the humanized beasts that made it out of Eternia had anything useful to contribute. That they numbered *few* didn't help matters either."

Irene shook her head at that thought. "Those talented freaks with their genius aptitudes. Couldn't even understand what they were trying to convey since we don't operate on the same level. What comes natural or easy to them is both trial and gauntlets of effort for us."

Her hand waved the mentality away as she continued. "The Incarnates are busy saving the world, and any and all dungeons that can be drummed up for the cause need to jump on that top-priority bandwagon pronto. So they're not available."

Titania understood Irene better now, adding her piece. "The Wisps likely aren't being helpful because they don't know how. I'm seeing the bottleneck here. Is that what you meant by problems Sunny could fix?"

Both human ladies nodded, Irene continued speaking since Jiivra had closed her eyes and was sitting back. "Definitely preferable! Though the gossip already made the rounds that Sunny in his damaged body can't get techniques to work. Lu did not keep it quiet. We've thus spread that news around in the hopes of a solution, but most of what we're getting back is unpleasant grimaces and soft mumbles that people would 'like' to help, but really can't. The only truly positive response was from the Gnome named Deverash, who had some light explode inside of his eyes before running his short little legs off to the strange floating platform he'd arrived on. Shouting something about 'The Katarina Project'?"

Artorian nodded, but didn't recall what that might be about. "I'll check in with Dev on the leg situation then. Redirecting people is just about the same thing as delegation, which is like ninety percent of an administration job. As to helping with cultivation, I'm going to reiterate that I really do want to go to the Skyspear and set up shop in a Headmaster's office. That notwithstanding, I should be a very good option for getting people from the C-ranks into the B-ranks. Lecturing I can do all-day, every-day."

He winked cheekily at Irene for stealing her saying.

Irene merely took it as a comfort. "That would be very helpful. Thank you. Now, since it's very evident we both need rest, how about you pull that Aura back in? You *devious* Sultan of Sleep."

Artorian's massive, toothy smile made it clear he was proud. "You noticed! Oh, very well done! Here I was doing my best to be covert about it. Yes, well. I may be in need of another quick short nap as well. I think Tibbins snuck a whole lot of sleeping assistance into that pot Wu brought me, and it's kicking in. A good nap for everyone then? We can continue this in a bit."

The ladies nodded and made to leave, so the old man turned to Titania. "Wake me when Amber is being decanted?"

"Sure, but if I deem you to need more sleep, then you're skipping it and catching up later." Titania replied in true caregiver fashion. She'd lost none of her sharp edge from the pre-Eternia days, though it was clear through the fondness of her tone that she remembered that they would always be on the same team. "Now tuck in. Or it's *the spoon* for you."

Artorian put his hands up, then tugged his covers over himself and curled in for some delicious shut eye. He loved a good nap.

CHAPTER NINE

Scilla awaited him in his bonfire space when the old man closed his eyes. Appearing as a set of pink irises living on the ceiling, her voice didn't sound too stable. "You don't look half as distressed as I expected you to be."

Artorian took a moment to fully manifest his being, sitting down on a silver outcrop of tree root. The place looked peaceful. Tranquil. Filled with a sunset that came with all the expected colors, and blissful silence save for the rustling of leaves. "Shouldn't I be asking you that? Last I recall, you stopped one of Odin's attacks. That can't have been good for you."

Scilla's discomfort was blatant, her form barely cohesive as she shifted through the space as a roiling cloud rather than a person who knew to use their feet. "Downright terrible. Blocking that strike took a vast chunk out of my 'lifespan,' or whatever we want to call it until I can't keep myself together."

Artorian made a throaty sound of thought, then wrenched his hands together as he made a snap decision. "We're introducing you to the family when Amber is decanted. I want you to get as much family and town-time as we can. How long can I wait on the Tribulation before it's a problem?"

Adult Scilla's keening sound had the old man reflexively open his arms for her. The misshapen cloud bundled into his offered spot, barely able to form the arms to hug him back. "I'm... I'm out of time on that front. Stopping Odin's attack took it all. A Liminal being isn't supposed to interfere like that, and my act did terrible things in recompense. If I could have you do the Tribulation as soon as possible, that may actually help me at this point. Previously I could afford to push and wait, but now I'm... *damaged*."

Artorian hummed, rocking her. "Will going through a Tribulation mend you a bit?"

"I think so?" The cloud was hesitant. "The extra flow from the rank up would let me mend my physical form back to something that lets me walk around, outside of your mental space, without me falling over myself every five feet. If I can't even keep it together here, I've got no chance in Cal."

"Was it worth it?" The old man's tone was gentle. "Or do you regret it?"

"Both?" returned Scilla's complicated answer. "I'm hoping I can make friends with Astrea. That would mean a lot. If I can't, that's going to hurt more than I'll be willing to bear."

Artorian rubbed the cloud's head, or what counted for one. "I'm of the opinion that this will be easier than you think. You *did* save her, and I've had to give them nothing but strange explanations this entire time. A Liminal being is just another tick on the list. All will be well. They'll *adore* you."

The kind words were a comfort to the cloud, which lost a significant amount of its viscous, roiling features as the mass settled into its makeshift cradle. "I hope so."

He patted the Caligene. "I know so. So why don't you put it out of mind for a bit, and flop into a cozy lounger next to me? First nap time, then meeting people. Don't worry about your physical shape too much. I will likely need to hold off on the Tribulation until I can talk to Dawn or Cal, because if I start and then explode due to my injuries, that gets us nowhere."

Scilla said nothing in retort, returning to the ceiling. Sunny let her go, and allowed his mental self to calm in order to indulge in that nap he suggested. Taking one's own advice happened far too infrequently. There would be much to do during the waking hours.

Like always.

A green light bopping on his head woke him in what felt like no time at all. Save that it was now clearly dark outside, the heat of the bonfire tickled his cheeks, and a lively barbeque was in full swing as some of the cultivators hauled in their latest hunting trophies. Artorian blinked at the view. "Is that a pile of *bears?*"

"Sure is!" Titania sounded an awful lot like Genevieve when she copied the cadence. "They're in heavy supply and rather invasive? Entire groups of them keep coming down from the mountains and head right for us. If we don't keep their numbers down, we might actually get besieged. Some of them did a number on the west gate as is. We're thinking Tarrean's honey bees are drawing them in from all over? Otherwise we don't know, but we have to deal with them anyway because they *just keep coming*. It's like the 'there are billions' Vanaheim Hel-cow problem. Except with bears."

Artorian made a high pitched 'huh' noise through his nose, but otherwise kept seated in his cot. "Ember would have a field day with her sous vide skills. She loves to chew on bears. Usually while looking something larger right in the eyes with a 'come at me' or 'whatcha gonna do about it' taunting expression."

Titania bobbed excitedly. "She might visit! Currently I'm waiting on a Mage or Immaculate-class beast to come pick you up and carry you to the bonfire."

The old man grumbled a little, quickly wondering if he didn't have something hidden in his sleevies that would let him avoid that fate. There was always something. A spare army, perhaps? No? Darn. Before he could get particularly far with pondering how Dawn kept a whole legion of C'towl tucked away in her shadow, Halcyon's nose poked in through the window. Based on the positioning, she was floating upside down in her Orca form above the house. Was it a house? Or more of a repurposed shop? It was big, sure, but now that Artorian wondered about it, what was this place being used for before he occupied it? Later, *later*! "Cy! Darling. Are you here to pick me up?"

Turning to properly adhere to gravity, she slowly adopted her humanized form. Reaching a giant hand through the window, she picked him up, blanket and all, before cradling her Dreamer against her chest. "Of course, my Dreamer. I am filled with happiness to be of such crucial help. This is a good feeling that many who know you deeply crave. Few have the opportunity to give back in a way that feels meaningful to us. I am in a very good mood! We have been trying to either do much of a tiny thing, or contribute to larger projects we thought you would approve of."

That statement gave Artorian both pause, and food for thought. His clever, playful quip never made it from his lips as he contemplated Halcyon's words while she brought him to a prime spot in front of the bonfire. Not too close. Not too out of the way. Sturdy table next to a lounger. Right side free for handshakes, left side supported by some well-wrought birch hardwood.

He recognized the material, but it clashed with an earlier statement. "Birch? I thought all the wood was cedar now?"

Artorian gave the table some test prods and squeezes, but stopped once a flood of people were all trying to make it to him. He frowned and snapped at the lot of them when the ruckus quickly became louder than his thoughts. "Settle down! One at a time or I won't stay. I have my own introductions of new people to make, and while I love your enthusiasm, you'll all behave."

"Or else *what*, old man!" Shouted Meg from the Bardic section, playfully antagonistic. The looks she got back from well over half the congregation made her abandon her well-earned seat and run for the safety of the Odeum. All they could hear at her swift passing was a full-volume, "Nyope!"

The sound of which broke the tension and turned their glares into soft, chuckled laughter. People returned to settle and make little groups, after which Wuxius stood on a stool and smacked a ladle against the bottom of a pot. "Hello all! We can't actually accommodate everyone who showed up, so please help a bit so we can make the best of it. I need at least four more people and two more fire-pits for all the bear meat to become stew, three for a good enough supply of fresh water as we have *already* run out, and seating… wherever you can find it. Please keep in mind that most of the furniture isn't Mage quality and will not be able to hold a lot of size or weight. Thank you!"

With Wu stepping down from his stool, he was ambushed by a dozen individuals wanting more information on how to help. He directed them as best he could, which for the most part was towards a very expectant Lunella. She, unlike the poor dad out of his depth, could handle that kind of people-flood. Poor Wu had no chance unless they were his horde of children.

When one of the helpers gave her some lip, on the other hand, Lunella called out, her finger squarely pressed into Karakum's human chest. "*Pa!* Do you know this curly-mustached fencer? He says he's not sure I should be in charge."

Artorian raised a brow and replied in equal measure, wildly gesticulating with his pointer finger. "Karakum, you better listen to her or I will kick your ass all the way around this bonfire! It will not matter that I don't have no legs! I will find a way, young man!"

Karakum instantly found where he'd kept his spare respect and promptly apologized to Lunella. Who gave him one of those motherly '*mhm's*' and got right to directing him towards making a new place for a fire.

Since he had everyone's attention anyway, Artorian then clapped his hands Mahogany-style. Getting that nice '*pop*' followed by a lull of silence. "Before we get started, I'd like to introduce a new member of the family right away. Some of you saw her for a short moment when Odin was using my face to wipe every speck of dirt from the ground. We'll get him for that later, don't worry. Scilla, are you managing?"

From Artorian's shadow, an adult human arm sprouted forth. "Need a little help!"

"*Alley-oop!*" Reaching over, Artorian grabbed her outstretched palm and pulled her free the rest of the way. "Better?"

When Scilla balanced on her human feet, bits and pieces of her broke off in swaths of cloudy darkness that did their best to reform. Her voice was shaky, but there was a smile on her face. Her way of saying she was doing her best. "I've almost got myself together? I'm going to need something to lean against or I'm just going to fa~aaaa—!"

"Gotcha!" Astrea caught Scilla when she leaned the other way too far and began to fall. Scilla needed to let go of Artorian in order to get one arm around Astrea's shoulder while the other tightly gripped the offered arm and hand. "You don't weigh much of anything, do ya?"

Astrea grinned through her obvious smile, ecstatic to meet the girl that had saved her bacon. "Hi! I'm Astrea. What's your name? Where are you from! How'd you join the bundle?"

The Caligene clung as best as she could. "I... I have weight that I need to deal with, and currently can't. You're just strong. I'm... I'm Scilla, from Chasuble. I suppose you could call me a rescue?"

The Liminal being's weak smile was met with a passionate outroar of applause and cheers. Plus one Tychus who added an arm under Scilla's shoulders to give her two points of balance in order for her to stand. He chuckled softly, a more heartfelt expression on his face that bled deeply into his words. "*Heh.* Aren't we all?"

Grim appeared from behind Ty to wink at Artorian, before making hand-signals that he was going to get these three settled. An assenting nod from Artorian, and the four of them whisked away to the sidelines. Where Scilla was met with the bombardment of people that Artorian had managed to avoid. The instant flood of positive attention towards her did something good for both his hearts as his eyes took in the view. The state of her body was all but forgotten as her face beamed a massive smile. Her hand reached for handshake after handshake as she relied heavily on Astrea for support.

Artorian closed his eyes, nodded as he could feel all would be well, and tore himself away. He spoke softly, his voice a whisper. "Welcome to the family, Scilla. Welcome to the family."

A squeeze on his shoulder had him look up, Halcyon there and present. He reached up to squeeze her finger in reply, solemnly nodding as he tried to let go of the feeling gripping his insides. Cy knew, somehow, that as important as this meeting was, the parting would be too soon, and bittersweet. Her voice replied in a whisper, which he could hear plain as day. "Food as distraction, or decanting?"

Artorian held her digit, then settled in his chair and sat up properly. He replied in his normal voice, getting a grip. "Decanting. The atmosphere is pleasant, let's keep the ball rolling. Can someone get Craig? As an old Guild-mate, he might be a pleasant face for Amber."

Halcyon nodded, then looked over her shoulder at Titania, who'd set up shop on the table next to them with some basic necessities. She overheard the matter, then turned herself as several smaller balls of light sped out from nearby woodworks in order to receive orders. A few whispers later and the newlights were off in search of Craig.

Artorian liked this already. "That's some good delegation."

Titania was a little smug. "We had things well in hand without you. Mostly we're using systems left behind by Zelia. She was the true mastermind of bureaucracy. Sadly, she and Yuki still need more Iteration-sleep, so she won't be joining us for a while."

The old man replied with a curt nod. "Well done, Yvessa. *Well done.*"

The compliment brought glorious warmth to her forest green light. The praise only intensified her delight as that was exactly what she'd been wanting to hear for the longest time. The validation made her feel like she stood on top of the world, and it took a chin-nudge from Halcyon to pull her back. "Caretaker? Any brighter and you'll start blinding people."

Titania huffed and prodded her back with some green light. "Hush you! That meant a lot to me. Let me bask!"

As the Orca and Wisp bickered, Artorian looked the other way, his eyes scanning over the crowd. He recognized most of them! Though, understandably, the Wood Elves that were here kept a healthy distance away from the roaring flame pits, preferring Essence lights in favor of 'oh-bark, oh-bark, I'm on fire'!

He waved at a few, got the reply that they were all busy with something and would get to him when they could, then wondered who he was catching up with next.

CHAPTER TEN

Given the size of the gathering, Artorian thought it easier to suss out who *wasn't* here, rather than who was. Top of the list of missing personnel: the big four. No Cal, Turnip, Tot, or Ammy. Then, none of the planar outliers. No Adam, no demons. Narrowing to the supervisor circle, very few appeared to be present. No Minya, Chandra, Henry, Marie, Aiden, and obviously no Odin. No Dev, no... *Wait.* Brianna, located! She was doing her usual eminence-in-shadow trickery, but he could see her as if that entire complicated obfuscation field didn't exist. A cute trick though! She had full control over who could and could not see her at a whim.

Save for sassy sunshine spirits.

He waved at her to get Brianna's attention, then kept on tallying. He felt jolly to see Decorum in the crowd, though a weight was hanging on his boy's shoulders. Well, Tisha was nowhere to be seen. That was likely the weight. A small tuning of the ears, and that appeared to be the exact topic which Gomez was letting flow from his heart to a small group of avid listeners. Other Chosen.

He decided not to butt in.

Valkyrie Valhalla, a Lamia-shaped Surtur, and several more that he knew he recognized, but couldn't place from where, were all lending the humanized Liger their ears. The story, it seemed, wasn't out of place, as more than a few of them spoke like they had been forced to leave people they cared for behind in Eternia. He had been told a detail earlier that only those who hadn't been naturally born and raised in Eternia managed to get back out, during Tim's great tipping of the bucket.

Yes, that made sense. Tisha was an Eternia native in that regard, while he'd technically brought Decorum in. That explained why there was such a large Wood Elven host, but none of the more poignant animal-based individuals he'd met. No Yorn or Yiba, for example. No Red Pandas, neither Rip nor Tear. He expected there would be some exceptions, but he currently didn't see any.

He gave a wave to Razor and Ali when they raised their bear shanks towards him, but they were content to keep huddled in their little group. Some of the traders were also here! Members from both the S.A.S. and Rica's group were in attendance, though both counted low in number. All the traders had huddled up in their own corner, entrapped in an embattled debate concerning the prices of goods, and their value in cheese. Artorian saw fit to leave that well enough alone. Not only did he not want to deal with minutiae like that complicated 'reputation' and 'requisition' math, but he'd been requested to delegate!

He was more than happy to oblige the women in charge.

"I am always truly impressed when you can simply *see me*, Administrator." Brianna spoke with a cutting edge that Artorian could tell she did not mean. "This is my best invisibility trick. Nobody else even got a whiff of me, if the expression of your strongest Chosen is anything to go by. Do not blame your nose, Halcyon. I am simply *that good*."

Artorian looked up at Cy, who was giving Brianna a look that she didn't actually believe the Dark Elf had merely *appeared* from open space without her being aware of it. When Cy looked down, he made a nose-motion that they should go ahead and chat, since a horde of newlights were zipping back to Titania with a flustered Craig in tow. While not out of breath, he did sound like he'd been interrupted. As much as a monk could be. "I was meditating! What is this hurry that I could not be left in peace?"

"Do you know High Mageous Amber, by chance? We're about to decant her and hoped you'd be a friendly face. This new place can be a lot to take in." Artorian took an offering of meat from Tibbins when the flustered chef hurried by.

Craig, delicate and graceful as he may be in his movements, tripped over his own toes at the name drop. "*High* Mageous Amber? I know *of* her. Portal Guild Mages come with hefty renown. I may have been in her vicinity during the Mountaindale days, but that's the most I'm willing to boast about."

"*Mmm.* I see." Artorian considered the provided flank of meat, not taking a bite just yet. "Still, are you up to the task of filling her in on missing events? I'm hopeful you were informed during your own bonfire decanting, and being a friendly Guild-face, I'd hope you'd be able to do so with minimal issue. If she, of course, starts throwing her A-rank weight around, just point her in my direction."

Craig rubbed some nonexistent sweat away from his forehead. "No. I mean, yes, I can do that. Celestials above, here I was thinking I'd be getting more students added to my roster. I'm at capacity as is!"

Artorian stuck his flank in her air with good news. "Two or three more teachers from the old Mountaindale school will be decanted shortly as well, in case you know of Snookem Bookem and Emilia Nerys. So that burden will lighten. Plus, I'll be helping myself with cultivation teachings, now that I'm here. Lunella would chew my ear off if I didn't contribute."

Craig appeared to know what he was talking about. A nervous flicker of the eyes darted to the village elder's location before settling back on the old man. "Yes. I understand. I will make the best of it then."

Artorian nodded, then looked over his shoulder at Titania. "Sounds like he's ready for Genevieve. Anything else you need from me?"

"Nope! Just the starting signal." Titania hummed a soft red, turning to face the monk. "Please follow the purple wisp that will be here shortly. We need some open space for proper decanting."

Craig nodded, and walked off with Genevieve shortly after she sped onto the scene. Artorian watched them go, then looked over his shoulder again before taking a big bite of his bear flank. "Alright, this really is *mighty* convenient."

Titania reverted to forest green, and replied with a question. "You mean me being here to give easy delegation orders, or Halcyon being a porter?"

"Both?" Artorian considered, confirming it for himself by

saying the confirmation out loud. "Both. Definitely both. I was apprehensive at first, but this works. Is this roughly how it's going to be for a while?"

Titania bobbed to say yes. "Essentially. Even if you can lower your density and weight to the point that Wuxius can carry you, Cy is a measure for everyone else's comfort. Unpleasant waves were created by people seeing you get smacked into the ground, and left so thoroughly injured. The story caused some fears in that event's wake. So Halcyon will be your back and forth, since most everyone is well aware of her might."

Titania then motioned at herself. "I have sort of always been your designated caretaker, so it's just more of the same for me. With the very convenient difference that I have my own network of... what do I call them? Gophers? The newlights mean well, but they can be rambunctious. I'm no Zelia, but the Wisps will get the job done. If we don't, the Gnomes get the job, and there's a lot of sharp eyes and sharper commentary on that topic."

Conversation abruptly ceased, heads turning to the outpouring of space-bending light vomiting up into the sky from the nearby open acre. A rather upset Portal Mage wasn't acclimating to her new surroundings well, which was honestly a surprise given their whole deal was leaving one place only to show up in another.

High Mageous Amber, top class Portalmancer of the now-fallen Guild, appeared to be in a less than pleasant mood when she fielded her Aura to get some personal space. A mistake that she would soon find she shouldn't have made. "No! You get your hands away from me! Where... What happened to the fight? I was in the middle of a fight between those High Elven mooks, some Barbarians, and an Amazon remnant. Who do you thi—"

"*Pipe down!*" Artorian howled back, his fingers reaching out to pinch her fielded Aura like the ear of some misbehaving sproutling, twisting the heavy blanket that was locking down or flattening an unacceptably large number of individuals in his happy little village. Artorian didn't know why he was suddenly thinking of a boat sinking under the waves because it needed to be quieter, but the sound of a nautical whistle didn't leave his head until Amber pulled her Aura back in.

Amber donned her power like an afternoon coat, a truly affronted look crossing her face. Her head snapped in the direction of the old man dressed in attire that she wouldn't wish to see on any of her rivals, who was now holding half a coconut with a tiny umbrella sticking out from the top. A pleasantry he'd been handed by one of Rica's foxy brethren.

"Better!" His fingers released the feeling of solidified jelly. Interesting how the Auras of others had different textures? The random idea to lick it crossed his mind, but he quickly stuffed that thought away into a pocket before the idea could accomplish anything. That would be rude. "Now take a breather, sit down, and talk to Craig."

He sipped his coconut as Amber stumbled backwards and fell on her rear. The ground did an amazing job of buffeting her fall, but that was Wisp engineering for you. The reason for which he was told via a murmured whisper by his Chosen. Halcyon had, apparently, fallen through the ground once due to her density where one of the wider sewer halls was laid.

Brianna, seated with one leg over the other at the edge of the table, added a rumbling *boff* sound effect with her hands spreading apart to simulate the foundations giving way to a massive sinkhole. A pouty look from the Orca made her stop, followed by the Dark Elf pressing an apologetic digit to her own lips.

Halcyon had been very unhappy about the sudden introduction to foul water, with Lunella doubly so about the gaping hole in her town. Especially since the dreaded smells were no longer *contained*. That problem had been promptly amended by a group of Wisps who took the newly discovered ceiling weakness of their sewer halls as a challenge. Something about 'showing those Gnomes'!

Artorian missed his tiny friends.

When the ball of the festivities resumed their roll, Craig and Amber were visibly engaged in dialectics. The poor monk was doing his best keeping up with the Mage's barrage of questions.

Artorian motioned at Titania. The green Wisp hovered closer, some smaller blue Wisps neatly waiting in a row on the table for her to return. "Any chance we can get Soni? Two people who think with portals would be better than one."

Titania bobbed her light to indicate that it wasn't in the cards. "Indisposed with Adam. Aside from the three turncoats, the rest are either fleeing to Olympus, or causing problems independently on Caltopia. Inside informants are prized."

Artorian perked up. "About that. Was that planned, or not? I have my suspicions and all, but shouldn't this entire problem be moot now that Cal is back? He can Ex Machina them all dead, can't he?"

With a sing-song voice, Titania performed a tiny twirl and a shimmy before speaking. "He has to let people live li~i~i~ves, and his 'definition stretching' and 'vagueness' has gotten him into a spot of trouble. So no squishing. No poofing. We're stuck with them for a while. More... ingenious methods of handling them will be required."

Artorian choked on his coconut juice as he deciphered her meaning. "Demon *diplomacy*? Oh Abyss no! Where's Dawny? I need *my sword*."

Halcyon sputtered with laughter. Both from her Dreamer flailing to get out of his seat, and from waving his coconut umbrella around as if it were a year of the sword calendar weapon. She pressed her hand onto his shoulders as Titania dropped into his lap and spoke. "Caretaker says: Relax. Yes, pushing the demons towards Odin's little patch was pre-planned. Though that was with the idea in mind to have a place where we could drop a large, nice rock on them by accident. From *orbit*. We have the rock in place, but now we can't use it. Still, nice to have backups in the back pocket!"

When Artorian's hands flopped to his seat, he threw his head back for a childish groan. "I don't wanna do demon *diplomacyyy*... It's bad enough that I have to tolerate their existence. Now I can't *go-a-smiting*? This is *terrible*. Someone get me a peg-leg from some guy named... I don't know. Wirt? Or something. Then I need Halcyon to fly me closer, I want to hit them with my sword. *Foot*. Otherwise I want a portal to catapult Killer Rabbits of Caer-bannog through. Preferably one where they can see me shake my fist at them afterwards, while I follow up with insults related to shrubberies, and maybe a questionable rock. We got any raccoons around here? They knew their way around inconspicuous acquisitions!"

"What's this I hear about needing portals?" Amber cut in, having walked up with Craig. Stomped was a more apt term, but the ground didn't give. The look on his face said he couldn't answer some questions. The look on Amber's said she wasn't going to take 'no' and 'I don't know' for an answer. "This world is nothing like the one I remember existing so much as ten minutes ago. Craig has made an adequate attempt to prime me, but I am suffused with jitters. Having my Aura *pinched* was also not something I appreciated. You are the only one here with—"

Her words stopped like cut reception when Halcyon dropped her gaze down onto the High Mageous. Cy was not pleased about the blatant disrespect or demanding approach, and an A-rank five Beast could make themselves *very* difficult to ignore.

"I... *err.*" Artorian saw the change in pace as Amber faltered in step. She had clearly expected her rank to muscle through any red tape that might be strung up, only to drop into dilation when her senses discerned a threat, to then find out she didn't have it available. With Amber already unsettled, she froze up.

Between an A-ranker who had the run of the place, another A-ranker who she *knew* was there but for the life of her couldn't *see*, a human-appearing Beast that instinctively felt like they could backhand her back into last week, and whatever that infinite source of Essence swirling around in that green ball of light was about... she felt out of her depth. Guild swagger would accomplish nothing here. The survival-war was arguably easier to parse. Though, that appeared to be over?

Artorian smoothly motioned to an open spot, grandpa-mode engaged. "Amber? Pull up a chair, dear. I was hoping Craig would be able to give you the full rundown, but it seems to have slipped my mind that A-rankers who have been A-rankers for a while don't quite see the world from the same height everyone else does. Take this coconut. Try a sip. Then why don't we lean back while you go ahead and tell us what's on your mind, and we'll do our best to get on the same page? Sounds good?"

Amber hesitantly accepted the coconut, unsure how a drink was going to have any effect on a Mage. Much less a High Mageous such as herself. She took the offered seat when another lounger was pulled close, then tried a sip when she'd settled. Amber wheezed out loud as her eyes watered, coughing like a first time drinker who had not expected to get punched in the back of the throat. Artorian didn't suppress his giggle. "Good, isn't it!"

Amber squeezed her vision, her left hand clinging to her sternum with a firm squeeze as she turned to look at him through blurred vision. She coughed out her words. "I'm an A-ranker! **Keff*. How?*"

Artorian clapped his hands together, distracting himself by doing the thing he was good at. Being grandpa. "Call me Sunny. Welcome to Caltopia. You hold on tight to that coconut. The story goes something like this, and you're going to be glad to have your hands full."

CHAPTER ELEVEN

Amber needed several coconuts, but they had those in supply thanks to Rica, for whom this had been a very long trip. The small fox in question had large eyes sparkling with intrigue as she zipped up to as many people as she could to meet them all with child-like wonder. She was the adorable distraction Artorian kept his eyes on when Amber lulled in comprehension and needed a moment to convalesce and nurse her drink.

The High Mageous slurred her words, drunk as a twisted kite. "So all you need from me is a portal from this place, 'New Fringe'—which, *please* find a better name—to some structure in the middle of some lost desert known as a Skyspear."

Artorian wiggled to find comfort in his seat. Halcyon tugged at the blanket he was laying on to smooth the fabric, before it inevitably wrinkled again.

Amber blinked un-evenly while slapping her hand down on a different empty coconut. Like they were location markers. "Then, a connection between here and the *moon*, where Halcyon operates. One from here to Rica's trading collective. Finally, one from here to where your Dwarven friends are currently 'striking the earth' in order to make it 'happy' as they build up the dwarf fortress that is Nidavellir. Yes?"

The other A-ranker confirmed that tentative plan for her with a humming sound.

Amber closed her eyes, downed her fourteenth coconut, turned it upside down, then placed it on her face to cover her eyes as she sunk deep into her spot. Her words were slow and labored, broken by breathy giggles. "There's that word again. *'Moon.'* *Ehehe*. Moo."

Artorian nibbled on a cracker before a feisty Lunella barged up to him with a pastry. He was provided the confection with a quick grumble that translated as: 'Tibbins can do better, my personal abyss.' Then was bored into by an unrelenting gaze as the matron crossed her arms. Her foot impatiently tapped the ground, which let Artorian look down and see the grinning face of Munch poking out from behind her right knee. The Slime also held a tray with a pastry on it, and Artorian quickly deduced that he had been duped into being the judge for a competition between opinionated chefs.

Given he was never going to win against his children, he observed the... eclair? Some cream-filled thing with a layer of sweet glaze brushed on top. Looked tasty. Biting away half of the sugary monster in one go, he considered the flavors. Some pensive chewing and particularly dramatic facial movements to make Lunella sweat followed, ending with the other end being eaten considerably faster as he licked his fingers clean before smothering himself in Aura. "Delish!"

"Heavy, though," he amended as Lu was doing the finger-on-bicep-taps. "The cream alone felt like I ate a steak. Tasty as it was. Plus there was so much sugar in that glaze, I'm not sure what it was actually supposed to be."

With a sharp inhale, Lunella narrowed her gaze and looked into the distance, then nodded as if she understood what she had to do and left without a word. Tibbins immediately got an earful from half the town away as she beelined to the kitchens. "Tib, I know you mucked with my glaze!"

Given that the person in question suddenly burst from the kitchen doors and ran for the hills with a suspicious tiny cauldron tucked under his arm, that was likely the case. "You'll never catch meee!"

"Abyss I won't, Tibs!" Lunella poured back, doing a decent job at chasing a cultivator. Though without gaining much ground. "Stand still!"

"I refoooooose!" he yelled back, adding a high-pitched accent on his specifically misspoken word.

Artorian chuckled, then stopped leaning so far over the edge of his seat as they ran out of convenient sight range. He instead leaned down, and accepted Munch's platter. "What's this then?"

Munch held up a small wooden sign, using some of his colored slime to create words on the plaque. "Berry tart!"

While the pastry was innocent enough, the fork that Munch produced and handed to Artorian was anything but. Frowning at the object, Artorian lifted his chin in time to see Munch flee the scene in a litany of mad and cackled giggling. Which sounded like bubbles being blown in a hot drink. Munch had clearly just performed impressive shenanigans, because the fork between Artorian's fingers was *the* fork. Giving the implement a wiggle, he then shrugged and enjoyed the pastry with bonus catharsis. Barry was finally giving back to society! About time. "Can't say no to a dedicated dessert fork when there's a competition to judge."

His justification admittedly didn't have the strongest grounding, but 'he felt like it' was good enough for now. Someone would be coming for this artifact sooner or later anyway. Best he had it, rather than some more unsavory alternatives. He also noted that Munch had the uncanny ability to sneak into places that were meant to be *secure*. He could tattle?

Tapping the end of the fork against his mouth, he decided against it. "*Nah*. Never know when you might need to pull a convenient rogue out of your back pocket."

"You can't pull a color out of your pocket." Amber mumbled back, her recovery slow only because she had no interest in hurrying it along. "And it's rouge, not rogue. Like that tart. Or do you make a habit out of sneaking off with confections?"

Taking the empty half off her face, she stuck the tiny umbrella in her mouth and clopped two halves together to make the sound of a horse trotting. Her clarity, on the other hand, was much sharper than she let on. "This is all so messed up."

Artorian put down his remaining pastry without commenting that he might, indeed, have the tendency to keep a spare pie laying around. Never knew when you were going to drop in on some freezing bards, after all. He cleaned the fork to pocket it, then laced his fingers and leaned her way. "What's on your mind?"

The High Mageous made vague motions to her surroundings. "I'm not even at grips with being *in* a Soul Space. Mine is *tiny*. I remember thinking the whole thing was a hoax. We were just in

75

some spot on a planet where Oath-contracts put a damper on what we could do. The portal I remember going through in order to get here? It was… celestials, it was amazing. The rest of the trip is a blur in comparison to how my mind pulls towards that one memory. The transition was smooth. *So smooth.* Like wet soap gliding across a gloss-finished panel."

"Why thank you!" Cal said, still sporting the scholar's body as he elbow-leaned in on the back of Amber's lounger. "Mighty kind."

"Cal!" Artorian intoned, pleasantly surprised by the dungeon's presence. "Nice of you to join the festivities. Here I thought you'd be too busy for the next two eternities."

The scholar pushed up, his face grinning warmly like he'd been provided an invitation on a golden platter. "*Oho!* Quips from the get-go? Alright, *Legsy*, good to see you too, bud!"

Artorian released a mighty, singular 'Ha,' then reached out his hand which Cal fist-bumped. The old man spoke fondly. "Outstanding, love me some hearty humor. The warm familiarity is also nice. What brings you, buddy? Anything we need to help with?"

Cal winced, but shook his head. "No, don't worry about it. I'm here to be social. Or try? Tim is working on his approachability, I got 'bud' from him. Dani crept around the edge of the door in the workshop, and the shiver I felt crawl up my spine told me it was time to put my wrench down. Is there a lot to do? Yes. More than I'm willing to admit. Should I never stop until it's done before I come see my people? Best not. What's happening? *Oooooh*, is that pastry? Can I try?"

Artorian grinned, offered him the other half of Munch's strawberry tart, then procured the fork for Cal to enjoy it with. The dungeon gasped in slow, rising tones as he gingerly reached out to accept both. His voice was a worshipping whisper. "*This is going to be delicious.*"

The old man did his best to suppress his giggles as Cal closed his eyes while nibbling tiny piece after tiny piece of the tart, making some explicit sounds not fit for the innocent ears of sproutlings. "*Mmmf.* I can taste the vengeance. The fine emulsions of catharsis and victory mixed with the sugary goodness of the treat I'm actually tasting. Not quite quality puddle-moss, but very good!"

Amber scrutinized the scholarly man with her eyes, turning to the other A-ranker for a question. "Is he okay?"

The old man grinned ear to ear. "He has rarely been better. There's more history for you to catch up on, but pretend you just found permanent success over a pain that's been a thorn in your side since before becoming a Mage. Not only did you win, but you got to *indulge* in your win."

Amber looked at the scholar again. "He's not putting enough feeling into it then. Give me another one of those coconuts and I'll show you what a fake noise of extreme happiness actually sounds like."

Cal choked on his tart and coughed as his face turned beet red, waving that away while making an 'X' with his arms. After hacking away his shock and finding the flavor of fresh air again, he shook his head as well. "*Nu-uh*. Big no-no. We don't do that here. This is a wholesome place."

Amber picked up her old coconut, her eyebrows raised just enough to appear nonplussed and cheeky as she looked away. "Your loss. You can always distract me with mechanical talks about portals. Those have been known to sober me up really well, I hear. Makes me a downright *polite* person."

Cal conjured a third lounger to slide himself right into the huddle. "I would *love* to suddenly talk about portals!"

Artorian had to look away, shrieking with laughter as Halcyon rubbed his back. His face red from the wheezing as his hand slapped the table. "Ha! She got you good, boy!"

Amber shrugged lightly. "You don't make it to my age without learning some skillful wordplay, Legsy."

The old man's wheezing laughter turned into a hand-to-the-chest gasp, leaning back into a far corner of his lounger as his gaping mouth pointed at the High Mageous. "You devious vixen! I am so glad to have another quipper-snapper in our midst! Welcome to the family!"

Forky was returned to the Administrator, Cal delving into some of the depths of Portalmancy with a not-even-slightly tipsy Mageous. Amber had cleared her fog up with a snap. There was thinking with portals to do! Artorian, in the meanwhile, pocketed the dessert fork, and leaned towards Titania. "Well, that was pleasant. Anyone trying to get a word in with me? I expect with Cal here, the rest of the squad will start dropping in, in due time.

The green wisp checked a ledger. "Do I get a go? The Keeper and Guardian gave you the primer, but there's more on Wispy needs."

"Of course!" Artorian beamed, one of his hands shooting into the air as he fully turned her way. Everyone else was easing into their own conversations anyway, and Cal was working wonders with Amber based on her general mood and tone of voice. Though the more she got her footing, the more her politeness and obvious business acumen began to shine through, more of her old self slowly recovered piece by piece as she found her groove. "What do you need from me, dear?"

Titania made a ledger visible and turned it around for him. "Megaprojects aren't cutting the grass quickly enough before it can overgrow. By which I mean that there is too much downtime for far too many Wisps who would otherwise make their own entertainment. They all *want* to help, given they're Spring Court Lights. Though, the dissociation between 'doing something too enthusiastically would cause a lot of potential harm' and 'can't sit still won't sit still' is a problem. Can you think of anything for them to do?"

Artorian squeezed his chin, his eyes unfocusing as pensive little noises hummed from his throat. "*Hmmm... Myesss. Myess.* That might do? Yvessa, how do Wisps feel about sustained tasks? Currently it's not a problem yet, but garbage, trash, and the like will begin to accumulate and pile up. Not everything will make it to the sewers, and we don't have a disposal site. Can we add anything like that? A clean home is a healthy home, and that scales up to cities and down to people. If anyone litters egregiously, I'd also like to know *who*. Their kneecaps might be in danger."

Titania noted it down, bobbing in approval. "Some will fuss, but public service might instill some sense of belonging and accomplishment. Most of the newlights are hiding in the cardinal trees. Some are shy. Others have apprehension. A few are still a tiny bit too frightened to be seen. The rules have always been to stay unknown and whatnot. With the bigger split between Courts, not everyone agrees on those old morals. However, Oberon's declaration that Wisps could freely change between Courts instead of staying stuck in one was the real twister. His whirlwind decree picked up the entire prior house of laws and chucked it right out of the window."

The edge of her green light turned rough. "A few Winter

Court Wisps are very much on his tail for it, trying to usurp him via the 'Old Rules,' though Abyss if I know what that entails. Little of the oldest rules make any sense to me. It's like a group of toddlers got together and non-verbally agreed on how to play the game, didn't tell anyone, and then everyone else had to play an interpretive game of charades to try to come up with an explanation that sounded cohesive enough to translate what they were doing. Was it a correct translation? Nobody knows. Most uppity Wisps, of course, stand on their coat-tails that *they* have the correct interpretation."

Artorian smiled as Yvessa fussed. Her huffy tone was often interjected with a nasally exhale as she bounced around in a hovering circle with tiny steam puffs coming out the top and sides of her light. He nodded sagely and with broad motions to show agreement, even if he didn't follow her lore half the time. When Titania was done and sated, she dismissed her screen and drew in a deep breath. "I'm going to take these lights and spread this idea around. See what we can do with it. You can be cozy, and don't cause trouble!"

"I'm harmless! I'll just roll the other way and rejoin Cal's conversation." Artorian giggled, then winked. A single threatening wave from a spoon made him turn quicker than planned before the Wisps shot off to the cardinal tree in the west.

CHAPTER TWELVE

When Artorian's ears re-tuned to the conversation between Amber and Cal, they were in the full swing of deal-making. He didn't know Amber, but puzzled her personality out as the conversation went on. Regardless of being a High Mageous, and when not burdened by a small mountain of stress and uncertainty, she appeared a caring and emotional person while recounting some of her personal history, for Cal to have grounding as to what he was working with.

Apparently, she'd cried for Dale after he became a Dungeon Born, because he looked malnourished. A small detail in the story, but a notable one.

The whole Baron Dale and Mountaindale Council business was a fascinating topic to hear about. Amber kept respectful to those who held power and showed intelligence. In addition to having quite the mind on her shoulders, it was quickly clear that she was a skilled negotiator. Building those portals wasn't going to come cheap for anyone!

Some of her subtler commentary clued Artorian into her inner workings.

She hated people who were foolish, naive, and might cost her or her organization well-earned benefits. Artorian felt like he had it on the nose during one of Amber's passing comments: She'd fumed when 'James'—someone under her in the old Portal Guild hierarchy—constantly acted belligerent toward Dale. Almost costing the Portal Mages their chance to build a Portal in Mountaindale altogether. This 'James' had been sent off for an enthusiastic walk by Dale, which suddenly brought Artorian's memory jogging to the forefront. While on the roof of 'ye old headmaster's house,' Dale had told him to 'get off his mountain!'

That made so much more sense now.

Alas, not all he learned of Amber was sunshine and roses. Clear disregard for the mundane problems of non-cultivators and lower-ranked cultivators was on such a bright display that Amber didn't even seem to realize she was doing it. Any non-Mage didn't so much as earn one of her passing glances, and when Wux showed up with refreshments, the look on her face might as well have been polite disdain. Which felt at odds with her storied recollection of interactions with Dale? *Ah,* but he'd been both a Baron and landowner, hadn't he?

Amber respected *power.*

Chalking that up to her being an older generation Mage with Guild-influences, he resumed his tally of her general skillset: Skilled businesswoman. Cared for others and her clients.

Good traits by themselves. She was particularly concerned about a story detail concerning a person named 'Nick,' who used an illegal portal jump. This was highly infuriating and insulting to her because those killed people, and could have killed others when he appeared where he wanted to go.

An unforgivable black mark upon her profession.

Artorian wasn't so sure what this part of the story was about. Was she referring to the 'Nick' from the Collective he'd handed over to Dani, or someone else? If anything, Artorian was more interested that 'Illegal Portal Jumps' were on the table as a possibility. He'd always considered portals and their ilk to be either a stationary fixture, or some tapestry Soni weaved with great labor and effort. He'd only seen Grace whip one up from nothing, so hearing there was more to portal madness was intriguing in its own way.

Any complicated task done quickly was bound to come with some sort of backlash, cost, or 'unfortunate consequences.' Especially given Amber's distaste for the event.

He'd have to leave delving around in that tool box to someone else. Artorian doubted he'd have the time to play with portals, as teleportation was already rough enough. He needed far more classroom lessons for his liking on the matter, because he'd been bumbling through that ability like a drunken bee. Without Zelia, he... probably shouldn't even touch it.

Back on topic!

During the olden days, Amber served as an advisor, took pride in her results, and possessed clear love for her portal work. That last one, Artorian could definitely work with.

Her mannerisms, now that she seemed settled, were easy enough to organize on neat little shelves. She was polite and informal in speech, generally sported a calm demeanor, was not shy about showing physical emotion, and wore clear biases right on her sleeve.

In short, he could work with Amber, but she wasn't going to be a good candidate to keep in this village. Skyspear would definitely need to be the place, because if she slipped and acted poorly towards Lu or Wu, he was uncertain that he wouldn't ask Bri-bri if she was still in the stabbing business.

"Actually..." Artorian turned the other way, poking his nose into the soft conversation between a cross-legged, seated Halcyon and table-edge-propped Brianna. There was no other way for them to get on an eye-to-eye level. "Bri-bri? Are you still in the stabbing business, or is that behind you? Just... curiosity asking."

Her luminous smile was matched only by the hopeful stars twinkling in her eyes. The Dark Elven assassin's words *purred*. "I have a special affection for being behind someone when a stabbing is involved, Administrator. Do let me know when that curiosity involves more than a passing fancy? We can speak then."

Artorian turned away after a tiny nod. Both terribly impressed, and *incredibly concerned*. Well... a rogue *and* an assassin in the pocket wasn't something to fuss about, but he had the suspicious sensation that his pocket was going to get quite heavy if he kept asking silly questions like that.

Now that he thought of it, perhaps he should not have done that when surrounded by so many twitchy ears. This surely wouldn't be the start of some bad rumors? *Naaahhh.* He'd be fine. Amber's sudden case of nervous sweating was likely entirely coincidental. So was her shaky grip on her coconut and accompanying big swig. Yes. Surely it would all be fine. He had in no way just spoken to an individual Amber could not see, but heard and possibly recognized.

Most others couldn't see Brianna, literally the best assassin currently in existence, when she did not want them to. Artorian pretended extraordinarily hard that he had not just asked a very overt question pertaining to a sudden and disquieting health check.

With full blasé attitude and aloof nonchalance.

Yes. Surely the bonfire was just getting to Amber a bit. He sipped his own coconut, looked at her, and smiled a large harmless smile. Why Amber's forehead dabbing momentarily doubled was a vast mystery, but she sputtered out her words in direct attempt to re-seat herself into a position of politeness and charm. "My apologies for before, *Administrator*. When you so kindly introduce yourself as one would a relative, I—"

Artorian shook his head and waved her attempt at diplomacy away. "Water under the bridge, my dear. All's well. Please don't mind me too much, I'm just an old nobody helping people I hold dear."

Amber believed that about as much as the distance she could throw the old man. She'd be lucky if she got her hand on his atrocity of an attire, given the sudden, incredible amount of eyes being very subtle about not looking in her direction. All that attention was incredibly keen on her actions and responses until the 'innocent old man' said she was in the clear. There were too many big crossbows here for her comfort.

She was in a direct conversation with Cal, the actual dungeon, on regional improvements. That was normally plenty of '*big oomph*' to keep around. Yet that was different from having the majority of inhabitants in a town give off the kind of feeling that it would not be safe anywhere, regardless of where one slept at night, to cross a person with an amount of soft power at his disposal equal to the dungeon's hard power. Amber thought to herself: *Don't abyss with the dungeon. Don't abyss with the old man. Easy peasy diplomacy squeezy.*

She smiled wide, her voice in full diplo-mode. "Well, thank you kindly. I will strive to see to the continued health of this pleasant and growing community."

That wording was cherry picked, and to her delight found its mark when the old man vigorously nodded in approval, raising his coconut to her. "Well said, well said!"

Silently releasing a breath she didn't realize she'd been holding,

Amber melted into her lounger. The more things changed, the more they stayed the same. A small smile did play on her lips. She'd be making portals again very soon! Possibly with an entire slew of lessons accompanying them! What she knew of portals, and what this place could offer her, were leagues apart. Her love for her craft tingled in her heart, and Artorian felt satisfied as he received a sympathy nudge from that connection.

He could leave Amber to her own devices. She would sort herself out.

<Your thoughts are loud, my Dreamer. I take it I will not be throwing that one into orbit?> Halcyon whispered through a private mental connection as her hand reached to touch his shoulder.

The old man placed his hand onto hers for a gentle tap, and to obfuscate the chat, while he noted this peer-to-peer option being available with a new touch limitation. He mentally replied, sounding sated. <Yes, all is well. You heard me puzzle out Amber? >

Halcyon confirmed this for him. <I did, my Dreamer. Proximity made your thoughts as clear as summer rain. A comfort that works as normal, honestly. The new mess with the Pylons has temporarily fuddled with the more convenient ways of speaking. I also have the suspicion that someone is listening in on normal Forum conversations. I have apprehensions about a certain 'Task Manager'? Something is interfering with normal mental connections, and they are being routed through the broken system instead. I suspect foul play. I will let go shortly, my Dreamer. Zelia taught me that clever ruses must be swift. I shall leave this portal maker be.>

Breaking her link by taking her hand away, the Administrator created a strike mark on his mental tally next to this 'Task Manager,' then returned to the flow of the moment.

Artorian enjoyed the general atmosphere for a good while. He sat back, sipped fancy drinks, and snacked on confections that fled from the woodworks and made their way into his hands. All in all? A good gathering. There was laughter, some light music, and heavy discussions all around. There was no difference between experiencing a 'big happy' and a 'small happy,' so he found this pleasant.

He'd expected to get mobbed more. This was certainly nicer.

Laying back, he pulled his soul item free and compressed the fluff to the size of an average face-snuggling device. "You poor thing. You're all beat up. All those pillow fights took the seams right out of you. Oh, yup, that's a tear right at the corner. Better fix that."

Sticking his tongue partially out the side of his mouth, Artorian concentrated. Condensing some Mana from the open air that he released from between his fingertips, he formed the energy-equivalent of needle and thread and fussed to himself as he patched up his pillow like a seamstress from ancient times.

He was lost in his task until, many hours later, the familiar voice of Tater Tot snapped him back to reality. Thankfully, with no change in gravity. Tatum's tone was high pitched on approach, his swagger indicative of someone trying to play off terrible news. His voice was intentionally drawn out and comedic as he stopped to lean against Cal's chair. "*He-heeey*, Boss-MAN."

Cal stopped cold and turned only his head to look at the half-smiling Incarnate who'd swaggered his way over. He already knew this wasn't going to be good, not buying anything the man was selling when Tatum clasped his hands together like a salesman that only used Ea-nasir's low-grade copper coins to peddle spicy dirt. "Hey, so, we've got a small problem."

Cal closed his eyes, inhaled with tense slowness, and breathed out his words like a foreman who'd just lost his last abyss to give. "I'm renaming you to *Ricky*."

CHAPTER THIRTEEN

"Sure. Call me Ricky if it helps." Tatum rubbed the back of his head, his expression sheepish. The man then made a small gesture to Artorian, realizing he should probably know now rather than find out later. The sly old man would be finding out anyway. "Sunny being informed might help in the long run, but I sadly do need to steal you away, boss."

Cal hung his head, then shook Amber's hand with some parting words that she could begin when she felt like it. He made a minor motion as if he were calling someone, then Cal was knocked right from his seat to the tune of *"Daddddyyyyyyyy!"*

Cal ended up thoroughly tackled, releasing a fatherly *ooof*! Like a stack of pins toppled by a heavy ball.

A Wood Elven group in the back appeared from the bushes in instant response, all holding up signs that proudly exclaimed: 'Strike'! Cal's seat also toppled when the Wisp bowling ball smashed in, his leg comically stuck in the armchair spoke as Grace took her daddy down to the ground with her. The scholar ended up fully splayed on the grass in an inglorious heap while Grace pressed into his cheek, creating a sound like a siren.

Everyone watching burst out in undignified laughter as Grace used Cal's head as a trampoline, the small Wisp gleeful and excited. "I'm heeeeere! You called, Dad?"

"Yes, I—" Cal sputtered as he interposed his hands between

his face and the bouncing globe of hard light. "Grace, would you just—"

"Oops! Gotcha!" Grace landed on the flat palm of Artorian's outstretched hand as he reached to catch her, allowing Cal to get up. Artorian chuckled at the instant pouty face he received as reply from Grace. She had clearly been intending to continue as her colors bristled, settling on the poutiest periwinkle she could uphold. "Very adorable! Amber, your palm, please?"

Amber upturned her palm, receiving the Wisp as Grace was gently deposited on her hand. She blinked at the globe of light a few times, not really believing what she was seeing. Artorian smiled, and filled in for her. "Please meet Grace, Cal's little one, a Wisp, and… infinitely better at portal making than you."

Amber's eyes cut through space to stab Artorian to death purely with a look from that blatant accusation. She puffed up, gathering the air to bury him in words. Air that expelled from her lungs as a wheeze when Grace joined the fray with a massive grin on her face. She made orange and blue *gates* on either side of her, which she put to use by juggling a piece of fruit through them! Grace dropped the item through one portal, and angled the other so it would neatly deposit the fruit back into the first one, without fail, in a cute upwards arc.

Grace stopped both advanced portals when the High Mageous's jaw fell, then let Artorian have the piece of fruit as it redirected during the next portal-hop for him to catch, and zipped away from Amber's hand like a bandit breaking for the edge of town. Amber flung herself from her chair in full-on haste, throwing herself after the beelining ball of light. "No, come back! How did you do that?!"

Artorian heard Grace reply 'aperture bath curtains and shut-ters' before she was out of audible range. He nodded and turned back to Cal, who was brushing himself off. "They're going to be great friends. I'm guessing a distraction is what you needed Grace for, and she caught on with flying colors?"

"She did when you got cheeky. My little girl is a lot smarter than she lets on! I love her so much." The dungeon gushed before pressing his hands into his hips. "As to friends? I think so as well. Still. I'm needed. Have you been to my secret workshops on the moon before?"

The old man shook his head. "Only some of Tot's hotspots."

Tatum groaned at the mention. "How did that nickname get ouuuut?"

Cal flashed a wide grin. "Just wait until 'Ricky' spreads around."

Artorian giggled, then motioned at his leg situation. "How do you want to handle this, Cal? I've already got the sense this is neither a quick nor convenient fix. Someone will have to carry me."

Halcyon picked him right up, bundle and all. "Clearly I am going with you, my Dreamer."

Tatum provided a nod of approval, and Cal clapped his hands to translocate them all without any further delay. A movement method that... Artorian didn't know how to describe, because there was nothing to describe. No new sensations. No 'pulling,' or being moved through a layer. No flying, or teleportation, or any such measurable alterations happened to him.

They were just... elsewhere now.

The new space was large, open, and riddled with hovering Iridium tables covered in all sorts of ledgers and plans. Artorian leaned over to touch a dark gray support pillar that felt like coarse stone, just to get a sense of reality. Which led to a ceiling seemingly made of soft light, which for some reason currently wasn't enough to quash how unsettled he felt.

He tackled it with a sanity check question. "We moved, right?"

"We did." Cal shoved his hands into his pockets as he wandered over to one of many, many work tables, away from the ones laden with ticking dangers. The table of choice was positioned near a thoroughfare, piled with documents of all kinds that had either a group of Gnomes or Wisps pouring over them while embattled in a debate consisting of hot whispers and slap fights. "This is the staging area for new projects. We can get anywhere from here. For anything sensitive, we go by one of the well-defended rivers. For non-sensitive matters, it's a walk to another floor or section. The moon is my oyster, so to say."

Artorian didn't understand, but there was too much he didn't understand all in one go to really pin down what he wanted to ask about. "I'm going to go with the flow for now? I need more grounding."

Tatum made a 'this way' motion, and began walking over paved and polished moonstone flooring. The gemstone variant.

They passed through the staging area leading to complicated architecture that very boldly said 'junction,' based on how it connected the staging area to several pathways and travel options. Some went up, some down, there were even a few slides, chutes, and ladders. Some local residents were clearly using break time to make a game out of those options, and Artorian began getting the gist that the method 'up' and 'down' was an idea determined purely with where the lighting was.

On their walk down a set of particularly wide stairs designed for a creature much larger than any of them, Vanilla zipped up to Tatum with one of those mischief-laden expressions. Her voice was no different. "What's hot, Tater Tot?"

Tatum closed his eyes, exhaled, and replied flatly. This was not a good time. "The flames of the abyss."

"Oh." Vanilla realized his mood only after he spoke. Then slid a small cauldron of soup piled full of roasted potatoes out from behind her hip. "Is it too much to ask for you to say 'what's cooking, good looking'?"

He placed a hand on her head, giving it a rub as they walked. "It is right now, 'Nilla. Later, perhaps? Important work needs to happen."

Pouting, she nodded, visibly deflated, and slunk off past them until mommy Halcyon swept her up with a free arm. Artorian relieved Vanilla of the soup cauldron, absconding the treat right onto his lap as he was being arm-carried himself. He had plenty of room for the meal, and as usual, Grandpa-torian remained the ever-present voice of support. "Now, we can't let this go to waste while it's fresh. So what's cookin', good lookin'?"

Vanilla's ears shot up, followed by a beaming expression as her dropped mood picked itself right back up. Artorian got a look from Tatum, but he shrugged back. "I'm either going to be distracted with food, or I ask you a barrage of questions when you clearly want to be talking with Cal right now."

Tot considered that, nodded in agreement, and instantly stepped up to be at Cal's side as he whipped secret documents out from his inner robe pocket. "Here are the improved schematics for the Demon-Banishing Runes."

Artorian choked on a potato, instantly regretting he'd chosen a snack over conversation. If the topic was slapping down demons, he wanted his nose so deep into the information that… Actually, he wasn't going to finish the metaphor. Instead, he made grabby hands.

Cal took the blueprints, leafing through them. "Here I thought it was about my Eternium suggestions. How *did* you feel about being the Divine of Coffee? You're slated for Dark and Water, after all."

The Incarnate grimaced. "That *wasn't* a joke? I don't... Abyss, Cal. *Dale* can have it for all I care. What am I going to do with coffee? I already have the jitters naturally."

"In before you get a follower named Joe, and you're the god of a cup of Joe. Personally, I think that is exactly the sort of quality punnery I'm looking for." Cal shrugged, then paused as he felt like engineering that a bit. "In fact. That's too good to pass up, and we were trying to figure out a limiter on those old punishments we're still working out. Limiting your first proper interaction in the working version to someone named 'Joe' is delicious cappuccino. I'm doin' it."

"Ca~a~al." Tatum groaned, making hand motions that pinched his fingers together. "Why do you do this to *meeee?*"

"You deserved it. Obviously! Don't fuss too much, it'll only be for the working version. You get to do what you want during the beta test. Eternium is going to need the help." Cal wore a massive, pleasant expression. He clapped the Incarnate on the shoulder, then resumed leafing. "Now what's this about? These look fine. You did misplace this one piece of vellum though. This is about Whispers?"

Tatum took the page and scanned it over, Artorian asking the question from behind them. "Would that refer to those strange words we keep hearing, or becoming aware of, or randomly jumping to the forefront of the mind? What *is* that about? Been happening constantly."

"To me in the olden days as well, actually. Before Xeno snagged them." Cal squinted, thinking about it.

Tot appeared to have an answer ready, and spoke like a collegiate lecturer. "I'm surprised you're getting them with frequency, Artorian, you're not an Incarnate. Then again, Cal wasn't either. The Whispers are very normal. They happen anytime a Heavenly rank is paying an unhealthy amount of attention to you."

Cal snapped his fingers, the knowledge clicking. "**Madness** did that to me!"

The Incarnate folded up the page and tucked it into his sleeve. "We believe so, yes. The occurrence happens more often than we find comfortable, but we can't exactly tell a Heavenly what to do, or what *not* to do. If you have their attention, then you have it. The longer it happens, the worse the Whispers get. The event is rarely beneficial, mostly because I'm working with the theory that the 'when' factor of their information does not line up with ours. Resulting in us ending up with an answer that we just don't know the question to, and that can get very troubling."

Artorian resumed inhaling soup while Halcyon mothered Vanilla, giving Tatum some blissful quiet time to invest in calibrations with Cal. He chuffed at the thought. "Cal-ibrations."

Tot's momentary distraction put Cal on a tangent. "The Essence-Calibration Project? I thought that was sorted?"

"The what?" Came from behind them when Artorian was between bites.

Tatum grumbled only a little, then felt it best to just explain. "No, that's running optimally. The E.C.P. is what we're calling the method in Cal's Soul Space by which we seamlessly swap from Essence, to Vaporous Mana, to Liquid Mana, to Solid Mana, to Spirit, and back."

A thought struck him, Tatum turning with a finger in the air. "Speaking of, please do not do what you did during the Odin fight again? Devouring massive swaths of Essence out of the stratosphere or mesosphere confused the abyss out of the Pylons. You could just have gathered Mana instead, by thinking about it. We know that, at the time, you did not know this, but abyss man, stick to your energy lane."

Artorian laughed in amusement and to cope with the feeling of sudden dejection. "I could have been pulling Mana that *entire time?* I shot myself in the foot!"

Cal giggled, then shook his head. "We're still reviewing the recordings, but haven't been able to make it a priority. My docket is fatter than a whale at a krill buffet. I remember it was pretty fun to play with the energy types like dough. Did you know they all feel different?"

He made motions like a baker molding bread. "Moving Essence and moving Mana, of any type, is a completely different sensory experience. I was wondering ages ago why Dale could freely play with his Mana without moving his Essence, and vice versa, but turns out that had a really simple explanation. Like, Mages can have some Essence in their Aura, but it will just... hang in there? Like a C'towl on a poster."

Cal smirked at his own joke. "Sometimes I think all the energy types are slightly sentient. From Mana and up, I really start to wonder, because I've seen it behave in both strange ways, and occasionally with hefty bias. Oh, Artorian! You're actually a case study in one of those."

"Because Mana loves me? The old man inquired, a pensive hand on his beard. "I noticed that aspect stuck around from Eternia."

"Yeah!" Cal was enthusiastic. "The technique Odin tossed your way took itself apart when realizing you were the target, and I find that mighty interesting. Because it does *not* do that for me."

Artorian beamed. "Jelly?"

"A little, yes, thank you for asking!" The dungeon shot back, before the three of them devolved into bouts of hapless laughter as the stairs gave way to a massive bulkhead of a door. "Alright, we're here. Ricky, show me the thing."

Tatum performed a silly salute, opening the doors without touching them. "You got it, boss-man!"

CHAPTER FOURTEEN

This new workshop was a vast monstrosity of available space, with tables on tables covered in equally whimsical and questionable thingamabobs. Some objects were in stasis, but looked primed to explode. Others already had, and were being dissected.

Aside from the entrance that Cy fit through like a charm, Artorian could not find any walls save for the one behind them. He even tapped on her arm to turn so they could both look back at the door. The bulkhead was very much there, but aside from the single natural wall of moon rock the entrance gate was nested in, the only visible thing keeping the ceiling from collapsing to the floor were questionably thin orange-colored metal beams placed equidistant from one another.

Based on some marks on the gemstone floor, Artorian deduced that the supports had moved... Twice? Eyeballing it, column spacing began at fifty feet, then expanded to... about fifty-five? Currently, optimal column spacing appeared to be sixty feet exactly between beams. Halcyon walked next to a support strut so the old man could prod at one, finding both grooves and a magnetic sticking sensation as he brushed his fingertips across. "Curious."

Peeling away from the beam's static field when Halcyon followed the other two as they advanced onwards, Artorian darted his eyes around for more goodies. He had to give the logistics here serious credit. Gnomes dressed in all sorts of colors marked with differing insignia zipped from square to square without ever bumping into one another. Regardless of the load in their hands. "How are they doing that?"

Cycling a little Essence to his vision, only for his Mana to perform the equivalent action instead, the hidden guidelines bloomed with color in his view. Dedicated walking spaces were marked out in stripy yellow lines of one-way-traffic, complete with glowing arrows that each were a work of art. A whole network of otherwise hidden specific-speed lanes was laid bare, and it was gorgeous. He guessed that the amount of chevrons dictated the *nyoom*.

Artorian couldn't see an arrow that didn't have some Wisp-influenced flourish to it. "*Oooh*! I get it! The Wisps did the markings. I'm betting that because they got to determine where Gnomes walked, they got extra snippy about it, and added all that flavorful flair."

Artorian's nose tingled when Cal groaned, handing a pouch to Occultatum as the lanky man smirked victoriously. "How do you always get that bet right? Have you lost one yet? Can you do that soon? These Cores are hard to make, Ricky!"

"*He he he.*" Tatum's mood bloomed like a spring flower. "Your own fault for betting against our old man in a contest of noticing details. Now I even have too many!"

Cal harrumphed, wagging his index finger at his colleague. "You just wait, I still have a chance to get those back."

The motion clued Artorian in that there was more. He tapped his lips and looked around, but didn't find anything particularly strange about the Gnome-powered warehouse until one walked up one of the beams holding boxes twice his size, straight up into the soft glow of light above them. "Now why would he need to walk up the beam?"

Inspecting the ceiling and bypassing the light, Artorian squinted his adjusting vision, then snapped his fingers. "The ceiling is another work floor! Which does not at all appear bothered by being upside down? Oh, hey! Gravity runes! Our floor must be their ceiling, and light!"

Cal released a pained throat-noise when he stopped to lean his head back. "Come *onnnn.*"

"*He he heeee!*" Tatum cackled and extended his hand, his fingers making a clear 'hand it over' motion while the schmoozing and pleased expression on his face oozed with cathartic luxury. "That's what you get for opening your big mouth! *Gimme gimme!*"

Cal slapped another Core into Tatum's hands, then marched on while mumble-fussing to himself. "Stupid Incarnate and his stupid friends and his stupid good guesses and his stupid bets that I keep thinking I will win, like a stupid."

Halcyon, carrying a very placated Vanilla and a glum Artorian because he was all out of soup, saddled up next to the beaming Incarnate. Cal hustled along in front of them to fume, so Artorian leaned over to sneak a peek at Tot's gains. "What'd'ja win?"

Tatum rolled the unimpressive crystal bismuth marbles between his knuckles, then held each up to his eye in turn. "Nothin' much. Two *Luminous*-quality Beast Cores."

Halcyon glowered at the man, grunt-growling from the back of her throat. She wasn't happy about that detail at all. "We have *enough* geese on the Moon's surface, *thank you*, Void Dreamer."

Tot winked up at her. "Don't *worryyy*, these aren't for geese. These... These are probably going to be for trade. My Honor and Requisition systems are just not working out well. Either they're used to extremes, like in Olympus where the logs all show them using the system to pull a fast one on someone else. Or people approach the topic with pure discomfort, and pretend it doesn't exist. I'm considering a spirit-stone-based economy test instead. Nutrition, Cultivation, and Monetary value all rolled into one."

Halcyon was not put at ease, her only recourse being to trot away from the dreamer and hurry behind Cal using a gait that was very power-walky. Ricky's giggling as he caught up behind them did not help either. "It'll be *fiiine!*"

Artorian poked his head over Cy's arm with his eyebrows raised. "We don't believe *youuuuu!*"

Cal was amused, but interjected. "Will you two stop elongating your words back there and come tell me which of these red zones needs my immediate attention? Also, why are there three? Ricky, you said we only had one problem."

"I did not!" Tatum clarified as he hustled to the front, crossing across an extra thick solid yellow line, then an orange line, then a red line on the floor. Each of which was easily a foot wide. "I said we had a problem. Not how many."

"Boy..." Cal broadly motioned at the three workspaces

where groups of Gnomes, in attire colorations matching the danger levels of their projects, patiently stood on the sidelines. "Well?"

Tot stopped, motioning at Halcyon. "Cy, don't cross the orange line, there won't be anything left of you."

Halcyon squeaked to a halt at the border of the yellow line, refusing to cross even that one. The glare on her face spoke volumes that she would have loved to know that information *before-hand*. Cal clearly thought that was silly and frowned, flicking a hand to add a red insignia to Vanilla's, Cy's, and Artorian's current attire. Even if Artorian's attire was making a few Gnomes faint at the atrocity of its very existence. Entire divisions were being hastily put together to remedy his clothing situation, because·if *that unforgivable sin* was what the Wisps were giving him to wear, clearly they were taking over the department.

One of the Gnomes, dressed in a dapper outfit that made Artorian think of Deverash's choice of threads, strolled past them with a saucer balanced on his white-gloved hand. He moved over the lines like they weren't there, and provided the dungeon an Americano and the Incarnate a fresh latte.

Tatum took it, but his expression faltered before slowly lifting his chin to sneer at Cal, whose mood was now what Tatum's had been previously. The Incarnate grumbled. "You did this on purpose. I didn't even notice you called a barista."

Artorian was far too busy snapping his head back and forth as he was dying to know how that Gnome had come and gone. He hadn't noticed the barista until the dapper man entered his sight, and barely noticed that same Gnome leave until the tattletale sound of a *pop* reached the edge of his ears. Artorian 'huh'd' loudly, then turned to Tatum. "He spent a whole teleportation on it too."

Tatum went 'pfffff' in an amused exhale, motioning at the table on the left. "Might as well go clockwise. Which is the easiest... Swanson? You want to tell Cal what's going on with the Banishing Rune?"

One of the few Gnomes still seated at the table turned on his stool. Though it seemed to be the stool which rotated, as the Gnome looked over the brim of miniscule rectangular glasses up at Cal with the bushiest raised eyebrow in existence. The short man spoke like a person who was already bothered about the visit when the day had barely begun, and they had the entire shift still to go. "Does bacon go with eggs?"

"Well, Ricky, does it?" Cal looked at Tatum with strong amusement, quietly sipping his Americano as the Gnome glowered at the Incarnate.

"Don't throw me under the C'towl like that, boss-man." Tatum had a hint of a pout, though he turned towards Swanson to placate the project manager. "All the bacon, and *all* the eggs, Swanson."

The Gnome nodded with profound understanding, grumping as he shot off his stool with his hands pressed behind his back. Tiny legs paced around the table as he got right into giving Cal an earful.

Artorian was distracted by a keening noise from Halcyon, who he turned to post haste in favor of overhearing Swanson's intro. "Dear?"

"I'm uncomfortable…" She whined, her eyes flicking to the ground which she had still refused to cross, then to Tatum for messing with her like that. Her existence meant a lot to her, and she squeezed her Dreamer a little tighter, like a teddy bear, for comfort.

Artorian followed her gaze, then decided Tatum looked far too comfortable in that relaxed, slightly leaning, hand-in-pocket pose of his while he sipped his latte. Meddling Technique: Stirring the Pot, immediately activated. He waited for just the moment when Occultatum was drinking, then spoke out of left field. "So Occy, what *is* your **Law**?"

Tatum choked on his coffee, violently coughed, had to put the cup down and lean his hand on the table for support, then slapped his own chest. Halcyon snorted at the sight, which to Artorian meant mission accomplished. Tot rounded on him, then accusingly stabbed a pointer finger in his direction, and wheezed out his words while still choking on his latte-chug.

Shouldn't have taken such a big swig!

Tatum swallowed his embarrassment before chastising the old man. "*No!* No, Artorian. Bad! You know better! I am not telling a soul! Everyone has been free and welcome to make their guesses and stick to their assumptions. I let the Chosen have their Void Dreamer. I ignore people's **Law**-guesses and whispers of: **Nothingness**, **Oblivion**, **Hidden**, **Unknown**, **Discovery**, all of it. I *cannot* tell you. We don't speak of Cal's because there's too much to unpack, we don't speak of mine because it is outright *dangerous* to bring up. You want to call it something? Try Aurora Borealis. That's innocent enough, and pretty to think about."

He faltered, kneading his brow as his hand pressed to a column. "I need to get my mind off it. What's a terrible thought? Right, Yuki, goddess of all things ice and snow, making me a caramel frappuccino with a heavy valley girl accent."

Occultatum shuddered powerfully, then opened and closed his hands to squeeze them. "Alright, I'm good. I'm good."

Cal overhead him and laughed from the other side of the worktable. "Ha-ha-haaa! Is that who first came up with the coffee idea? I was wondering where it came from."

Tatum righted himself, grumbling as loud as Swanson. "Of course it was Yuki! Timed right on the cusp of the comment where Vanilla said I looked hot. We were tuning Elysium, of course it was hot! We were *in the sun*. I was having a great day, feeling smug, and she took me down several pegs with nothing but words and a few wrist motions. Then there was a frappe in my hands and not a soul who saw it has ever been able to let it go."

Tatum vented with momentary anger. "That icy, frozen... *Oooohh*."

"Can we get back to it, please?" Swanson rumbled with begrudging respect. There was a cup of pure black liquid in his hand when Artorian knew them to have been empty prior. Perhaps that barista had a personal teleporter? Swanson's voice droned like a foreman who wanted to get to work. "The banishment effects failing across the board is but the first and least of the current issues in this sector, and I'd like to move on to the Northmen Tattoo Dilemma, and... *boh*... I don't know, time acceleration Pylons cascading catastrophically?"

Cal handed the blueprints he still held to Swanson, who took them and spread them out on the table. The Gnome then shot Tatum the stink eye. "Was wondering who *nicked* the originals."

With Halcyon finally brave enough to venture across the lines, the lot of them filed in behind the Gnome as he restarted his explanation. "As I was saying..."

Unfurling the full and proper document on the Demon Banishing Rune, Swanson stabbed his stubby finger down on the section where a Rune had been circled several times already. "I told the boys last time, and I'll tell 'em this time too. This configuration does not tighten the bolt remotely well enough for the 'X' being banished, to be returned to the 'Y' plane of origin. The Chains of Chaos get a right giggle out of the attempt, then play Wisp ping-pong with the demons being sent back. I swear that each time we get one slapped back into one of the Cores, the chains go: *Olé!*"

Swanson grunted. "Bottom line, the entire project needs to be discontinued. We can't spare the Gnome-power. Not to a project where we know the outcome won't satisfy the minimum requirement. These runes cannot currently perma-banish demons."

Cal drummed his fingers on the table. "This feels like it needs more of a 'say so' from me than any actual thinking, tinkering, or choices that need to be made."

Swanson nodded. "The D.B.P. began under Wisp jurisdiction. We can ask you to cut through the red tape, or we can spend four months breaking the Fall Court's door down."

The dungeon exhaled, waving the entire idea away with the back of his hand. "This project is scrapped. End of discussion."

"Can do, boss!" Swanson the Gnome beamed with delight. He loved it when problems received a direct, neat, finalizing pin to stick in them. Furling the document right back up, he walked over to the next section.

Artorian noticed the red and orange stripes around the D.B.P. area clearing away as everyone left it. When Swanson arrived at the next section, the work area they had left was fully converted to tinker away on another project entirely.

The header on the table now said: S.G.R. - Sugar Glider Racing.

Artorian was interested, but he still wanted to know why he'd been dragged along on this trip first. Then, there would be delicious troublemaking. Several of these sections he wanted to deftly poke his nose into. He whispered to himself. "Soon."

CHAPTER FIFTEEN

"Next on the docket. *This mess*. I have seen some devious patterns during my time as a foreman, but this beastie takes the sprocket. *Shlum*, if we didn't know that an infernal dungeon put this together, I would be having serious concerns about our ethical committee." Swanson shook his head while unfurling the designs on Northman Tattoos and their... unsavory details. "Boss, please tell me that whoever you got this from ain't on our Silverwood tree?"

Cal leaned his elbows on the table, then shook his head. "The Northmen's 'Voice of the People' infernal dungeon and its 'Wards of Fek'koff' were no joke. I offered, but they refused me. I'm fairly certain they knew they were going to die after I left, unless that suave speaker was really so delusional to think it would be fine. We have other infernal channel Cores on the Silverwood, but none of them with that kind of personality. Current theory is that the mind in that specific Core was from another plane, unless my entire hypothesis about intelligent Cores is bunk and they all become that cold and heartless. I don't even remember it having a Wisp, and it was not suffering from Dungeon Madness."

Cal motioned around at the sinister designs on the table. "Now what's the problem here? Ethical or not, a tool is still just a tool. We're not going around blaming the arrow when someone gets shot by a bow. It's always the wielder."

Swanson dropped his thumb on a poster-sized blueprint. "This is part of the project on how to sustainably and safely transfer one ability, from one person to another, *without* relying on a Pylon for transfer, or memory Core to double as housing. Wood Elven head-bonking yielded no fruit we deemed worthy of eating, and was moved to another table."

The Gnome clarified. "We encountered a problem in the stage where we tried to copy a set of memories mid-transit, specifically because it *didn't work*, and we're not sure why. Currently, the bolts are on genetic coding, but it doesn't explain some… oddities."

Cal nodded and made the chin motion for more of the project to be unfurled and revealed. "Give me the quick and short of it. This sounds like something we can table and back-burner."

Swanson rubbed his hands together. Progress! "We had to do some digging through Old World lore, as the Northmen weren't going to be forthcoming with any information. We asked a few, but they clammed up, and we didn't have an otter around to break the shell open."

Making a motion for some other Gnomes to bring in some history books and open them to the correct pages, he turned his finger into a light-pointer when the dusty tomes were propped up. This way, Swanson could designate the highlighted section without needing to crawl onto the already packed table. "I'm going to have to break this down into the W's for this to make sense."

His onlookers nodded, so Swanson got to it. "Who are the Northmen barbarians? When did this set of flesh-runes come about? What are these tattoos actually? Where are they useful? Why would this need to exist in the first place?"

Cal's expression turned unpleasant. A history lesson was not why he was here.

Swanson appeared to be aware. "I just needed the questions spoken, Boss. The boring stuff I'm keeping short. Northmen is the name of a set of people—mostly derived from human ancestry—who survived in brutal colds and inhospitable environments due to the help of a dungeon who was playing with them the entire time."

Swanson's hand dropped a paragraph. "They referred to the voice of the dungeon as 'the Voice of the People,' and it's the popular theory that all the Northmen were either its dungeon born, or otherwise contracted. Given the limitation that dungeons can't directly speak to anyone who has an Aura in the way, we lean to the former. If the latter, they either didn't know, or part of the deal was that they forgot."

He moved his pointing finger. "This might tie in to the Northmen being obsessed with being *body* cultivators, as their skills and weapons were focused far and over anything Aura related. We are working on the assumption that the dungeon was a very controlling and conniving one, and that the idea of its knowledge bleeding out into the world was something it despised. Because otherwise, we're not sure why such specifically cruel and brutal containment methods were devised."

His line of light moved to another book as the first was removed. Table space was prized. "The society built up in 'Voice of the People' land... I'm going to call 'questionable,' and move on without further comment. We all know about the militancy, hard adherence to rules either unspoken or forgotten, and fanatical values placed on their 'Honor.' There's a shameful amount of similarity with current day Olympus. The mechanics of 'Honor' were something I needed a Wisp Marquis for in order to have explained, because the cultural nuances went over my head."

Swanson widened his pointer light to highlight a thick section in the flint-spined tome. "Bringing us to the interesting stuff. Sometimes, Northmen had to leave this society. Not always under positive circumstances. In the events where the dungeon deemed that some of the toys it provided should not see the light of day, it devised reasons for that knowledge being left behind. Causing some... truly grueling social applications on how that got interpreted."

Sections of a Rune came into view. "The method in which the Northmen 'retain' someone's power when sending them out into the world is with a 'flesh tattoo.' Most interesting for us is that this tattoo can be stored in another medium. Say a memory Core. We have a different team working out correlations."

Swanson shook his head; he didn't like this next part. "The only way to really take someone's power, and make it unavailable to them, is to take their memories both of that power, and of how they got it. Which is part of what goes with the 'flesh' of the tattoo. Cells are retained."

He righted himself, and soldiered on. "What a person loses isn't just their 'essence and cultivation technique.' This containment method also takes the knowledge of everything they did to get, practice, and use those methods."

Unpleasant grunts and nods from other Gnomes made the rounds. You could regain abilities if you remembered the process to unlock them, but without that, it was working from square one. Swanson was given a small piece of cloth to dab on his forehead. "Taking memories—rather than copying them—is dangerous as all abyss, because that's how you break a person. In exploring our case study—Tom, if you were wondering—we uncovered some bewildering data. As an example of a lesser side-effect, it explains why Tom turned out to be *much* older than he thought."

Swanson needed some strong spirits, but was provided with them since they'd expected this was going to happen. He had them poured right into his mug of dark roast. "When you take memories from a brain, you can take those pathways, but you cannot take the nodes or synapses. So if a person acted 'good' before those memories were taken, they will still act 'good' after. Their *inclinations* remain. You can't just *take a mind apart*, as much of a mind relies on all the parts being there to work as intended."

Swanson conjured up a complicated diagram of a skull. Within, some lightning appeared to move inside in a set, repeating pattern. "Problem one: when you take memories from the brain, you can undo those experiences, but all of the other pathways formed because of them still remain. Taking all the leaves off from a branch doesn't mean that branch won't regrow leaves where they should belong. A person will still behave the same, even without remembering why. Meaning that people are still likely to make the same *type* of choices and decisions. Even if the details change."

The lightning in the skull then changed colors. "Problem two: because pathways are what determine *specific* thoughts and memories, and those were removed, it means that *all* memories related to that pathway were removed as well. Even if the pathway builds itself anew, in the exact same pattern, it will not regain any of the losses."

Swanson placed the spirits on the table, only for them to be whisked away before he could change his mind and swig a larger gulp. "The devious bit is… in the *pre-planning* that seems to have occurred. In every case—and I do mean *every case*—we have gone over, it is why 'memories of a mother figure' are always left behind, and why memories of the 'father figure' are almost always completely gone."

Cal needed a moment to process. Tatum's eyebrows went up. Artorian turned instantly furious.

Halcyon abandoned the topic in order to attend to her Dreamer. Her voice did its best to be soothing. "My Dreamer?"

Artorian angrily pointed at one of the diagrams on the table. "That detail right there irritates the abyss out of me. Are we sure this dungeon didn't have a demon in its Core? The modus operandi stinks of one."

Cal turned, curious. "Why?"

Artorian fussed. "Loving memories are required for a person not going insane. Have you been around kids much? Down to the barest essentials, they will abandon food, milk, toys, and anything else when they need you to hold them and be there with them. They will choose it intrinsically, without knowing or understanding why. Yet they will choose it, they will cling to you, and only when that is satisfied will they go back to any of those other needs. If that most primal of comforts was ripped away from a person, then anything built on that foundation crumbles catastrophically."

He angrily pointed at the discolored electricity. "In most—not all, but most—societies, it is the case that the mother figure is also the primary love and caregiver. Those most basic of building bricks are required for people to be people, or people would be demons. So to hear that this containment technique—if I'm understanding what I'm hearing correctly—takes away memories in order to take away powers, then this dungeon knew that taking away certain memories left behind only a broken person. Meaning, it pre-planned memory patterns not tied to these foundational building blocks, which it could take away if needed. Swanson, tell me that in Northmen society, it *wasn't* purely the father who taught combat?"

Swanson closed his eyes, and shook his head. Because... no. "No, I'm sorry, Administrator. That was exactly how it worked. The father taught cultivation, fighting, skills... the rest."

The Gnome brightened in expression as he thought of something, his light ending as his hands folded behind his back. "The only good news is that we can confirm the inclinations carrying over are nigh-guaranteed. We have Tom's hammer as a direct case study. The trunk of the tree stands strong."

The table was cleared of books as Swanson spoke. "Even though he did not know of his history or proficiency with hammers, Tom still leaned in that direction. When he once again knew his skill with 'Thud,' the name of his old hammer, it was legendary. Throughout all that walking a new path in life, he was the same pleasant, warm-hearted, jovial man. Regretful about his mistakes. Mournful for his lack of control and the people who perished because of it. Genuinely heartbroken that he couldn't have done better at the time. Then, seeking to do better. So it was the first time, and so it was the second."

Artorian grumbled, but Cal took the floor. "I'm seeing what could make people rather heated about this. Back to the arrow and bow issue, and without assigning blame, is there a safer and non-invasive way to do this? Or is that not the problem here?"

Swanson walked next to Tatum, then leaned in to drop his finger on another blueprint. "Right here. Our 'safe' method of knowledge transfer is honestly the memory Cores. We already had something better, the question came up of how we'd do things if we were suddenly without. Your Soul Space is great, boss, but we're getting used to random sections failing all the time."

Cal could only nod, being very aware of his to-do list. "I see the need for looking. Please continue your talk."

Swanson moved an inch of vellum to note a detail on the blueprint. "This bit right here is what has us stumbling. When Tom got his tattoo back, it was kept in a memory Core. That by itself was convenient. The baffling thing is... as far as we can tell, recreate, or deduce from research we've been willing to do? That memory Core would have only ever worked for Tom. *Just Tom.* Nobody else."

Cal frowned, his arms crossing. "That's not right. That's not how memory Cores work."

Swanson pointed at him. "Correct! Which is why it's twisting my bacon."

Tatum tentatively raised his hand while his other grip firmly held his chin, after which his raised hand pressed down on some text in one of the blueprints. "This might be it."

The rest of them flocked around, reading the relevant entry a few times in silence. Artorian wasn't following this time, but the Incarnate and dungeon both began to nod and mumbled positive mentions. He looked up at Tot, then made a noise at him for attention.

When Tatum looked at Artorian and saw the visual request for clarification, he pointed back to the same section. "Do you remember how I roughly told you the same thing about memories and intelligence just being patterns? Same story here. If you also remember the bit about how that changes for Mages, you'll find the piece of insight that allows this to make sense. The mind and the soul become the same thing. So if a piece of Tom's mind was removed, then, via the technicality of it being connected to Essence, so was a piece of his soul. This puzzle piece can only be placed back in the puzzle it was taken from, because unlike with a perfect memory Core, there is *so much baggage* with a flesh tattoo."

Artorian frowned, and rubbed at the crease. "I didn't have that problem with the Wood Elves, and that head-bonk effect sounded even more direct than this?"

Cal shook his head no. "A sharing of experience, and a gifting of experience—which is what you went through—don't match up with what happened to Tom. You got a new, self-experienced version, or a copy. Tom had a piece of himself removed with so much of his specific information in it that the only place it could return to was Tom. I think I know why this information can't be copied. This piece of knowledge in the tattoo isn't a *copy* of other information, it is *the original piece* of information, and information can't be destroyed. To copy this, since perfect copies are... admittedly not *aaaaactually* a thing? Would be to destroy or alter some part of the existing data. Universe says no."

Artorian rubbed his forehead crease harder. "Preposterous? Things frequently get destroyed randomly with no chance for recourse or recovery. Information is lost all the time."

Tatum put his hand up, and Artorian tossed him the proverbial ball. "I think I see where you're at. You're thinking if a book gets burned, anything in that book is lost forever, even if it was an original?"

Artorian considered that, and nodded. Tatum then pointed back to the floating electric skull. "That applies only to information that isn't in some way bound to both a soul, and Essence. We're not talking about a book here, we're talking about a piece of information that has become a universal constant. Think... a soul attached to information makes it Ur-information, like Traviticus of Baldree was the Ur-Travis."

He attempted to be more specific. "The only way for that extra suffix to drop away is if Tom were to die, and all living memory of him ceased to exist. Then there is nothing for the shard of the soul to tether back on to, and you are, in fact, at the book example. Nothing 'extra' makes the piece of information 'special.' Essence is one of these qualifiers, and is a big reason why we *did* successfully get the Wood Elves back: as *them*. Their bodies died. Their information didn't. It's why the soul-tethering you saw when you were visiting me in Elysium behaves like it does."

Before a problematic question was asked, he shot a warning glare. "This does not mean it is easy or convenient to perform this process. This entire endeavor of resurrection is impossible without Cal and his frankly insane energy allowance. Bringing back a single person costs as much as it does for me to Incarnate, as if starting from an F-ranker. If it was not critically important that we got all those souls and minds, we *would not have done it*. There are dangers and downsides you do not know about, and I will *beg you* not to meddle with it."

Artorian gave him a serious salute. "Message received. Do not play with resurrection."

Tot turned. "Swanson, have you tried this with someone who is already dead? Does my hypothesis hold?"

The Gnome paled. "Beg your pardon, sir, but I wouldn't do this tattoo business to a living soul. Not only do I not have research done, I *refuse* to do it. I was very specific earlier with the mention: 'Research we have been willing to do,' I'm afraid."

Tatum pulled back, his hand tucked to his chest. "That... is very reasonable."

Tot wasn't going to touch that any more than he'd already stumbled into. He clamped his mouth shut, then looked to Cal, who had decided on the outcome.

Cal declared his will. "This sounds very simple to me. I don't want to see this come up ever again. Not only is taking original memories out of someone a big red flag for me, the flesh thing mouse-squeaks my friends out, and I have zero interest in getting dragged into an argument between scholars on how souls and soul-bound information *might* work. Much less the ethics, which I surmise from Artorian's reaction to be, at best, dark and dubious. I want this entire project scrapped, and shoved into the blacklist vault. This never comes up again if we can help it. We stick to memory Cores, and make sure we can keep making them. This tattoo thing is banned. Swanson? Tell the other teams you mentioned earlier to shelve this."

A relieved sigh from Artorian was met with understanding nods from Tatum, and a whole host of equally relieved Gnomes who packed the table up like every single document was coated in acid. Cal pushed himself off the workspace, and turned away. "We're done here. Next project? My time acceleration Pylons not working sounds *actually* important."

CHAPTER SIXTEEN

When the group arrived at the 'time and relative dimensions in space' table, Cal actually sat down. No leaning into view with his feet ready to move. This was a sit down and hash it out until it was done kind of deal.

Artorian immediately considered escape routes. This was clearly going to take longer than he had patience for, especially with so many other interesting projects out and about.

Vanilla wiggled her way out of Halcyon's grip, settling on Tatum's lap like a small child eager to be involved when he sat down next to Cal, though she kept her hands out of sight. Probably not for mischief...? Nah, clearly there was going to be mischief. Neither of Tot's chosen were the kind to behave for long.

When Halcyon moved close enough so Artorian could see details of the table, his piqued interest fell on how it looked like a flawless duplicate of the giant clock used during the old supervisor meetings. That or... This was that very table? Several of the inner works were on the fritz, or just dead. Unmoving when they should clearly be ticking along.

For a moment, Artorian tuned his ears to the work zone next to them as this one was setting up with all sorts of... incomprehensible four-dimensional models. The first peek, two Gnomes chatting? "I was under the impression that higher processing speed was an indicator of high intelligence. I was wrong. 'Bigger brains' doesn't mean they're smarter, it means they can be stupid *faster*. I swear… *humans*."

Artorian blinked and pulled his ears away. Maybe he didn't want to listen to that one… A thought occurred, so his eyes trained on Cal. "Say, buddy, with the demons and the banishing rune thing. Conveniently getting rid of them doesn't sound like it's in the hand of cards I've been dealt. Tell me I've got another option aside from diplomacy?"

Cal looked up from reading a primer he was going through. "De—? Oh! Right. Umm… No, I don't think so. I need all living souls to essentially live out a life, I definitely need you not to ask me the details. Making a deal may have to be the way to go, because banishing rune power doesn't matter, and if you send them to a memory Core… I'm sorry, bud. I *have to* let them back out."

"I… I see." That last bit of the information put an especially nasty vice into Artorian's side. He considered **Compassion** as an option. "What about… if they're *perma*-perma dead?"

Cal slowly put down his pamphlet, looking Artorian right in the eyes. "Sunny. Concerning Ghreziz? The only reason you got away with it is because, at the time, I was neither awake, nor the rank I currently am. Becoming a double-S rank of **Acme** has put some *serious* pinch in my ass, and the Heavenly of **Oaths** is directly breathing down on my neck. Please. *Please.* Don't. I would really love *not* to have to invoke the deal you have with me here."

Artorian put his hands up. "I'm not gonna make ya. You grasp why I had to ask?"

Cal relaxed, exhaled, then nodded. "Yeah… yeah, I get it. Demons have you by the beard and always will, and I'm not exactly *thrilled* about any of this either. Bottom line is actually pretty easy. No perma-kills, normal kills only get them back in the Core. Cored creatures that haven't lived a full life, as dictated by the breathing on the back of my neck, get re-decanted, no questions asked."

"Ten-four, I suppose." Artorian dropped his head in resignation, not knowing why he was thinking of red and blue lights at the moment. "How does that work out with Urcan? He's a sword right now. **Sorrow**, to be specific."

Cal sat up and checked, then shrugged. "Feels like that's fine on the **Oath** stress-check? It's *a* life. I'm not getting a 'you will be bopped for this' sensation."

Artorian perked up. Then a little more. Then he sat up, and perked up *significantly* more. A cheshire grin spread across his features, his hands forming an upside down pyramid. "Oh? *Oh.* Well, that's good to know. So it's merely a matter of them not being in a Core, and them not being 'dead,' but their form of function is... arguable?"

Cal frowned, fully setting his pamphlet down. "Where are you going with this? If you abyss-up some insane little idea and one of the **Oaths** goes pop, that's it for all of us. Spill it. Now."

Artorian's face looked like a fox making a lucrative trade.

"Well, the nice thing about Urcan right now is that while he might be a demon, he is also a demon that can't do any harm unless someone swings him around for a while. While I fully expect that sword to be able to influence wielder decisions and actions, in some respect." He motioned at himself. "I just happen to be a hardy and difficult target for such effects."

Artorian then motioned towards a random book on the table. "However, if it's acceptable that a demon can live as an object, such as back in the day with Port-Ellis the portcullis, then... Why do I not fill a library of empty shelves with books? Books that might happen to be... a little arguable in nature? A little *eldritch*, as Traviticus would say?"

Tatum leaned into the conversation, his gaze intrigued. "That can't work... Can it?"

"Can it, Ricky!" Cal snapped back while referencing the metal container, his eyes screwed tight in contemplation as he chewed this scheme over and prodded it immediately. *Mnnnngrlmn...* "No. Abyss. They would have to *agree* to be books, or it wouldn't count."

Artorian snapped his fingers, clicked his tongue in disapproval, and punched his arm into empty air. *Tsk, bahhh*. "I have to resort to... *Diplomacy.*"

Cal stabbed a finger in his direction. "Now if you can come to some kind of agreement or accord, that's different. If they *willingly* do the book thing, then it *will* count."

"Accords, you say?" Artorian mulled it over pensively, leaning back in the crook of Halcyon's arm. "*The* Accords? A terrible thought that could go wrong in all sorts of horrible ways which we only find out about later… Turning demons into books, though? A problem shelved for later? That might just be worth it. We really need them not to be a problem *now*, right?"

"*Now* would be an exceptionally bad time for anything new to be a problem. Demons especially. This time-thing we're about to start discussing? That's old hat, a problem of effort and duration." Cal then turned serious in both voice and expression. "Active and malicious entities roaming around my Soul Space that I can't squish or box up? *That* gets my goat."

Artorian nodded precipitously. "Sounds like I know what I'm doing!"

Tatum leaned in towards him. "Are you telling me that you, Mr. Sunshine, demon-despiser extraordinaire, is going to *gab* with a whole conclave of entities he wants to see turn into granulated powder, and convince them all to become books?"

Artorian beamed. "That's me! Who else was gonna do it?"

The Incarnate shrugged. "Henry or Marie, maybe? They've been going on and on about how to run the new version of their monarchy. Seemed like something they would include."

The old man pulled a face. "A monarchy, during *this* iteration? In *this* economy? They would never financially recover from this. This is a terrible time to practice kingdom management. Our people are out and about during this iteration! I don't want them tangled up in their *practice* sessions. H and M can do that in Eternia. They can take a break and run a cheap clothing store for all I care. Focusing on kingdom management instead of supervisor tasks will cause problems for everyone."

Tatum moved his hands palm up. "You'll have to hash that out with them. I'm sure they will drop by your little village in due time. I believe they did once already? Your adopted daughter threw them out because they crushed houses by existing."

"And I'm proud of Lunella for it!" Artorian replied, his arms crossing as a firm nod of approval accompanied his statement. "Now, I believe I've distracted from the currently tabled discussion long enough. We are here for some sort of time-thing?"

Cal nodded and picked the pamphlet back up. "*Mhm*. Administrator, when it comes to the demons and accords topic, let me know when you need something. I want that project… *expedited*. Please pick some Gnomes and Wisps and work on it when availability permits. The sooner I no longer have to be concerned about demons, the happier I will be."

Sunny thought about it, but snapped to his answers nice and quick. "Easy, Titania and Deverash. Souls I can work with. A few people yet to be decanted might also be mighty helpful, if you could let me time when to unpack them. If you need them *out*-out, of course, please ignore my request."

Cal nodded in approval, considering that sorted until he was needed for the next stage of what was now labeled 'The Accords Project' or 'Tap' for short. Surely that wouldn't come back up as some kind of pun relating to magic and gathering. "Work with other dungeons as Pylon bearers and network support, if you need to Tap some lands or creatures for more 'oomph' to work with. You've got it. I'll skip over your few decantees remaining, until I really can't. Perhaps Lunella will think of me more kindly if I don't force her horde on her right away as well…"

Cal nodded, satisfied.

Artorian took the proverbial ball when offered. "I'll let Titania know if I need more operational space. Now, did you actually need me for this, or did you just want me to be aware of it?"

Cal looked to Ricky, who rolled his wrist to motion at the latter mention before answering. "I just wanted him to know that this workshop exists, and what all happens here, rather than any particular and specific projects. Sunny being able to get here officially felt relevant. Instead of him stumbling in, or sneaking in, or any of the other methods we've set up auto-kill wards and protections against."

Tot pointed at the red stripes on the ground, and felt that was enough to make his point. Cal tapped the table twice with a finger. "Sunny, listen in on the primer, but aside from that, most of this is going to… I'm sorry, bud, this is all technical talk between engineers that's going to fly right over your head. No philosophy here. Expect lots of references to specific Pylons, numbers, and jargon that will make your head spin. Fun for me, not so much for you."

Artorian appreciated the heads up. "I will sit in for the primer then. Afterwards, if Deverash is around here somewhere, I'd like Halcyon to take me."

"Sure." Cal returned his attention to Swanson. "Alright, I'm caught up. Explain to our philosopher at the table what the problem is. Maybe hearing it in simple terms will give me some fresh perspective."

Swanson unfurled his prized golden-hemmed blueprint across the table, being extra careful with the product. "In simple words? Well... Let me see. So, time as it passes in Cal, and time as it passes outside of Cal, is not happening at the same rate. Honestly, feel free to pick a word that suits you."

Creating a diagram that shone out of his prized blueprint, Swanson worked the images like a professional stop-motion modeler. "Outside of Cal, time works the way you remember it. A second actually means a second. An hour actually means an hour. Mages muck with this concept, not in the sense that the actual time passing differs, but how much time they perceive is passing. The more powerful the Mage, and the denser their Mana, the stronger this divide. Again, a second is still just a second for everyone else, but to a Mage who isn't handling themselves right, that one second could be *hours*' worth of time where the rest of the world essentially stands still."

Artorian nodded. "Last I recall, that's named 'dilation.'"

Swanson waggled his finger with an approving smile, as that tidbit told him he wasn't explaining this to a complete novice, and he could skip more of the basics. "Outstanding. Now the bit that isn't common knowledge is that this dilation can go both ways. While a Mage experiences a 'slow down' even if their perception of time speeds up, the opposite can happen, where a Mage 'speeds up' by letting their perception slow down. You can stand in one spot for an entire season, watching the trees grow as you remain there unaffected and unharmed. Because let's face it, you're a Mage and who is going to do anything to you? During this, you can allow the time *you feel has passed* during that one season be no more than... a minute? Two? Up to the Mage, really."

Artorian motioned that he understood. "Could spend a season in a minute, or a minute in a season, depending on which way you bend your density. I only know the one where I can spend a season in a minute, but I'd love a book on the other one sometime later."

Swanson had it noted, then continued. "In Cal's Soul Space, we have been coasting along using the option you don't know much about. We have been slowing down everyone's perception of time, so that more of it passes relative to our experiences. As, until the Chain of Chaos bindings get released, there's not a whole lot we can do save for waiting our journey out, and I'd rather not go insane waiting. So given the option to feel like 'one minute' has passed in trade for 'a million years' if need be, that's a swap I'm wholeheartedly making."

Artorian again motioned that he understood, and settled in for more.

CHAPTER SEVENTEEN

Swanson rubbed his hands together. Time for the big cheese. "Going as hard and fast on that change as we could was a whole lot of zeroes too slow to make actual headway. One minute for one million years is not a formula we were close to. Not even remotely. Using some cleverness combining Pylons for **Calibration** and Cal's access to the **Time** law, on the other hand—plus T.C. *if he ever leaves his garden*—acquires us some really delicious numbers. Problem being, to keep those numbers, we needed Eternium, Cal, and whole hosts of Pylons to all stay neatly synchronized. That... didn't happen, and now we have to clean up all the broken and destroyed debris before we can start over to set it up again."

Artorian crossed his arms, no longer following. "I'm not seeing a problem here. This is just cleaning up and rebuilding."

Swanson made the 'hold up' motion with both his hands. "Not that simple, but I can see how it sounds like it might be. Second problem is that we don't have the same conditions as we did last time, in order to restart. Eternium has some bad things lingering inside of his Soul Space that he can't get rid of on his own, Cal's system has advanced past what we were using, and the entire idea needs a ground up revamp, and finally... there's the *exiting* problem."

Artorian turned to Occultatum, a detail clicking. "Is this the body problem you told me about?"

Tot nodded. "Sure is. The issue comes down to 'now that we know we can meddle,' do we actually rebuild the Pylon system allowing us to go fast again? Or do we influence events as best we can to make sure that there is a world outside of Cal for us to actually get back to? We can do both, but we can't prioritize both."

Tatum illuminated a different section of the chart. "Preliminary results so far all fall into the category of 'not good.' Complete Essence deprivation of a whole planet notwithstanding, I am worried that we don't have the time to get the dilation Pylons up and running again before we have a far different, and far more pressing set of problems. Having the bodies to go back home is one thing, but there needs to be something to go back *to*, and if the 'something' we go back to is entirely inhospitable to us, what then?"

Swanson pulled Artorian's attention back to the diagram. "Currently, we are slowing down at the rate we sped up. Jumping up or dropping down to a different dilation range doesn't just happen with the snap of a finger anymore, I'm sorry to say. Our estimates show that by the time the current rubble is cleared, we will be traveling at only the speed that Cal's reverse dilation is able to skate us by on. No **Time**-law boosting. That… may be where we are forced to keep it."

Artorian held his hands up, requisitioning a pause. Vanilla took this opportunity to get her fluffy ears under his falling hands for some quality scratches. "Now it sounds like we are discussing two different topics that are in the same book, but not on the same page. Backpedal with me."

Swanson slowed down and looked at the ceiling. "I suppose we sort of are branching this out too much as is. That's the problem with trying to keep a complex topic simple. This table is for 'if we do revamp the dilation system' how are we going about it? Again, that's *this* table. Which is why I'm assuming the boss gave you the 'jargon you're not going to like' warning."

Cal put his hand up. "Be that as it may, I'm in the boat with my Administrator on this, because after hearing the simple version, right now I don't feel like rebuilding this system in a hurry is as big of a rush as it initially sounded. If we are millions of years away from the Chains undoing, then yes, this is a valuable project. However, if we're dealing with 'the chains might undo, but we have nothing to go back to,' that sounds more pressing to me.

Especially when I have already nosed through the reports that we've successfully gotten something *past* them. Not *easily*, but we did. If we can schedule events so that a life outside is possible, that holds more importance to me than running at top speed towards the finish line. Because while I am content with holding everyone for *right now*, I already want the life back where this place was empty."

Tatum chuckled. "Trying to get rid of us?"

Cal turned, more serious than intended. "Tot, I *can't escape* you. You are literally in me, and I like peace and quiet too. I like work, but this is so much work that my craving for entertainment is sky high. Plus, if I don't work, then nothing will ever get done, because I have foolishly set up the majority of the systems to not work without me. I am deeply moved by the notion of turning that around, which is why I have so many other dungeon Cores assisting me."

Tatum paused, then folded his hands. "I'm sorry, Cal. That's stressful, and I'm not helping."

Cal frowned, then shook his head. "No... you're fine. It's fine. This is just how life is and we're all trying to make the best of it. Being a double-S ranker came with some changes I haven't coped with yet."

Tot eased into an understanding expression as that made a lot of sense to him. Sadly, the rest of the table looked at him like a horde of lost puppies. He shrugged apologetically at them. "If you think this talk is complicated, you're not ready for the struggle that Incarnates roll through on a daily basis."

They dropped it, and Cal tugged the edge of the golden-hemmed blueprint closer, to the gasping sound of Swanson as he reached for it with undue worry. Cal cleared his throat. "I can see why this was initially a big emergency. Pylon Banks: 'Mossbag,' 'Vaati,' 'Hagubomosho,' 'EBCDIC,' and 'Mcguffium' all held some pretty important information. Oh, Artorian, this is the jargon bit that's not going to make sense."

The old man mouthed an 'ah' in sudden comprehension, then nudged Halcyon before pointing off in a haphazard direction. "Cy, I will not be some boat plodding along the river of this plot. Take me over there! Let's cause some trouble!"

Cal looked right up from his notes. "Could you not?"

Artorian giggled. "Son, you knew well and good that when you took me down here, I would not be able to resist a literal ware-house of goodies to stick my nose in."

The dungeon grimaced. "Fair point."

Artorian stuck his arm out further, pointing to the distance like some captain motioning towards the horizon while standing captain-ly on the prow. "Dev! Prepare the hugs! I'm comin', buddy! Cy, activate the zoomies! *Leggooo!*"

Cal sighed, rubbing his eyes. "Was that supposed to be 'let's go'? Oh my *me.*"

Tatum snorted as he watched Halcyon lift Artorian like he was the figurehead of the ship, and run forwards between the work-shops along the designated walk lane. "Well, that's about what I was expecting... I'm surprised we could make him sit still for so long. So, what are we doing about these Pylons, boss?"

"Ricky." Cal exhaled, propping himself up with one arm. "We are not doing *anything* with these Pylons. This project is scrapped. We have other projects to prioritize before this one is even worth revisiting. Swanson? Full cleanup protocols. I want everything of the old project recycled and the empty space made available, but once that is done, this entire division is shelved. We do not need to look at accelerating to the finish line until there's something worth calling a finish line."

Swanson saluted, and Cal turned to the Incarnate. "Tatum, set up the committee that knows anything about anything pertaining to bypassing the Chains. I know Zelia is a key component, but I glanced at her health and that Core is in extreme need of R&R, so I want as much prep set up as possible. Up to the point where she wakes up naturally. I am *not* jeopardizing our best chance to succeed on this. Plus, not **Time**-law forcing the iterations will make recovery a much smoother process. That addition has been mucking with the rest and recovery cycles for eons. No more."

Tatum nodded, and got up from his seat. "We'll have to itera-tion shift more organically from this point, boss. No help from this project means our quick-reset days are over. Soul Space changes both here and in Eternia's new version will have an actual history, rather than resets. Are you alright with that?"

Cal nodded, also getting up as the Gnomes began clearing the table. Swanson's prized blueprint was back in his grip as he whis-pered to it like a baby. Cal pulled his eyes away. "For the best, even if it's unfortunate. Keep the iteration changes under wraps for now.

We might be able to simulate the effect by mass-coring everyone for some sleep, and waking them when we've made all the changes that would be bad for their health if they'd seen it. Full resets are out, but with some clever finagling, we can get close."

The Incarnate nodded, very much in that same boat. "Not a bad plan. Hinges on Artorian getting the demons to cooperate though. With everyone being an auto-decant, non-cantibles are a fat problem. Pushing the big sleep button doesn't work unless it's everyone at the same time."

"He'll trim it down to size." Cal mused. "Plus, he'll have help when he needs it. Now, Ricky, jokes aside, Artorian is long out of earshot, and none of these were actual catastrophes or problems that badly needed my direct and immediate attention. Can we get to it? What's the emergency? These were all distractions."

Tatum inhaled firmly, then made a Spirit-quality orb-shaped barrier around them, blocking out all soundwaves save for Cal's and his own. "Eternium is badly hurt. Zelia needs more time to recover than is going to be convenient... and... there's a particularly nasty wire-tear deep inside of the Silverwood that isn't healing. Dawn and I are pretty sure it's because your Core is cracked. Your actual, real one, outside. You took personality damage during your double-S Incarnation, right?"

Cal gave a single sharp nod, and Tatum continued. "That's more than likely the culprit. The only way to fix your true Core is outside in, and inside out, at the same time. We can't reliably get past the Chains right now, so don't push Spirit energy expenditures."

"Abyss." Cal groaned, burying his face in his hands. "If it's not one thing, it's another, huh? Did we get any good news?"

Tatum waggled his hand. "You're potent, for one. Double-S opens up a host of new options for you in terms of toolbox. The real trouble is that your biggest vulnerabilities all stem from factors barely in your control right now. Artorian can step on demons, Ammy is already rooting around in Eternium when I'm not, and... well, it's good that she's a master of destruction. With you two synchronized back to the same wavelength and timestream, the hiccups have abated and the stasis lock was lifted. That did mean some timed issues have begun counting down, and until we can throw people in there to retrieve the 'gifts' preventing Tim from making sweeping changes, progress will be akin to trying to plug three holes in the boat with only two stoppers, and shoveling the water out with a rusty bucket."

He shook his head and soldiered on, not wanting to think about Eternia problems while focused on Cal. "Back on topic: Odin is honestly a liability. I would snap his neck and call it done, but unfortunately he has to be let out again soon, unless he genuinely chooses to stay in his seed Core of his own volition. That's our only grace. On that topic, Odin is on everyone's abyss list. And don't tell anyone, but Chandra badly, *badly* needs away-from-it-all time. A concept you just told me you need too. We found a temporary reprieve, but I've got no information on if it will work as a longer term solution."

Cal nodded, rolling his wrist for more. "What else?"

Tatum drew a breath and kept going. "Our supervisors of old don't really get along, and forcing them to work together is going to do more harm than good. Aiden and Henry have beef they're going to need to work out in Eternia, because doing it here is bad juju. That's going to have to be the 'pleasant' solution for most of the old crew. In that same vein, Henry and Marie are butting heads with a lot of people right now. Their antics were fine in Eternia, but here… not so much. Artorian hit the nail on the head in his commentary."

Cal held up a hand. "I grasp it. Other topics?"

Tatum held his own hands. "We will, and I mean as an eventuality, lose most of our current Pylons. The cascading failure thing was not a joke. While our backup banks are sitting abandoned and covered in cobwebs, our useful ones are dying. We can recycle them, but… those minds aren't coming back, and those souls are *expended*. Remember Minya and her mental burn out?"

Cal *mhm'd*. "We went through the humanoid populace on the matter already. Are you telling me we just lost, or are about to lose, the animal populace? Insects and the like didn't qualify for Pylons. Not properly. We're out of sapients in that case."

Tatum nodded. "I am, and we are. Now, as good news, we once had a way to make synthetic Pylons that didn't require being grown from a Beast Core or mind, is that still on the table?"

The dungeon grumbled. "It's a pain in the Calcite to do, much slower and more difficult than Beast Cores, not to mention expensive. However, if that's all we've got, then that's what we're doing. No more sentient minds as new Pylons it is. They all need to rest. I remember the reports. Their next eye-opening needs to be a life worth living, or it's all going to go downhill. We technically have capable candidates left in the form of entities Tim carted along, but... I am not happy about the sudden idea in my mind about using demon minds as new Pylons. That's going to go bad in a fast way. Items by themselves are... asking for trouble, but that still sounds better than demons having direct system access. That's *begging* for problems. I do not want a Barry two point oh. But, sweeping the matter under the rug..."

The Incarnate could not disagree. "It's asking for trouble later, and it would buy us time right now. We're going to have to deal with it eventually, but if we could avoid dealing with that particular problem right now... I'm liking the value proposition."

Cal hung his head and sighed. "Yeah, I do too, which is part of the problem. Alright, is that the list? Run me through solutions."

Occultatum pulled a hidden book out of his inner sleeve, visible only to himself and Cal as he rifled the pages. His personal book of secrets. "Eternium we can help by getting the 'gift' problems out, and letting him run the beta. I'm thinking it's similar to the 'can't see Liminal items' issue you had in your own Soul Space. He knows there are issues, but not what or where. We can't reset his world, but if we can send Ammy and Artorian in as a team, that's... three books and it's sorted. A problem finder and a problem solver. Boom. Abyss, it could be the entire beta run if we get lucky with our cards."

Cal raised a brow. "We're counting in books now?"

The Incarnate smiled weakly. "You started it. Can't help that we thought it was a good idea when you brought it up."

The dungeon rumbled. "Ha-ha. How soon can we implement that?"

Tatum flipped a page and ran his finger down a chart. "Not this book, probably not the next one. This volume, Artorian is going to have his hands full with the 'Tap.' Accords don't write themselves. Next volume... I'm honestly expecting a small civil war because Henry is socially clueless lately and Marie seems to have forgotten how to quit being a Queen. My copper is on the next book being all about that being handled, and the rough edges of society in your Soul Space getting smoothed out. Might be a good time to slip him your ice canopy notes? H and M are playing with lives and passing it off as betterment, but you know Artorian isn't going to let that fly. Not this go around. You heard him earlier."

The Incarnate tapped an entry in his secret notes. "The next three volumes after that, though? That sounds like good Eternium beta-run material. If we aren't back out in the real world after that… then I have serious concerns we will have to address when we get there. We're going to have to find a way to send people out into the real world, and while we have a few options, there's nothing stable just yet. Note that, if we do this, we will be heavily influencing the history of whoever comes before us exiting your Soul Space, and I mean all of history."

Cal disagreed. "No, not history. Set it up so that we influence mythology. I want everything we do kept out of history. I want misunderstandings and plausible deniability, until we are good and ready to disembark, I want the whole deck in my hands. The planet doesn't even get dealt cards until we're good and ready. I already know how to sort the planetary Essence problem; that's me shedding a manly tear and shutting off my ley lines. Move on to the 'me being injured' solution."

Tatum scribbled in the orders, and flipped a page. "Fixing you is as difficult as getting someone who is at minimum a double-S ranker out, all set to apply raw spiritual energy to the crack in your Core. It won't fix the lost personality, but it will mend any other issues pertaining to disembarking. You having a full and healthy Core sounds much better than you having a damaged one, where… we're honestly grasping at straws for what the effects might be."

Cal waved it away. "Whole is better than not whole. Makes sense. Continue."

Tatum moved onto the last paragraph. "Zelia needs naptime. That's the full and short of it, and the last note on the 'actual serious problems' docket."

Cal inhaled deep, then released the held breath easy and slow. "Let Zelia sleep, and let's have a world she can be proud of ready and waiting for her. Y'know, I was expecting to take this much worse? This isn't so bad. We can do something about all of this, even indirectly. We'll need to draw up a timeline and order of events to finish tasks with the least aggravation to my injury, but this all sounds feasible."

Tatum smirked. "So long as Artorian can convince demons to be books, yes."

Cal sighed hard as Tatum dropped the privacy field. "Ricky..."

"Yes, boss-man? I *am* the potion-seller." The Incarnate put on a wide grin. His eyebrows bounced wildly because he'd said that last part very much on purpose. They trusted Artorian, but poking at Cal for it was never going to get old. "Do you need my *strongest* potion?"

"Get out." Cal whined, dropping his hand towards a door neither of them could see, but knew was there. "Before I do more than Eternia-limit you to speaking to people named 'Joe.'"

CHAPTER EIGHTEEN

<Did you get all of that?> Vanilla asked through the private forum connection.

<I did.> Artorian mentally kneaded the bridge of his nose. <Thank you for letting me listen in to the conversation between Tot and Cal. How *did* you keep that up? Same as my Halcyon?>

Vanilla huffed, proud of herself. <I'm a sneaky sneak. They forgot about little Vanilla! So I tuned in where Tater Tot's shield couldn't stop me. I'm not sure why he thought that trick would keep us out more than once? You can't un-think your own thoughts! Occy can't un-hear what goes through his ears either, both of which nosy chosen are privy to if they do more than sit pretty and listen. Anywho. That's my end of the bargain, I expect you'll have yours when it's ready?>

Artorian confirmed the deal. <You'll have it when it's ready, Vanilla. Tell Munch I appreciate the... opportunity for conversation. I didn't know that there were functional off-network Pylon bank copies not overseen by the Task Manager. 'Redundant back-ups' don't seem so redundant now.>

Vanilla explained. <A bonus for not destroying and deleting old work when a new version is set up and left to run. Besides, I've been needing to tell someone all this since I heard it the first time. Munch and I both want what's best for our Dreamer, to borrow Halcyon's words. Cal... alright, we exist because of Cal, but our

hearts move for our Tater Tot. Better you knew, as according to our good friend Genevieve, it's better when you do.>

The old man soothed her. <She is very correct. I'll help however I can, of course. I hope the pre-payment of where Tibbins keeps his secret recipes tides you over until I can provide you with what I promised. Have a lovely cookout, 'Nilla.>

The connection closed. Artorian slumped in Halcyon's arms, then firmly bulged his cheeks with air and slowly let himself deflate like a balloon. "I knew it wasn't going to be anything simple."

Halcyon's calm voice was a blessing in disguise. "Is it something you can handle?"

Huffing, Artorian crossed his arms, frowned, and then provided a single, sharp nod. "Yes. I can help. Keeping hurt from me was never an option, the silly-buggers. Most interesting is the… *civil war*, next volume. Glad to know about that likelihood ahead of time. Tatum was right, though, I'm going to be all-in on the Accords this volume. Afterwards, I've students to teach, C-rankers to pull into Magehood, demons to parlay with, and minutiae to attend. If I can do all that in this volume, that might be a miracle. More than likely these events will be spread out. The sooner I can hole up in the Skyspear, the better, I think. As soon as Amber has that portal up and running, it's going to be decant-o-clock, and then we hit the ground running."

He waved violently when Dev came into view. "Speaking of running! Dev, my dearest rhombus! Tell me you have legs!"

"I don't!" The floating eight-sided die beamed before quickly morphing into the very Gnome that Artorian knew and loved. Dapper bow tie and everything. He then pointed down, now very much in the possession of feet. "Except that I doooo!"

On closer approach, Deverash then looked stricken, a horrified expression on his face. "What are you *wearing*? I thought a lack of legs was the problem! Why didn't you warn me about *that*? Most profane of rusty sprockets! Good greases, *why*? Are you sure it's the legs you need help with? I need words of profanity for what you are doing to my eyes. Oh… blessed wrench. I… I'm going to be sick. Take it away from me. Begone from me!"

His friend was hamming up the performance, but Artorian just crossed his arms with a bemused smile. "Well, slap some legs on me and I can go ahead and do that! I heard you were the only one with a solution!"

Dev rounded on him, a stern hand pressed to his own sternum. "Of course I would have a solution. You've had me working on it since the Eternia alpha-run! Katarina went in peace, and with love, by the way. You were her final, and greatest joy. I doubt you've had the opportunity to be told, so I wanted to make sure you knew."

Sunny felt like all the wind had been torn from his sails. "She... *Oh*. When?"

Deverash squeezed his fingers into his palms. "Seconds after she sent you on her way. She was proud of it. Eternium was proud of it. She earned a permanent spot in the night sky. A star to shine down upon all who would be as pure and righteous as her. Or due to your legacy quest, but the first idea sounds more heartfelt."

Artorian closed his eyes, letting himself feel the loss. Katarina deserved that from him. "She... She was magnificent. I hope her descendants find her footsteps too large to stand in, and follow the path anyway."

Halcyon set Artorian down on the side of the worktable where Dev stood, his floating-die friends hovering around them while making welcoming face-images at them. "I would like to hear the stories of this Katarina sometime, my Dreamer."

"Of course, dear." Artorian nodded, then motioned to Dev. "Bud, transition to some good news?"

Deverash hopped up on the table next to one of his best friends, Artorian getting a thigh-pat. "Plenty. The legs project we began for her. The one out of repurposing a racer? That's done. We just need to attach them to someone. We didn't design them for a Mage, so there might be some connectivity issues with the current Cores. Once they're on, though, they should work like a charm. That initial energy flow is going to be the hiccup. Otherwise, Katarina did have a daughter. Though..."

Artorian raised a brow.

Deverash shook his head. "You asked for good news."

The old man grit his teeth. "Lay it on me."

The Gnome relented. "Fimbulwinter does not a hospitable environment make. She has abandoned her name, and is now simply 'Duchess.' Yuki would love her. She's had to freeze her own heart, be cold as a tyrant, and has already needed to make some brutal decisions in order to drag what could be saved from her civilization into frostpunk survival land."

"She's hanging in there?" Sunny pondered out loud.

"She'd be doing much better than just 'hanging in there' if she had more to work with. Her upbringing gave her the means for a sharp mind, but her circumstances have driven her to be a cunning city planner. Every inch of space gained from the elements is a war of weeks, and she is determined to win. Every curve, every path, every angle of every street matters. Each degree of heat is one that she will claw to keep."

Artorian felt taken aback. "I take it that I can't go help."

"Not unless you can get into Eternium!" Dev had a weak and pained curve to his expression. "Sorry, Sunny."

To Dev's surprise, the calculating old man appeared less bothered than the Gnome expected. Instead, Artorian mumbled to himself. Something about 'volumes' and 'timelines.' He didn't pursue and let his friend come back to his senses on his own time, which happened right when Halcyon sat down on the bench and caused the whole thing to creak.

She blushed fiercely. "Oops."

Dev frowned at her. "Cy? This is horribly impolite. I must know. How much do you weigh? I know what that bench is *made* of. I now have concerns about *you*."

"I don't know whether to tail slap you for that or just answer you." Halcyon's tone was flat, taken aback that the Gnome had the kind of steel orbs to just go ahead and say something so daring and controversial. "Get me a scale later, and I'll stand on it, but one beached whale comment and your rapidly ascending form will be renamed to Cloudpiercer."

"Deal." The Gnome turned his head to Artorian as the man inspected his widdle leg-nubs and waggled them. "Sunny, what's with the glaring? Willing them back into being won't work."

Artorian hummed. "I'm doing that thing where I'm wiggling my toes. I'm convinced I can still feel them; that they aren't there to perform the wiggle still puzzles me."

"Phantom limbs." Dev helpfully added. "Actually rather common. Helpful for our purposes too, since that is the feeling you'll need to flex in order for us to test if all parts of the mechanical replacements work or not. Do you want the run-down, or to see these speedy beauties first?"

"Obviously I want to see them!" Artorian perked up with a smile. "Where are they?"

"Ta-daaaah!" Dev cheered like a celebratory birthday-announcer. Whisking a tarp off of the table they sat on using telekinesis, he revealed a gleaming spectacle that Artorian's eyes interpreted as a marvel of engineering. Even if he didn't understand a lick of the design save that both items were vaguely leg-shaped... if applying the term graciously. "They're... pretty? Shiny mauve chrome? With... stickers in places. Dev, what am I looking at?"

"Legs!" the dapper miniature man cheerfully retorted, his face all smiles. "Aren't they gorgeous!"

"Oh, they're gorgeous alright, buddy, but are you sure that these things are legs?" Artorian motioned from the feet-bits to... what he guessed was supposed to encompass a hip? "I can't make heads or tails of this artwork. Except that my knees go... in those sockets, there. I think?"

Dev scratched at his chin. "How about you sit in the middle of the table, we install them, and see if it doesn't make more sense then? Do you really care so long as they function as legs? Granted, they are two-hundred percent made from racer thrusters, so if you hot-pump energy into them, you *will* smash into the ceiling. Their output is no joke."

Artorian returned his eyes to the 'legs' with renewed wonder. "This I need to see. Cy, dear, move me, please?"

Halcyon gladly did so. Once in position, the table modulated and altered, firing with pistons and springs as both steam and an electric hum moved Artorian to sit in the fanciest, most modular operating chair he'd ever seen. Each movement of his form was accounted for, springing him back to a cozy neutral position once his surprised wriggling ceased applying tension. *"Who-how!* It moves! Well... only so long as I move. Quite cozy now, actually. I'm enjoying the springiness of this chair, Dev. I want twelve."

One of the floating octahedrons took note, after which they hovered around him in a circle, calibrating before starting a spin cycle as waves of concentrated light scanned over him. Artorian sat cozy as the dice Gnomes took their measurements, being able to watch as a second group in a lower circle adjusted the mechanical art pieces to fit together in more succinct three-dimensional shapes that... "Ah! There we go! *Now* they look like legs. That artistic license is still there, but at least I can recognize the idea clearly now."

Deverash nodded, humming a ditty tune as he checked off box after box on a checklist he was holding. Given he was keeping a stack of three such clipboards, Artorian expected this stage was the easy part. "Want to walk me through this? Undue anxiety is still not something I want."

Dev looked up from his mark-infested clipboard, then looked down to realize he'd been doing all his talking in his head, but not out loud. "I wasn't talking this whole time? Oh, bother. Of course, Sunny."

Tucking the boards under his arm, he cleared his throat. "Currently, you're going through the measuring and sizing stages. We planned *these* thrusters for a non-cultivator, female, old lady. We're now adapting them up to cultivator level, sizing them to a male of your stature and type, and saving the settings under 'codger.' Which is a joke from one of the newer Goggle-heads that I'm too amused by to change."

"Goggle-heads?" Artorian inquired as his pants were turned into shorts. "What are those?"

Deverash rambled it off. "Young Gnomes, their eyes bright with the spark of invention. We give them goggles as a first birthday gift to keep *other* sparks out of their eyes. Ingenuity is great! Going blind from looking directly into a welder, not so much."

Artorian laced his fingers, honestly not too bothered by all the prodding he was subjected to. One of the charts on the table was coming alive with information, and some of it surprised him. Two hearts not particularly counted, the question marks next to his species, and a line stating 'Nascent Being' assaulted with several underlines caught his eye. "There's that Eternia skill again... Dev, just what did Tim do to me?"

The Gnome paused, took off his beret to scratch at his head, then slapped it back on. "Wish I could tell you. By which I do not mean that I know and am prevented from telling you. I mean I do not know and am stumped by some of these findings. You are welcome to look at my file. It is sadly... very vacant. Unless you like question marks and angry Gnome rambling on theories that got scratched out later because we found something else that didn't make sense. This is the first time we've gotten a full and direct opportunity to put you through the scanning wringer, so while I might have something for you to drink later, right now you're looking at an empty glass."

Artorian hummed. "It is the empty space that makes the bowl useful. Such is life. Any theories, though? Any at all? Give me *something* to hold on to."

Dev chuckled in amusement. "Back to being profound, I see. Speaking of, was: 'the assassin you sent after me is part of my family now' also you?"

Sunny frowned, then shook his head. "No, that one is news to me. Sounds like an interesting story."

"Sprockets! One that I've been trying to track down for months!" Dev snapped his fingers. "Guesswork wise... Best I've got is that the pattern of your soul looks at the primary being you are in order to record information and experiences. Like... being a human that can turn into a rabbit? No problems. Suddenly being a rabbit that can turn into a human? That's your pattern turned upside down. Think of a basic charcoal rubbing technique in art. The shape showing up on the paper no longer conforms to the original design the artist expected, and is now left to scratch their heads."

He tapped the clipboard to his chin. "I remember in Eternia that the system was all sorts of confused as to what your actual base race was, and it did weird things with your empowerment formula."

Dev made a tally mark on his pad when prompted by an octahedron. "I think the Dragon Evolution options were Tim's first attempt at a fix, which is how having two hearts became a standard for you. Same with the bonescripting. The Nascent Being alteration is the second attempt at a fix. For what purpose and to what end? No idea. I do have the nose-tingle that these pattern changes are why easy body swapping and easy replacement bodies weren't on the table. Again, I hunger for these details just as badly. Anywho, stage one is all done. Ready for initial fitting?"

CHAPTER NINETEEN

Artorian shot his friend a thumbs up, most interested in how this would work. "They look like legs now. Sort of. Very... animalistic, in a sense? There's open space where I expect mass to be. The metallic nature of it all baffles me. I'm not seeing a single spring, cable, or pipe, and while I am pleased about not having a pulley installed in my hip, I don't see how these would be operated."

Dev telekinetically handed him a whole book from the table. "We wrote this for Katarina. This manual includes the basics on Essence cycling and the manifesting of Meridians, since she would have to connect the ones in her legs to the Cores we've installed in the Striker Mark IX."

"I'm sorry, the *what?*" Artorian snapped back, glad for the book, but caught fully off guard by the naming convention. "That makes these sound like weapons."

"Not quite." The Gnome kept clinically calm. "The first version of these thrusters were called 'Strike Witches.' Which was nothing more than a tube with balancers, some hydraulics, a gyro, two rotors, and an exhaust slapped on the ends. Couldn't rightly call them legs, but they got the test group off the ground and into the air, so we knew we had something to work with."

He smiled at a pleasant memory. "Then we had to backpedal because Titania reminded us that we were working on prosthetic legs, not a way to smash your face against a solid cloud faster. We were in the middle of the 'Stratos' version at the time, and all collectively slapped our foreheads. We were so proud of making it to the stratosphere that we'd forgotten entirely someone was supposed to walk on these. Classic Gnome behavior."

Artorian motioned to the incomprehensible design of the legs. "What led to this then? With prosthetics, I'd have known they were legs right away, but here… the foot is all separated into parts and spread out. Like claws? A lot like 'Tekka's claws, actually. Except they're all mechanical pieces. The ankle looks like it's a complicated mess of ball joints that… I have no idea how those all connect. The shin is some plate with reinforced lattice behind it? I can understand how the next lattice piece would enclose around my knee, and the plates after that around the thigh. If Mana skin was real skin, the breathability of the lattice and gaps would be nice, but for the bits where there's no leg? I don't… I don't see the purpose of the gaps."

Dev kept silent as his friend did an acceptable job of puzzling out the outer structure of his new legs. When Artorian looked at him pleadingly, Dev pointed with his utensil. "The interlock plates around the thigh are meant to copy the functions of a cast meant to set and keep bone in place."

His pencil motioned down. "The knee and ankle joints are the most complicated parts, and the short explanation is that a solid connection of Essence will keep those key points tethered. Mana, in your case. The version for Katarina needed… less flexible parts. Bulkier. More mechanical, interlocking, restricting solutions. With you, we can shift right to options we'd discovered during the Stratos version. The change you're seeing happen to the legs is a whole fresh batch of updates we're all loading in right now."

Artorian frowned, watching the shape change before his eyes. "How is metal responding and morphing like that?"

Dev blinked at him. "It's… Iridium. *Our Iridium.* Duh?"

The old man slapped his forehead. "Laevateinn! Right. It's not like I spent celestials-knows how long trying to recover every scrap of it from all the realms!"

The gnome threw his head back and laughed, recovering by leaning on his clipboards for support. "*Ahhh*, never change, old boy."

Smiling wide and shaking his head as he wiped a tear away, he flipped a page and tapped it with his eraser. "The empty space inside of the leg is to account for flexing and movement. If you stand in place and turn your midriff to the right, some of the support lattice in the legs will move and shift to accommodate the change in density and weight... up to a point. I can guarantee you that any density over A-rank one will crush them. Or at least, *this* model will crumple. In fact, just expect this version to crumple at some point from probably... something stupid that shouldn't have broken them. Unlike bodies of meat or Mana, the adaptability of this Iridium cannot keep up with some of the stresses you will inevitably put it through. Each time you break one, we can find out why and make new ones. So if you break them often, honestly, that's for the better."

Dev motioned at the knee. "I'm actually surprised you weren't thrown for a loop by the brick of metal protecting the front of your knee?"

Artorian shrugged. "That honestly made sense. I'm going to bump into things and it's better a bulkhead takes a beating than the support structure. I wasn't bothered or concerned by any of the big chunky pieces, because if I'm going to slam into things, or punt a demon through a cloud, I wouldn't want to do it with the lattice. The plates seem to be there to protect sensitive parts like all the round bits, and the Cores you've got tucked away all over the place. There's a single Core in each leg that looks more important than the rest, but if anything, I'm not sure why the foot is so large."

Dev nodded. "We needed more surface area to grip in case you leaned forwards. Normal Mage feet can very precisely alter where all the weight goes without you falling over. These don't have that kind of sensitivity or precise motor control, since we're just not at a version where we can provide you with good enough haptic feed-back. So, bigger feet. It's not like their weight will affect you."

Artorian crossed his arms, his focus on the claw bits of the feet. "Well, alright... how come some parts aren't connected in any way?"

Dev had to pull up some visual schematics for that one. "Mag-netics. Once you've got Mana flow up and running, you should be able to connect from the new Meridians to the Cores, and give them some juice. When you do, you *should* get delicate control of all pieces that function via magnetics. We couldn't mechanically replicate Ammy's sword-floating trick. Tried, though."

Turning the image somewhat, Artorian could see an example via a set of images that had a test Gnome wiggling his mechanical 'toes,' even if those bits of metal were not connected to the rest of the foot. The old man needed to rub his eyes. "Aaand we're past what I understand."

Dev considered the difficulty. "Well, do *think* of it like Ammy's flying swords, and how they always keep a set distance behind her no matter how she moves, or how fast. They tether into place and stay put, where she wanted them to stay put. Usually it's a delta formation. Same idea for the disconnected feet bits."

Light bloomed in Sunny's gaze. "Oh! That helps a lot! Alright, enough questions. How do I get these on?"

His devilish Gnome friend grinned. "They are on! You think all this talking was meant to do something other than distract you?"

"Why you little…" Artorian breathed out, not actually upset. If anything, he was mildly impressed Dev's squad had gotten the job done so swiftly. "Fine. What do I do from here?"

The Gnome checked his clipboard. "A not so easy part, I'm afraid. There's plenty of Essence and Mana down here, but now we need you to nap. By which I mean you need to stay put and concentrate on making the new Meridians until we can get you out of that chair. Or we have to do the whole thing over."

Artorian made an unpleasant expression. "Would have been great to know before I sat down. Other things need doing and my naps are question marks in the timeline. What about Halcyon?"

Cy bumped her Orca nose on the top of his head. She was floating belly-up for fun, her tail waving lazily. She spoke via a direct mental connection while her nose touched him. <I'll be here. I refuse to leave. They can fight me to make me try. It will not go well for them.>

He reached up to pat and rub her nose, then exhaled to agree. "That's how it is then. Alright, I'll settle in, and hope the world doesn't end before I open my eyes again. Rough estimate on how long this will take?"

Dev shot his friend a questioning look. "How would I know? You're the Essence scholar. You figure it out. How difficult was it for you to make Meridians the first time? There's no corruption to clear out and a lot of work went into making the Striker's pathways ready and pristine. The knee Cores functioning as part of the joint are also proper Cores, and they can definitely hold some of the slack. Speaking of, that will also help with the problem of completing an internal rune. I heard about your wake-up migraine from Lunella, but recommend against pulling that stunt again for now. I can't stop you from trying the Astral Celerity pattern-fix trick, but it might have unintended consequences unless we really have these dialed in. Beasts do all their ability activation completely in their Cores, rather than their bodies. While they are external help for you, it works the same. Which might mean that the pattern being fixed is... not yours. Hold off. My Electrum coins are that you will be done in five minutes. Tops."

"Oh." Artorian flashed a look of surprise. "Well, that's not so bad at all. I will definitely hold off on pattern-mending. I know a double-edged sword when I see one, especially when it's not leaning in my favor. I can wait for proper legs, there's these now, after all! Excuse me for a moment!"

"Don't blow them up!" Dev snap-yelled at his friend as he settled in and closed his eyes. "Too big a strain will ceiling-smack you. Connect, not k-thunk!"

Snug, Artorian rubbed his hands together in his bonfire space. Closing his eyes there and dropping into his center, he blinked at the sight of the impossible geometric shape while no more than a celestine mote of light himself. <Right! I forgot I made a Penrose Triangle here, that'll just have to stay put.>

From this point, reaching out through the gaps at the edges of his center was elementary. Connecting Essence from his wrecked legs to the Striker Cores, which directly pressed into the underside of where his legs used to continue, was easy cookie baking. Getting Meridians up and running was a breeze with the channels pre-carved. All he was doing was pouring hot water into the teapot. When it came time to stir, he could already feel the sensation of his old ghost limbs and his new metal ones moving at roughly the same time. Not with synchronization, but that was a matter of time and practice. <I'm easing into these new shoes like a smooth criminal who's going to moonwalk out of the cobbler with them.>

His toe-claw movements provided him excellent synaptic feed-back. The physical sensation especially brought him great satisfaction. <Well, that's one of those small joys in life, isn't it? Defeating Odin? Nuthin'. Wiggling tiny metal plates? Boundless joy.>

Swirling Essence through the system, Artorian felt disconnected from his new legs on a fundamental level. They were there and present, but they weren't him, or part of him. They were... a crutch he was leaning on. Something to pick up and put away. He'd have to learn and live with that. <*Hmm.* Would stuffing in some Mana fix that, or does that cause the face-meets-ceiling problem? A *little* juice couldn't hurt.>

Doing as intended, Mana replaced the Meridian channels. He instantly woke up to a sudden pain in his neck, and when he opened his eyes, found himself buried in some ceiling rubble. "Ow!"

"I warned you not to step on the gas, Sunny!" Dev yelled from below. Or, above him? Was he upside down?

Artorian extracted himself from the workspace that used to be functional and bustling, apologizing to the Gnomes whose project he'd flattened. "Sorry, sorry. Dev! How do I get down? Up? I can't fly."

Halcyon made it easy by sky-swimming by and giving him a broad, easy platform to grab a hold of. Transitioning the layers between gravity runes was a trip, as up became down only to feel like up again as he passed through a thick blanket of static. Deposited on the chair he'd rocketed out from, Artorian brushed the debris out of his dusty beard. "Whelp. Any Mana at all causes a smashing success. Of the ceiling-face variety."

A loud shattering sound made everyone look at Artorian's legs as they lost a significant amount of glow and luster, the control Cores in the knees completely destroyed from the Mana strain. "Well that's not good." Dev replied. "That means we... Sprockets, we need better Beast Cores. Strong quality isn't bolting down the screw. B-ranked Cores can't handle A-ranked Mana. We'd need Beastly as the minimum. That's a tall order. The supply of upper ranked Cores is sparse. An Immaculate Core would be ideal, but I don't think I'm getting my hands on an S-ranked Beast Core."

Artorian lolled his head back and forth, then leaned down to relay a detail he'd picked up. "Tatum has two Luminous ones in his pocket right now. He said he was going to trade them. Would those help?"

Dev didn't even question the information as a light filled his eyes, the gears behind then turning like a racer's power supply in overdrive. Double-S ranked Cores? He *wanted* them. With speed, he dropped his board and huddled up with his brethren. Some very hand-movement-intensive discussions later, they split and zipped away, leaving only Deverash behind. "The good news: we will probably have those soon. Might cost us, but still. The bad news: I know the Strikers are not very useful right now, and you probably can't stand on them for support. No control Cores means no proper toe-plate wiggles, either. You'll get minor movements, at best. The magnetics will keep all the pieces together now that they have some charge. Good news two, good idea boogaloo: having them at all might help the mind?"

"That I can feel them does help, Dev. Thank you for the artistic prosthetics." Artorian confirmed, making grabby hands for Halcyon while planning ahead. Dev was giving him the silent 'you're not going to want to be here when they get back' look. "Once the new Cores are in place, what do you think the next step will be? Also, anything I should avoid doing while these are on?"

Checking the live readout on the worktable, Dev squeezed the end of his tiny moustache. "Good you asked, or I would not have seen this. Likely… you will need a vast influx of Mana to synchronize with the Striker Mark IX fully once the new Cores are in. Think of it as going at full-blast to make everything *feel* the same, new legs included. I think you've done Tribulations for full heals and recovery before? This falls squarely in that boat. Otherwise, try not to shapeshift in any way. Size-changes ain't good neither, so keep your dragon tucked into your sleeves."

That was easy to understand for the bearded geezer. "Turning into a Long isn't going to be in the cards for a while. Gotcha. You think Tribulations might fix this? A small convenience, that. I'll have to speak to a few people to pre-plan Tribulation seven. Still, progress! Lunella is going to give me an earful about the destroyed pants, though."

Dev scowled, waving at Halcyon to take Artorian away before his own words decided to become uncouth all by themselves. They were dark and flat as was. "I consider their demolition a public service in the name of the greater good."

CHAPTER TWENTY

Halcyon ferried her Dreamer home, checking on his surprisingly quiet form as he looked over at all the colorful and interesting workspaces they were passing. "My Dreamer? I thought you would be asking to poke your nose into more places. You are being uncharacteristically quiet."

"*Hmm?*" Artorian looked up, his thoughts living elsewhere. "I suppose that's reasonable. No, dear. My mind has been on the Tribulation ever since it was mentioned. Scilla might not have too long, and I don't want to dwell on that possible loss. I want her to live with her newly minted friends and family, after all. I know she requested I hurry up with number seven, but the prior information where she asked me to wait is being a source of conflict. I both do, and do not, wish to do the Tribulation. I was thinking over who to talk about it with, other than Scilla."

"If you inform Lunella, my Dreamer, I guarantee you that whomever needs the news will mysteriously find themselves in possession of said news." Halcyon hovered to an opening in the seemingly endless interior wall that was labeled as a 'cooling tower.' "The New Fringe has a way of getting people what they need. Particularly the lost and injured. The Old Fringe may have been a place where one ended up, but the New Fringe is becoming a place where people can begin anew. Lunella has kept the door wide open, and the meals plentiful. No matter how much Jiivra fusses about wanting more walls."

The door gave her no difficulties, and Cy smoothly sped up through the open cylinder. Exiting out onto the surface of the moon, defensive fortifications came into view before the landscape did. Soon enough, as Cy climbed higher, Artorian recognized that they had left a star-shaped fortress, albeit a different one from last time. There was no flower-shaped main structure in the middle. Merely the gaping hole they flew out from, before that opening was obscured with a growing illusion that spread across the gap like a tangling mesh.

"You're right, Cy. I'll tell Lu and Scilla and try to put it out of mind. Dawny, too, in case there's any explosive concerns with getting started. I forgot to ask Cal." Artorian inspected their improvised exit as Halcyon increased the pace of her flight. "Isn't that a rather obvious weak point that someone nefarious could hop on into, thus infiltrating the workshop?"

Halcyon grinned at the suggestion, her tone that of an intrigued dungeon master who pretended to be supportive of a player's endeavors. "They can certainly try. Now, where to?"

Artorian shrugged and dropped it. The moon, based on the little descriptions he'd pieced together, was one giant ball of pure death-trap. Soul-stealing rivers, mind-eating plants, strangely convenient and suspicious 'cooling towers.' Or was it mind-stealing rivers and soul-stealing plants? Y'know, neither of the options made any of it sound any better, so he dropped that line of thinking too. "Home is likely best. I think that if Anansi or Hulk needed me for anything, they would find their way to me. I don't have anything for Anansi either. If he asks, do feel free to tell him he's welcome to drop by? I have the feeling that until Skyspear is available, I'm going to be glued to my bedside window."

Halcyon nodded and breached lunar orbit, starting the trek to Caltopia the old-fashioned way as she confirmed the heading. "New Fringe it is. Don't want to drop by El Dorado, Nidavellir, Atlantis, or Olympus?"

Artorian made an uncertain noise. "Never heard of the first one. I don't want to put a toe over the Olympus line until I'm good and ready to step on them. Atlantis? That must be Aiden. Aiden, I'm going to leave alone until I have the trade goods we spoke about last time. Thank you for the reminder; I will quietly sneak those over to Lu as well. As to the Coast of Rica... I think it's best to delay until my extended Dwarven family settles down from their crafting frenzy. They should... get to do what their hearts sing for. Before that, nobody should interfere, lest they accidentally find a cask of amontillado and plaster themselves into a wall like a teleport gone awry."

His chosen snickered, amused. "As you say, my Dreamer. Is there anything I can do or help with when we get you home?"

Artorian considered the request, focused on wiggling his new metal toes... or the plates that represented them. He had very minor control currently, nothing that he'd consider actually useful. He sure was happy about the wiggle, though. Proof of concept was key. "Well, I need you to go anywhere, dear. Are you alright with that? Otherwise, let me think... What *am* I doing once I'm home?"

Contemplating, he collated a list while Halcyon made a happy and excited Orca pod-call. She was definitely in pleasant spirits at being her Dreamer's trusted ferry. Her Dreamer praised her for her positivity with a well-pressed rub on the nose, as he considered himself somewhat of a burden that he was saddling her with.

She beamed a proud pink in the cheeks, doing a shimmy and a tail-heavy hip-dance before nudging his cheek to get going with his list! He chuckled good-naturedly. "All right, all right! Not in order: Tribulation, in conjunction with synchronizing with these new legs. Accords, in conjunction with demon diplomacy. Decanting, after the Skyspear is set up."

He snapped his fingers. "Ah, there's something right away. I'm not going to be able to walk around the place freely, though I do recall our cultivators want first crack at any possible hostiles who have tucked away in there. I'm sure they will see it as some kind of 'immortal-combat challenge-tower.'"

Tucking his arms back in, he continued collating. "I need to mend my Soul Pillow. I was going to ask about some kind of mental communication that didn't involve the Task Manager, but Vanilla handed that to me on a platter. I got much more out of that deal than she realized. Actually... There was a mention of cobwebs? Anansi might be exactly who I need here. Cy, could you inform him of the backup Pylon network that handles peer-to-peer connections? I'd like a more robust web connection at my fingertips while I'm stuck being stationary with my stationery."

Halcyon nodded, then looked at him with the clear message that she wished him to continue. So he did. "Astrea, Ty, and Grim asked for Infernal channels with a cherry on top. I'm sadly not sure I can still supply that sundae, save for the cherry. I'll deal with Henry, Marie, and any other supervisor when they choose to drop by. Decanting Snookem early might be useful? That or he will find a corner to nap in and we will never find him again, like some obstinate owl. I'll hoot-hoot hold off."

Shaking his head with a smile, he restarted his count. "I want to do some scribing, but there are other things to prioritize. Some administration work. Getting a few C-ranks to the B-ranks. I've half a mind to expect a visit from Dale and his party? I'm not sure what his plans are now that he's fully separate from Cal. I bet he's got a few stories for me. Gomez, too. Cy, am I going to have to deal with the S.A.S. at all?"

"I doubt it." Halcyon replied calm and smooth. "When the year contract you made with Scout is up, maybe then? She is more likely to approach Lunella for the renewal at this point. Currently they're all busy at work making connections and establishing supply lines. Voltekka discovered a newfound passion for trailblazing, and flattening ground into roads wherever he zips and treads. That helps the prior."

A positive note from the old man told Cy he understood, though a thought caused distraction. "Alright then. I was initially keen to try Tatum's reputation currency system, but now that I'm revisiting the topic I'm… not so sure. The more I think of it, the stranger it is. Like, I won't say no if it comes up, but there's something about it that doesn't fit right."

Halcyon had a crack at it. "Would it be that there is no stick accompanying the strangely large carrot, save for the Requisition effect?"

"Maybe. I think Tatum mentioned a detail that seems to bother me as well." Artorian rumbled, musing out loud. "It might be that it seems too easy to rack up really large numbers, only to then get horribly abyssed-over later? I feel like the entire experiment was one big honor system to see who can get a big number, and *not* use it up. Some litmus test for morality based on currency. My stomach doesn't like it, and that's enough for me to be wary. Demons with access to this… I'm only seeing a series of unfortunate circumstances narrated by someone with an exceptionally long nose and nasally way of speaking. Someone who likes lemon and is snickety."

Halcyon snorted and had to look away. "Then do not use it, my Dreamer. The Void Dreamer did mention Olympus did not fare well with the attempt. We will find other ways. Besides, most who know you are far more interested in hearing what you might need, and how to implement it. The cost of the task is... not so important."

Artorian felt unpleasant. "That's... that's getting awfully close to me being some kind of king or ruler, and that beats right into my wall of discomfort too. I appreciate it, Cy, but I think I will stick to gently requesting help when I have ideas or needs. Delegating on such a high level makes my fingers curl into my hands and squeeze. I'll stick to administration, and directing workflows. The New Fringe may feel like a new home, but it's Lunella's basket of eggs."

Halcyon looked like she was about to object, but decided not to, bumping her nose against the top of his head in acknowledgement. She believed his feelings on the matter might be stronger than her Dreamer thought, but she would leave that topic to rest until he discovered it for himself. "As you say, my Dreamer."

Lacing his fingers, Artorian tried to put his list in some workable order. "Alright, time to allot a timeline. What event is locked behind some gate, and what can I do anytime?"

He held both his hands up in front of his face and made himself a flowchart. Artorian began with his left hand, folding in his thumb. "Pillow mending I can do in my sleep. Teaching cultivation I can do while snug in my cot. Scribing, while I would prefer a big mahogany desk, can happen anytime. Talking to visitors happens on the schedule of the visitor, but so far there's nothing I cannot put on pause to attend to a heartfelt chat. Lastly for list leftie, administration is ferried by that same boat."

His focus fell on his right hand as he counted down, his left hand placed in his lap. "Then we've got the gated events. Tribulation. Diplomacy and Accords. Skyspear. Decanting adults. Decanting children."

He popped his cheeks and rolled his knuckles as if tumbling a coin across them. "That needs some more structure. So to do the Tribulation, I need checkmarks from Lu, Scilla, and Ammy. Accords... that's the end of the list. Skyspear is waiting on Amber, and I can't guesstimate a timeline without Titania sneaking me the intelligence. Decanting adults comes before decanting children, but both are gated by the Skyspear being both available and secured. Unless there's demons, and then we stick Richard on 'em."

Closing his hand, he reopened his fist to fix his list. "So actually, Tribulation, then Skyspear, then decanting, then Accords. With leftie's list able to substitute for the empty spaces between these events. Which makes the current difficulty…"

He considered the requirements. "Cy, do you know if Ammy has time for me?"

"Of course I have time for you, silly boy." Amaterasu appeared as a patch of void next to Artorian, opening up in a reverse black hole that unfurled to form a miniature sun. "Cover your eyes for a moment, I don't have **Teleportation** fueled through the **Sun Law** down yet."

Artorian was so surprised that he wasn't on the ball or quick on the uptake. Halcyon covered him with a massive Orca fin, making it very dark for a moment before her brightly outlined protective fin pulled away as the shine did. Revealing a cheeky Incarnate flying lazily along next to them; as if she was lounging on an Elysium palanquin loaded with fine wine and expensive grapes. Ammy was draped rather than dressed in clothing composed of elegant finery, the colors of her attire mimicking a golden sunrise.

Ammy's voice was honey. *"Hi, sugar!"*

CHAPTER TWENTY-ONE

Ammy propped her cheek up with her palm, smug as a pouty plum. She fluttered her eyelashes at her speechless bestie. "C'towl got your tongue?"

Artorian sat up violently, worked off the top half of his atrocious winter sweater, then mightily threw the bundle smack into her face, the sweater thrown with enough surprise force to swat Ammy right off her pretend-palanquin. "*Dress*, you insufferable prankster! I know *trees* with better manners than the heart attack you just tried to inflict."

Choking on her laughter, Ammy shrieked while holding onto the bundled up sweater like it was an unmovable anchor in space. She wheezed and turned red, barely able to contain herself as Artorian had seen right through her abyss, and called her out on it without a moment of hesitation once the pieces clicked.

After some hiccupped giggling on Ammy's end, during which Artorian glared at her with the expression equivalent of him impatiently tapping his foot, Ammy worked herself into the insult to nature and wiggled her sleevies. They were so long that her hands didn't even show, while the bottom hem covered all the way over her knees. "*Ahh*... that was so worth it! Oh, I forgot to adjust my size back. I'm still in smol-shortstack-mode. What do you think? Compact, Dawn-lithe, or Ammy-muscle today?"

"Which one can I hug you in?" Artorian flatly retorted.

Ammy rolled on her axis in space with one of the sleeves pensively pressed to her mouth, then she smashed face first into his chest before speaking, her arms squeezing his ribs like the man was a rubber duck. "Any!"

H-hoompfh! "D-Dawny! You're still dense as a star! I can't breathe!" He wheezed with newly regained liberty when the four-foot nothing miniature version of Ammy rolled over and released him. She chose to sit on the new metallic legs, prodding them with interest while Artorian slapped his chest in the hopes he would recover faster. Empty hopes, but hopes nonetheless. *Wheeeze*. "Does your design matter when the contents are the same?"

"It does to some people." She hummed back, rolling one of the ball joints in the left ankle. "Doesn't usually matter to you, so I asked. I think I'm feelin' Dawny-lithe today? Small was good when I was tumbling around with the animals. Give me a moment."

Rising up from her seat, Ammy glowed with a swirling dark-ness from within that visually appeared to showcase a star dying within the confines of her shape. When she sat her butt back down, she was the shape Artorian had always known Dawn to look like in the pre-Amaterasu days. Reds to oranges galore on a tanned tapestry.

Her voice was no different regardless of her looks. "That's better."

Wiggling the sleeves, she got her hands through the ends just fine as she adjusted the sweater and properly looked at it with a severe frown. "Okay, *what*? Is someone trying to kill you with a broken fashion sense? Zelia would have an aneurysm."

Artorian released a high pitched noise from his throat. *Hmn*! "Lu made it for me. So, like a good Grandpa, I wear the thing. That it can kill small rodents at a glance is something I'm choosing to gloss over. She did her best."

"Huh." Ammy held onto the bottom hem, her thumbs brushing over it as regardless of the explanation, her dislike for the piece only seemed to grow at a steady rate. "That's… very sweet, Sunny. Very *you*. I'm returning this to you, and sliding something much more worthwhile out of the Autarchy's Closet."

Artorian was about to ask her if that was a location he could visit, because it very much sounded like a prominent location he wanted to nose about in. When she clapped her hands, the wardrobe transformation instantly completed, with Ammy dressed entirely differently. The atrocity-sweater was back on him, which he chose to keep quiet about, while Ammy had settled on flowing robes in the design of a loose kimono. One of Zelia's personal favorite styles, even if the Arachne preferred them exactly fitted, trim and modest.

The white and gray color scheme wasn't doing it for Ammy on second inspection, so she pressed her finger to the metallic color of Artorian's mauve and chrome Iridium legs. Artorian likened the following transitional visual experience to a wave of paint washing like water down a canvas, originating from the touching finger to surging across her robes.

Settling into place as she pulled her digit away, the metallic purple hues mingled like a sophisticated tie-dye. "There we go! Mauve and chrome kimono! Matches the purple gradients on the end of my hair, too. This liger mauve wouldn't work too well as muscle-Ammy. I prefer my yellows in that form, but this fits current-me great!"

Artorian crossed his arms, and nodded during inspection. "Very stylish. Not even a contest."

She flicked his shoulder. "Don't sound so pouty. When you're done being Lunella's mannequin, I have some exceptionally nice things Zelia put aside for you. They are *very soft.*"

That detail perked the old man right up, complete with a smile as he punched both arms into the air. "Woo!"

Ammy settled in his lap and lounged, claiming both his hands to hold when they came back down. "That's a much better reception! Now, I was free when I heard you say my name, but I will admit I am not aware of any of the context. You caught on quick with my cheeky-as-abyss entrance, but if you need something, then I'm going to need the story."

Halcyon grumbled. "Well, it is exceptionally difficult to hold you *both* in the curl of my fin when I'm trying to be so careful about my Dreamer's legs. Could we shift this around? I'm having difficulty flying now, Fire Dreamer."

"Right, my density! My apologies, Halcyon darling." Ammy realized that Cy was doing all the heavy lifting. "You deserve a break, even if you are so dead set on being a diligent dirigible. Slow down to a stop, I'll pull Zephyr in. She's been bored out of her mind bobbing around in drydock."

Halcyon gladly did so, allowing Ammy to prepare a section of static space to feel more malleable than the rest of the emptiness around it. Artorian was enthralled not by the sight, but by the distinctively different energetic feel that glob of space had. "Alright, that is *fascinating*. I can feel the rough intent, but what *is* that tingly sensation creeping into my fingertips when I reach out for that spot? The area feels like a mixture of the creepy chill you get when passing through a gate, but it's flavored like teleportation."

Before he got a response, Artorian could feel that an object the rough shape and size of a boat was going to exit into the prepared section of space. On the cue where he thought it, Zephyr filtered line by line into the cuboid space at what must have been the speed of light. Her form stretched and bent unnaturally before fully entering the space, after which Zephyr filled out to the standard, expected size. Was that his perception at play, or had her form actually been altered during the move? He couldn't tell.

The current vessel appeared to look identical to the rich yacht Artorian remembered seeing the first time! Well, almost identical. There were some detail changes, some material choice upgrades, new hull plating. Regardless of that, the boat still screamed to his senses that the object was Zephyr the person, rather than some boat that happened to share the name.

Artorian ran his fingers down his beard. "I want so many answers."

Zephyr unfurled her sails when the space around her returned to normality, feeling no different from the rest of the empty void around her. Artorian tapped his lips at the thought. Even the 'void' here was technically full of Essence, so was it right to call it a void? Breathing and talking was currently not remotely impeded. So, probably not, but that was a problem for later.

Ammy motioned her arms out to her Elven friend, a full-sized luxury yacht. "Ta-dah! She's okay! You did a great job with the emergency healing, Sunny. By the time we got to her, we were able to bring her into triage right away. Physically, she's tip top."

That specification concerned him. "Mentally?"

Zephyr pushed open a porthole, leaning on her elbows from the inside of her ship. The blasé High Elf smirked as she showed off being able to uphold two forms at the same time. "Mentally, I want time and space in spades. Though something to do doesn't mix well with not wanting to be bothered. So let me play boat, don't grill me until I'm ready to come out and talk on my own terms and on my own time, and we won't have problems. Now come aboard so I can drop this Elven form and focus on being the ship. Just because I can do the trick doesn't mean I want to uphold it."

Zephyr closed the porthole window and vanished, prompting Artorian to shoot Ammy a look that only asked more questions. Ammy shrugged with a smile. "You heard her. The earlier process was Incarnate magic. That space that tingles your fingertips? That was all Spiritual energy, and you're not there yet. The process of getting Zephyr from drydock to here, we are designating with the term 'warping.' We've dabbled before, but now we're actually doing a proper project. Or we were, when there was extra time for it. Think of it as another way to get 'thing A' across a vast distance, and arrive at 'place B.' Warping is neither teleporting nor gating, instead picture it as folding a 'bubble' of space out of reality and then folding it back in at the destination. Think of it as a 'next step' that doesn't even work without Spirit-oomph involved. Very experimental, volunteers only. Do not try this at home."

She flicked Artorian right in the forehead as she took over carrying duties from Halcyon, who adopted her humanized form to board the vessel. "*Do not.*"

Artorian rubbed his forehead, his scheming expression dropping away. "Alright, alright! That hurt!"

"The pain will help you remember." She half-teased, her eyes burning extra bright novas at him for a moment before an innocent smile overtook her facial features. "Now swing your arm around my neck. Zephy provided us fancy deck-chairs and I'm settling you into one so you can get to telling me stories."

Artorian did as he was told, deposited shortly after in a very luxurious deck chair where he could lay and stretch out. The decor around him caught his eye again and again, little details rampant in the structural design. "Feels like some kind of miniature mahogany palace. Everything is fancy. *Everything.* Even this table, and are these glasses you're filling with water made of some kind of twisted crystal? How did the engravings end up *in* the glass? Is it even glass?"

Zephyr popped open a tube on the deck, the flap of which moved as if she were speaking. "Old man, I may not like my heritage, but I am still a *fancy* lady. I like my quality. I like to shine. I like things that make High Elves rhyme. Now settle in, enjoy your Elysium water, and quit prodding before I practice my barrel rolls. I have already made so many star-foxes by hurtling them from my deck to deep into the beyond that there is now a dedicated clan named the McClouds. The only reason I still tolerate them is because they are designing a whole new line of pirate ships after me that they're naming the Arrrrr-wings. The sleekness of the idea is gorgeous. *You*, I tolerate because you gave me the chance to stab Odin in the eye, and then patched me up afterwards. Do not presume that this lease of respect comes with an inexhaustible line of credit. I *just* told you not to prod. Do not test my sails twice."

Artorian put his hands in the air. "Aye aye, Cap'n."

Ammy grabbed the front of his sweater and tugged him in after filling everyone's water steins. Her fingers made eye-to-eye motions. "No. Look at me. I am the captain now."

Artorian felt mighty confused as his eyes darted between Ammy and the pipe, which lasted about two seconds before neither of the girls could keep a straight face, or the equivalent of one. Bursting out in highly amused laughter, Ammy let her bestie go very gently, depositing him back into his seat, while the lower-decks howled in amusement. Was this some inside joke he wasn't in on?

Artorian was genuinely worried he'd offended someone, but Halcyon rubbed an amused hand over his bald head as she pulled her chair up to be closer. "They are playing with you, my Dreamer."

"Oh!" Artorian realized with a loud exhalation, his form slumping. "Oh good!"

Ammy recovered and pulled her chair right up next to Artorian's, then laid sideways to settle in with her glass of water in hand. "Just prodding, sugar. Nobody's upset at you. That was a recurring joke from an event that keeps happening. We keep having random people board Zeph and think 'finders keepers,' after which they declare themselves the captain. It goes very poorly for them, to the great enjoyment of the rest of us. Now drink some water, and get me up to speed."

Artorian looked at his glass, downed the contents in one go, and placed the cup upside down on the table as the remaining thrill and aftershocks of the events washed over and through him, leaving only him behind as he cleared his thoughts, and got a handle on himself. This had just been sproutling pranking, and he was none the worse off for it, given the smiling faces he was surrounded by.

Falling right into grandpa-mode, Artorian got into the swing of it and informed Ammy of his recent adventures, and worries about Tribulation seven. "The story goes somewhat like this."

CHAPTER TWENTY-TWO

Ammy chewed on the end of her miniature drink-parasol as Artorian spent hours recounting, passing the time both by listening, and getting fed up with looking at the atrocity sweater well past the point where she wanted to deal with it. Ammy made him stand and Rosewood-pose while recounting his tale as she fitted him with some nicer, Zelia-quality charcoal black and currant red robes. She'd have Lunella's gift nicely packaged and sent back to her for 'safekeeping.'

Dev had taken time out of his busy schedule to make that delivery personally.

The sweater... *probably* made it back to Lunella.

Artorian barely noticed, consumed by storytelling. He needed to vent for so long that when Zephyr arrived in Caltopia's orbit, she decided to do some cloud-surfing and globe circumnavigating instead, as it was clearly the case that there was still much more steam stuck in the elder's think tank.

A non-issue, since they weren't truly pressed on time until one of the gated events had its conditions met. Halcyon went ahead to fill in Lunella, Jiivra, and Irene when the yacht hovered high over the New Fringe, leaving Artorian to quibble like an ancient seamstress to an ever-attentive Incarnate. During this, he diligently worked on his soul item. The task kept his hands busy in between keeping Amaterasu amused, as Ammy giggled when he slid off-topic and began a soapbox tantrum that ended up demanding the use of both his arms for visual elucidation.

The man spoke with his hands, after all.

To Ammy, the scene was occasionally reminiscent of an old play she used to watch; one of an overzealous and purple felt-faced doll who once bought a bookshelf off of a gumtree, only to be wrapped up in an increasingly implausible series of events with ever increasing urgency and panic. Only to flee, lose the bookshelf to a shrubbery, and be recognizable in the far distance by the sheer virtue of its powerful arm flailing.

When Ammy returned from her trip down memory lane, Artorian was out of steam, the old fox snoring the night away in his chair having fallen asleep mid-rant somewhere after thinking that curling over on his left side for a bit of comfort would surely be alright, as he wasn't tired. He'd just adjust his pillow a little like so, accidentally bury his face into the fluff a bit much, and now he could get back to...

Snoring, as far as a very entertained Ammy was concerned. She eased out of her chair, tucked him in, and bundled some extra pillows into the gaps for good measure. When she was done, she pressed her hands to her hips and sighed with a nod. Bouncing on her toes, she then stretched her arms out above her head and leaned back until her back popped, causing enough satisfaction for her to lean her elbows onto the gunwale. "Sunny sure can talk, huh?"

Scilla stuck her arm up and out of Ammy's shadow, prompting the Incarnate to lean down and tug her free until she could stand on her own two feet.

"Standing all on your own is good progress." Ammy's tone was complementary, brushing Scilla's green attire off even if it wasn't necessary. She was imagining the creases. "How are you feeling, hon?"

Scilla joined Ammy's gunwale lean. The act was easier than standing. "Getting there, Mom. My dress is fine!" She fussed back, her hand weakly beating at an over-attentive Incarnate's preening. "Sunny being able to drown politicians in words is nothing new. He looked very cozy getting to tell you everything on his mind and get you up to speed at the same time. Do you think you'll ever get to do the same?"

Ammy nodded with certainty. "Without a doubt. I, unlike our

dearest, feel no grand push or inclination to gush unless it is truly pressing, or necessary. All these Incarnate-only headaches would be a massive burden, and I've no interest in adding so much as a feather of it to his shoulders. This work is mine, as is the weight. Zelia knew that balancing act well. If we start bogging our philosopher down with weight for his mind, what must get done will not get done. One day that will not matter, and I will get to spend years and years, snug as a C'towl in a cowl, nested in the crook of a couch, prattling his ear off. Like a granny who has dirt on the neighbors."

"He'd like that far too much. Plus, you're already a granny, you just hide it well with that pretty face!" Scilla was bemused and her fingers harmlessly poked Ammy's ribs. "He'd smile, sit back fondly, and relish in your tales and experiences well past the point where he realizes his tea has long gone cold."

"Oh hush!" Ammy fussed, playing hand-slap with the Liminal being for a moment before curling an arm around her shoulders, tugging Scilla's head in under her chin. "Now, no more deflecting. How are you *feeling*?"

Scilla tensed, but relented. "A step above terrible, but not okay. This is the best I'm able to do to stabilize my form until the Tribulation, and at this point, even if he completes it, my clock is ticking. Making friends was really nice? Astrea's a treat. Total troublemaker. Ty means well, but is on the bandwagon and in the back of the cart before I've realized there is one, and Grim is sitting in the front with a hand on the reins wondering what's taking me so long. I'm *obviously* coming."

Ammy smiled. "Sounds like a merry band of troublemakers alright. Is Grim correct? Or are their schemes not your tea?"

"*Pfffff.*" Scilla's head moved backwards from the statement, her chin dipping. "That brat hasn't been wrong yet. I am on that cart with Astrea in record time, we pick Craig up along the way, detour to fetch Frank, and giggle our way onwards to adventure."

The Incarnate tapped her fingers while looking skywards. "Frank... Frank... I don't recall that one."

The Liminal one enjoyed feeling the breeze on her face, and spoke in a matching tone. "Frank was a Wisp that Sunny met in Eternia. One of Tim's little background experiments with inviolable information. In the same vein that Dev had his entire race restored from the backup kept in his own memories, and the Wood

Elves from their shared experiences, Frank used to be some Guild... Leader? Master? Someone from the Mountaindale days who died near a Chaos Portal. Restoring him fully was fraught with trial, but Tim figured out a way to get him back as a Wisp, **Law** included. Which... is a little problematic, but that was an unavoidable side-effect."

Scilla blobbed some wet orbs into being above her hand to keep a tally for herself. "If I remember the order correctly; Dale saw Frank die to a Blight effect from some necromancer, Cal later got a full copy of Dale's memories, Cal then isolated Frank-specific memories and gave them to Tim. Tim found all the matching memories from everyone else in a Core who knew of Frank, Tim then had enough of what constituted 'Frank' to tether those experiences into a seed Core. Once enough of the pattern was in the Core, the soul snapped right to it from... I actually have no idea where. Only that this effect is both automatic and replicable. Then suddenly we had 'Frank' the B-ranked Mage when the inviolable soul information overwrote the gathered memories, restoring them. Except as Frank the Wisp, instead of Frank the Guild-daddy."

Ammy leaned on her elbow as she let Scilla go, her confused frown only deepening. "Clarify that first part? I have a rough working understanding of the souls bit, so not that. I helped Tater Tot put the first spellforms for the tethering process together. Why is a Wisp with a **Law** a problem? That happens all the time with bonded Wisps."

Scilla waffled her hand from side to side while showing her teeth, her expression detailing a 'sort of.' "A bonded Wisp that gets their **Law** in conjunction with their Dungeon? Yeah! No problem. That's normal Wisp Ascendancy. Like how Dani got hers when Cal did, except that they still encounter the Incarnation node-limit problem. Well, that *used* to be a problem. Dani took the first-step slot when Cal got himself into the second-step slot. I'm actually surprised that the open slot didn't go to Dale?"

The Incarnate shot that detail down. "Dale and Cal have the same soul. It's a strict one soul to one node ratio. Soul-splitting doesn't change that, it just reduces your power. Bob's split was even, so they all had the same **Death Law** access, no matter how diminished. Cal could recoup Dale and the rest of his soul if he wanted. The mixture would all just be 'Cal' again. My vote was that having Dale around was safer, even if it's only relevant when we can be back out and about again. Normalizing healthy behaviors is smart. Never know when you need a backup body in case some mad cultivator rips the Core out of your chest and dramatically crushes it. Y'know?"

Ammy rolled her hand for Scilla to tell her more about Frank. "Newlights?"

Clearing her throat, Scilla watched the clouds split below their passing. "A Wisp that gains a **Law** by themselves, on their own merits, or otherwise without the help of a Dungeon or bond, is called a 'High Wisp.' Like a High Mageous, sort of, it's a title descriptor to differentiate between the two. A High Wisp is a faux-pas in most of Wisp society, so Frank doesn't hang with them. His personality also…"

Ammy laced her fingers, expressing a mixture of intrigue and amusement. "Well come on, spill the tea."

Scilla cocked her head to judge her mother with one of those: 'You're scheming something, aren't you?' looks. She explained regardless. "Pre-Wisp Frank was a character. At his core? He had good intentions at heart. In execution? He slipped around being just a little too sketchy to be a straight arrow. He loved clearance sales, had a strange anxiety with taxes, despised paperwork, or really most work in general. He preferred keeping coins in his pocket, and his attention on matters that he had fun with. Like secretly sneaking the camp cook information on provisions that Dale could provide. Otherwise, he was nice to the kid, and snuck off to his hobbies."

Ammy smirked. "Like trains?"

Scilla instantly dismissed her wet orbs as she needed to squeeze both her eyes and hands shut, her closing palm pressing down around her mother's. "Do *not* let Sunny see those. It will be the end of days."

The Incarnate snickered, her shoulders bouncing. "Oh, I know. The entire technology department is a hardened off-limits Black-Star site. Black-badge clearance only, and that merely to perceive the location. Caltopia is Tech-Age limited unless someone on the surface puzzles something out on their own. Even Wisp-swarms are restricted to Antiquity-Age blueprints. Cal has made it very clear that inventions are to be supported, but not handed out."

Ammy patted her own hand on Scilla's. "Back to topic. High Wisps are a problem, why?"

Scilla grunted. "I mean, they're not for us, but somewhere in ancient Wisp lore, High Wisps were deemed to be problems because in order for a Wisp to get a **Law**, they would need to be able to get Essence by themselves. Without relying on a parent-Dungeon to provide it for them."

She recouped her hands. "Personal benefactors are an itchy topic, but we know it was done. People secretly keeping a Wisp in their pocket, taking care of it with their Essence, and the like. Rare, but we have plenty of recorded instances of it happening. The Lion Kingdom's rise was a great example. The real kicker is that the story, and stigma slapped on High Wisps specifically, is that they accomplished Magehood without any of those factors. Meaning personal cultivation. Which... for some reason that remains hidden to me, the older Wisps have a massive bias against."

Ammy considered the information, then deemed it not to be particularly dangerous. "Makes sense to me. Wisps as a pattern for cultivation techniques, the kept-in-the-center kind, are some of the best and most potent ones out there. Unless you dabble in impossible shapes, or whatnot. Though I don't recommend those either way."

She shot her snoozing Artorian a squinted glare immediately after making that statement. "I suppose the problem comes down to Wisps being considered neither a Beast nor a cultivator?"

Scilla perked up at that thought. "Now that you mention it, I've never seen a Wisp with a Core of any kind. Nor any with a cultivation technique. They don't even know how to make one, or how to drop into their own centers, if the conversations with the cultivators in the New Fringe are anything to go by. I also don't think they're counted as curators?"

Ammy nodded in confirmation. "They are not."

Scilla felt like her mind was pinball-tilted, like a boat being overly affected by a capsizing wave, whilst the rest of her body hadn't caught up with standing sideways. "Wait... but... *huh?*"

The Incarnate felt incredibly amused. "A cultivation technique is a poor man's copy of something else's basic function. Wisps can't copy something into themselves when their own pattern is already the 'most-bestest' version of the idea that it could be. If you let rogue Essence or Mana permeate a space, then sure, the space is going to go all sorts of winky wonky wonka. However, the first kind of intelligent and sapient creature you will get out of that very rampant energy *is* a Wisp. They are direct manifestations of energy coming alive. They are Ur-Life. As pristine as it could be."

Ammy rubbed Scilla's head to comfort her, adding in a tasteless joke. "We, in comparison, begin as fleshy meat-prisons with extra baggage, scrounging for scraps that happen to provide power. So I find it most amusing that even as this theoretically purer life-form, they quibble, quip, and scheme worse than we do. I wonder what that says about life? More of a Sunny topic, that."

Scilla's hands gripped tight to the ship's gunwale, her eyes wide and staring thousands of yards off into the distance. "I don't like this topic anymore. Can we talk about something less earth-shattering? Like Tribulations?"

The Incarnate squeezed Scilla's head into the crook of her bronze neck, nosing up and down Scilla's temple. "What's there to talk about? He's safe to proceed, Sunny isn't in danger, nor expecting damage by going through number seven, and *you* won't instantly be lost to us. You even have a strong chance of a firm recovery. Sounds like a win-win to me, sugar."

Scilla relaxed, calmed, and buried her face into the neck of her mother. "Thanks, Mom."

CHAPTER TWENTY-THREE

"Mornin', sunshine!" Artorian woke to Minya violently opening the heavy curtains covering her barn windows. "How long are you going to lay there snoozing? Dale has been up and out since the crack of dawn and is cruising!"

Artorian blinked away the spots in his eyes, pushing himself up from the straw mattress he was currently laying on. When had he transitioned? Wasn't he just on a boat? He could swear he'd been on a boat, cozily roaming the warm skies. "I'd—who—what?"

He barely had the time to look over his shoulder at a mid-motion Minya before another face shoved into view from the outside of the window.

"Well he~ll~ooo there!" Hans had a twinkle in his eyes, his puffed cheeks resting on the knuckles of both hands as he leaned into the window hard. "Long time no lecture! Oh, does Dale even know you're here? I was so curious who got sneaked into the barn in the dark of the night."

Minya's quick exit made Hans gasp, his eyes and mouth wide. "Ohhhh. Nobody knows! I'm going to milk this like I milk the cows! Gonna take my ti~i~i~ime. Better to savor the flavor."

"Hans! You're late! Where are you?" The voice of a ran-out-of-patience-ten-minutes-ago Rose was booming. "If I find you napping in the hay again, you better hope you're more fire resistant than you claim, because I will set the whole place ablaze and make you build the next one by your lonesome. No Tom to help!"

Tsk. Hans clicked his tongue. "Duty calls. The grapes of wrath require battle once more. I'll be back later! If you're looking for the ladyfolk, they're in the olive fields. If you seek the menfolk, follow whatever yelling is the most prevalent. May not always be our fairer halves! Kids are *loud*."

Hans vanished from his window like a breeze that decided it was time to go. Artorian had to crawl up some and stick his head out, looking both ways before he could figure out where the C-ranker had fled to. Most likely culprit? The location of the lovely motherly lady with the small tyke on her hip. "That blazing troublemaker is a father now? I should reconsider getting up."

"Even if you did, where would you go? Can you go?" Chandra pushed a bale of hay to the side, dressed in an outfit made entirely of spring leaves. Very much not a Zelia style either, this had Rosewood's fingerprints all over it. "Close that gaping mouth of yours while you're at it, Administrator. Or is it head-master? I wasn't fully informed which role Cal wanted you in. Dale calling you the headmaster all the time has gotten me confused."

"Chandra!" Artorian pleasantly exclaimed with a big smile, his arms up and open for a hug. "It's so good to see you! Last I heard of you from Tatum, you might not be doing too well. I was so worried!"

Chandra paused her stride, her expression melting from stoic work-mode to one of warmth and sweetness. She put down the clothing in her arms on a hay-bale acting as a table, and slid over to squeeze the old man with a hug. "You darling old soul. You're just saying that! Don't be too worried about me, I just needed somewhere to put roots down. Dale's farm is a good spot. We'll fill you in as time allows."

Artorian was helped to sit upright, but wasn't going to be able to go much further without help. He nodded to show understanding, then held Chandra's hand for a bit as he felt the need to quietly sit there and breathe. Chandra sat on the hay next to him, barely leaving a dent. "You all right?"

Artorian frowned, then dipped his head. "I think so. If not, I'll get there. I had a moment of emptiness. A weight pressing on my shoulders, of which I could not discern the source. The burden just squeezed me without warning, and only now is slowly ebbing away. I'll be fine. Are we on some kind of farm, then?"

Chandra allowed some flowers to grow on her palm, then join together in the shape of a clasp. Which she plucked in order to fix the front of his open robes, neatly keeping them tidy and closed. "You are. We're calling this our family farm. A spot away from it all. Your place was not a good option. Everyone sort of knows where it is, and it's centered on most currently available maps."

"Oh. That…" Artorian held his beard. "*Hmm.* I will come up with something. That's not how I was hoping it would go, but I'll roll with the punches. More importantly, family farm? Is Dale a farmer? I remember making a joke once or twice, but that's sort of it."

Chandra leaned back, motioning out of the window to a herd of sheep. With her helpful guidance, Artorian could easily pick out Dale's form tending to them. "He's got a surprising gift for the wooly ones. Yes, family farm. Brianna is currently here as well, as we want to support Rose and her newest family addition. Given Rose comes from an intermingling of Brianna's and my family lines, we thought ourselves directly responsible to step in and help. Especially should the little one be born with the same affinities as Rose, because that was a labor of legend and a half."

Artorian rubbed over her hand with concern. "Is all well?"

Chandra inhaled heavily, releasing an exhale scented as a fresh lavender breeze. "Yes. Yes, the little one turned out to resemble the father more, both to our… chagrin, and relief. The timing worked out well with Minya's tyke, though she's a little ball of snooze in her crib right now. Hans' boy has all the hallmarks of a curious mouse sniffing out trouble. We're not sure how he got out of his crib and on the roof, but he's done it twice, both times with a very distressed C'towl tightly bound in his grip."

"I'm not sure if it would help…" Artorian released her grip when she sat back. "However, Lu and Wu over in my neck of the woods have a whole host of kids that so far are still contained in memory Cores. When the Skyspear is claimed, we were going to set up a school, classes, probably daycare given the needs. They're welcome to come. I plan on being there as much as I can while I deal with my assigned work."

Chandra pressed both her hands together, then eased them close to her mouth in contemplation. "That would be mighty helpful. I will need to make sure they eat well. On that topic, did Tibbins win that strange pastry competition over in N.F.?"

Artorian's face of doubt made Chandra hang her head. "I knew short lessons would not be enough. Thankfully, our resource woes are minimal. Anything we cannot grow ourselves, we can trade for with fair ease. Even if we know that the Spring Court cheats and magics goods into existence like they're playing in creative mode."

The old man didn't know what that meant, but nodded regardless. "I'm sure that everything easy will eventually fade, leaving us glad we put in the hard work to have control over our produce."

Chandra firmly agreed. "Having run a restaurant, I know for certain that I want both a tight hold on any goods or produce grown, and the means of their production. I need *reliable* sourcing. Not rabbits pulled out of Wisp hats. Who knows where those bashers have been?"

Pulling a hay-bale closer with some carefully grown vines that crept out of the ground, she then grew a copy of the farm atop the makeshift table using different, detailed variations of moss.

She began by pointing at a barn. "We are here. Hay storage. Only the girls know you're here, as you were supposed to be a surprise for Dale. He's been having big depressive bouts mixed with nostalgia and homesickness. Ammy had the thought that another friendly face would help. Plus, he needs someone to talk to. He can't talk to Cal at all, and the dungeon doesn't visit."

"I'll mention it to Cal, depending on my chat with Dale. I don't yet know if that idea is a detriment, or for the better." Artorian pushed a finger into the moss to test it. "Spongy!"

"Well, it *is* sponge moss." She picked up his finger, then hovered it above a field outlined in brown. "This is where Dale farms coffee, and where coffee elementals are cultivated. This space has been conditioned to conform to a tropical climate where there is no frost, ample sunshine, and plenty of water. Please keep your Aura reeled in. Too much direct sunlight or hydration can have a reverse and detrimental effect, and if I recall correctly, your kind of Auric accents cause *both* at the same time."

"Accents?" Artorian inquired. "I thought you'd have said effects."

Chandra shook her head. "I find accents, like the types which differ during the spoken word, better illustrate the subtle little differences when two otherwise identical Auras should be at play. You taught Dale the Starlight Aura, I believe? His Aura acts completely differently from yours. It feels different. Abyss, it even *tastes* different. You can tell from the plants and spices anytime you eat food affected by his accent."

She then poked him in the chest. "Your Aura turned back on when you woke up, which made me hurry over here with your washed… clothes? Ammy said I wasn't allowed to burn them. A Wisp brought them in after a Gnomish delivery went awry. You've already affected the hay here, and I was originally planning to tell you to tone it down and get back to work, but you *had* to be such an insufferable, caring codger."

Artorian chuckled pleasantly, reeling in his Aura as requested. "I'll keep my emanations under wraps. I'm currently a touch more interested in how you and Brianna are family. Rose, I believe, qualifies as a Half-Elf?"

Chandra cocked her head, her arms crossing. "Her parents had her through Silverwood means. Normal rules of conception aren't considered, nor the genders going into the mixture. The Silverwood will make it work, because much like the written lectures we found from some old miser, intent plays a big part for that tree. Silverwoods are also very…"

"Arrogant? Or is that the wrong word?" Rose interjected as she joined the huddle, done with her fieldwork. A cheek-to-cheek kiss was provided to Chandra before her butt found a seat. She shot the older woman a look with her eyes, then wrapped an arm around the Nature Mage who momentarily looked sheepish. "I could *feel* you gossiping about me from two fields away, Grandma."

Rose then turned to the old man, and spoke while Chandra composed herself. "I love both my dads, but I think that tree pranked the celestials out of them to end up with *me*."

Artorian raised a brow at her, allowing her to sneak in a helpful addendum. "My parents are Chandra's son, and Brianna's brother. You can meet them if you'd like? They're sweet as all sugar, and grow canes of it near the lake."

Artorian beamed an enthusiastic smile as Chandra retook the reeds of conversation.

"I'm still baffled to see them again. It's *them*-them, too. Not just their faces with a different mind behind the eyes. I thought I'd lost my boys forever, then Tim comes by like it's no big deal and introduces them." Chandra chewed on her words, her hands waffling. "I'm not going to say arrogant, Rose, because Silverwoods don't hold what they are over you like some kind of hammer to a nail. However, they have very particular personalities, and certain traits that they all share, which can make them very difficult to get along with. Because if and when they do not agree with you, or want to do something, then *forget it*. It's not happening. A Silverwood will fight you on the grounds of spite and principle, and they can hold some root-gripped *ground*."

Artorian pondered out loud. "Seemed to get along with me well enough."

Chandra glared, her tone sarcastic and pointed. "Can't say I'm surprised a Silverwood wouldn't adore the bark-detailed abyss out of *you*. That's like putting two old wide-grin foxes together and expecting them not to start plotting with their arms wrapped around the other's neck. Speaking of, I heard Richard might be joining us soon? That is exactly the kind of situation I'm fretting about."

She waved her hands like she wanted to be far away from the topic. "Short version! Silverwood influences helped make Rose look like a Half-Elf, so she doesn't trigger a human's uncanny valley problem, but also doesn't get insta-slapped with Dark Elven bias when someone first looks at her. It... it worked out. The Essence channels were honestly the bigger problem, but that wasn't the tree's fault."

Artorian felt the need for a change of pace, thus changed topic by pointing at the brown patch of moss. "Coffee is a word I've been hearing thrown around lately. I think I first heard it from some coconut crabs who held it in... far too high esteem."

Chandra smiled, glad for the complete conversation flip. "It was supposed to be a joke, originally. A prank. Coffee is full of something called caffeine, which when blended and used as grounds to strain hot water through, results in a drink that can directly stimulate the central nervous system. Leading to increased alertness, wakefulness, and such. The downside is that it can make people jittery, increase heart rates, or as we accidentally discovered with one of the Chosen, make people *vibrate through the floor*."

Her smile bloomed, a full on smirk proud on her face. "We tried giving it to some plants after that, and they clipped through the wall, floor, ceiling, anything. When the coffee ran its course, the plant was stuck there. Not great for anything more than a prank because it does play havoc with the Essence keeping walls as walls. However, it was just too funny. We've called such sightings the 'Bethesda Effect.' We wanted to give some to Cal in the hopes he'd slip right through the floor and finally fix all the holes still rampant in the world, because the Incarnates haven't been able to get to them all."

"How did it go?" Artorian asked in full amusement. "Success?"

Chandra's expression fell slightly. "He sipped. He liked it. He threw the cup on the ground. Demanded another. Made some *impressive* facial twitches. Then... I think he ended up in an alternate reality somewhere because Dawn and Occy had to go get him, but there was something funny to it because Dani stayed behind and she could *not* stop laughing."

"Couldn't see the events yourself as a non-Incarnate?" Artorian surmised.

Chandra sighed. "Could not. Occy refuses to tell me what happened. Every time I tried, he would suffer a weak bout of giggles, trying to hide his snickering as Cal shot him sharp and dirty looks while my sweetums stumbled away, trying so hard to keep himself together. Dawn just stood there with her arms crossed, entirely unamused, which killed Dani downright dead with additional shrieking laughter. She's on the ground every time she sees Dawn make that flat, stoic as stone face."

Artorian shared in the amusement, then poked another part of the moss. "Sheep?"

Chandra returned to task. "Cows. They need large grazing pastures. Sheep are over here. Vanilla fields are here. If you see a large, round, fat, red, dragon-looking thing attending them, that's just Chonk. He tends to the vanilla fields."

She pointed out a few more places, then stopped on a patch of purple. "This whole section is Tyrian's olive grove. Us girls prefer spending time here, both to tease poor little Pim, and for delicious girl-gossip time. Tyrian likes manually making oil, then posing. It's a fun game of 'show-off' that we take turns with."

Artorian frowned, tapping the area. "I know... I know that name. She was an Olympian? A girl part of Odin's group, protective of some smallish bird boy."

"That's her." Chandra confirmed, making some of the diorama grow more details. "Tyri had a massive problem with her bird-boy being picked on. There wasn't even a need to convince her to change sides. There's a lot of fight in her, and all of it was directed at the mountain she came from. She's not the brightest soul, but give that girl a task and she'll get it done. A very 'can do' attitude lives in her."

Artorian suddenly had flashbacks of another soul who defined such a can-do attitude. He shook himself from the memories living in Socorro, and just accepted they were up a friend and down an enemy. "That's how it is then. Show me the rest."

CHAPTER TWENTY-FOUR

Minya had periodically joined them at different points in the day, initially meaning to 'check up' on Chandra and the gossip, then choosing to remain and get snug on a compact wad of hay to share in the tea. Tea that Minya had slipped away to acquire, so they all had refreshments to match the entertainment.

The **Nature** Mage turned out to have much to get off her chest. The sun was long down by the time the map of moss sat forgotten on the hay, Chandra venting her feelings, frustrations, and furies in full force. Manifesting plants all about her like nature herself pitching a fit, only to calm like a volcano, have some water, then get heated over the next topic that caused the barn to become overgrown with wild vines.

The whole structure became covered tile to rooftop in amalgams of wildflowers. The colors were sure pretty, even if the occasional tremor through the building tested its foundations. The cracks of which were patched by growing greenery.

Artorian at this point felt like the barn resembled an overgrown shrub rather than some kind of structure. He was surprised that none of whom Hans had referred to as 'the menfolk' showed up, but figured that any source of Mana-empowered snapping was reason enough for them all to stay away. Lest they be either dragged in, or become the subject of the A-ranker's attention while she was in full 'And-another-thing!' mode.

Minya poked at a few of the moss patches, commenting that being a farmer was tough, but the plants grew on you. This got a giggle out of the group until Hans attempted to squeeze by, resulting in the three ladies squinting at him in pointed silence. The man swiftly fled before he could land his clever comment. Bravely running away may have been a better description. Like Sir Robin, from the olden tales told by the performance group, Monty's Python.

Artorian motioned at Rose when her person escaped silent judgement. "I notice that treatment works every time. Is there some other meaning to it?"

Rose sipped her tea and flicked her eyes to Minya, who filled in. "We squint at the sun because it's bright. We squint at people because they're not."

Sagely nodding followed from the other two, so Artorian promptly dropped it with a deflecting comment. "Hans didn't look like that bad of a lad? Some prodding enjoyment, but certainly no malice?"

Rose waggled her cup. "My largest boy, much like my smallest, loves poking his nose into any matter where it doesn't belong. Some of our boys are sweethearts, like Dale. Some, like Tom, are thrill seekers. Others, like Hans, are just trouble. They aren't who the more severe of silent looks are reserved for. My Hans took one look at my face, saw I was having a good time, and realized he'd only detract from it right now. So he split. Or, I'm being too generous and he thought of something even worse and is now doing that instead, before we suddenly find him snooping again."

Chandra grumbled, her own experiences matching the mood. "Tot is a scatterbrain. Well-meaning or not, a stiff smack to the rump is sometimes necessary to retain his attention."

Minya was the only one who made a foul face. "Dale is a good sort. Most everyone I spent some time with before him, on the other claw... taught me that it's better to never assume malice when incompetence will suffice as an explanation."

Chandra's expression copied Minya's for a moment, making an amendment. "I've heard that discussed. The Clarkian scholars of old, I think? 'Sufficiently advanced incompetence is indistinguishable from malice.' There's a point where ignorance becomes malice, as there is sometimes no way to reconcile a person's actions with what is reasonable for them to know. On some matters, there is simply no way to act that obtusely ignorant except if it is both deliberate and malicious. Don't lend those people your voice or your ear, just stab them."

"I arrive at the *best* parts of conversation." Brianna smoothly unfurled herself from the shadows. With silent steps, she deftly made her way to Rose without leaving a single indent in any of the moss. Brianna provided Chandra and Rose a cheek-to-cheek kiss with a loud 'mwah.' After which, she settled down next to Chandra, who gladly helped a full cup of hot tea into her cold-looking fingers. The warmth filling her hands improved Brianna's mood by an immediate step. "*Mmm.* Two good things in the same minute. If only the rest of my work went so smoothly. I also know of the argument of which you speak, though only the ending, because it amused me."

Chandra asked Brianna to say more with a look, which she gladly did while sinking into the hay. "Some scholar named Hanlon was sick of being kept awake by their bickering, and chased them all out of the hall with his shaving razor. Shouting that they were the stupid ones for keeping him up all night. Hanlon's razor became an adage for that very discussion."

Rose copied Brianna's good idea, also settling back into her spot on the hay for renewed comfort. She then picked her tiny spoon out of her cup and pointed it at Artorian. The old man understood why he experienced a sudden fear response, but that didn't prevent it from happening. He had it under wraps when Rose spoke. "So were you actually Dale's mentor back in Mountaindale? Or is that a different story?"

Artorian put his own cup down, glad for the segue. "That was me. Dale caught me while having difficulties as a baron, whilst also in dire need of quick, sudden, explosive growth. Survival and all, you know how it goes. He was going to give me valuable information to take him as my private pupil. Which, while I definitely didn't want a pupil, was so clever and lucrative of an offer that I had to bite the arrowhead. I barely had the chance to teach him anything though. Just some minor trifles, and a way to slap people."

Minya squinted at him. "Would those *minor trifles* include that monster of an Aura he tromps about with on a daily basis?"

Artorian pressed his hand to his chest. "Starlight? It's not *that* good. There's no specific function, just a little bit of everything that helps. It's no Regeneration Aura. Has some downsides too, if you ever use it in a tavern where people want to remain hammered."

The ladies laughed in unison, Brianna leaning over to sweetly pat his shoulder. She spoke with dark amusement. "Administrator. Bless your heart. Dale has an Aura that was built to perfection, using some of the most potent methods known at the time. Your particular mixture is more than 'a mere trifle,' given that it really does help with *everything*. Including that which you did not realize you needed. It's *insane*. My Blade Aura may exceed it when it comes to fulfilling a singular purpose, but a Starlight Aura is a weapon of *convenience*."

Artorian put his hands up in surrender, which made it easy for Ammy to float in through the window and grab a hold of them like mooring points at a harbor. She was in a great mood, her voice melodiously playful and sweet. "Gotcha!"

He looked up, and beamed a smile as Brianna let go and pulled back respectfully. Artorian spoke up at the floating Incarnate wistfully. "Hello dearest. Come join the girl-gab?"

"Mhm!" She musically retorted with a chipper noise, slowly altering her hover path so she could slowly and easily plunk herself down next to him. "Brianna is right, by the way. Starlight Aura is a *trip*. Try not to confuse it with Sunlight Aura? Now that I'm in that seat, there's some subtle but surefire differences between the two. Starlight is your utility spread that used to erase blight, and now improves anything it touches. Not that I see people complaining about the fatigue-fixer, but still. The Sunlight variant is definitely more useful when it comes to melting undead down to sticks of butter, and pairs nicely with frying demons."

"Is *that* how Dale's juju works?" All eyes snapped to the open window, the voice suspiciously Hans-flavored. Ammy frowned, then leaned through the open space in order to pluck out a weed. One shaped strangely much like Hans, who was completely covered in flowers, fronds, and plants for effective camouflage. She lifted the man into plain view, allowing the others to judge him with their eyes as Hans blinked excessively. "*Oops.* I said that out loud, didn't I?"

Artorian felt baffled. Amused as could be, but baffled. "How did nobody notice you? *I* didn't notice you."

The man-shaped shrub shrugged, his smile gleaming as he looked apologetic. Though he only *looked* apologetic, as the gesture was made either way. "Nobody was looking! You'd be amazed how many noses you can slip right under if you pretend to be mundane and part of the scenery."

Artorian firmly looked him up and down, then frowned. "Hans? What is that—I'm generously going to call it '*an attempt*'— roiling in your center?"

The man nervously half-laughed. "*Urhm.* My cultivation technique that I stole fair and square? It... uh. Well, it *was* working well enough. Works great for Rose, though!"

Artorian's gaze did the rounds, which was where Rose learned that protective veils of any sort over their centers were more of a polite joke to chuckle about when it came to the old man's perception. He paused his eyes on the window that Hans was being dangled from. "Dear? He brought a tiny friend."

Ammy bothered to look, then raised a brow as the corner of her lips curled up. Reaching down with her free hand, she picked up Hans Jr. The child was equally well-camouflaged as a shrub-cosplay. The Incarnate's voice was smooth. "Well, aren't you two the brightest nuggets of gold in the river?"

Hans thought this a great chance to do some quality deflecting. "People do say I have a way of lighting up a room!"

Rose grumbled him right back down to ground level. "That's called arson and those people are witnesses. Why is my son dressed like a shrub, why is he using a sugarcane reed as a pacifier, and why is he looking at you with bright eyes, happy to be imitating Daddy? Look at him go on that pacifier."

Giggling all around saved Hans from the worst of fates, Artorian busy shaking his head with a smile on his face while Ammy patiently waited for a verdict. She observed Rose, who narrowed her gaze as devious gears turned behind her eyes. "You know what? This calls for punishment. You want to be a cheeky waffle, teaching *my* son like that?"

Hans pressed his grass-clad hands together, pleading like a puppy. "Oh c'mon, this is harmless! I'm but a mere shrub!"

Rose looked to Ammy for ideas, who looked to Artorian, who caught on right away. Immediately, he pretended to be old and frail, acting like he was on Hans's side. "The boy meant well enough. A *light* sentence would do? Why not keep it fair and give him the same kind of rundown you used to give me in the Muspelheim desert? *Light* exercise."

Hans smiled ear to ear with his teeth. "Sounds fair to me!"

Artorian hid his terrible expression, for he should be ashamed of the schadenfreude he was committing on this poor father. Ammy grinned, handing the shrubbery-baby to Mommy's waiting arms. With an approving nod from Rose, she then tossed the shrubbery-man straight into the sky with a flick of the wrist. Her voice boomed after the projectile, full of excitement. "Combat practice it is!"

Artorian cheered supportively. "Good luck!"

Hans realized a little late that this was, in fact, a terrible fate. Somewhere between joining a delta formation of birds, and then leaving it again. He made the best of it as he sang terribly off-key, arms wide and flapping. "I believe I can flyyyy, I believe I can touch the skyyyy."

"That's not quite how that works." Rose watched Hans smack and plume-smash into a large brown spot that was... hopefully mud. Yes. *Mud.* Not something else that began with an 'm' and ended with 'anure.' Her voice filled with satisfaction as gravity worked like gravity should. "*That's* how that works."

He shot upright from the 'mud,' and raised his arms to the sky defiantly, undaunted since he did not yet realize what he'd fallen into. Hans was, if anything, a man of infinite bravado. "Even brown, my fire will burn strong!"

Rose bounced her baby on her knee, yelling through the open window. "Whatever you say, Mr. Brown Fire! Serenade me then!"

Hans dropped his arms, a bit more squeamish as all eyes were on him, and the smell was starting to register. "I can't do it when you're watching!"

Rose had never been given a better quip opportunity, and capitalized hard. "That's becoming a real problem, Hans!"

Hans's hands flopped to his sides, at which point he recognized that he was not only dirty, but that he was *exceptionally* dirty, instantly freaking out and attempting to flee the location so he could plunge into a river to vigorously cleanse himself. A feat made a little difficult by his current, extended tummy girth. Curse him for loving Wuxius' mead shipments so much! Or possibly his own grape wine, but best to blame someone else.

"Getting a little old and fat, dear?" Rose prodded at him from the overgrown barn.

"I'm not fat!" He paused to knead at his own belly when the horrible realization finally arrived. "Oh my celestials, I'm fat! Tom? Tom! Train me! I have to lose this weight! I am to be a lithe flower! A delicate willow!"

"Training, he says?" Rose grinned, de-shrubberizing her youngest. "Ammy, could you please?"

"I would be delighted to use a brat as a broom!" Leaning as she began her hover, she kissed Sunny on the top of his head. "Do your Tribulation, sugar. Lu and Scilla know."

He frowned pensively, then settled into a state of visible comfort before nodding.

"C'mere, you sneaky-beaky stalker!" Ammy howled while speeding from the open window. They all heard Hans screech like a chicken and flee the other way as an over-enthusiastic Incarnate tailed him. "We're going to whip you into shape, fix up that cultivation technique, and make you *presentable* for your lady!"

"Rose, save meeee!" Ammy snatched him up, turned a begging Hans into a brown fireball, and hurled him towards the nearest desert. On the plus side, he arrived squeaky clean, even if his complaints were still off-key. "Think of the children!"

Ammy three-point hero-landed close enough to send the man tumbling away across a high dune. "Oh, we are, Hanselbread. *We are.* That is why I will be gentle! Hans Jr. needs his dad to come home. That it might be with a fresh tan is a sacrifice I'm willing to accept."

Bouncing on her toes, she then rolled her shoulders and popped her neck intimidatingly before hovering ominously from the ground. Her tone darkened playfully. "How crispy he is when that happens... Well, that depends on your *sincerity*, Hans."

"What...?" He stuttered, having trouble finding his feet in the sand as he did his utmost to retain every hint of suaveness he could scramble to keep a hold of. "What do you recommend I do for that?"

Her voice loomed, the smile on her face terror-inducing as reality behind the Incarnate bent and twisted uncomfortably.

"Lesson one. Never stop moving." Ammy let her entire body

catch with golden flames, her silhouette imposing and overtly dangerous while the suns in her eyes swirled. She gave him the most curt and laconic advice she could as Hans booked it. He was the first to be subjected to her Trial of the Golden Sun, color-matching fireballs forming as miniature novas above Amaterasu's upturned palms. *"Run."*

CHAPTER TWENTY-FIVE

Artorian watched the show, his smile slowly fading. Kneading at his forehead, he picked his metal legs up one at a time to lay down properly on the makeshift hay-bale bed, tucking his charcoal and currant robes in around them afterwards. "Sometimes I envy those who are on the Power Gathering track. This Tribulation business is so uncomfortable a thought in comparison. Completing it might be out of my reach."

Chandra formed a thin, fresh blanket of interlocked vines to serve as a new duvet cover. Artorian gladly pulled it close, not even surprised that it was soft as cloth. Brianna and Chandra nodded slowly, deep understanding plain on the A-rankers' faces as they thoroughly understood his current growing pains. "You remind me of a work by Traviticus of Baldree."

Artorian laced his hands, his attention on Chandra's words. "Please, do share?"

The **Nature** Mage scrunched up her face to recall the wording. It had been ages since she'd seen the performance. "I believe he was orating on the topic of comfort versus success? He was in the process of referring to 'a deeply uncertain feeling you get, when you know you're not doing things the way noteworthy or successful people are doing it.' Contrasted by the sudden knowledge that if 'your efforts are actually working,' then to 'just remember that that's what having a competitive advantage feels like.' He goes long in depth to describe that success in the face of what should be insurmountable 'usually doesn't feel comfortable, because it is, by nature, uncommon.' He finished his soapbox speech with the confirmation that 'this is a good sign—unless what you're doing *isn't* working, in which case, you know, um, it's the other thing.' He trailed off after that. Possibly distracted by a distant dais while reaching for his knife, the need for murder glinting in his eyes."

Artorian cocked his head as he tried to think of how an old speech could apply to his situation. A piece of general advice was never a direct measuring stick for one's issues, for no such advice could work in each instance of differing specifics.

Still, he didn't dislike Chandra's recounting of the scroll. "I believe it means that even if my path is difficult, because I am seeing success, I should not be concerned about the discomfort that comes from comparing myself to others. For there are no others I can compare myself to in order to understand where my median, and thus my measurement of comfort comparative to my success, actually lies."

He chewed on his cheek. "Sadly, that doesn't mean I don't feel the discomfort, success on my track or not. Having a competitive advantage does feel nice? Being able to refill my Mana in a snap is a terribly powerful wildcard, regardless of the cost."

Brianna commiserated with the old man. "In my opinion… the Tribulation track is uncomfortable in practice, particularly compared to the other two tracks. I feel *that one* possesses the most unique and unpleasant of drawbacks. The Power Gathering track is very straightforward. The Exemplar track has its own difficulties, but I would not trade it for the trials of the Tribulation track."

Artorian ran a hand over his bald head. "Now it feels like you're exaggerating."

Brianna raised a brow. "You became a child during your A-rank one Tribulation, didn't you? When we met you during one of your first round-table meetings between all of Cal's supervisors. Had that occurred to me, I would have had powerful negative reactions. Ammy told us Scilla is holding your Liminal energy for you, but being able to sleep in peace is a small comfort compared to the hectic changes we have seen you undergo."

"I suppose I bobbed along like a raft, given my circumstances."

Artorian fidgeted with the currant robe. "What's the Exemplar track like? Sounds like that's yours?"

Brianna nodded, leaning into the hay as she quietly listened to the sounds of Hans running and screaming in the far distance, like it was an experience to be paired with fine dining. "Well, A-rankers tend to get saddled with the track that is guaranteed to be the most difficult for them. A **Law** with little complexity to it, combined with a person who has little they need to self-reflect on, tends to get pushed onto the Exemplar track. The point is to make something of yourself, where otherwise the path was easy. Alternatively, that **Law** is desiring to be more well-known, or in some way gain fame, thus requiring the bound Mage to acquire both."

She twirled a dagger for fun, though its origins were a mystery. "A **Law** with little complexity to it, combined with a person who has much they need to self-reflect on, tends to get pushed onto the Power Gathering track. People who are busy struggling with or against themselves, may find it difficult to focus on esoterica. The lessons of the A-rank by themselves may be more difficult than the act of gathering the Mana that allows the increase of a rank, so the focus is not on the energy as much as it is the Mage who requires work."

She wagged her finger knowingly. "Being 'bricked' for any length of time is a most frightening experience. Merely becoming an A-ranker is a daunting task that is not without cost. While some people will stand up from that pain and stride onwards, many will merely lay on the ground and clutch themselves."

The dagger vanished into particles of Essence as Brianna interlaced her fingers. "Lastly, a **Law** of significant complexity, regardless of who is bound to it, can opt for the Tribulations Track. I have heard, and now seen firsthand, that these trials are devious, dastardly, and downright destructive. Severe intelligence is required to excise matters close to a Mage's heart so deeply, and never have I witnessed it done with the Mage in question finding it in any way easy or convenient to keep completing the tasks. 'Tribulations' was not a word chosen without thought. Being struck by lightning a thousand times would be more favorable to a Mage on that track than whatever heart-wrenching feelings they must endure in order to willingly take the step to face the next one."

Artorian was now the one nodding along sagely, as that was most certainly the case.

Brianna smiled, then amended her prior statement. "Complex **Laws** have also been known to choose otherwise, and provide their bound Mages either of the other tracks for reasons I can only consider incomprehensible. Cal is one such clear example, as I would swear on my favorite dagger that he is on the Power Gathering track. Yet, he has the occasional Exemplar task trickled in?"

She put her hands up. "So it may be the case that these tracks are merely speculation of what we have been able to observe and no more. Perhaps the Heavenlies are laughing at us for understanding so little of their divine puzzle. Perhaps there are no tracks, or perhaps there are five and we are short two. This truth, I do not know."

That got a pleasant chuckle out of Artorian, his warm expression back on his foes, woes laid by the wayside. "I forget, at times, that you have the silver tongue of nobility, Brianna. All that just to make me feel a bit better? You sly, cunning creature. Thank you for this kindness."

He sighed, then laid back. "I wish I knew how to get in contact with Dev. He wanted to do something to these legs before I did my Tribulation."

The ladies leaned in for a private huddle, whispering back and forth before they all got up and brushed their clothes off. Hay tended to stick to fabric. Rose left first, carrying her youngest—who had fallen asleep on her shoulder—back home.

Brianna and Chandra gave him some parting words, with a mention to visit them at Tyrian's olive patch when he was all done. This left Artorian alone with Minya, who he gave a wide smile. "Strange how the times have turned, no? Here I was suddenly thinking of us all sitting around a large round table, Bob still present."

She chuckled, then shook her head as she procured a ring from her pocket. Artorian could faintly make out the words 'Odds and Ends' engraved into the side. "That was a very long time ago, Artorian. If we were to go further, I'd still be proselytizing for the Cult of Cal!"

They both chuckled to that. Minya equipped the ring, then summoned forth an unremarkable orb from its storage-space confines. Artorian cocked his head with interest. "How do those work?"

Minya held up the orb in question to return his question.

"Items? The Gnomes have a dedicated warehouse space with heavily encoded teleportation runes. Think... Each item receives a number, which when keyed to an object such as this ring, gains its own alphabet code. It will be called a creation code if you ever see it on a prompt."

She turned her hand around a few times. "This ring has the alphabet code: I.C.B.M. Then pretend the orb has the item code: 4-5-1. It's actually much longer, but I'll shorten it for convenience's sake."

Artorian nodded, so she continued. "When I place any object into this ring, I am actually teleporting it to a warehouse where dedicated floorspace has been carved into squares, and set aside for use with only this specific ring. Specifically, warehouse I.C.B.M. Each object requires a set amount of space, and thus 'squares' which it takes up in that real warehouse. Your old racer, if that's a good example, would take four such squares."

Artorian popped up a finger for a quick question. "I remember the racer taking just one slot in Eternia. Is that similar?"

Minya nodded. "There's some size differences between Cal's warehouses and Tim's warehouses. For now, at least. The Warehouse Inventory Project is slated to undergo several improvements. Don't be surprised if, when you visit Eternium's playground again, the item will suddenly take four spaces. Racers are big and bulky, they should take up more room."

She then held up the retrieved object. "This orb, even if it is a small item, would take a single square. To make problems like the math for 'volume' simple, both objects will be considered to take 'all available space' within the warehouse squares, in order to be certain that there is no overlap between one item location and another."

Minya rolled the orb between her hands. "Think of item 4-5-1 here as an 'entity' rather than a thing that merely has density, volume, and mass. One entity per dedicated space allotment. It's one of the new guidelines to assist with avoiding spectacular mishaps, like all materials in a warehouse compressing into one big amalgam of... matter? Stuff? A mess. No idea why it happened still, all the Gnome did was cross into a different Eternia realm. We expect our problems with storage are far from over, and eventually someone is going to get their hands on a storage item 'of holding' that doesn't act like it should, because some detail wasn't calibrated right. Just file the report to the Gnomes."

Artorian nodded again, so Minya handed over the orb. Right as he touched it, he could feel that it was similar to the lump of coal he'd stolen from the messenger demon in Eternia. A messaging device! He then frowned at it, mumbling. "How do I simply *know* that this item is what it is?"

Minya tapped the top to activate the item, the orb glowing a faint blue. "That's what I meant with 'entity' versus 'thing.' Some items, specifically any item that has an item code in number form, is stored as information that is revealed when touched, unless blocked out by certain conditions. In Eternium, that condition is a combination of the Perception attribute and a hidden value known as 'Clearance.' As an Administrator, you will never be barred by the latter. So when you hold this item, given the rules it follows, you know what it is and what it does. That's sort of the entire point we wanted to achieve when making these. What good is a special item with a boatload of special features if you have no clue what those features are?"

Artorian rubbed his chin. "So this is actually an Eternia game item that has 'crossed the border,' so to speak. Since those work the same out here as they do in there... I can just call Dev?"

Minya beamed. "Never need anyone to explain things to you, huh?"

Artorian immediately put his hands up in swift rebuttal. "Not at all! Perception doesn't equal understanding. I wouldn't have grasped any of this at all, had you not explained it like I was ten. Which is very helpful! Please feel free to shoot for eight or seven next time."

A shrewd expression crossed his face when he saw her smirk. "I have the strange feeling you've become habituated to doing this kind of thing for any boy you talk to."

Minya released an amused *pfffff*. "I live with *Dale*. He might have all the affinities, and the mental capacity to balance them out one day, but he's an Earth Essence boy at heart, and stubborn as a mule. If explaining the easy way gets my point through his shale rock of a skull, I will keep that method in my pocket for basically anyone."

She wrote the warehouse code for her ring in the air with some Mana. "Alphabetical codes come with four markers. The first is which world or Soul Space the item was made in. The second is which world the item currently resides in. Y'know, so it knows what rules it needs to adhere to."

Minya then motioned at herself. "The third is what category of tether the item currently has. The fourth is a marker for an item being keyed to a *specific* person, under the previous subgroup. There is supposed to be a marker five and six as well, but much of the Gnome-power had to be assigned to more immediate problems."

Minya held up her hand. "In the case of this ring, it was created in Incursus, one of the dungeons helping Cal. If you ever need to find him, that's easy. Follow the signs labeled 'Forts,' and the calls of 'Everything is on fire!' or 'cannon rush.' There's your 'I.' Currently the ring exists in Cal's Soul Space, for the 'C'. I am considered a supervisor, so my tether designation is 'B.' As an Administrator, yours would be 'A.' Please know that I'm not jealous, or some such. I don't want that thought to ruffle feathers later. I'm happy being a farmer girl and occasional hunter, snooping around for high-end goodies."

She smirked when Artorian appreciatively bobbed, returning her attention to the item. "Lastly, I am designated under the marker 'M' for Minya. This is why markers five and six would have been helpful, as the current system can't handle first-letter duplicates."

Artorian crossed his arms, rolling the oversized blue-glowing shot-put messenger-marble between his fingers. "I think I get it?"

Minya tried another example, when a sudden scheme came to mind. She would only be able to do this once, but abyss, she couldn't help it. "Say that an item was made by Bacchus, another dungeon, which currently resides in your Soul Space. Held by... let's say a Wood Elf, which would belong to designation 'K,' by someone important named Acacia, for the 'A.' The alphabetical code result would be B.A.K.A. You baka."

Artorian's arms crossed powerfully in response to some small nudge to the side of his head; then felt his mouth move before his brain did, speaking words in quick succession even if he did not understand them, nor why he was offended. "Tsun-tsun-tsun-tsun."

Minya cackled, howling with laughter while Artorian held his chest looking like he'd swallowed a bug. Minya spoke between hiccups. "I love how that works, every time! The 'Dere' Pylons are sooooo busted! I crack up at this every time they trigger."

"Get out of here, you Pylon-abusing jokester! That was a mental push just now! No! Unacceptable! Out! Ten years dungeon!" His voice was shrill. Artorian then picked up stray pieces of hay, chucking them at Minya as her cackling intensified.

Chased out of her own barn, she giggled uncontrollably as she joined the woman-huddle taking their time walking away, easily in time for her to share the gossip. When Artorian heard the entire group laugh, he hid his face in both his hands before tugging the vine-blanket over his head like he wasn't here.

His voice turned pouty. "That's it. I'm calling Dev."

CHAPTER TWENTY-SIX

Dev pulled open the protective blanket Artorian hid under. A vast, amusement-filled expression covering his tiny face. "You know that messenger orb lets me hear everything once you've told it to call someone, right? Mr. Tsun."

"I will accept Tsu! Not that anyone would use it regardless, and we're all better off for it." Artorian puffed back from beneath his covers, his finger stabbed to the air imperiously. "At least Tsu was actually one of my names once. I will not be subjected to nick-names via a Pylon prank."

Dev prodded the bundle with his Iridium wrench. "Whatever you say, oh vine-clad one. You didn't want me to be here putting Luminous Cores into your Strikers, then?"

Artorian pushed a pillow on his face to make an animalistic sound. When he pulled it away, he reset his views and met his Gnomish friend with a gleaming smile. "Dev, so good of you to come! Yes, I very much wanted to see you. I'd love the leg-patch."

Deverash bent backwards with laughter. "What was that half-reared political circus act?! That doesn't work if I saw you in an unpleasant state first, you oiled cog."

"I tried." Artorian grumbled, lifting his arms just to aimlessly drop them on the hay. "Still, good to see you, old friend. Did the trade with Tot go well enough?"

"Most certainly!" His tiny compatriot held up a crystal bismuth marble in each hand. "I even got both! So we can do both legs evenly!"

Artorian lifted his messenger orb, looking at the no longer shining sphere. "Wasn't this Core aglow? Here I was wanting to compare sizes, but now I'm wondering why neither this nor those are glowing. Aren't Luminous Cores supposed to be blinding? They were pretty unimpressive the first time I saw them as well."

Dev firmly gave a single affirming nod, his hand on his tool-belt. "If you don't know what you're doing, then that's right. Beast Cores will blind you when containing Essence that is moving. As to the messenger orb, it only glows when it's working. So when I got here, it stopped. Don't need to talk to someone at a distance when I'm right here, no? Plus I needed to test the new Bifrost features."

Sunny looked out the window, checking for the bridge of that name. "I don't see any stairways to heaven?"

Dev grinned. "Nor highways to Hel, I'm afraid. The new Bifrost bridge is more of a pick up and deliver service. It'll pick you up in particles of hard-light, and move you over to the other end of the designated recipient point. We want the end result to be a spectacular sight. I'm going for a rainbow theme. This time, sadly, no special effects just yet. I arrived at the front door to hear a group of ladies giggling, if that helps your timeline."

The old man pulled the vine blanket back over his head. "Secondhand embarrassment murders me. Firsthand barely phases me, but the other one? Cold crawling sensations right under the skin. It's terrible."

He sighed, throwing the blanket back off his head. His hands hit the hay a bit hard, but his friend didn't comment, letting Artorian work through his abyss. Coping didn't take too long. "When can we start on the leg upgrade? I can't say I recall what it was supposed to do."

Dev walked up on the air like a solid staircase, conveniently making his way to the art installations pretending to be legs. "Do you want me to remind you, or just make this work so you can do your Tribulation, and can go for a walk when you wake up?"

Artorian chewed weakly on his lower lip. "*Mnnn...* I'll take the prior, if you'd be so kind. The short version, though."

"Forgot you smashed your face into the workshop's ceiling by pumping the tiniest bit of Mana into the cracked Strong-quality

Cores currently in those legs?" Dev half-asked, half-joked. "Must have hit you harder than I thought!"

"Just *tell me*, Dev." Artorian groaned.

"Alright, alright." Dev's tone still sounded like he spoke in jest. "Your artificial legs need to be able to sustain the same Mana pressure as the rest of your body. Mana forms have to be synchronized top to bottom to work properly, so your existing form will reject the legs if they can't hold up to a sustained stream of A-rank one Mana. Aura doesn't count. I'm still not sure if the legs can survive a pressure higher than A-rank one Mana, so just... keep it there if all goes well until some results come in. Unless you feel like breaking them right away, and spending more time in bed before we can get you the next version."

Dev had the internal components of the legs open in a jiffy, his deft hands juggling and replacing Cores like it was second nature. "The Strong Cores weren't good enough. Luminous ones should be *too* good, so the new Cores will not be the point of failure. I expect the rest of the Strikers to fail first. Keep that messenger orb in your pocket, you never know when you will suddenly need a leg mechanic."

When Artorian leaned to look, Dev was already finished, his tiny hands clapping together. "There we go. Not even a hint of component rejection. Just what I like to see! Sprockets, I love our Iridium."

"That fast?" Artorian wondered, his words breathy.

"That fast!" Dev jovially confirmed. "I was just giving you a hard time to be here a few minutes longer, but sadly, I'm already needed elsewhere. Your Strikers are all set and ready for a big Mana influx, so if you were going to do that Tribulation, now's the time. I'll get out of your beard. Oh, to use the orb properly, just think of wanting to talk to me when you hold the sphere, then tap the top. It works with anyone who has an orb like it. Mine glows green!"

They shared a quick high five.

Dev hopped out of the window, then walked in a circle for a bit before settling on a patch of grass and saluting. As he did, the Gnome shot skywards in a beam of light that appeared and disappeared in a flash.

Artorian gawked. "*Huh.* So much for there being no special effects yet."

Afterwards, he was alone with only his thoughts, the hay bales, and moonlight streaming through his open window. More of a hollow at this point, given what Chandra had done to the building, but he'd call it a window for convenience. He tapped a tune on his stomach, uncharacteristically nervous about the Tribulation. "Where was it this time? The old Fringe? That's going to be an adventure after seeing the growth in the new one."

He exhaled firmly through his nose. "I really should suggest a rename. New Fringe doesn't roll from the tongue easily. *What*, though. The name of the next volume, maybe?"

Adjusting the cloth-bundled hay under his head, he finally decided that this just wasn't comfortable. Summoning his Soul Pillow, he propped that behind his head and back instead. "Vast, instant improvements. Making this thing a pillow was a genius decision. Even if I can't use it in combat with any sort of clout. I should fix up this one, finish it, and start on a second one. Maybe a blanket for maximum giggles."

Settling back, he called it time to get started, and closed his eyes. Descending into the bonfire space, he hadn't expected to find it empty. No Caligene girl waiting for him? "Scilla?"

Asking out loud provided no response. He looked around, made some arm motions that would allow for a really easy joke to be made at his expense, then adopted a pose that would make it even worse. No clever quip snapped from the ceiling. It was just him and the Silverwood in his bonfire space.

Sitting on one of the roots, he looked down to wiggle his toes. "Fun how I still have functional dancing implements here. A comfort, that."

He sat there longer than he should, watching the reactive wave of the leaves as they moved in a breeze. There were no fancy lights to any of it this time. If anything, his bonfire felt mundane. Simple. The space may have been small, but he'd never needed it to be big. Just him, a cup in his hands, maybe some hapless bundles of boundless energy to watch over as they stumbled across one another in the distance.

He got up from the root, pressing his back to the silvered trunk before he fell into a seated position with a grunt. Patting the root system coming from the base, he eased back and watched the tapestry of colors unfold upon the walls of the bonfire space. "Another pleasant sunrise."

Artorian didn't notice the transition between his dreaming state and Tribulation state. The flawless, gentle, paint-brush differences brushing across his senses were applied with careful, caring, loving grace.

————

On a hill, one of many, with his back pressed to a tree, Tzu—no longer much of a tyrant—clutched a map. He'd found the place, or so he'd thought. A big flat lake with shallow water, with the smell of salt ever pervasive in the air unless a light breeze carried it away. A tiny village nested opposite the bent crook of a riverbend that even he couldn't consider natural. Not with how the river had cleanly bisected a hill without any signs of natural erosion. He'd seen sword cuts less clean.

There was very little difference in the look of that hill and the thought of someone using a tiny knife to cut pudding in two. Tzu's younger voice sighed. "I miss pudding. Never did learn how the Lion chefs made it. Very different from Phoenix pancakes."

Brushing his legs free of sticky grass, he blocked the sun's rays with a hand as he got up. His skin stung from all the travel. Bruised joints and expended supplies aside, he had to come to terms with this barely-a-hamlet collage of cobbled structures being the goal. Turning back was never in the cards. Certainly not now. Plus, it appeared he'd been spotted.

He waved at the man on the cart, though it was the donkey pulling it making the majority of the ruckus. Resulting in neither of the men being able to understand one another until their spoken words turned to shouts. A short jaunt to a dirt path that couldn't rightly be called a road later, and he was shaking hands with a regional trader.

This man took salt from here, then brought back sundry items, cloth bolts, some iron tools… Nothing fancy. Tzu traded some possessions for an ease of journey, but couldn't get much out of the trader. He was a stoic youth from Rutsel, the brooding man in some kind of foul mood after Tzu clearly hadn't offered much worthwhile.

Enough for the trip. Not enough for the youth's interest. Just like this particular route, it seemed. The youth was jittery to hand it over to another trader. Tzu was certain he wouldn't remember this man from Rutsel. There was too much greed in his eyes, carrying the silent story of promises left unfulfilled, and riches so far left unattained. Tzu commented that if the youth should invest in anything, then it should be the cart. The ride was horribly rough, and without a hooded cover, the sun could get unbearable.

The youth appeared to begrudgingly take the suggestion, but spoke to him no further until the donkey was braying up a storm. Then he mentioned he was going to get horses as soon as possible, because this wily thing was driving him mad.

Artorian disembarked from the cart to be met, and passed, by a flood of children who all beelined for the noisy animal for a chance to pet it. A well-hatched plan by the donkey, as far as Tzu could tell.

"Him, I know." An older man with a braided beard and a hunched posture croaked. The man looked like the skinniest toad Tzu had seen when he turned to face the swampy voice. How could a person have such fatty cheeks, yet be thin as a stick? "You. Are a mystery."

The aged elder's plucked tree branch poked into Tzu's shin. So Tzu began to answer him. "I was looking for this place. I am—"

The elder shot a hand up, stopping him right away. "This place is not one where one journeys to, this is a place you end up. Skip the circumstances, the wear is written all over your face, the tear is clear on your body, and if I have to contend with that haunted look in your eyes much longer, I'll start believing in ghost stories."

The elder motioned a trembling finger towards another elder, one who was shuffling towards them from a longhouse with scholarly patience. "You can be *his* problem. I'm here to talk trade with our fresh-faced Rutselite over here."

The trader grumbled out a dissatisfied grunt in response, clearly unhappy with his lack of facial stubble being pointed out for yet another season. Something the toady elder smiled about before waddling the trader's way. Tzu thought that the people here must not have much in the way of entertainment, so they made their own.

"You're a sight for sore eyes, son." The elder was wearing a turtle shell as a hat, using a tone much more inviting than that of the huffy toad. Stopping in front of Tzu, the turtle elder rubbed his three remaining fingers over his chin. Tzu could tell that, much like himself, this elder had seen bad times firsthand. The recognition in his eyes when they traveled over Tzu's scars and injuries was tell-tale. "Likely feel more sore than you look. Come along, we'll get those tended. You're clearly staying, so there's a few things about this place that you should know."

Tzu fell into pace with the man when he turned to shamble back the way he came. He was curious now, hauling his bag over his shoulder. "Like what? Also, no introductions?"

The turtle elder nodded like he'd seen this coming. "What's there to introduce? I'm an elder. The little ones are sproutlings. The adults have names that make their profession clear. Adults without such names are still but children, save…"

He paused for a moment, motioning to a large child sitting by himself and chewing on a piece of firewood. "Save for some, who were blessed by nature and the heavens in a different way. Choppy is a good boy, but will need extra… luck."

Tzu looked, and could tell by the shape of the child's face that he was different. 'Blessing' had been a kind choice of words from the elder. The kid was affected by the kind of gift where one thing would consume them, at the cost of all else. At that one thing, they would excel over all others. Problem being that, to integrate comfortably with all the others, those other skills were direly important. Tzu spoke before he understood what he said. "He'll do great. Nothing that can't be helped with a little love, care, and attention."

The turtle elder paused to raise a brow at him. "Have a gift yourself, do you? To find the good where others see a needy bundle of tantrums and screams. Or…"

The elder's eyes flicked over his pack, after which he scrunched his eyes shut, nodded, and moved on. "I see. Forgive my callousness."

Tzu instinctively reached for a throw pillow fastened to the side of his pack, giving it a squeeze as his heart clamped, eyes moistened, and jaw grit. The feeling lasted only a moment, but it was enough. The conversation was cut short, and didn't resume until the elder stopped in front of the door to the longhouse. "I'm afraid I can't put it off, now."

Opening his palm, he raised it to Tzu like he was requesting a coin.

Tzu's face scrunched quizzically, not following the elder's intent. "I have nothing valuable left to give you, unless you don't mind an old bow, a worn axe, or clothes that have seen better days."

The elder shook his head, his own face plastered into a forced mask of stone. One that kept breaking as the elder seemed to think he was asking for something more valuable than Tzu understood. "No... nothing like that. To live in the Fringe, you have to leave your old self behind. So it was for me, and those who came before me."

The elder squeezed his hand shut, then opened it again. "I need your *name*, please."

Tzu felt his teeth grit again, jaw set as the rest of the world melted away, his eyes set on the weathered, three fingered, open palm. Options flashed in his head, but he lifted his chin to meet the elder's green eyes. "Which ones?"

"All of them, son." The turtle-hat grandfather replied. All of them."

Tzu felt himself choke up rather than express it, eyes once more on the open hand. "I don't have a physical—"

"*Pretend.*" The elder cut in, apparently being the de-facto go-to person for this kind of thing, based on the looks Tzu realized he was getting from others in the hamlet when they came to attend to the commotion. "It will help, if you pretend. Or... One moment, perhaps I have something better."

Tzu waited for the time it took for the elder to enter the long-house, and return with a few poorly made wooden cups. Including a carving tool that fit the turtle-shell elder's hand very well. They must all have been his. "Here, carve them in this."

Taking two, he felt his heart sink into the blank canvases on their unmarred sides. When the carving tool made it into his dominant grip, he didn't think, he just worked. What was the worth of a name, when it left one's heart so easily? Though perhaps he should have paid more attention to the silent tears trailing down his cheeks.

Finished, he observed them, swallowed, then placed both one at a time into the waiting elder's open hand. He spoke the words as he gave them away, a deep void arriving where his stomach had been. "Merli, of Morovia."

The elder nodded, making room for the other. Tzu felt like his mouth was both dry, and full of slime at the same time, the words so difficult to say. "Tzu, of... Alina."

The elder took that cup as well. Then, pressing them together, reduced them to crushed splinters between his palms before he would speak at all. Parting his sturdy crafter's hands, the remains fell haplessly to the ground, swept away by the salty wind to be deposited in the lake. "Dear lost soul of the Ancient World. I meet you at the dusk of the loss of a brand new friend. Feel welcome, and let us both mourn, and celebrate his passing."

The elder then turned, and parted open the door of the long-house, welcoming the nameless man inside. "My wonderful, interesting new friend. I see you are a sproutling, but one who has grown tall. Would you share tea with me? I would love to discover what to call you."

The nameless man felt hollow, and empty. He looked at the open door, and the fire within. Then he looked over his shoulder, at the borders of a world he no longer recognized. Wordlessly, the nameless man nodded. His expression lacked life, but for a moment they saw the expression of a large child chewing on wood. The child saw him, then. With a raucous smile, the wood-chewer pulled the piece from his mouth, and waved it at him with a sound of excitement.

That was enough for the nameless man to feel his heartbeat, the edge of his lip curling upward before waving back. He nodded at the elder, and made his way inside. "I think I'd like that."

The elder closed the door behind them, revealing Artorian in the empty space left behind. He sniffled hard as he leaned against the wall. Then, with wet eyes, he looked up at Choppy for the first time since ages past.

For a moment, his idyllic little hamlet was gone, replaced by static shifts and aggressive alterations of the entire scene. One where instead his world was made of burning smoke, and blight-whispered fog. The memory restored itself soon enough, but Artorian knew what he was contending with from that flicker alone. "Hello darkness, my old friend."

CHAPTER TWENTY-SEVEN

Artorian shifted the scene forward in time. There was going to be nothing of note for a while. That discussion in the longhouse added an ever-increasing stream of elders, on ever reshaping topics of discussion. He knew those old badgers, toads, and turtles had all been pointed in their topics to get a rise out of him, but he would have likely done the same when an addition like him arrived at a hamlet with intent to stay.

He'd waved at a few snot-nosed brats poking their heads in, caused more than a few hushed rumors, and at some point fell asleep in front of the fire after several hours of deeply argued medical care. The young ones were shooed away when it came to his more… widespread injuries. The aged and seasoned people didn't care, though they did ask him to keep his tapestry of scars under wraps.

Some stories should remain buried.

With the nameless one pending the decision of his name, the elders of the Fringe first spent hours, then whole evenings, then whole handfuls of evenings in argument and noisy, cup-throwing talks. By then, the adult sproutling had been provided an A-frame home to live in. The position wasn't great, being so close to the bonfire. The elders prized lakeside housing considerably more. Less walking to do in the morning.

Artorian recalled not minding one bit. Warm and breezy was a big yes-pleasy!

The old man living through this Tribulation sat on the roof of said A-frame home, watching the goings on from an advanced height. He'd used this spot in the early Fringe days after Tzu had arrived, but it had not taken very long for the tolls of his injuries to demand their payment, keeping him rooted to the ground. "I really did begin to age quickly after those first two seasons of river-bathing. Look at all that messy, rancorous corruption covertly biding its time. I know she's not Zelia yet at this time, but with the Scar's hidden little dangers so well concealed, I'm honestly wondering how and why it ever included the mental push to make a person strive for the goals of their heart, rather than those they'd convinced themselves of."

He shook his head. "For the better, in the end. Tarrean became a magnificent father. Tibs has the gift of the cook. Irene found her happiness. Good tidings all around."

A commotion below made him look down. "Ah, here we go."

In the window of the A-frame home, a horde of sproutlings peppered the nameless man with an endless barrage of questions. Some were… pointless. Others, more pointed. Some were interesting. Few… sensical. Artorian watched Tzu have physical trouble as he made the critical mistake of trying to get the horde to move at his speed, flowing to one of his well-versed and established orders.

None of it worked.

The cloud of children went at only one speed. Their own. Anything else was conveniently forgotten, thrown to the wayside, or outright ignored in favor of the brand new idea or question that came to the forefront of a mouth. Artorian chuckled at his old self. "Poor tsun tsun. So flustered!"

He giggled at the joke this time, finding some humor in it. "Alright, maybe that perversion of the nickname isn't so bad, or harmful. I'm going to give Minya an earful later about that trickery with a mental-push-inducing Pylon, though. That's a no-no in my book."

He put his hands next to his mouth, shouting down to the crowd that couldn't hear him. "Good luck, ol' boy!"

The nameless one's door burst open, breaking right off the hinges, never to see a proper repair. "Sproutlings! To the field! I cannot keep up with all of you. If we're going to play, let's play! I will show you the meaning of exhaustion!"

Artorian watched the rest of the day play away as, true to his word, the nameless one conjured increasingly complicated games, with rules that went and came, only to collapse himself by the end of it. The man kneaded the bridge of his nose as the sun set, sore all over as he laid on the grass, listening to the horde of play continue on without him. "Children. I was bested by *children*."

"*He he heeee.*" The turtle elder giggled sharply as he crested the hill, groaning as he sat down next to the breath-heaving newcomer. "That would be our sproutlings! Unpredictable. Inexhaustible. Uncontrollable. Inexorable. Inconceivable!"

The nameless one squinted up at the turtle-shell elder. "That word... I do not think it means what you think it means, Vizzini."

"Nonsense!" The elder gave a know-it-all scoff. "I have managed to get that bunch to listen to me, so clearly my choice of wording is correct."

The nameless one squinted far more powerfully. "That's not... that's not how that works. That's not how anything works!"

"Hahaha!" The elder laughed at him, rocking back and forth in amusement. "Too inflexible! How do you expect to get along with the little ones if you expect them to grasp your perspective? Have you even grasped theirs?"

"Not yet, then, I suppose." The nameless one turned pouty, his head bobbing from left to right while he crossed his arms. This elder was giving him such *lip*! "I'll figure it out, turtle-man. Humans have never figured out how to give up, even when all hope is lost."

"True!" The elder's mood was emboldened by the chagrin oozing off from the nameless one. "Yet even that, you may have to leave behind."

That tiny statement was something Artorian watched his past self chew and puzzle on. He'd gotten settled in one of the tree branches, enjoying the view with them. He listened to them quibble, only for the turtle elder to become ever more successful in prying the knife under his protective plates one tiny comment at a time. Worse still, the elder was thoroughly enjoying the entire process, giggling each time Tzu's discomfort spiked.

Artorian couldn't help but laugh at his old self as the nameless man stomped off back to the longhouse, the steam practically coming out of his ears while a bouncing elder kept on his heels with that abyss-eating ear to ear grin.

Artorian watched as Tzu entered the longhouse only to find more of the infernal elders. When pushed inside by the turtle elder, it took a single quip from the old man for all the others in the building to suddenly be on board with prodding poor Tzu to pieces.

The poor newcomer ended up snapping at the congregation, a sturdy finger pointed at an elder that he was going to name Threads, because the man was well dressed in a village of few means. Not naming them was going to cause him a headache otherwise. Elder was insufficient when there was more than one! He wanted those delicious suffixes and affixes! "Alright then, what do *you* think about children?"

Threads shimmied in his chair, then calmed, his expression one of dolor. "Sproutlings are a journey you get to be dragged along with every day. Seeing the world again through their eyes is an adventure you get to enjoy. You willingly sacrifice everything for them. You would die for them. Kill for them... And smile the whole time."

Threads broke from his dolor with a quip. "Also, they usually smell bad, and break all your nice stuff. Throw them in the river, often!"

The newcomer noted down that last part specifically. His eyes sharply flicked to the next elder, whom he was going to name Dagny. An older man of powerful and portly build, but Artorian could now clearly see—even better than before when he was seeing only through Tzu's eyes—that all that portliness was muscle. This elder moved mountains in his spare time, and when he spoke he sounded aggressively friendly. "Keep them alive. Love them uncon- ditionally. Teach them right from left. And wrong. Also, hear the lamentations of the enemies' women."

The man seemed to realize where he was trailing off to and quickly shushed himself with a swig from a mug, making a hand motion for the next person before he could say anything more. Artorian and Tzu followed the motion to the next elder as they mentally tallied 'support the acquisition of lamentations.'

Dagny coughed. "You're up, Xian."

The name mentioned escaped only Dagny, while everyone else pretended that it hadn't been said. Artorian bent back to laugh, realizing that even the elders had trouble with their own system! Xian, however, pulled his nose up. "They leave food everywhere. They don't even eat it. They just break it and stick it to things. They pursue you to no end. Ask ceaseless questions, tell stories that make no sense, and make painfully obvious comments and give arguments rooted in nothing. They wake up at stupid hours and raid the pantry, leaving the remains of what was supposed to be *your meal* scattered about the house. They scream at the slightest inconvenience, they torment the pets, they torment each other. They torment *me*."

Tzu, the currently nameless, decided it best not to bother that particular elder a whole lot. Artorian, on the other hand, just about had his nose in the elder's face, studying him intently. He rubbed his long beard while muttering to himself. "This wouldn't be the same Xian that the city of Xi'an was named after... would it? What was the story I heard again? Some mayor? I'll have to pick up the old books."

"I'm done. You go, Ka'Ren." The attention of the room fell on a lady that pinched and twisted Xian's leg in response.

The elder lady turned to flash then a smile as if nothing happened, answering the topic. "You love them from the second they're born. They're utterly exhausting. Frustrating. Rage inducing. Yet fabulous fun. They force you to question your values and preconceived ideas. Children are absolute contradictions. They can break your heart with pain, and burst your heart with joy. Sometimes in the same moment."

Tzu got 'allow the questioning of contradictions' from that, but nodded all the same. His attention fell on... Drat, nobody was name-dropping this time. Fine, Elder Stubblefield. The man spoke like he had some experience in the matters of children, possibly because it was clear from his glance at the window that he had many. "Realize that your job as a parent is not to keep them from every hardship or disappointment, but to teach them how to respond to those with kindness instead of anger and retaliation. To admit your mistakes quickly, and never let pride make you think you are better, prettier, smarter, or of more value than any other person you come across, no matter how they look or act."

The last elder, a truly ancient lady with vitiligo, had been studying Tzu this entire time. When it came her turn to have the baton, she asked a question instead of answering one. "Are you a father?"

Tzu winced, squeezing his hands over one another as flashes of an old life crossed his eyes. His hand subconsciously moved for his pocket, holding a tiny pillow. "Meeting the prerequisites of one sadly did not mean that I was afforded the enjoyment of being one."

That shut most of the elders up. All but Elder Viti, who had Tzu's eyes flash over her skin condition with growing worry. She smiled, and gained his attention with a smooth motion of her hand, before she pressed a finger to her own cheek. Then to her chest, then her forehead. "Skin color doesn't matter, only what's in your heart and what's in your head."

She then clapped her hands. "Now, it is late, and we have duties. We shall resume this tomorrow, for the candles are spent and the topic has soured. It's no good to poke fun at a soul that is actually hurting."

Tzu was glad to be dismissed. He skipped dinner and curled in early, or would have, had Elder Viti not been sitting in his home's window like she was a stalking four year old herself. She jump-scared him nearly right out of his skin when he turned over and saw her perch.

"*Ha ha ha…*" She slowly and weakly chuckled as the ex-soldier scrambled. "I can only pull this stunt once. Glad to see it still worked!"

CHAPTER TWENTY-EIGHT

Tzu sat up, pulling his covers around him for protection, given the inquisitive eyes he'd shot over Elder Viti in the prior meeting were now being returned. "Can... Can I help you?"

"Me?" She tasted the words as she looked to the stars. "No, lad. I'm on my way out. Though..."

Her gaze dropped, far softer and sweeter this time. "I have this feeling that there are many you *could* help. Both in terms of people, and politics. Ka'Ren will soon be replaced by her daughter, Switch."

Viti's words turned complicated. "There is... There has been darkness in that child. A willingness to swing the branch too much and too hard. The time when that girl was a child has long passed, but I still blame myself for failing her. There is balance in the elders, as we are now. Yet, with Ka'Ren and myself soon to fade... I would ask if you are perhaps interested in adding your light to this motley little group? We would sneakily get you some other task to do before I cede the spot, of course."

Tzu frowned deep, confused. "That's... a *leap*. Why me? I'm nobody. I just got here."

Viti sweetly gave him a smile filled with the kind of open warmth that only a grandmother could conjure. "Dear boy. There is nobody that is *nobody*. Never in all my years have I met a single person that did not matter. Not a one. Not. A. Single. One. Some worry about being useful, but that's pish posh. Some worry about being beautiful, but they are the very artworks of nature itself. So is true for all of a mortal's worries."

Tzu understood, but his stance hadn't changed. "Still... Why me? I'm sure you have plenty of people who—"

"We do not." Viti cut in, short and quick. "You think good people grow *on* trees? No! Good people are grown *as* trees. You get out what you put in. You grow as you are fed. You dig roots to resist the direction of the wind. You sway with the waxing and waning of the seasons. You weather storms, and you stand tall and proud on sunny days. Then shelter those less fortunate with the breadth of your branches on wet ones."

Viti shivered a bit, her eyes squeezed shut at the recollection of some terrible memory. "The village is filled with good seeds, but the people who could make them grow good and proper have seen a bad winter. We have not known conflict for ages, but any and every time a soul with eyes like yours finds us, we are reminded of its truths. Then we see you from our homes, and we see you carry around the child that many others hate. For no reason other than his looks, and his unfortunate circumstances."

She was off the windowsill in a moment, her hands clamped tight on his shoulders. "Do you understand? *You*—only you— looked upon that sproutling and did not preconceive. You did not judge. The elders saw your heart break, but your roots hold firm. We did not see a lost soldier who wandered in from some war, no more hope in his burned out soul. We saw a *father* with no child to embrace. That is why I asked you in the longhouse. Because I wanted to be *sure*."

Tzu did not fight the grip, but he was moved more than his words could say. He swallowed, but felt there was more Viti needed to say. "Sure of what?"

Viti released him, her sudden burst of speed and strength gone entirely as she sat on the little bench next to the bed. "I wanted to be sure, Merli of Morovia, that I could answer your question. For I refused to say in the longhouse. My answer is not for the others to hear."

Tzu was dressed under his covers, so he wasn't truly in a precarious position. Now that the gaze had come and gone, he looked upon the elder collapsing into herself and slid from the bed, wrapping his blanket around her shoulders before joining Viti on the bench. She smiled, her voice cracked, and face wrinkled. "Oh... look at you. You don't even know or understand, and yet you move anyway."

"I'm going to admit that you still have me at a loss, elder." He was trying to be polite, and the confusion bled through his voice. "I understand there's a good behind the scenes reason that you might want me somewhere, but that's already how I heard this place worked. I'm not following why what you have to say is secretive, or why I'm getting the visit."

Viti calmed at the question, her thoughts finding some order. "Boy, if you think the elders get along, you're mistaken. Like all societies, we have our own little groups. We also have... slightly more secret rules. No *elder* has ever been a person who grew up in the village."

That detail caught Tzu's attention, and Viti could tell.

"Aren't you a clever nugget? Look at you putting that together from a tiny comment. It's written all over your face." She shook her head. "Switchy will be the first natural-grown elder, and she did not grow up as the most *receptive* dandelion."

Relaxing as she pulled the blanket bundle around herself, Viti squeezed it to her face. "As for why I wanted nobody else to hear, it is half to avoid a few months of argument that I won't live long enough to see the conclusion to, and half due to *some* flat-out not understanding. They would not understand for the same reason that they don't occupy themselves with the sproutlings."

Tzu puzzled the pieces. "You did mention a bad winter?"

Viti chuckled, the topic not one she wanted to touch, but ventured through anyway. "Lives have a way of being intense and... short in the Fringe. You notice how I look... say, eighty?"

"I would surmise a healthy seventy." Tzu tried to quip and be sweet. "A flush sixty-five."

"I'm forty-four." Viti cut in with a half-mocking, half-joking expression. "I have kept an exquisite count. You're a peach, boy, but even *my* estimate was generous. I look ancient. That's just how it goes here. Some of us are tenacious. Some... leave us far too soon. We lost most of the people who were good with sproutlings this last winter. The cold hit us exceptionally hard."

She eased one hand over the other. "We were watching you try and fail to corral them. My argument was that it didn't matter if you were currently failing. You were the one out there, spending time with them, while the rest of us focused on matters closer to our interests. Those sproutlings have been running rampant for a while, and with nobody having much in the way of spare time, save for us elders…"

"I can see where the ball stops rolling when looking through the eyes of expectation." Tzu was on board with where this was headed. "You want me as an elder not because I would be good at the things elders normally do, but because there's a massive niche that needs to be filled, and I'm a good candidate."

He looked about the inside of his new, tiny house. Trying to find something for his eyes to settle on. "I'm not sure I'm the best choice for that. I'm—"

"The choice I want." Viti clarified. "Tell me, when you were falling over yourself herding them, what were you thinking? Not the frustration, or the methods. Your feelings. Tell me your feelings."

Tzu wished he had that blanket back, but the answer, as embarrassing as it was, came easily. "I've never felt more afraid of anything in my life, than I was when looking after children. Anything could hurt them, and yet when they smash nose-first into a tree, they barely notice. They are blind to the details of things, and any issue not overt might as well be invisible."

Viti listened to him go on for an hour. That tiny question had been the crack in the dam, and now the water could flow where previously there were only carved earthworks. When it came to her turn on answering her question from the longhouse, Tzu was receptive to change.

Viti spoke carefully. "You have to be like water to handle them. You must allow their chaos to flow over you, through you, with you. You must match their flow, or you will lose them. You cannot force a child to move to your flow, and expect it to willingly remain that way. That will only teach the child to rebel, even on the matters where what you do is best for them. When they clearly do not know it."

Tzu nodded, and Artorian watched them gab. The sun was nearly up by the time Tzu got shuteye, though he woke a mere few hours later to the very squirrely horde he'd been speaking with Viti about. Roused from slumber, the half-asleep nameless one looked upon the flow of the children with bleary eyes. He did not see their forms. Only their direction of movement, shrieked words, and half-baked plans.

The wind passed through his fingers, and it soothed him while encouraging the flotilla of thoughts that he should play along. Tzu found the wanton will to be lacking. That would merely move him, but he was not who needed moving.

The heat of the sun bled into his skin, warming him after the loss of sweet embrace provided by a well-wrapped morning blanket. The warmth, too, spurred him to move and follow his heart. Tzu found the draw of passions burning bright to be but a thought that should ebb away. For with that inner heat came an anger for which there was no room here.

The light piercing the clouds laid on his shoulders, like hands from a prophet, already whispering sweet words of direction and guidance. Tzu listened, but found himself immune to their pull. No words of great weight would hold sway here. No stoking of the other factors deemed acceptable.

His mind instead lingered on the words of the elder.

Artorian, too, watched carefully. "Was it here, then? Yes. It is *here.*"

Tzu got to his feet without thinking of making the movement. His body merely moved as one of the children called. He didn't even know what was said, but the call was clear. His eyes looked, but they did not see. They did not need to see.

Lost in his head, Tzu abandoned sight. The wind cleared, and he heard clearly. His heart beat steady, and his body hit homeostasis. The light dimmed and brightened, but he could be blinded no more. The Phoenix kata fed his movements, and led his steps. His ears listened only to the sounds from small souls, and parsed their chaos out from the rest of the world.

His thoughts moved to their activities, their drives, what they searched, and what they yearned. Tzu abandoned himself beyond the loss of a name, his movements seamlessly bringing him within the raucous circle of children. He tapped one sharply, then moved away, using another to block an easy approach as they bowled into each other and laughed haplessly. He listened to their flow, and in an instant, ran for the hills.

Their game had changed at a whim, their rules as fickle as the direction of wind itself. So Tzu changed himself along with them. The new rules, the real rules, were both easy and simple. There was no Tzu. There was no adult. There were minds engaged in a group activity. Nothing more. Nothing less. There was no higher thought. No reason. Only the flow as a sparse comment from an outlier changed the game again, and thus Tzu changed with it.

No longer running, he now laid prone on the grass, crawling along as any space above knee height was now dangerous for no reason at all. The sproutlings picked up on the change inherent in the nameless one. They were no longer around an adult supervising them, or to yell at them. They were playing with a legendary 'big kid.' One who understood. One who moved with them. One who moved *as* them.

Artorian watched as the vestiges of Tzu left the man who had given up that name. He also watched as a weak water affinity broke through the internal dam of his Essences, finding root in the constant, endless, swaying waves of change. Willingly drawn. Willingly accepted. Like a songstress out on a rock, beckoning a ship closer, the affinity found itself welcome, and made itself home.

Artorian nodded in profound understanding. "Air, from rebellion. Light, from loss. Fire, from passion. Water, from relinquishment. My lesser channels lie revealed. Their attainment, a secret no further."

The old man left Tzu to his performance as the mantra of 'I do not matter, they do' found a home. Flicking his gaze to the village, Artorian noted that Tzu was currently watched by multitudes of eyes. Artorian instead considered a phrase that passed over his thoughts. 'Quis custodiet ipsos custodes?' Cocking his head in confusion, the meaning translated, he spoke the words. "Who watches the watchers?"

Looking again, he supposed he should not have been surprised that Dagny and Viti were cultivators. Both of them were incredibly surprised at what they were seeing, as they shared a look across the breadth of the village, even with several hills and buildings in the way. The connection was unmistakable. The nod at the same time was also hard to square away, that and Dagny making a face while holding up four fingers. While he faced a wall, completely blocked from Viti's direct view. She even held up four fingers right after Dagny in an equal amount of shock.

Artorian chuckled and shrugged. "That's the Fringe, after all. A place you end up. Not a place you go. I'm renaming the New Fringe. The meaning isn't applicable. That place is a center, while this was an escape. It's been hammered home now, and I'm convinced. I will choose something... starting with an A."

"Well, that was clean." Scilla slid into the Tribulation's reality next to him. "I didn't even show up on time, and here you are at the end of your seventh Tribulation."

Artorian smiled, tensed his shoulders, then dropped them before returning his attention to the scene and layout of the village below him as he kept rising higher. "Are we at the end? Is this not the beginning?"

She slapped his shoulder. "Stop trying to be so sweet. I see right through you, mister!"

"I refuse!" He beamed a smile. "Turtle-elder Vizzini had the right of it, and I see where I got it from, now. Still. What Tribulation? I was expecting... something more?"

"No." Scilla shook her head as she sat cross-legged in the air. "That was it. You're all done. This one wasn't a regret, it was something you needed to tackle. A reminder to hold firm. Or perhaps I'm just horribly sentimental now, and wanted to see a bunch of little kids smile their grass-and-dirt-coated teeth up at a big kid who approved of them."

"I was on their team, after all." Artorian nodded. "Now what about you, dear? How are you holding together?"

Scilla moved so she could lay in his arms via a princess carry, and Artorian obliged her. "I'm holding great. I feel my timer. A couple good years, then I'm either out with a pop, or a high-five to my replacement. I'm thinking the latter, yeah?"

"Always go out with a bang!" He smiled, and danced on the clouds with the Liminal one in his arms to the sound of violins that they could hear, but did not exist. Artorian then tossed her high into the sky and clapped his hands together with extra oomph, causing a Mahogany-style cannon-pound *wub* as he yelled "Boom!"

CHAPTER TWENTY-NINE

Dale's prized barn exploded in shards of wood, rapidly conflagrating hay, and flaming bales that spewed in every direction as a mighty pleased Artorian punched through the overgrown roof and pierced the skies. He could be mistaken for an arrow of prismatic light, shooting up from the hole-of-debris blast zone. Concentric rings of air and energy echoed around the arrow as it flew, circling ever farther outwards before the source twisted an awkward U-turn midair and slammed back into the ground.

Artorian had no time to feel concern, as the impact had not dented his momentum. With his leg panels open and releasing powerful, sustained jet-streams of Mana that kicked him around the farm like a Wisp on a bad ping pong day, his flight path became rowdy, hectic, and erratic, but the wild cheering erupting out from him told the new onlookers that all was well.

Dale, so far blissfully ignorant, tipped his straw hat at the sound. Looking up from tilling as he leaned on his shovel, his senses held to the sound of... some kind of old man? Hollering 'Whoooo-hooooo!' while the fizzing pops and bangs of a few alchemy labs blowing up in sequence traveled ever closer to his—

Dale yowled when the Gnome-rocket crested the hill. "Celestial feces!"

Artorian burst onto the scene with a smile full of grass and dirt, his hand reaching out for some kind of handhold to keep him grounded. Instead, his open palm found Dale's shirt! He then clung, gripped, and tore the man away from his work as his ancient disciple let out the girliest of screams. Dale's shovel flung to the winds while his straw hat saluted him on the way out, landing where Dale's feet used to be.

Artorian's old disciple loudly shrieked out a high pitched, goblinoid "*Reeeeeeeeeee.*"

Which was enough for the old man to consider some less-than-insane aerial maneuvering as he yelled to his old disciple. "Hold on to your butt, Dale! I'm trying to get control of these spooky scary skeletons! These babies go fast! Oh darn, that desert is coming awfully close!"

Exploding a sandy mountain only to roll along with Dale copying all his movement, both of them ended up legs-up at the apex of the next dune over before spitting out mouthfuls of sand. They both coughed, then looked at one another, and weakly broke down with child-like laughter as they let their Auras do their work. Artorian's legs sputtered loudly, but cutting energy was as easy as supplying it in the first place, so the old man stayed put.

Artorian flopped back on the sand dune, his new legs venting with a puff of air as they rejected all the sand stuck in the mechanism. "*Ahhh,* what a ride. Hello, Dale, old pal, how's the non-baron life treating you?"

"Hah." Dale smiled, shook his head, and copied his ancient mentor. "I thought it was you Minya tucked away in the barn. Nobody else has the Auric signature of a Starlight effect."

Artorian nodded, but waited for Dale to actually reply, which he did right after. "I've... Y'know, I was going to say 'I've been better,' but I'm not doing too bad? I've had to re-prioritize my life somewhat. Nice to see you again, headmaster. Or is it Administrator now? I have a really hard time getting access to details of late, and bribing Hans is *expensive.*"

"Consider my current services extraordinarily cheap, with discounts! Dale, help meeee!" Hans cried as he skidded between them like a ballerina skating across the sands, as if the course material beneath his feet was ice. "She's on my tail! Hustle!"

Dale growled at him, getting on his feet and falling right in line along with Artorian as he too shot up and bolted. The old man seemingly knew better than to rest on his laurels and believe he was safe. Dale let his friend have it. "Abyss, Hans! I get my first chance to actually talk to someone I can pour my heart out to, and here you are dragging me right back into the fire!"

Artorian looked over his shoulder to see an *incredibly enthusiastic* Amaterasu crest a dune. Vanta-void-black corona flames swirled around her hands while an equally black sun-themed flag hovered like a cape behind her back. "Oh, biscuits, we better run faster, boys! That's not fire."

"Is *that* why I'm not immune to it?" Hans sputtered back incredulously, having been subject to one of Ammy's... exquisite lessons, for a while now. "She has been shouting instructions at me this entire time, and if I do not follow them to the letter, it gets hot, hot, hot!"

"Hans!" Ammy's voice thundered. "Circulate that center clockwise, now! I want to see every wide curve of that refinement technique swirl like you are taking Rose on the most expensive dancefloor that you haven't managed to steal yet!"

The assassin's incredulous gasp and dramatic press to his chest made Artorian think of a slighted bard. "One I have *not* stolen? Just how poor of a—"

The assassin dodged to the right as a missile of golden-onyx flame seared past where his head had been a hint of a moment earlier. The missile course-corrected of its own accord, chasing him around a dune just a fraction faster than his escape speed. "Clockwise, Hans! Clockwise! If I don't see that Perfect fire channel put some bustle in your hustle, I'm swapping to proper fireballs! You are distracted and keep checking if you have an audience. Only Rose is watching!"

"Not the fireballs! Hilfe!" Hans squeaked out while Dale and Artorian booked it in a completely different direction. Both mumbled silent apologies to the assassin as they left him squarely in the dust. Dale didn't want that trouble, and Artorian knew better. They both knew Dawn wasn't going to go gentle on him when—in a moment of brief, and very sudden overconfidence as he dodged a vivacious gout of flame with a beautiful pirouette— they heard Hans brag. "Rose! Not even these burning suns can blind me to your beautiful appearance, and if anyone makes a song about this, I'm going to kill them!"

Artorian chuckled. "Yuki will hear about this."

Finding that 'the opposite direction of explosions' to be the correct angle of travel, the old mentor and disciple made themselves scarce until they both came to a stop at the top of a particularly large sandy hill. Dale exhaled hard, his hands on his hips. "*Pffff*... A Mage-ranked body, and I feel no different than a D-ranker on the run. Cal made this place *weird*."

Artorian cleared his throat. "Yes, well... Along with all variations of the word fear, Ammy has a way of putting the *humble* into someone. Venerated A-ranked Mage? More like a puffed-up displeased kitten if she sets her gaze on you. You'll yowl, and then run away. There was never any winning."

"I'm married." Dale retorted in a half jest. "There's never any winning regardless."

Artorian raised a brow. "Isn't there, or is life just better when Minya is happy?"

Dale grumbled good-naturedly. "Okay, okay. I'm always happier when my Minya wins. I love her, y'know. I'm just a sour-puss about it sometimes. She treats me well, I'm a happy man, I'm delighted to have a family... I think... I think that, cultivation aside, I'm happier with a life like this. No baron of a mountain, no noble with duties, but a farmer of a tiny patch of dirt, packed with a couple of sheep."

"And a this-and-that?" Artorian added. "Heard about coffee, and the like."

Dale snorted. "Oh, that? That's to kick Cal in the pants. The snoot never talks to me anymore. I know he's here, too. He just... avoids me, I think."

The old man nodded. "Aside from that. I did hear through the grapevine that some things were on your mind, and a scraggly old coot like myself would pose a good ear. What can I help with, my boy?"

Dale flopped onto the sand dune, watching the sky and releasing a heavy sigh. "I... Y'know, before Hans rained on my parade, I had a mind full of worries. Now they're all breezes in the wind, and I don't remember a single one."

Artorian settled next to Dale, and copied the studying of the sky. "Understandable. How about we just... gab? Never know what might come up."

Dale pointed at the horizon. "The sun, currently."

Artorian reached over to slap his knee. "Leave the puns for Cal!"

Dale grinned. "Wasn't a pun!"

Artorian growled. "Oh, you think that makes it better, do you?"

"Of course!" Dale giggled back, his hand trying to grasp a star that was impossible to reach. "I've got to have *something* over Cal."

The old man was starting to see where Dale's brain was stuck. "Cal sounds like the topic jabbed like a thorn in your side, old disciple."

Dale paused. "Yes, also, speaking of. I heard that our deal sort of dissolved after we entered Cal?"

His mentor nodded. "I'm afraid it did. Even if you could tell me what the details for the permanency of the headmaster position was, does it matter now? Even a little? Would you have learned what I had to teach you? You busy little bee, you."

The grandfather soft-nudged his fist into Dale's shoulder, but the farmer just smiled and chuckled before speaking. "I got leagues of use out of the Aura. I don't think I ever really used any of the light techniques or attacks you showed me. To test them, maybe? Not afterwards. Not that I recall. The Aura is worth its weight in gold, though. Don't let anyone fool you! Starlight Aura is bafflingly useful. Anyone with the affinities for it would try to sell you entire continents to be taught the skill."

"It's not that difficult…" Artorian mumbled.

Dale moved his hand to slap the old man on the knee instead. "Excuse you. Aura is *difficult*. There's a whole bunch of steps needed just to make one, and then using it is like walking through a palace made entirely of mirrors, where if you bump into something, you need to start all over. Knowing the exact essence combination is one thing, but if I hadn't been affected by it to understand the intrinsic feeling, I likely would have mucked it up. Dale the adventurer just 'punches things good,' thank you."

Artorian considered the matter, then dropped it. "Very well then. So what's with you and Cal? Aside from that he hasn't poked his nose in."

Dale's arms fell onto the sand, then moved to hold his stomach. "I've always had Cal, in a way. Or vice versa? I overheard the Master chat about it with Minya, over how I'm more a part of him than he is of me. I... I really don't know how to feel about possibly not actually existing?"

There it was, Artorian surmised. The crux of the matter. "Of course you exist. Silly boy. You can think, you can talk to me, you're sharing this moment with me, and it is exclusively yours to share in."

"Except when Cal subsumes me... right?" Dale asked with a complicated tone. "Then I'm gone, and Cal has everything I am."

Artorian shrugged. "Cal has a copy of everything I am as well, but I don't let that bother me. As far as I am concerned, I am unique. A pure, inviolable perspective upon the universe. As far as I am concerned, so are you. Cal can't take that away from me as much as he can't take that away from you."

Dale frowned, his head turning. "Existence really doesn't bother you does it?"

Artorian chuckled fondly. "Does exist. Does not exist. What is tomorrow? What was yesterday? Does it matter? Or does it only matter that we are here, now, at this moment?"

He stuck his old finger to the sky.

"An ancient, wise turtle once said: Yesterday? That is history. Tomorrow? That is a mystery. But today? Today is a gift! That is why we call it the present." The old man beamed at him. "When you worry about things too big or small, you lose the perspective of the path you are actually walking. What does it matter if you are Dale, a part of Cal? Or Cal, a part of Dale? You are separate, and have differing views and opinions. So I will treat you as such, and I will treat you as such regardless of how anything works in the world. For while I am with you, you are my world, and I am yours. We share in this existence. This memory. This reality. This... now."

Artorian winked. "That is enough. It has always been enough. You do not need to prove more, nor does more need to be proven. If you can worry about it, then you have—in part—already found the answer. For if there was nothing to worry about, there would be nothing to know. If there is doubt, then there is no doubt."

That last part was too cryptic for Dale, so Artorian broke it down for him. "In simple words. You are you, because you can worry about being you. You are not anyone else, unless you want to be someone else. Then you will slowly begin adopting their traits. That's just how it works. So the only question you need to bother asking is easy. Because that which comprises Dale is not at all what comprises Cal. So: are you Dale, or are you Cal?"

Dale blinked at that, feeling the epiphany as lightning struck his brain. "Well, that makes it simple... Of course I'm *Dale!*"

"And it never needed to be any more complicated than that!" Artorian smiled, before diverging from the topic. "Now, I must know, as I do love some good gossip. I haven't seen Tom at all. Is he well?"

"Tom?" Dale's train of thought got on the new track, not at all opposed to the change of pace. "He's doing his own thing. One of the mockingbirds—Sileet, I believe?—tweeted up a storm about how Tom might be in a relationship with his hammer."

Dale paused. "That might need explaining. Heavily enchanted objects become sentient and gain personalities. Thud was one of Cal's original enchanted masterpieces, and has ventured through every realm that Tom has dragged and swung it through. Gaining in might the entire time. Now, Thud might be more than a mere hammer. So, I suppose you could call them an item? Together, they smash a lot."

Artorian couldn't stop his sputtered giggle. "I'm happy for them! I was worried for the big man since I heard trickles of him being left out here and there, but now it sounds like he was never alone to begin with. I am sated! What about you and Minya? Details, boy. *Details!* How did you meet?"

"Well... she thought I was Cal for a while." Dale flushed hard, and didn't realize the old man had mentally put on some tea. "Mountaindale days? Rough history. I'd rather not touch on it. The Soul Space days, on the other sickle... *Wow.* How did I get so lucky? Did all my luck from getting tumble-dried with stab wounds get tallied up to get me a goddess like Minya? I don't deserve her, but man does her smile mean the world to me."

Artorian beamed, and kept silent as Dale blabbed. "She's the entire reason it's all gone so well. The farm. My halcyon days. The kid... I once tried to plan the perfect date! Only to have every-thing that could go wrong, actually go wrong. If I ever catch that abyss-piece of a raccoon... I am strangling Murphy before turning that little mongrel into a scarf. The whole event was in shambles, and this legend of a woman kissed my forehead and told me that even when the world goes wrong, I am somehow still wrong-er. I fell for her head over heels, and that is something I have never regretted. Not once. Then there was this one time, at band camp—"

Dale gushed for hours, as his old mentor only replied with fond smiles. Artorian wiggled his metal toes as they listened to Hans scream in the distance, followed by the occasional musical 'boom' and Amaterasu's villainous laughter.

CHAPTER THIRTY

Dale improved his sandcastle, his verbal stories still jumping back and forth entire perspectives while telling the tales of the fabled 'Divine Dungeon' universe. Or everything he experienced while it was him and Cal on Mountaindale. "So really, if I hadn't made deals with Frank and Richard, then the entire outcome would have gone very differently!"

Artorian frowned, then paused digging his mote. "You've mentioned that second name a few times now, but this wouldn't be Richard *Demonbane*, would it?"

"Yeah!" Dale was jovial, his finger pointing at the old man standing in his own sandcastle. "Him! He was with the church. An A-ranker for sure!"

Artorian pondered, then nodded. "Don't suppose you've heard of Emilia Nerys?"

Dale squinted at his sandcastle floor. "I thought it was Amelia Nerys. I could swear the name sounds familiar, but A-Melia, or E-Melia… Wait, I remember! It's Emilia. E at the start, and I in the middle. She was on one of the documents for the college. I got her confused with Amalia Iuliana Chitulescu, a bird who makes cover art. Why do you ask?"

Artorian froze for a moment, realizing he'd been getting the name wrong this entire time. He'd fix that and try to stick to the correct spelling as he mumbled the name back. "Emilia Nerys. E at the start, I in the middle."

"Your old mentor plays the architect of fate, my old friend" The chorus of Adam's voices trimmed down to but a single recognizable one as the celestial descended from on high. Hovering near the ground to steady himself, wayward down feathers fell near him only to dissolve on contact with matter. When his bare feet landed silently on the sand, not a single kernel showed an indent, his arms opening to invite Dale into a welcomed hug. "He schemes for his friends, and maneuvers the landscape to be beneficial to his loved ones. This new stratagem is no different."

Dale was up in a flash. His arms hug-squeezed around Adam the moment that the celestial touched to the ground, the old friend accosted by a blind, head-first Dale-tackle. Which Adam took to the stomach like a true champ as Dale knocked the grace and elegance right out of his wings, the sparkles and fluffy down all still hanging near Artorian as the effect hadn't realized its user had been stolen away.

The bullrush tumbled both Dale and Adam down the entire dune, the event highlighted in the background by Artorian's laughter. Adam's sudden complaints for his friend to *please* release his wings from this death-grip fell on the deafest of ears. Dale was busy making loud farm-animal noises in order to drown the celestial's pleading out, so he could squeeze Adam for longer. Like a Lion that hadn't seen its caretaker for years.

Artorian hollered down the sandy mountain, chiding Adam for the meager few minutes he'd spent with them in Eternia. "That's what you get for leaving them hanging, feathers!"

"Why aren't you helping me?!" Adam exhaled back at the old man through tightly squeezed ribs. "I didn't see this tackle happen. Deterministic fate showed you're supposed to be helping me!"

"I *am* helping. Just not you!" Artorian cackled. "Sorry, old boy! I'm an agent of free will! I think your visions pranked you. This architect thinks this is a much better fate to occur than some alternatives. So take your rib-crushing hugs. They missed you, ya winged doofus!"

"*They?*" Adam wheezed, his wings completely pinned in Dale's far-too-skillful grip as the hard-headed, stubborn mule of a man barked to the air while rolling around. Like it was some emergency beacon. "There's more?"

"*Adaaaammmm!*" Hans was crying, thick tears running over his marred, soot-covered cheeks and glass-coated hair, a rolling heat-wave right on his heels. The completely tanned, scorched, nude as nature assassin howled with wind-empowered fire as he crested the sandstone hill. Running slam-dunk first right into the cuddle puddle to add onto Adam's wing-squeezing. "I should've saved *you~u~u~u!*"

Hans likely knew that saving the old Adam had never really been in the cards, but from Artorian's point of view, the man was too scorched and delusional to think of that right now. At least Ammy had been decent enough to provide him... decency with that well-positioned leaf in the way to block any and all question-able topics and leading questions.

"Hans, you are naked!" Adam cringed as his upper lip pulled up in discomfort. Struggling in vain, Adam had to deal with Arto-rian laughing, Ammy hugging the old fox from behind so he wouldn't fall off the other side of the dune while *also* not coming to his aide, Dale being a donkey, and Hans—most infuriating friend that he was—*joining* Dale in the cacophony of the improvised farm. Adam had no choice, he had to stab one of them where it hurt. "Hansss... you smell like... *mud.*"

The neat-freak assassin let go in an instant, shrieked, and rolled in the sand while whining "Get it off, get it off, get it offff."

"Ha, freedom!" Adam cried, only to be squeezed back into submission as Dale suplexed the celestial while still refusing to calm down from his animal parade. He coughed out his next words with extra breath. "Dhaaaale. *Please.* I need to dress Hans. Leaf or not, it's unsightly!"

Dale replied with a rooster's morning cry, then let Adam go. Bent over backwards and twisted wrong-ways, Adam gulped in a deep breath. He then pointed at Hans, and coughed. "Clothes Beam!"

The sound of a piccolo accompanied the shrill flash of light, and when the luminance faded, Hans was both perfectly clean and immaculately dressed in strange monastic attire. Like not a single embarrassing event had ever occurred, Hans jumped right to his feet, tipped his new turban like he'd lived with it all his life, and flashed a sinner's smile. "Why, hello there!"

A powerful flash of heat from the top of the dune made all the color drain from the assassin's freshly tanned face. The Incarnate rasped, a huge evil grin on her face while her hand made a claws-up grasping motion. "General Kenobi!"

Hans ran.

No quips. He just *ran*.

Artorian laughed, Adam laughed, Dale laughed, the dune laughed. Adam and Artorian both instantly triggered, launching flat-faced, super-serious, Mana-fueled laser beams through the sand-buried mimic to kill it outright—then continued their merriment like they hadn't just paid tribute to the **Law** of **War**. The dune was dust and rubble, and their sandcastles were toast, but that was alright. The celestial and architect hovered into place to mutually catch Dale, as the man had been sent sailing in an arc through the air when they'd insta-gibbed the buried threat, catching him.

"Ope! Gotcha!" Artorian mused supportively, putting his ancient disciple down as they both flared their Auras at the same time. The duo then smiled wide and pointed finger crossbows at each other until Adam copied them both like it was no big deal, joining in the three-way pointing procession while they all turned to the other with big, dumb, open-mouthed smiles. All three of them loudly went "Eyyyy!"

When they were done unknowingly performing the traditional greeting of all spider-men of the Autarchy, they shared handshakes, more hugs, and then held Dale because he was the one who needed the most support. Unlike Artorian who could make it all wait until later, and Adam who had all his mud in a bag, Dale wept.

To be expected, really.

Some more sitting in the sand and watching Hans get hunted like a basher later, Dale and Adam had caught up a bit. Occasionally interjected with grandfather commentary from the old man, in order to get Dale back on his feet. The farmer nodded, then grabbed Adam's shoulder for a stern shake. "Really, man. We missed you, badly. Rose loved you. Cried her eyes out more than once. Those couple minutes were… ground-shattering, and we've been thinking it might have been some dream. Come have dinner? Everyone needs to see you. *Properly*, this time. I can get a message out to Tom."

Adam smiled, then nodded. "Of course, old friend. We do

have a few tasks we must complete beforehand, as I'm afraid your mentor here will not be attending that gathering."

Artorian puzzled out the meaning, then sighed. Nodding in agreement when Dale's head snapped to regard him. "Is it Richard-time, then?"

Adam smirked like a snoot, winking. "If you choose to, free will man. The Demonbanes must meet and greet. Don't think I missed that 'ope' there earlier. Friend of those from the 'Mines of Sota.'"

The grandfather huffed, pouting at the celestial. "You little abyssalite! I'll have them sneak you some of that brandy. See what you say when your stomach turns into a twister, sending you on the kind of storied drunken bender that Yuki would savor."

The celestial's shoulders bounced, silently laughing. "I can neither be shaken nor stirred. I am no drink to be sipped to check for poison, nor am I uncertain of myself. I am Adam, of the Celestial plane. I am no abyssalite, regardless of the amount of cheek that I give you, **Love**."

Dale squinted at his old friend. "Was that directed at me? I know you said it to the headmaster, but that *distinctly* felt aimed at me."

Both Adam and Artorian brightened at Dale. Artorian in particular beamed out his words. "He's learning! I credit Minya."

"Hey!" Dale punched Artorian in the shoulder, then cat-yowled and pulled the wounded appendage against his chest. "Yeowch! What? How! Your pressure-feeling… thinger… is lower than mine! I should have gotten through!"

The disciple frowned as he forgot his cultivation-specific terms. Artorian just looked overly pleased and smug. "My body might be stuck at A-rank one to equip these sexy legs that I could make roadside carts pull over with, but that means the rest of my 'oomph' is going into my Aura. I am *good* at Aura, even if the way you made yours is a little better than mine. Very pointed, direct function. Some learning capacity in there too! Mine has it swapped. Lots of adaptive learning, not so much pointed function. Well done, my boy! That's a gorgeous, perfect artwork of an Aura. You could get shoved into a powerful energy beam strong enough to blow up a moon and come out decently unscathed!"

Dale flushed at the sincere compliment, his old mentor scanning him over studiously. This allowed Adam to speak and explain. "You are correct, Dale. Those words were for you, as you are the

DENNIS VANDERKERKEN & DAKOTA KROUT

one simmering down from inner turmoil. To explain in complexity, I am a deterministic creature. **Determinism** is the philosophical view that all events are determined completely by previously existing causes. To me, all of history has already happened, and I am merely acting out my part, during my time. In a way, I am made entirely out of celestial corruption. Do you recall—when I was the Adam you knew—my moments of future-sight, or how I was able to see an attack coming *so far in advance* that our group had a small conversation about needing to get out of the way? I see existence like that. The flow of life, space, and time, is *set*. Nothing new can happen. All events have already come to pass."

The celestial motioned to the old man. "Artorian is my opposite, as a being of **Possibility**. To him, nothing is set in stone, certain, required, or fated to occur. His very presence and belief in the malleability of reality, by itself, contributes to making existence malleable."

Adam pressed his own chest. "I am certain of myself. All questions I could have? Those are answered, all avenues explored. Everything, including both in terms of choices and actions, has a right answer. I don't choose these outcomes so much as... I merely do them. To me, Determinism has won. I am a static point, not an agent moving between them."

Dale squinted at his friend with powerful confusion and a complete emptiness of understanding. The farmer let out a single sound that solidified Adam had not gotten any part of his point across. "*Huh?*"

Artorian cackled, wiped away a tear, and put on his most innocent smile. "He's gold, isn't he? Adam, I think you had a point. That 'fated to be' stuff only works when you're not around people with the agency to muck with that established order of events you say is visible to you. There might be a set amount of outcomes you are privy to with those special eyes of yours, but we've already proven that the actual events which play out do not match what you see. Thus they are not the established truth of the matter. No matter how comforting you might find that determined outlook to cling to regardless. I can already tell that I will never change your mind, so... Please don't be too upset with me when I crash right through your 'way the world must be.' Again."

Adam considered it, checked the future, sighed, and gave up.

His allotted outcomes were no longer in his favor. The celestial's exhale was full of crass dejection. "I swear... *Philosophers...*"

Dale looked between the two. "I am *so* lost."

Adam considered that, then flicked his wrist, making **Compassion** appear in his hand. That got the attention of both cultivators, their words unified. "You can just *do that?*"

The celestial grinned, then waggled the blade while keeping eye contact with Artorian, making a very strong point that, unlike the old man, he was not undergoing any kind of change. Not a hint of gray, flick of color, or other alteration affected Adam, where Artorian would be having all sorts of emotional adventures right now. Especially without **Sorrow** to balance the emotional load out. "Sure can. Not a difficult trick. They can even do it by themselves if they feel like it."

"Can you two stop flirting?" Dale blurted out. "Is this to help me, or not? You both lost me in the next desert over ten minutes ago, and I'm still standing there wondering if you're coming to pick me back up. Also, Adam, I appreciate the attempt, but really. *I'm good.* I'm Dale. Dale with a loving family, a farm, and spastic coffee elementals that are likely already vibrating out of their planter boxes."

Adam peeked away to snort out laughter, while Artorian went flat faced. The old man then slowly moved a scandalized hand to his own chest, pressing fingers into his own sternum as he was momentarily touched by Hans's bardic inspiration. "You wound me, old friend. Fine! We'll call it off. Our noble houses clashed too much, the families would never approve! Neither Capulet, nor Montague!"

In response to Dale's unamused expression from his mentor's ad-libbing and making up words that didn't exist, Artorian resumed a normal pose. Adam then straightened up in response to the old man stopping his antics. The shift in playful grandfatherly demeanor to an Administrator's poise was both firm and direct.

Artorian shifted topics into work mode as he addressed the celestial. "Did you bring friends?"

"No." Adam, his expression unreadable before, now had a slight curl to his lip. He spoke curtly while releasing the grip on the sword, letting it vanish. Adam wanted to get one last joke in before it was truly serious-time. "I brought family!"

Timed exquisitely, that was the exact moment a portal opened right next to them, revealing Soni, Caro, and Corvid as they walked through in adorable, matching, debonair outfits. Soni then closed the portal behind them with a snap of his tiny claws. "We heard somebody called Dibs! Demons respect the law of Dibs. What can the double-Oh squad spy out for you today, oh most shiny Q-ball?"

The three of them saluted in unison to the Administrator and Eye in the Sky. The corvid began speaking, a new nametag showing a chosen name of 'Ludere.' "Double-Oh six, seven, and eight are reporting for assignment."

CHAPTER THIRTY-ONE

"All done playing around? Excellent timing." Ammy spoke from above as she dangled an unconscious Hans by the ankle. The rest of him hung upside down from her grip while tiny mockingbirds flew circles above his head. "I'm all done with lessons today. I heard my boy get serious from the other end of the desert, and Rose is running this way at full tilt. I'm going to make some accommodations. Yes?"

Nobody said anything against the notion, so Ammy moved her free hand upwards in a snapping motion. As she did, part of the desert came up along with the sharp movement. Those sand particles were made to shift, flow, and compress into a hot red and white emulsion before finalizing to products of cooled off glass. "There we go. Instant round table and matching chairs, plus coin floor. Everyone, take a seat."

They all did so, though Artorian motioned to Soni. "There's a lady running over here at top speed. Can we get a shortcut?"

Soni leaned out of his comparatively tiny seat to look past a sand dune, then made a circular motion with his tiny bat-paw. A portal opened, and they could see Rose speeding to it from the other side. Artorian waved her over, and the woman detoured instantly.

Sprinting through the gate before it closed, Rose released a howling cry of "Adaaaam!"

To which the celestial responded in mild, paralyzed panic. "Oh no, not again!"

Shortly before getting tackled right off his freshly taken seat, his cries of wing-crushing protest fell on deaf ears as his words were deafened by more animal noises. Rose had apparently attended Dale's school of not-wanting-to-hear-it.

Artorian laughed, Ammy laughed, Adam laughed, Dale laughed, and another dune laughed. They all shot the dune, turning it into an obliterated pile of flickering glitter and fireworks. While the lot of them glared at the cratered remnant, now nothing but cinders, smoke rose from their pointer-fingers. They all brought the digits to their lips, then blew the effect out like a night-time candle in unison, ending the smoky emanation.

"It's the Muspelheim desert all over again, isn't it?" Artorian asked Ammy as he pretend-tucked his finger into his belt, whose annoyed 'mhm' told him everything he needed to know. "So it's not just Cal needing to bury his bad experiments anymore?"

Ammy huffed. "You'd be surprised how few options there are for getting rid of things that you don't want destroyed, and there's no better place to sweep something under the rug than a sand carpet. What are people going to do in order to find things? Bring a giant comb and go through the desert? That's some Spaceballs madness. Nothing reasonable people would try."

Dale put his hand up, glad to have been included in the stationary skeet-shoot. Dropping the prior subject, Ammy addressed him like he was an adopted child. The tenderness in her voice surprised a few people. "Yes, sweetie?"

All except Dale, it seemed, who spoke to Amaterasu like she was his grandmother. "Can I know what the Richard thing is about? I knew him decently well. I have a few stories if we need them."

Artorian perked up, getting cozy in his seat as Adam was freed from Rose's attentive, crushing grasp when she noticed her larger child needed help. Attending a passed out Hans instead, they all got seated at the table before the old man replied. "I would love to hear it. In short, we're decanting a few people from the Mountain-dale days. Next up are Richard, Nerys, then probably Snookem Bookem. We have… a couple of problems to tackle, and they might be suitable to help. If they choose to. Please, yes, tell us about Richard! You look far more comfortable all of a sudden!"

Dale sheepishly pointed at Ammy. "Oh, well. My grandma is here, and that always makes me feel a bit more confident. Everything gets *done*. Also, when I was a baron, these kinds of meetings were drilled in. I sort of missed sitting around a big table getting to feel important and included? There's a strange, tingly, comfort sensation."

Artorian looked wide-eyed at Ammy, but she just playfully shrugged back at him. "He's a sweet little baby. I have soft spots. Shush!"

Artorian put both his hands up, then turned to Dale with his full attention. The old man asked calmly, prompting the start of story time, even if some people had already heard some segments and were going to get a round two. "Richard? The arrow-point version."

Dale slid into the segue with gusto, glad for the change in conversation as he tallied on his fingers. "Father Richard hates demons and anything that has to do with necromancy. He was either in an Infernal monster or demon hunting order for the church, which specialized in fighting against such. He has an immense desire to prove himself and his ability to the church, to which he is exceptionally devout anytime it comes up."

Adam nodded to agree.

Dale dropped his hand to move it about with a gesture, and lost his physical count. Looking at his hand and mouthing where he'd been, he just started over when he couldn't remember. "Richard is a kind hearted person, a good teacher, and stalwart mentor. Which Adam here can likely attest to, as he was Dick's disciple for a while. He taught me about binding runed items to myself."

Adam repressed a small smirk, shifting one leg over the other as he added a comment. "Richard attained his skills from Cardinal Kere Nolsen, famed Slayer of Shades. The Adam of old was frantic and uncomfortable when the topic first arose. He was a fan. The current Adam finds the methods overly flashy, though attacking the shades of a color will always be an amusing trick. The niche to defeating shadows lies in meddling with the careful interplay of what a shadow requires to exist. Fascinating find, really. Shame he rarely used it, favoring his black-and-white Justice effect."

Artorian motioned for a pause. "You changed Richard's name

suddenly. I know how that works for some other people around here, but not him. I have insufficient context."

Dale sat back and made an 'oh' expression. "You mean 'Dick'? That's an odd nickname that anyone named Richard appears to be assigned."

Adam pleasantly chuckled. "A joke that manifested before its time. One must love the cyclical nature of things to really appreciate it."

"So a joke, then?" Artorian clarified. "I'll stick with Richard. Please continue, Dale."

The farmer nodded, then kept recounting. "Father Richard is responsible for pulling me up into the D-ranks, I believe in trade for... was it a spot of land for his church? The one with the solid quartz floor that was see through, collecting celestial Essence? He was mighty proud of it."

Artorian leaned in his glass chair with an amused wrinkle to his nose. "I should show him the Cathedral of the Luminous Prism if there's ever the chance. If he thought a quartz foundation was fancy."

Dale slapped the table with a stern laugh at the thought of showing a Cathedral to a Father, then pulled it back to shake it in the air. "Ow! I hurt my hand on a glass table? It's glass! I should not be the one injured here."

Ammy winked at him. "*I* made it, sweetie. I may have restricted myself to Essence when chasing your brown flame of a friend here, but this is Spirit glass. I used *my* oomph to get it done in a hurry. If this entire continent went up like a powder keg, this table still wouldn't have a scratch."

Artorian narrowed his eyes at the thought. "Ammy, don't suppose we can travel with this setup? Would be mighty helpful when demon diplomacy needs to be on my plate."

The incarnate replied with a curt nod. "I'm expecting Titania shortly. I'll have her slap some item codes on all the pieces. She's better at it."

"Diplomacy?" Dale asked, not believing his ears. "*What?*"

His old mentor winked at him. "You'll see. In fact, I might even ask you to be included if you feel like it? I'm only taking Mages and up with me when I go and have the big meeting. The more the merrier!"

Dale pressed his pointer finger to his chest, making sure he was really the person being addressed. Artorian closed his eyes for a moment to nod. "Yes, son. *You*. That's an A-rank nine body you're sporting, even if you are clueless on how to use it, past living in it."

Dale thought about it, then beamed ear to ear with a massive smile when he looked at the grandmother who'd adopted him. Ammy approved with a single nod. "I'll need to run it by Minya, but she will likely ask to come along for... *acquisition* reasons. If I end up not being there... Well, she said no."

"Odds and Ends?" Rose quipped. A small laugh went around the table, after which she set Dale back on topic in order to be helpful. "Anything else notable about Richard?"

"Depends on if you're asking only Dale, or everyone." Hans cut in, having recovered in time to hear glimpses of the conversation. Rose instantly had him by the ear, pulling him back into a glass seat rather than let the problem child stand up and pace. "Ow! I'll sit, I'll sit!"

Dale chuckled, speaking about Richard. "He's cheeky, clever, and wise, much like yourself, headmaster. But he does have problems with anything that gets in the way of teaching others about the church, or church activities. I'm not sure if that will stay pertinent with the entire faction... missing."

Hans smirked, adding very different details. "He got disgusted when Frank told him he should be paying people to come into his church in order to watch the dungeon boss battles rather than them coming in to learn and worship. That quartz floor gave a clear view of Cal's lower floors."

Artorian filed that note away, thinking of a particular question. "Do we know anything about his **Law**?"

Adam stuck his wing up like a hand. When motioned to, the celestial answered. "Father Richard is bound to the **Law** of **Sonder**. That being: all individuals are unique but connected; sharing bonds, the realization that each random passerby is living a life as vivid and complex as your own."

Artorian found that very useful, then laid his eyes on Hans, who was glad for the attention. "Anything more under-the-table?"

Hans showed his teeth and popped his knuckles, finding his moment to gab and shine. "Richard has a disregard for the mundane problems of both non-cultivators and lower-ranked cultivators. But which Mage of our time didn't have that kind of mind-set? More interestingly, he's a wheeler and dealer kind of guy! It's a common story that he used three plots of land instead of one when he started building his church, as he couldn't dig down due to the dungeon being there. The fun bit was that he never *asked* for that extra land, and played it off when people found out. A forgiveness over permission outlook. He also bought dungeon-drop pendants from people at the low-*low* price of fifty silvers, then happily sold them for a higher profit."

Artorian chuckled with a nasal exhale.

Dale growled, crossing his arms in a fuss. "I caught him on both of those too! I was like, 'But they're worth more!' And he just went, 'Only if you can activate them!' Then he winked at me when I caught wind of his little resale scheme. Otherwise he's polite, refers to people younger than him as 'lad' a lot, can be silly, is usually rather casual in conversation, but he does tend to get very pious when he speaks. Unless he catches you when your chips are down. Then with great amusement asks if you're hiding like a scared little Forest Elf."

Artorian motioned that he had enough gossip, as the stories were leaving the territory of usefulness. He instead angled his nose towards the three demon spies. "You've all been rather quiet. You three alright?"

Soni uncomfortably cleared his threat. "Sunny, you are talking about a person who sounds like he would see us and bring the sky down. On principle. We're sweating nervously and turning ever deeper shades of pale. I can confirm our shades are feeling very much attacked at the moment, and he's not even here yet."

Hans sneered. "*Nah*. The nose follows power first. Always know whose feet not to get in front of. He would politely turn to Lady Amaterasu and succinctly bow."

"Are you sure?" Ammy questioned, not too sure about that. "I would not be surprised if he appeared, squeezed his grip around the front of your robe, and accused you of a crime that you'd deny, and yet probably did."

Rose shook her head to defend her large child. "I think his eyes would do the rounds, pause on me because of the affinities, then come to a rest and stop on Adam before he gasps loudly."

Adam blustered out a weak laugh, then countered that claim.

"Oh? Here I was of the opinion that he would see me first, and his mouth would gape!"

Ludere and Caro both raised an eyebrow at that mention. Then like laying a pile of chips on a velvet table, Caro the raccoon spoke. "Want to *bet* on that?"

Adam's eyes glinted, his voice supremely amused. "To see who the Father's attention will truly fall on first? *Yes*."

CHAPTER THIRTY-TWO

Father Richard Demonbane needed an abyss-cracked *moment*.

Some old man had just thanked a glowing orb of green light for her help, while Richard was standing in front of a round glass table that seemed to have been haphazardly deposited in the middle of a desert. A desert with some rather suspicious nearby craters for decoration.

All of that though, was a tithe's pittance compared to everything else accosting his eyes all at the same time. Where did he *begin*?

"So anyway, he started blasting." The monastic-dressed man with a painfully familiar voice was trying to steer his attention away from the considerably more interesting options to lay his attention on.

Hans lost his part of the bet when Richard did not pay a lick of attention to either him or the comment. Instead, Richard traced his fingers across his hollow cheeks and high, pronounced cheekbones. Brushing them up through medium-length graying hair that swept neatly to the back, before the Father made a questioning hand motion as metaphorical geometric forms and equations danced before his eyes.

Richard then blinked, tried to say something, stopped himself, tried again, then walked away to lay in the sand with his hands on his stomach, fingers laced. "I quit."

Raucous laughter broke out from the table, joined by calls of dissatisfied anguish and groans of bets powerfully lost. Dale made a broad motion of swallowing up all the imaginary chips on the table with both of his arms. "Jackpot! I won!"

Richard's head jerked up from the sand, his expression scandalized. "You bet on me and I don't even get a cut? Pay your tithes, boy!"

Artorian fell off his chair from laughter, too busy turning red and pink in the face while holding onto his ribs. Not due to Richard's outburst, but rather in response to Adam burying his face into both of his hands. The celestial had been *so sure* he would win.

The three demons cheered in unison for not getting insta-gibbed, getting up on their chairs to perform a little dance jig. Hans got up to curse and kick at some rocks in the sand while Rose couldn't stop herself from giggling madly. Also not at Richard's outburst, but rather Ammy's purely laconic and stoic flat-faced expression that didn't at all match the mood.

Dale grinned like a fool, imaginary winning clutched in his arms. "Tithes? Sure!"

Richard sat up in a flash, his arms pressing him upwards.

Dale's grin then grew three whole sizes before the next words left his lips. "A percentage of nothing is still nothing!"

Richard's enthused face fell flat, before the rest of him unceremoniously flopped back down into the sand. The green orb hovered over to him, then reached out with some molded light to pat his shoulder, accompanied by a motherly tone. "There, there."

The pious man scrutinized the sky. He narrowed his gaze and stuck his finger up, but no particular words came to him. He sat up to regard the table again, laid back down, looked again, then fell onto his back and re-folded his hands over his stomach. He pinched his own cheek, didn't appear to find the response he was looking for as he did not in fact wake up, then released a severe sigh.

When he did get to his feet, he stared down the tiny Bat, Corvid, and Raccoon all performing a childish dance while the animals held paws and skipped in a circle. He dropped his finger towards them, and spoke. "This will wait."

He then turned to Adam, pressed both his hands together as if they were clasped in prayer, moved them to his lips, then dropped them outwards towards the spitting image of his old disciple, who now instead appeared to be carved from the very heavens he used to worship and give praise to. His vision squinted, mind needing to set this incomprehensible mess in some kind of order. "This, too, will wait."

He then turned to the only person who had retained any sort of serious face throughout this entire affair, and quickly understood his place in the pecking order. He pressed a hand to his heart, then promptly and immediately, with maximum politeness and poise, bowed. "Grand Saintess."

Only after this concession did Ammy's face change from a stoic statue into something resembling a humble smile, prompting another bout of hilarity and laughter from everyone else who was already feeling weak in the gills, unable to contain themselves.

Richard ignored the petty thief, the lady attempting to corral the large man, the old academic howling on the ground, and his environment as he turned to Dale and finally revealed how he felt about this entire debacle. "Dale. *What*, in the entire celestial realm, is this *abyss*?"

He inhaled deeply.

"I did not wake up with enough tithes in my pocket to deal with this." Richard adopted a sermonizing tone, entirely too sober for this. "Yours is the only face out of this entire circus—no offense meant, my Lady Saintess—that I recognize without feeling a need to run, attack, or become paralyzed with fear. Please... Explain."

Dale gently raised his hand into the air, his mind still entirely on his ill-gotten winnings. "Before that. May I ask who your attention actually fell on first?"

Richard wanted this done and over with, so he pointed at both Adam, who was still burying his face into his hands, and the demons, who were now playing pattycake. "By the thinnest of margins? Those fell beasts and the literal slice of heaven devoured all my attention."

Dale squinted, voice slowing. "What margin?"

Richard understood that there was no escaping this until the game came to an actual conclusion. "Initially? The demon daycare."

Dale's face fell hard, his fists raised to the sky before he shook them. "Noooo! I am thwarted!"

Adam pulled his face up from his hands, the celestial's expression incredulous before he slapped the back of Dale's head with a pristine white wing. "You feel thwarted? The future is all sorts of chaos. Do you have any idea how big of an impact these tiny ripple events can have? You could make an entire 'What If' spinoff series about them!"

He raised his hand to the sky, gripping an unseen energy before shaking his head and pulling the force to his heart. "Oh celestial above, give me the strength to not *slap* my dear friend silly. With my prayers."

"You already slapped me!" Dale complained. "With your wing no less!"

"That was educational." Adam flatly consigned. "With my prayers."

"I didn't hear any prayers!" Dale whined, louder this time as he just didn't understand. The man then had an epiphany, and rounded on Richard. "Also no mention of margins!"

"No, no. The celestial has a point." Richard seemed to understand very well. That or he was throwing Dale under the cart for not actually answering his question. Distracted by the demon daycare trying their best to shove invisible goods—that simply did not appear to exist—into their physically fattening pockets.

Richard caught the amused glint in Adam's eye. So even the heavens had a sense of humor? Well then, no reason to hold back! "Very well, Dale. By the tiniest of margins—of say twenty-eight to twenty-four?—the literal angel who is the mirror image of my favorite student has it."

Adam beamed, his local luminance rising as one of his trembling fists rose with holy might to the air. The celestial calling upon the cry of the legendary Captain 'Ninety-Nine Holt' as his voice filled with resonant relief. "Vin-di-ca-tiooonnnn!"

The pockets of the demons instantly deflated, along with their expressions as they fell to their knees, cried in lamentation, and then slunk back off to their seats like blobs of sapient gelatin who had suffered a serious defeat.

Feeling like that outcome had been the only right one, Richard then addressed the C'towl in the bag when it came to the mystery bet. "Alright, so is there something there or not, or is this entire charade meant purely to toy with me?"

Hans leaned into the scene, finger extended. "Yes! The most valuable of—"

"They're messing with you." Amaterasu cut in, ending the pleasantries as the rest of the table—busy keeping up the charade —groaned, as that indicated the fun had thoroughly been nipped in the bud. That, and if Artorian turned any redder from laughter, there might be health concerns.

Everyone retook their seat at the table, taking a moment for a breather. Artorian was provided several napkins by Titania, who hovered up to his side like a diligent caretaker. When they were settled, Ammy motioned for Richard to take the open seat between Dale and Adam. The two people he was most likely interested in speaking to.

"I appreciate that a Demonbane is able to keep their calm in the face of such obvious targets." Ammy wore a wry smile on the edge of her lips. "I suppose that makes two of you at the table who understand that prudence is wise."

"Prudence is a powerful virtue, Grand Saintess. I give my humble appreciation for your esteemed deliberation." Richard spoke with the prior punctual pose, and a light chest-bow. The man was putting severe effort into being polite, and not upset an unknown S-ranker that clearly had the run of the place. Saints did as they pleased. "I admit that I still feel out of my depth, but given there were friendly faces and power present that had not already quelled the obvious threats, I surmised there might be more to this, no matter how deeply the call to *smite* coursed across my ears. I can still hear the Cardinal shout at me to apply justice."

Richard then paused, picking up on some of her language. He pondered aloud, fully expecting the Incarnate to denote herself. "May I ask who the other Demonbane is?"

Artorian gave him an adorable little wave, while Ammy spoke with a flick of her eyes that the old man was the intended recipient and target. "That would be Artorian, who, during your time at Mountaindale, was headmaster of the local academy. We have much to explain of the time that has been ticking during your absence, as when I checked the records, you were Cored rather early on during your Soul Space days."

"*Ah.*" Richard rubbed the back of his neck in embarrassment. "Yes. *That.* A disagreement with some of the guildies who did not abide with the suggested… or, well, *imposed* new ruleset. One of them got me in the back. It was very unbecoming of me to be so caught off guard."

Hans interjected. "Happens to the best of us. Had the same problem with arrows and knees, but my Rose is a masterful shot with any bow. I was bound to lose eventually."

Rose went *dawww*, then patted his cheek.

Interlude over, Richard fidgeted and didn't know which way to turn first after seating. He still expected answers from Dale, had a mountain of theological questions for Adam, but the moment his eyes met with Artorian's, the heavens parted. There was an instant moment of brotherly kinship as lightning connected their gazes. Like two warriors meeting for the first time on the field of battle, and knowing in that moment, without doubt, they were cut from the same cloth.

Both old foxes grinned, and that spelled the end of the world.

Or so Titania thought, as she could see the schemes from both these old codgers leave their bodies as fully formed spirits, striding across the empty distance between them to shake hands and wrap welcoming arms around the neck of the other. Marching ever onwards to spell the end of some poor, unsuspecting nation that had no idea it was about to lose all of its gold and valuables.

"If we had a functioning currency system, I would be so worried about those expressions." Titania was succinct, glad they were doing things without that metric for now. Tatum wouldn't let it stay that way, but she felt this way all the same. To distract herself, she also demanded her charge's attention. "Sunny, do I decant Nerys while I'm at it?"

Artorian was plucked from the moment, blinking to turn and address her. "*Hmm*? Oh, not yet, dear."

He then paused and waffled on his decision. "Well, on the other hand. Why not? It will save us from needing to explain twice, and all of Emilia's questions will likely be in the same vein as Richard's. Oh, speaking of. Introductions!"

Artorian went around the table, introducing everyone so the Father would have a name to put with the new faces. Once he got to Hans, the A-ranker had the snively wretch tight by the front of the robe while Hans instinctively put his hands up. "I knew I recognized you! You're the miscreant who stole an entire reliquary!"

"I put it back!" Hans hurriedly defended. "Maybe a little lighter than when I found it, but…"

Richard dropped Hans back into his seat and whisked himself

back to his own assigned spot, throwing his hands into the air like he just didn't care anymore. "I'll be mad later. Answers now would be very much appreciated. Also, I know Crimson Whip Nerys. A-rank four, member in the Healing Order of the Bloody Hand, notable F-rank mentor, famed necromancer hunter. Though, why you want to pull a seasoned Blood Mage into this mix is currently beyond me. Unless you're aware that her Mountaindale history was fouled with the amount of high-rankers that were leaning on her. Nobody is themselves when a Saint is staring you down expectantly. Dale? I still expect a full rundown from you."

Dale nodded, but had to give Artorian the floor for the other question. The old man smiled, making Richard forget all about the sudden ups and downs in his day with a couple well-placed words. "We have a demon infestation. I'm looking for people skilled at problem solving, and *diplomacy*."

The divine look Richard gave him told Artorian that the Father was the first person in the entire soul space to understand what he actually meant. Richard's elation was unstoppable, his words smooth and buttery as he hung his metaphorical coat onto the mission rack. His fingers steepled. "Pull in Nerys, and please, tell me *everything*."

CHAPTER THIRTY-THREE

Emilia Nerys needed an abyss-cracked *moment*.

Some old man had just thanked a glowing orb of green light for her help, while Nerys was standing in front of a group of people that looked plucked from the world's most chaotic grab bag.

Hans couldn't stop himself, the jokes immediate. "A priest walks into a bar and sees an angel, a demon, and an Incarnate sitting together at a table. Who does she address first?"

Emilia blinked at the man dressed in monastic attire. That wordplay didn't suit the position to which he seemed to aspire. Nerys's uncompromising face spoke volumes for her, as the assassin's words went right over her head.

"None?" She questioned, Her voice entirely new as she moved a hand to the front of her neck on noticing the change in pitch. Not at all what it had been. "My injury is gone?"

The Nordic, 'every word was delivered with punctuation, like a slap from the back of a hand,' must have been a Mountaindale stress-tic, because currently it was missing altogether.

Now, Nerys's voice indicated a more southern, calmer drawl. Pragmatic was a good way to describe it. Like the words and person were somewhat detached from the topic they spoke of. Artorian's memories caught the change right away as well, aware she was no longer enunciating every word like a Shatner's play.

Nerys finished answering the question, the moment short lived. "You went to a bar. You go to the barkeep."

The smugness wiped from Hans's face, but Nerys wasn't paying attention to that at all. Instead her attention zipped around, the nervousness creeping right back into her demeanor. "Where's Barry? I don't feel…"

Ammy took this moment to grab all the wind in the area, hold it still for a moment, and then let go. When Nerys snapped her attention towards the Incarnate, she winked at the Blood Mage, her nose moving towards an open chair.

Direction helped the unsettled Mage immensely, who fell right into step and slid her butt into the seat. She wasn't sure why everyone was looking at her with puzzled expressions. Nerys kept her calm, the expected anxiety-enunciation in her words still missing. Her hands pulled close and balled rather tightly due to sudden surprise, stress, and lack of something to distract herself with. She took a deep breath before speaking. "Is there egg on my face?"

Richard received her gaze by replying first, and everyone could see the recognition click behind her eyes. She knew the Father, her attentiveness spiking. "No, lass. Providence provides, and so it seems to have provided you the attire that I recall you having from the days before you took up a teaching position in the Mountain-dale Academy? You are in your Crimson Kit. Red heels, scarves, flowy dress, and all."

Emilia hadn't thought to look herself over, the southern sweetness in her tone increasing. "Well, I'll be sugar on a morning pie, it's my good outfit too. This one has pockets."

That raised a few eyebrows, but right after the moment of unexpected warmth, Nerys slid right out of her kindness, easing into a more comfortable, standoffish seating position. She didn't even seem to realize she'd done it. Her eyes then scanned the crowd, still lost on who to address or why, until she landed on Artorian.

Her face gained a sudden chill to it, words fearful. "The *paperwork* man."

Artorian needed a second, then vividly remembered Snookem! His fist had endlessly hammered the academy grounds as he'd attempted to cope with every additional wrinkle and frown that built on Emilia's face during her review. Her growing dread had provided the Air Dean endless, heaving, rib-aching laughter.

"Good to see you again, Emilia. You must recall me as the Phantom Academy Headmaster? Outstanding! One moment, please."

Artorian half turned in his seat, speaking to Titania. "Pull in Snookums, would you? They know each other, and that will make this all much easier to explain."

The green wisp made a sound of amusement at the name-twist, then directed her unseen newlights, organizing who needed to be decanted when, and where. With a silent puff that sounded like a sneakily passed breeze and played off like a trumpet, Snookem Bookem, prior Air Dean of the Mountaindale Academy, stood before the table completely dressed in his pajamas. Nightcap and fluffy ball at the end included. His reaction to the gathered individuals was entirely different than either Richard's or Nerys's.

Snookem Bookem spoke mirthfully. "I don't know what people woke me up for, but from a glance alone, I know that I wouldn't want to miss this for all the snoozes in the world! I love a good show. The last time I saw one of these, Preatoria and Nazeem got their comeuppance. Please tell me I have a ticket for a seat."

Artorian gladly motioned for an open one, and like a gust of wind, the man occupied it. His fingers were already drumming on the table in full expectation of pending amusement. Some people just had different priorities it seemed, so the attention fell back on Nerys. She appeared to still be waiting on Artorian to speak, holding on to 'a moment.'

The old man thought she might be a touch more literal than the rest of them. Her expression was cold, but she was trying to be helpful in her own way. She was also stealing glances at the rest of the table. A few in particular at the S-ranker, followed by small patches of concentration that appeared to be focused on the wind. Perhaps she was interested in Ammy's area control trick?

He stopped musing, and spoke. "Thank you for holding, Nerys. Now, to the freshly decanted: I'm sure a lot of you are both very confused and sprawling with questions. I'll keep introductions short. If you recall entering Cal, the dungeon of Mountaindale, you are correct in assuming that you are in his Soul Space. The quick and dirty of it is that, regardless of our multiple efforts to straighten the place up, we have… unwelcome visitors. Visitors that require the gift of a more skilled touch. In addition to that need, we are decanting everyone that died prior. By which I mean, they were saved in a memory Core of sorts, and are now coming back."

His attention momentarily fell on Emilia's crimson clothing. "Though in the case of some people, it appears that the Wisps doing the job are adding some flair, if the attire is of any measurement. I was hoping to hear how to avoid a 'round two.' Round one went poorly for everyone."

With that said, Artorian turned squarely to the freshly decanted. "So, Richard, Snookem, and Emilia, consider this whole affair a 'brand new leaf' ordeal. New story. New you. New chances. The old society is gone, done, and dusted. The old factions have been gone so long that they aren't even named here, and I'm hoping to connect everyone in favor of striving for a common cause."

Artorian's voice then leaned in Emilia's direction. "Unless you give a pass to the unfriendly demons, as well as the friendly ones?"

Nerys had been coasting along with the explanation until right around the end. Which was where her blood boiled. She'd been at a comfortable homeostasis because everyone else was, but her vampire-themed attire didn't appear to be merely for show when topics relating to necromancers and their summoned annoyances came to bear.

The reds on her scarves flared with streaks of angered blood, but then she suddenly simmered down. Her default state became a smile, a hum, and her hands keeping busy with something. In this case, tracing the patterns on the glass table. She began speaking slowly, her back straightening as some hints of nobility slipped into her speech.

Artorian had not known that Nerys was such a ball of complexity. He was starting to recognize the distinct signs of a person who had traveled often, picked up bits of culture and manners of speech from each area, and carried it along to the next place. The clashing cultures inevitably mixed. In Nerys's case, her specific emotional state seemed to make her lean toward one more than others.

"I do not 'get' jokes, Headmaster." Emilia said without feeling. "Neither am I particularly adept at telling them. I know they are funny. I laugh at them when others do. However, I frequently have no idea *why* they are funny. But they are definitely funny... Possibly."

Artorian laced his fingers, wondering where this was going as Nerys continued. "That is why, when I tell you that I find your statement to be of equal amounts insult and *hilarity*, I want you to know what that means to me."

The Blood Mage leaned forwards, both hands pressed to the glass. "I *despise* necromancers. With a passion matched only by my fury for their kin."

Her eyes, irises swirling and red with Mana, flicked to the animal circus trio in fancy little suits. She addressed them with venom. "You are not goop on the floor because I have not yet understood what is going on, and for no other reason."

Soni and company gulped, then chose the wiser option of saying nothing. This deflected some of Nerys's darker attention, her ire refocusing on the old man who had made the very poor jest. "My life is molded by those pests and their summoners. They killed my twins, and my dreams along with them. That my left arm is forever claw-scarred by my demon-possessed dead husband is nothing compared to the loss of my Ceylia and Ceron."

She exhaled hard, opening up since there was no point not to. "Before it all, I used to gush about being a beautiful woman from a noble family with great potential. Then my world shattered, and I shattered with it. I changed into a hunter, as no matter how skillful I am with blood, I simply do not have the gift of a healer. It was always *easier* to rip the vitality out of my foes, and give it to my friends. Not that this made me very popular when it came to the seedy adventuring parties I tagged along with, before finding the church."

Richard gave her a silent, but complicated expression. Nerys winced, and corrected herself. "Rather, the church found me. My hunting prowess was useful, but I was never again without a controlling hand on my shoulder nor without eyes digging into the back of my neck. It was the worst on Mountaindale. I had a bad day *one time*, and people made a thousand embellished reports about it. That was my attempt to *help*. As no matter how much I like being a mentor to those fresh in Essence, I lack something crucial that lets me fit in."

She picked at her white hair, fingers needing to fidget. The pale skinned woman brought the single hair to her brown eyes as the red hue faded, then blew the hair away. "I am three-hundred and seventy-one years old. I am a **Blood** Mage. I take from my enemies, and use it to empower myself. I live for the ghosts of the people I lost long ago, and wouldn't know how to keep living if it wasn't for them. I died long before Mountaindale, headmaster. I am the phantom of Ceylia, who wanted to be the best healer; and the phantom of Ceron, who loved to dance in the wind with his scarves."

Her hands squeezed each other. "There is no new leaf for me. Nor one that I want. There is only the hunt. Because children should be protected from the evils of the world, and no world ever seems to be short on evils. So tell me your joke again, headmaster, so I may laugh. Then level with me, and point me in the direction of the *kill*."

Artorian did not repeat himself.

Instead, he slightly tilted his head, eyes on the table. "There are... a whole host of children. Small, innocent, and untarnished, who will not have many to look out for them when we decant them. We will have a place, and likely plenty of time... Yet, nobody who is ready to watch over them as their hands learn to reach out, and touch the boundless Essence of this world."

Artorian did need to look at Nerys to be fully aware of her heart melting, and discomfort spiking. He just spoke, and soldiered on. "Must I truly point you in the direction of *kill*? Surely, I trust you to be skilled at it. However... would you perhaps walk, not with a fussy headmaster, but with an old man who needs a spot of help, to a place where bright eyed hopefuls need you more? Your spirit may be weighed by phantoms, but I have the strangest sensation itching the side of my nose that both the tremble and fidget in your fingers would vanish outright, if you so much as held theirs. Would you consider it, Emilia?"

Nerys almost didn't know what to say. "Why would you do this for me? I am nobody. A monster in Mage-flesh. You have no reason to trust me with the greatest treasures of the world."

Artorian met the eyes of some of the people around the table, and knew just as well as they did, that it was only Emilia who did not understand why she was a perfect fit. Even Richard nodded in solemn approval, but he was a sucker and sap for arcs of redemption.

"I offer it, Emilia." Artorian repeated. "Would you consider it?"

CHAPTER THIRTY-FOUR

Titania rang a tiny bell after it had become quiet for long enough for the atmosphere to become uncomfortable. Nerys had retreated into herself, deep in thought. "On that quiet note, this is where I tell you that Oberon just forwarded me a most interesting memo. Skyspear is claimed, Amber's portal is up and running, and all the cultivators are tackling floor after floor like a swarm of starving locusts."

Artorian snapped towards her. "Already? That's so fast! It's only been days since we decanted Amber!"

Soni perked up, the name familiar. "Would that be the crazy lady who was chasing Grace around? We got that gate finished yesterday! Good on her for getting it up and running."

The old man rounded on the demon Bat. "Boy! The last time I had to oversee all the materials being processed into a portal, the effort was a massive undertaking. Occultatum was still 'the Master' then, and the work was both endless and frustratingly labor intensive. I sent in more reports to Cal on requisitioned materials than all the words I've spoken to him total. No way we got that logistical nightmare sorted already. I was expecting this project to take upwards of a year."

Titania answered smugly. "*Grace* was with her. Scarcity is more of a polite joke. They were short on nothing, ever. The entire

Mayev Spire is now accessible. Lunella is crowing like a rooster about not being ready for the children. Or the extras."

Artorian's ear twitched, his gaze turning back to Nerys. Her answer was important, and the timer had run dry. "What'll it be, Emilia? The hunt? Or the children?"

The Blood Mage squeezed the hand rests of her chair, the decisions ticking into place behind her eyes. Her words became resolute. "Take me to this Spire."

A soft round of applause broke out from around the table, a feat that forced Nerys to squeeze into the backrest of her seat as if she was trying to hide behind the clear, see-through glass. Her cheeks were flushed, eyes unwilling to meet anyone's gaze. Her words lost their strength, becoming shy mumbles. "That didn't need applause..."

"Yes it did." Richard wore a proud smile. "That was excellent of you, Sister Emilia. You deserved that praise, and social warmth. You might be pressed onwards by your phantoms, but nobody missed that tremble in your hands. Nor how that tic stopped entirely when the headmaster here gave you the offer."

Nerys mumbled, uncertain as she folded her hands to hide them. "Is it even his to offer?"

"It is." The Saintess declared as a matter of fact. "Work on the assumption that my Artorian directs most matters of import not directly overseen by an Incarnate. Even then, we would lend him our ears. You would do well to give weight to his words."

This confirmation straightened Nerys up from her sunken posture. There was no source more absolute in her eyes than an S-ranker giving a yes or no on a matter. She steadied herself with a breath, and inclined her head in the speaker's direction. "As you decree, my Lady Saintess."

Richard then grabbed Dale by the scruff of his farmer's shirt. "Now that it is clear we are splitting up, I am holding onto our dear ex-baron here. I still want my answers, and yes, I want them from *you*, Dale."

"I am concerned." Dale wiggled uncomfortably.

"Don't worry, buddy!" Hans gave him a feisty grin. "Rose and I will be right there with you. Isn't that right, sugarplum?"

When Hans turned to look at Rose, she already had Adam's wings captured and crushed with her arm like he was an escaped hen. He was going nowhere except with them, no matter how much his arms flailed and struggled. "*Mhm!* With company!"

Artorian had a sudden thought, his finger shooting to the sky. "Before we part! Emilia, Richard, I must know. This has been bothering me for *ages*. What was the whole business in our old world with the eye colors? I know a girl from Chasuble with pink eyes, and it was some big deal. A whole social caste was dictated on this detail. A big reason children were taken from my village also ended up being that they had green eyes. Apparently the old church had the answers? What gives?"

Richard choked on air, turning slightly pale while turning to avert his gaze while Nerys let out an uncharacteristic, boastful laugh. Her voice cut through Richard's discomfort. "That old superstition? They never disproved it?"

Richard grumbled, clearly knowing some darker details that Nerys didn't, but she knew of this story and would say her piece. It had been asked of her, after all. Emilia turned to Artorian. "The eyes thing? Superstition based on some vision or prophecy that never came to pass, written in some poorly made rhyme."

She adopted a comfortable speaking stance, and began. "I know only the first half. Supposedly; Green sees potential, held by those whose fates will be torrential. Eyes of pink can see the divine, listen close, for the words they bring will be finer than any wine. Blues are dreamers, deep and cloudy, whose eyes see past the sky no matter how rowdy. Browns are grounded, strong and daring, the muscle to which one keeps firm with effort unsparing."

She shook her head, disappointed in the malarkey. "Unique corruption manifestations in naturally occurring eye colors were a topic of 'study' that the church tried to control in order to exploit. They did this in an attempt to develop a variant of non-Essence eyes that could show the church something otherwise invisible. Supposedly, all those who did replace their original pair with Essence or Mana supposedly couldn't see 'something divine' anymore. Which caused a whole stir. The whole prophecy was a sham, and thieves responsible for sneaking information in and out caught wind of this prophecy. Then spread them as badly misin-formed rumors, rumors that caught like a wildfire."

Richard looked increasingly uncomfortable, a detail which escaped nobody. Artorian turned towards him, clearing his throat. The Father defensively dabbed his beading forehead with a piece of his sleeve. "The truth, unfortunately, is nowhere so rosy. So, yes, and no, in retort to Sister Emilia's version. Yes, there was a prophecy. No, it was not so minor."

Interest grew around the table, people leaning in.

Richard cleared his raspy throat. "Please let me preface and say that I knew of the project. That does not mean I approved, nor was I *involved*. The early theory in some of the darker corners of the Church was that certain eye colors would be predisposed to certain affinity channels. The draw of an easy marker for power was... difficult to brush under the altar. Especially when so little was understood of how Essence channels were gained. It's of no heresy or consequence to say this now, but many Vicar ranks were struggling to increase or improve their strength, when people with more open channels shot past them sheerly due to having a stronger basis to build from. Jealousy and envy are powerful motivators, and there's a limit to how often you can rely on a cleanup crew."

He laced his fingers, getting to it. "In short, pink eyes are the sullied mark of a failed experiment, where Essence was used to both strip the eyes, and yet add an effect that would make that iris color more susceptible to picking up Essence effects. The goal was to see *ambient* Essence, so non-cultivators could be sent out into the world in frankly ridiculous numbers under the guise of missionaries."

Richard was now scowling. "The plan was for these hordes of disposable followers to find undiscovered dungeons, or places of power, then report back to the Church for a Vicar's personal gain. My refusal to toe the line is part of what got me stripped from my position and sent to the boonies."

His displeasure palpable, the Father wrapped up his explanation. "The ideal to connect eye colors to Essence channels ended up entirely fruitless, yet the insistence of many Vicars to keep looking regardless caused a sort of... societal byproduct? Green irises, as example, became held in high esteem due to the prophecy mentioned by Nerys. Green eyes became synonymous with leadership qualities, high growth potential, and a smattering of stories that all pointed to 'this person is bound for great things.' Even if nothing ever came of the actual prophecy."

He unlaced his fingers, and sighed. "In other words, fools acting foolish and refusing to fess up to being the fool, being all the greater of a fool for it. Continued by the eternal pigeonholing council. I would like to bury this topic now, if people would be so kind. A change of scenery would not go amiss either."

Amaterasu agreed. She got up first, clapped for attention, then laid down the law and points of action. "I'm glad we made solid progress. Now. Dale, Hans, Rose, Adam, and Richard? To the farm with you. Soni, Caro, and Ludere? Take Snookem and Nerys. Follow Titania to check on Amber's portal work. Double-oh squad, when you're done with the checkup, infiltrate Olympus. I want a run-down of our foes. Snookem and Nerys? Join the cultivator locust swarm and clear that entire Spire of hostiles. Non-cultivator children will be playing around in there, and I don't want to see so much as a G-ranked patch of aggressive moss when I come look. Sunny, you're with me. Titania? Join us when you're done."

Everyone saluted, as nobody was going to tell an S-ranker *no*. They then got up from their seats as Soni began opening portals to various places. Sunny began sauntering towards one, but was stopped by Ammy. She instead pointed up where Zephyr, the luxury yacht, was breaking through the clouds to descend. "We're not taking a portal. Cal wants to see us."

People's ears twitched at the mention, but nobody chose to say anything as they went their separate ways. Artorian partially expected Snookem to have questions, or Nerys to show more discomfort, but neither of those concerns were founded. Nerys instead seemed to have a quest in her eyes, while Snookem moved along like a breeze, just happy to be there. To him, this was all nothing more than a good time.

Richard badly wanted to ask about the dungeon, but a hand on the shoulder from Adam moved his priorities with a vengeance. He had catching up to do with both Dale and his fallen disciple, now returned in celestial flesh.

Hans appeared happy so long as he could make someone else's life more difficult, and Rose was already doing her due diligence in dragging him off by the ear. Dale, on the other hand, was a bundle of joy to behold. He was bouncing around like a puppy, happy to be surrounded by new people he could talk to. He did shoot a hopeful glance at his old mentor for a last minute tag-along, but Artorian just shook his head and winked. "Not this time, Dale. See to your farm, and your people."

Dale relented with a sigh, determined his turn with Cal would come.

Ammy wrapped her arm around Artorian's neck, pleased as she watched Zephyr touch down. "Small correction from before, Sunny. I keep hearing you referred to as headmaster? It's *Administrator*. Cal says so."

The ears of the people leaving through portals twitched again, but shoved their feelings away. Envy was pain at the good fortune of others, and they would not be the cause of any problems today. Artorian waved the last people away from his position against the gunwale before Soni moved through his last portal, closing it once on the other side.

Artorian then leaned on his elbows, addressing Ammy without turning his head. "That was very heavy-handed of you, dear."

Amaterasu grinned ear to ear as she laid on the gunwale next to him, rebuking the call of gravity. Her tone on the other hand, was deadly serious. "Sugar, to you, your position and place holds little value. You would be everyone's personal, loving grandfather if given a choice. The rest of us, however, need to make sure work gets done at pace, and for that, you need a social-pressure foot to put down. Use the weight that comes with the Administrator title. I heard you had some difficulty when Amber was decanted? I expect this to come up more than once. So just remember this interaction, alright, dearest? If you cannot, or choose not to, drop the hammer when it must fall, then get out of Ember's way. If you won't do it, then *I* will."

Artorian quietly nodded when the Incarnate pecked a kiss on his forehead, then floated away to go open the cabin door. With the old man distracted, he did not see Grimaldus, Tychus, and Astrea sneaking up on him until he was swallowed up in a surprise hug. He *oofed*, arms shooting up as he looked about to see smiling faces.

The trio beamed at him. "Surpriiiise!"

Artorian swept them all up, squeezing them to push his mind away from the other things. Perhaps slightly too hard as the attempt to crush-hug the old man turned into a sprawl-fest to free themselves from the very crush that the trio had wished to inflict. "You precious darlings. Oh, good news! I should be able to allot the Essence channels now that I've got my legs! Three Infernal cherries with the channels on top! Right?"

The trio looked at each other, then back at their grandfather as he released them. Ty pressed his hands to his knees, while Grimaldus saw serious spots and needed the gunwale for support, so Astrea did the talking. "You weren't told?"

He hurriedly scanned them over before releasing the heaviest exhale of relief. "Sweet mercy and kitchen crackers. Don't you scare me like that! I thought there was a problem, not that the three of you already acquired the channels all by yourselves!"

The trio pruned their lips, apparently not having thought of that in their rush to be pleasant. Astrea cringed out a half-smile, trying to lighten up the situation. "Surprise?"

"You three will be the death of me." Artorian looked at her and joked, then slapped his hand over his eyes. When his hand dropped, so did the worried mood he'd been pointlessly holding on to. "I jest. Congratulations! I'm proud of you. Now, if you're done trying to give me a heart attack, walk me to the fancy loungers. I want to hear every detail of how you accomplished this!"

The grandfather's warmth put the pep right back into their step, Tychus grinning as he wrapped his arm about the old man. Strange, was Ty significantly bigger all of a sudden? Tychus, *definitely* larger than before, eagerly began the story. "So there we were at the base of Mayev's Spire. *Minding our own business!*"

CHAPTER THIRTY-FIVE

"Ty! Do I hear you telling *lies?*" The door leading into the yacht burst open, occupied by a thin, mousy girl as Alexandria had heard her larger brother make a claim, disbelieved him on principle, and stormed up from her cabin to dress the big man down. "Momma Halcyon is going to wring you like a towel when she hears about this!"

"Nononono!" Tychus abandoned his story, rushing through the open door when Alexandria vanished below deck. A place that already sounded rowdy, filled with myriads of voices. Everyone could hear the large man hurry after her, his voice one of panic. "Alexandria, it was a joke!"

Astrea and Grim wasted no time in chasing after their brother, if only for the sake of damage control. Grim yelled over his shoulder. "We'll come find you later!"

Artorian enjoyed a singular 'ha' before Decorum prowled through the same door to end up on the deck. He politely closed the door the others had zipped through behind him, then smiled as he leaned on his gnarled walking stick. Finding a friendly face, he sauntered up to Artorian to provide a firm handshake. The human liger's voice was as stately as ever. "How pleasant to catch you on this boat, brother!"

"Indeed!" Artorian fondly replied, his eyes snapping with an unspoken question to Ammy. "I'm sure this is all very off the cuff, not at all planned."

"Not at all!" She lied, winking back at Artorian before motioning behind him.

He turned to peek, where very… effortful attempts were being made by Tyrian to squeeze through one of the now-open hatches. Brianna and Chandra appeared to be doing their darndest to perform this completely silently and pull her hips through, in cahoots to catch the old man off guard.

Artorian suddenly knew what Richard had felt like. There was a bet at play here! He cleared his throat at them, making them all look at him like deer caught in a sudden light. "*Ladies.*"

Their stunned silence lasted a touch too long for his liking, so Artorian decided to call the jig what it was and settled into his luxury lounge chair. Several people around him were already doing the same, except that they all seemed to be ignoring a particular seat. One positioned too close and too convenient to not have been filled already. He skipped the procession and went right to the pertinent question. "Alright, Cal. I see my people are decanted. Do I need to tune my ears in order to guess all that noise was children running amok below deck, or are you just going to fess up?"

Cal appeared with a thunderous expression in the open lounge chair. His sudden arrival was more of an invisibility effect being dropped, rather than him having been elsewhere. Artorian's guess had been on the nose. "You weren't even looking at me! Your eyes weren't even tuned! How did you know I was here?"

"Hmmm?" Artorian hummed. "How could I have known, Cal? It's not like everyone was trying to stay hidden. Plus, Alexandria should still be on my wall, and this little routine is suspect. So, what's the bet, and who won?"

Groans went around the yacht as a pipe opened, Zephyr hooting with laughter as she took off properly and sailed into the cloud layer. Given Cal made a lemon-face, Ammy was laughing, and nobody in the vicinity was claiming any kind of victory, Artorian scrolled through his options and blabbed an answer. "Alexandria then."

Grumbles from the losing parties confirmed he was correct, but sadly that didn't tell him what the bet was. Ah well. Artorian got comfy as he watched everyone settle in around him now that the ruse was foiled. "Alexandria it is. So what is the commotion about, and how are so many people fitting on Zephyr? I could have sworn that she..."

The sudden cessation of noise from the lower decks cut his words off. The detail bothered him so much that now it was time to cycle his vision and see. Using enhanced sight to peer through solid matter, his eyes widened when they landed on a fully functional, stable, dedicated portal room. "You put a gate *in* the yacht?! That can't be good for Zephyr."

"I'm perfectly fine." A nearby pipe sounded offended at the notion. "I am a *fancy* lady. No nice dresses? Fine, I will have a nice portal instead. See if you can delegate me to small background tasks now! Ha!"

Artorian surmised he'd missed some recent history, but he'd pry the details out of people soon enough. "I see. Well, so long as you're alright..."

Cal cleared his throat, getting everyone's attention. "So we ran into a snag, and this was the cleanest solution."

Chandra waved before Cal could finish. "Before you get into it, we only snuck in to try to win the prizes. We're going to head out, alright?"

Cal, still using the body of Kota the scholar, nodded in understanding. "Thanks for playing. Unfortunately there's no consolation prize. The pagoda of Mayev's Spire goes to Alexandria's new library. I'll let people know the game for the next segment once I think of something."

Brianna smirked wide. "Don't let Chandra fool you, she came to make sure our Administrator was in good shape. The new legs are holding him up well, even if they make me think they belong to a predator. Tyrian here is the one who thought it was all good fun and games."

"I love good fun and games!" Tyrian blurted out, excited to be included. "I performed marvelously in the Olympics! Even if the idea of the place sours me. They can meet me in the coliseum if they want to complain about my defection. That's what they get for harassing my birdy Pim."

She turned to the ship's bow, then aggressively shook her fist at a mountain in the distance. "Hands, maws, and claws off my birds!"

The three of them waved goodbye after Cal had a good laugh, then took the hatch shortcut to the portal room, where the ladies were back at the farmstead before anyone realized they'd been gone. With gates up and running, travel suddenly became convenient! Zephyr's mention about feeling useful also now struck a chord in Artorian's head, as there was much less use to an airship with those functional and prolific. The S.A.S. should be happy? He'd find out later.

That thought made his nose tingle, attention turning to Decorum. "Gomez, my boy, what brought you?"

The stately figure twirled his walking stick, then pointed the butt end at Cal. "Our most gracious host has allowed me to help with some of the more bothersome paperwork and minutiae. Which I believe is the topic he wished to bring to your attention. I have been coping with being apart from my most darling Tisha by burying myself in piles of work. Cal conspired with Zephyr, and now I have an office here. By 'here,' I do mean one of the rooms on the vessel. *I* may not need to be anywhere in particular, but some key documents do. Not everything can be handled through the World Wide Wisp Webway. Not with the Pylons being put to pasture. I would provide the acronym, but four Ws is just so hard to say."

That got a chuckle out of Cal, who waffled his hand. "I'm still trying to come up with an acronym for Wisps. For funsies, y'know? Nothing in the pipeline yet, but I bet I'm going to drink from an information-heavy well one day, and like a blip of light, it will come to me."

Artorian turned his head when Alexandria stormed back onto the deck, marching in a straight line right towards him before swallowing the old man up in a squeeze. Her tone was flat and to the point. "I forgot the hug. Hug attained. Back to biting the Troublesome Trio's ears off."

Artorian laughed when she power-walked away at the same pace she'd arrived. She'd likely randomly thought of that in the middle of making Ty's life difficult, turned on a copper, and was now getting right back to it. The grandfather was so looking forward to the gossip. "I want to say 'poor Tychus,' but if they are causing trouble and already have both Alexandria and Halcyon chasing them down, I'm convinced it was all well-deserved."

He shifted his vision, checking on people's Essence channels. "Looks like my 'Troublesome Trio' has attained a natural version of Weak-quality Infernal channels. Interesting how their other channels were not swallowed up. Did you have a hand in that, Cal?"

The dungeon nodded proudly, pleased as punch to get the recognition. "I did! I sprinkled in a bit of Zelia's old dungeon effect through my entire Soul Space. Not enough for the mental push, but *juuuust* enough to make the otherwise annoying little side effects miss the mark. I want to cater my Soul Space to Mages and up? Non-Mages are... I understand I have them, but in the grand scope of tasks and problems that I'm looking at, anyone not at a Mage-rank at minimum is just not going to be useful. Perhaps that's not fair, but that's the reality I need to contend with."

Artorian squinted one eye shut. "Is that why Mages have been at an easy equilibrium, while the non-Mages are shooting up in rank with seemingly endless fonts of Essence at their disposal?"

Cal confirmed his assumption. "Precisely! I don't want to dictate anyone's life, nor life-path, but I am most certainly going to make the ones I need convenient to attain. If people choose not to? Very well. I will respect that choice, and we will have some precious non-cultivators to love and take care of. Which is part of the snag I mentioned earlier."

Artorian leaned towards the man, indicating Cal had his attention. Cal saw this as an open invitation to keep speaking. "First. My apologies for barely being able to wait any time at all before we had to decant the people in your Cores. All the children, including Alhambra and Wo'ah, were below deck earlier. Your little guess was on the nose, as they tend to be. They have used the gate to move to the cleared floors of Mayev's Spire. To clarify, Mayev's Spire is the name of the overall mountain, and is divided into three sections. The base is a massive pagoda, an up-sized version of the structure the Dwarves made that ended up getting the Mayev's Spire name in the first place. The middle is the actual Skyspear mountain as you remember it—still shaped like a menhir, stairs and all—while on the top we have the old Skyspear Academy."

The dungeon made one of his extra-detailed three-dimensional Essence models appear to show what he meant. Artorian had missed these! The diorama's detail was exquisite. "Your Chosen weren't happy with merely re-creating the original designs over and over. Once they got to reconciling the differences between the version before the Skyspear blew up, and the version from when it had become the Spire, they began taking creative liberties and merged the two instances together."

Artorian pointed at the base of the spire, motioning at hexagonal shapes and arches dug into the rock. "Was that building carved straight out of the base, then? In the old world, that pagoda was a replacement for both the Skyspear and the Academy. Now it looks like the base of the mountain *is* the pagoda."

His face became grim. "I do recall that the whole mountain needed to go in order to address an oath-problem. That's not a memory that I'm going to forget."

Cal understood well, his face full of empathy. "Which is how we lost Ephira in the first place. Dawn—I mean, Amaterasu, explained the story to the Incarnate table in detail. I'm up and up on the timeline."

The lady in question confirmed with an upside-down thumbs-up as she was floating around the sails, her attention on mending one of the seams.

Artorian definitely appreciated that, then prodded himself in the chest. "To work then. I'm touched you want to keep me as an Administrator. What do you actually need me to do? I can give you a brief rundown of my prior plans, if helpful."

Cal shifted in his seat. "Please do."

With that allowance, Artorian ran down the full task lists he had allotted to Leftie and Rightie. A filing system both Decorum and Cal found highly amusing for how basic it was.

"If Alexandria ever gets wind that you kept it so simple, she will throw an entire filing cabinet at you." Gomez chuffed pleasantly. "I tried filing my own way, and she took one glance at the attempt before the steam came pouring out of her ears. I now use a system that has an entire page of organizational details on it before ever getting to the material, and may Cal help you if that front page isn't completely filled out."

"I will not." The dungeon giggled in retort. Cal then dissolved his Spire diorama, scooting one leg over the other. "To be serious for a moment. I think it's amicable and sweet that you want to make yourself available for people. I have nothing against this, but would like to ask that the *booking project* gets top priority. I had to let Odin back into the world right before we began this lovely jest, and the game was my attempt at a distraction from it. If we could get those Accords done as soon as porrible… sorry, *possible*. Not used to this tongue. Then—"

Cal had more to say, but he had lost everyone's attention with the flub. They were too busy laughing, and the dungeon needed to lean forward and hold his own forehead. They were never going to let this go.

CHAPTER THIRTY-SIX

"I will say, my office *does* come with a massive mahogany desk. Buried in books and scrolls, but it's there." Gomez grinned, having liked that the random detail had prominence in Artorian's leftie-list. "Would you like to come see it? The texture is purrrrfect."

Laughter once again broke out as Cal covered his eyes with both his hands. "What have I done? This is worse than Pag's 'womewhat.' Nobody is letting him live *that* down either!"

Artorian got up from his chair, patting Scholar D. Kota on the shoulder. "All will be well, son. It's just a friendly little jab. I will go look at Decorum's spot. Can I assume that you want me to do the same thing he is doing? One does not need an Administrator when there is nothing to administrate, after all. Ferried by a literal boat, this time!"

That dumb little mention did put a smile on Cal's face, who dropped his hands to slowly sit up straight. "That is correct. There's an empty cabin right across from Decorum's. Both are in the hallway that connects to the portal room. I thought that if I needed people to gate in and out quickly, doing the same with information when more and more Pylons are guaranteed to go down would be prudent."

Artorian hummed with a nod. "Sounds like Alexandria's filing system isn't going to see much push back?"

Cal scoffed. "It is embarrassing just how much better her filing system is than that of the Wisps or Gnomes. Tim took one look at it and walked right up to her, asking if she was at all interested in being an **Order** Mage. He wants to sponsor her, and that was before she showed Tim some of her more 'detailed' ledgers. They are currently *still* hashing out some maddeningly complicated mess in one of Eternium's workshops. Last time I looked at it, they hadn't gotten past section one, distracted by a debate on mono-spaced font, and 'funny business with the margins.' I am *so glad* that I didn't go to **Order**."

The dungeon then made a 'please go ahead' motion before laying back in his deck chair. The man looked like he needed a break, his words heavy with breath. "I've been going non-stop since my rank-up. Sunny, the short of it is that our high-tech *Pylon* ways are going to become low-tech *paper* ways for a while, and I need you to make sure nothing that isn't supposed to catch on fire actually catches on fire. In an emergency, blame Pag."

He rubbed a hand over his face. "For now... Titania is waiting for you in that empty room, she just arrived. All I need from you is to get the Accords done. Get them done *now*. Get whatever paper-planning work you need, pull in every able body you require, and get *rid* of these demons. The situation is becoming more precarious and while, yes, we will still have to deal with them later, it is para-mount that we take them off our plate *now*. I—"

Artorian mightily squeezed Cal's shoulder. "Son? Rest. I've got this handled. Administrator Artorian has understood the assign-ment. The problem will be gone by the end of this volume. Then we'll tackle the Pylons going down. Then, when I'm not needed, I will be in the Skyspear, teaching. You find me if you need me. You delegate the Wisps to send my work to my office. You nap. Or I put time aside to chase you with my sleep Aura."

The grandfather winked, then softly tapped the spot he'd squeezed. He'd already known most of this thanks to Vanilla, and mentally had the time to prepare. Now the task was upon him, and his eyes gleamed with anticipation. "Gomez? Lead the way, please. I have *diplomacy* to plan."

Something about the way his brother said it made Gomez lean away, his own squinted eyes glinting until the metaphorical lamp caught fire above his head, only to promptly and violently be replaced by a lit Nixie Tube when his mind caught up to the full meaning of that implication. "Oh. *Oh.* Of course, brother! Right this way."

With the pair of stately old men shuffling into the bowels of the ship to appreciate some fine mahogany, Ammy touched her toes down onto the deck, sitting down at the foot of Cal's seat. "Told you it would all work out fine. He wasn't going to leave you hanging, and he's clearly forgotten that he was supposed to be mad at you. Besides, I'm certain to be called in shortly for this 'diplomacy.'"

"About that." Cal exhaled. "What does he mean? A few people seem to have caught on to some kind of secondary plot I can't seem to suss out."

The Incarnate considered it, then smiled broadly. "Consider it a *surprise.* Those things you're so very short on. If you want a teaser, Sunny is likely to, with bundled scrolls falling out of his pockets, stride right up to Olympus and request a parlay. Since Odin's pride feels so stepped on that not having a chance to turn Artorian into mash with words would be an insult of a missed opportunity, he will be let in. With his... friends. Then there will probably be a long debate. Strong words. Many nights of difficult deliberation. You know how diplomacy goes! Lots of disagreements in a confined space."

Cal didn't understand. "None of that sounds fun or like a surprise."

Ammy's grin didn't let up. "Well... since we're referring to these little jaunts as 'volumes' now, the brighter minds will have sussed out that a theme has been missing in this one. A theme that will not be allowed to remain silent until the fat lady sings. You'll see!"

Cal gave up, his arms flopping. "I'll see, then. Does this make it our cue to skedaddle back to the moon? Is Tot back from Eternia yet?"

"Yes to the first, no to the second." The Incarnate extended a hand. Cal's version of spatial movement was faster. "We're all wrapped up here, and will only get in the way. As to Tatum, no. Eternia is in a very bad spot, and he's doing what he can to make the in-roads for Sunny and I to pile-drive in there and wrap up the loose ends. We need to stabilize the local problems before we can do any of that, so don't fuss about Eternia. We have people on it."

Cal stared at the sky for a short moment, then slap-grabbed

her hand in agreement, picking himself up both physically and mentally. "You're right. Let's go. We've got chains to rattle."

With a pop, they were gone.

Down in Zephyr's hold, or the remodeled space now acting as an empty room that would soon become an office, Gomez, Artorian, and Titania paced to get a feel for the space. Scurrying back and forth between Decorum's overstuffed version, and Sunny's vacant one, the old man was already seeing improvements. "Bookcases would be a good start. Cover every wall, and if we can make my ceiling a skylight, that would be good for mental health. I don't need a dark roof over my head and I can make my own light if there's no sun out."

Titania scribbled it down.

Since the entire room was completely empty for now, Artorian filled it by letting his soul item flop out, puff up, and stuff the entire room. "I have improved the space."

"So soft! That's mine now," Zephyr said as the door. "You dropped it. I found it. Mine."

"What? No! That's not how this works," Artorian swiftly rebuked. "Mine!"

"No, mine!" Zephyr disagreed.

Artorian stared at the door like it was a misbehaving toddler. He glanced at his pillow, then back at the door, and finally back at his pillow before the gears in his head reached a favorable conclusion. "Try to take it."

"I already have!" Zephyr proudly responded, a sudden gasp tearing from the hallway when the entire pillow completely vanished from the room. "No! My pirro!"

The way of speech made everyone remember Cal's recent flub and bend over with laughter. Much to Titania's incredible confusion as she hadn't gotten the memo yet. When Artorian recovered, he left the vacant room and motioned at Decorum's fancy chair in the other. "May I?"

"Please, feel free!" Gomez's stance at the door indicated he would love to burn the sight of his brother finding a home in that chair deep into his memory. There was a pride and pleasure to seeing one's patriarch-equivalent find comfort and approval in your place of residence. Titania appeared to share the thought, waiting patiently for the same sight.

The puffy leather chair creaked when Artorian sat, its fatty cushions deflating to allow the indent of his weight. A pleasantness overtook the old man before he pulled the chair in, scooting it closer to the mahogany desk so liberally covered in all sorts of parchment, scrolls, vellum, ink, and feathers. With fondness and yearning for the simpler life, a quill found its way into his hands. Dipping the silvered nib, he unfurled a piece of vellum unmarred by words, then touched the tip against the empty canvas.

The movements flowed like wind and water, Artorian's wrist dancing across the spread like a broken-hearted scribe having found a long-lost love. On the second line of the page, the quill no longer scratched across the empty canvas meant for words. Instead, each movement gained the sound of fresh earth being tilled.

The unmatched sharp stroke became a spade that cut through topsoil, releasing the scent of fertile ground, and that very smell began to permeate the small office. Mixed with notes of heavy sunshine, the tang of freshly cut green grass, and the rustling of wind as the feather of the quill breezed through open air.

Both Decorum and Titania stood mesmerized as the tiny office, confining walls and all, faded into the background of imagination. All of Artorian, the desk, and his many myriads of paper adopted tones of sepia-brown bark as a charcoal and currant gazebo formed around him.

Welcoming browns that interspersed with grays overtook Artorian's color scheme as the scribe worked on his tiny task in the wealth of a rapidly expanding worldly forest; the gazebo surrounded by great birches, trunks of mighty mahogany, and sprouts of rosewood. With a passing gust of wind, all the trees tinted with fall-red leaves that flourished vibrantly the closer to him they were.

In the painting that was his work, Artorian became surrounded by oaks so oversized that they held up entire mountains, the sea of canopies in the distance turning an equal shade of healthy red. On the source that he worked, a single silver sprout with a matching single silver leaf grew from the very vellum that the ancient scholar turned into art.

All that was missing was music as the minutes ticked by.

"Done." When Artorian spoke and the quill left the manuscript, colors seeped back into normality. The walls of reality replaced visions of the wood, and the sepia filtered away to wherever it had come from.

"What did you write?" Decorum's voice was a near whisper.

Artorian needed to pause and process the question, looking over his own work as if he did not know himself. When his eyes flicked across the words, his expression bloomed into a spring smile. "An ode to an old leaf."

Placing the quill back, he inhaled firm, then exhaled deeply. "I'm ready to begin. I have found a path through the foliage."

Before picking it up again, a corner of a scroll caught his eye. Reaching for it, Gomez suddenly took a step forward as if in response, his hand outstretched. "Wait."

The Administrator did so, his eyes looking at his brother as if they gazed over the rim of square glasses. "Is it private, brother?"

Gomez chuffed, walking up to the side of the desk he usually did not occupy. Plucking that very scroll free, he undid the golden clasp and rolled it open on the desk while Artorian neatly filed away his prior work. "Not at all, brother. I want to present it, rather than it being a find."

When the scroll unfurled and he saw the contents, Artorian slapped himself on the forehead. "I didn't think of that at all. That was an option this entire time!"

Gomez barked with laughter, needing to sit down in the chair opposite to the old man while Titania zipped up for an explanation. She looked at the diagrams on the scroll, but they just looked like... geometric animal parts? Her words were a touch crass, like a caretaker who was already busy and just got slighted by exclusion. "Can someone explain this to me?"

Artorian and Gomez shared a look, the burden falling on the old man. He leaned his elbows on the desk, and rested his chin on his hands. "So, before the Eternia alpha test, the one where you went with me? Cal was conducting trials on the system both in his own Soul Space and in Eternium. Terribly messy. During this time was when one of my Tribulations snapped me into the epiphany that I had the means to bring Decorum here, into the world of wonder. He has direct ancient history with me, and the short version is that I did wrong by him when I was young. After I used some... very high access Pylons, Decorum lived once more, and I was kept in a trapped state for a while. You know how that goes."

Titania mocked an exhale in Wisp format by expelling light from an invisible nose. "I know. Get to the point."

Artorian nodded. "When I finally had time with Decorum, a lot of subjective time had passed. Instead of me teaching him, he lived a full life, and was the one to teach me. Which brings us to *this* scroll."

Gomez spoke since Titania gave him a stern eye. "I always worried that my brother would be disappointed with the life I had chosen to lead, because all I knew was that he wanted me to run wild, and run free. A happy, blissful existence. I instead found my drives elsewhere, such as statesmanship. To ensure I did right by him, I gave him the full breadth of my memories using Wood Elven transfer tricks. For the first few hundred or so years I was alive, I experienced life as a Liger. Wild and free. How I moved. How I ate. How I napped. How I stretched. All feelings, sensation, and knowledge that makes the perfect foundation to *be* a Liger."

He motioned back to Artorian, who picked up the thread as panels of light were already forming around him. He walked around the desk, and winked at his caretaker. "A Liger that can be formed by purely *external* means. A trick that does not strain the inside of a Mage's body with the patterns of techniques, because this is no internal trick. This? This is Aura, and Presence."

Rather than falling to all fours, Artorian was sucked upwards into the chest cavity of a solid-light construct that resembled a Morovian hunter, his form all teeth, fang, claw, and prowess as the oversized cat filled most of the empty space in the room. Titania and Decorum backed out just so they wouldn't be flattened when the massive Liger of light stretched out. From within, Artorian's voice spoke pleasantly, even if it was the mouth of the beast that moved. "A method of movement, free from metal legs."

Titania released a slow, understanding **oooooh** when her copper dropped, and it all made sense. He could have used this right from the start of him waking up, if only he'd thought of it.

The nose of the luminous beast touched the top of Decorum's head, releasing a fatherly rowl while providing the cat-like affection of a nuzzle. Gomez clearly appreciated it. The motion completed, Artorian pulled the hundreds of panels back into himself, landing cleanly on his metal feet with a **ting**. The old man was mighty proud, his hands on his hips as he stretched left and right. "Well done, Gomez. Thank you."

The stately man shot him a massive smile, leaning on his walking stick in satisfaction. "Of course, brother! We are in this together. What next?"

Artorian clapped his hands together, tuning back to the desk. "For diplomacy, I will have to speak softly. Therefore, I'm going to need... a *big* stick."

CHAPTER THIRTY-SEVEN

One week of paper-fueled toil and turmoil later, Artorian stood at the border of Olympus. The gateway and entry point of the border was located at the base of a canyon that looked to resemble 'the dark places' where adult lions told their children never to venture.

His pockets were full of scrolls, vellum, spare quills, and more. While over his shoulder—attached by a boat's mooring rope—he was hoisting an entire crystal-glass gourd worth of ink. The black liquid could be seen sloshing inside, the fluted tip stopped by a massive cork. In his other hand, Artorian squeezed a Silverwood Bo-staff. The very same one he'd made last time with Purple Heartwood's instant Bo technique. Attached to the top were some rounded baobab fruits, ready for eating.

Scilla had found it in the hands of a baboon named Rafiki, and upon receiving it, the baboon had dubbed the weapon with its new name: 'The Last Straw.' Something Artorian was certain to reach, given the weight of the task he was about to wrestle into the mud like an ornery swine. Except that, much like philosophers arguing, the swine liked it.

Behind the Administrator dressed in scribe's regalia stood a whole host of mighty individuals. Cal had not been joking when he said he'd give Artorian priority.

Divided in battalions based on the difference in legion, a veritable army had been fielded. An A-rank seven Artorian served as the tip of the commanding triangle. At his left hand, Amaterasu the double-S ranker hovered menacingly. At his right hand, Admiral Halcyon stood immovable as a mountain as an A-rank six. Directly behind him in a line; an A-rank five Father Richard, A-rank four Gomez, and A-rank three Surtur, were already itching for parlay to break down.

Behind them stood the war host.

A sign and symbol of strength that even Olympians could wrap their heads around.

Leading the first armor-division, currently a brigade of Mage-ranked Bashers, stood Colonel Raile. Humanized as a B-rank four Granite Dwarf with a grudge against all warhammers, Raile was leading a force three-thousand strong, sporting a thick lump of wood that he kept between his gnashers and stuck out the side of his mouth, the end stoked with internal fire. Raile had forgone the offered military outfit in favor of thick granite armor with overlapping stone-plating. The armor plating covered his entire being, floppy ears to toe-claws. The only reason anyone could tell where his face was at a glance was thanks to the smoking stick of wood.

Raile insisted on calling it his 'cigar,' to the complaints of every single member of the five-hundred medical-oriented Glitterflits in his ranks. His personal guard composed of the Hops-Ecutioners only smirked in response, joking about how Raile's favorite command to give was 'ramming speed.'

Next to the Basher Brigade stood Major Snowball, B-rank six, at parade rest. Snowball had chosen to properly wear the military uniform that matched a wintered pattern, leading a cohort of four-hundred and eighty elemental Mage-ranked cats, complete with a special elite squad of all-Affinity C'towl, fondly referred to as the A-team. This brought the total feline unit strength up to a clean and even five-hundred.

Major Snowball was as cold and calculating as his whiskers were sharp and clean. A clean separation for Colonel Raile's propensity to smash both the heads of his troops, and his own, nose-first into the fray. Snowball preferred to strike unseen from a bank of fog, or steam.

Behind the Basher Brigade, Major General Manny the Manticore stood at the head of a veritable legion of freshly Mage-ranked goblins. The numbers easily delved into the twenty-five thousand mark. His legions sub-divided with the various heads of goblins who'd proven their leadership qualities. Manny had opted for the serious outfit option, which he proudly boasted about and wore due to the piece being personally tailored by Zelia in the early days.

That comprised the troops that could be seen out in the open, but not all of them. Every commander had a sneaky little 'surprise' stashed away. Raile's surprise hid under a rock. Or to be more specific, lurked in a nearby marsh. Led by a Dwarven Sergeant named McShane, who had a bit of an alchemist streak in him as he'd become famous for feeding his boys nutrient mixes called 'protein shakes.'

McShane had also developed a highly nutritious new snack for a different military branch called a 'crayon.' The new favorite treat of many a Dwarf. They even came in a variety of colors!

McShane led a squad of men known so far only as 'Dwarven Marines,' otherwise operating out of a dingy hole in the ground called Tun's Tavern, which wanted little to do with the crafting madness still ongoing in the Nidavellir capital. McShane and his boys had instead taken it upon themselves to quietly remove threats to the patriarchs' society-building endeavors. For now, he and his boys—along with a second squad led by Corporal Kellen Shadowbeard—lurked in the muck, ready to pounce at an opportune moment. None would see or hear them coming until the combat knives unsheathed from the holsters.

Before Administrator Artorian, a field of demon-possessed Olympians glowered and glared at him, each with their tiny little moustaches that bristled when his gaze landed on them.

"You know why I'm here." Artorian was cold and calculated. "Make a path. He's waiting for me, in his gilded palace on that little mountain of his. I've come to parlay."

Several demons were formed as blobs of tar, sitting on the shoulders of their hosts like little imps of mischief. Several, Artorian even recognized. Pencil, from Midgard. Hanekawa, from Muspelheim. Moo, from Vanaheim. He knew it was Mu, with a 'u,' but Mu was *also* the name of a friendly dungeon Core, so he was going to make the distinction. Lastly, Robar, from Svartalfheim. That one he recognized from when they'd all ganged up on him in space, before he'd unloaded on them with the Diffusion Zone Attack.

Best keep that one in the pocket, it was a tad costly.

Artorian also recognized that they all lacked the special protection Ghreziz must have provided. The demons seemed to be of the firm opinion, however, that the old man wasn't going to be using his shiny fields and sunny Auras. He did show up without it deployed, after all. They seemed to have an understanding of the stakes, and lack of permanence in mortality. A game they were far more skilled at than the pillow codger.

Artorian had thus decided to bring along some people who had *experience* in these matters. No demon was going to best the chrome-lined 'we-live, we-die, we-live-again' records compared to even a single one of Cal's goblins.

Pencil scoffed, the Olympian brute whose shoulders he was riding on lumbering forwards. Even if he was puny in comparison to Halcyon. Pencil spoke in his prior, small, mousy voice, loud enough to be heard by everyone nearby. "You again. I despise that it's all come to this."

He spat out the word 'parlay,' then turned with the brute hand-folding behind his back. "Follow then, if you dare. Zeus of Olympus waits to accept your inevitable, unconditional surrender. Miscreant."

Pencil said nothing about the visible troops, also far more interested in this all going to the squeakers and a massive brawl breaking out. Artorian broke ground and breached the border, his foot crossing the threshold to move forwards. His close cohort followed into step, the synchronized movements of the war host causing a vibration to tremor through the land with every footfall. A calculated move done on purpose to make life a little annoying for the demons living in the canyon, and especially the pompous ones at the top of the mountain.

"Not Odin of Azguardia? Or Asgard. Or As-go-go-gadget, or whatever silly name it is now?" Artorian instantly stoked the fire before they were ten steps into the journey. He then glanced at Ammy and nodded, who rubbed his bald head before shooting skywards. "When these events become recorded, you're only going to confuse readers and narrators if you change locations and people's names too much. Pick one. Stick with it. Or Traviticus of Baldree will shank you."

"The only thing getting shanked here is you and all the friends you brought once the surrender is made official, you bearded brat.

Sending your strongest powerhouse away was a *foolish* play." Pencil grinned, thinking he'd gained a sudden advantage with the S-ranker leaving. After all, Zeus had beat the ancient Administrator into the ground last time. Halted only by intervention of the dungeon itself. "Easy, 'Olympians' is correct. We are composed of the mightiest warriors from every race before Moonfall! Every Mage who saw reason has joined our ranks. True-seers of Asgard. Amazon defectors. Wise High Elves. The Guild's finest. Now willingly merged with my abyssal kin, to be even more superior over you than they already were!"

The demon forces moved alongside the war host, some flanking to trail and pincer the Administrator's forces in from behind. Artorian did not appear bothered. He merely crossed a line off from his checklist. "Is that so? Thank you for putting my worries at ease, Pencil. Here I was worried you had more."

Pencil the imp turned on the brute's shoulder while the big Olympian kept walking. "Don't. You. Dare. Insult me like that. Or attempt to wiggle your little schemes into my mind to get information out. You get nothing, pillow man. Nothing!"

"I dared. I did. You good little imp, you!" Artorian gave him a celestial smile. From his pocket, he conjured an Iridium tonfa. "You've also already failed, but that's no different than last time. Maybe we'll practice playing catch some more after all the paperwork is done? You were such a good sport about it."

Pencil fumed. The Imp's eyes darted from Moo to Hanekawa, but they were dead set on keeping their flanking positions. "Fine! Bura, A-gust-ist. Lead the war criminal to the esteemed one. I refuse to be around this silver-tongued dervish any longer."

Pencil retreated into his host, which promptly grew massive bat-like wings before vertically removing him from the situation.

Artorian sweetly hollered after him. "Toodle-oo! Don't forget to write!"

Bura and A-gust-ist both fully subsumed their hosts, coating them entirely in black tar before the more demonic features could properly manifest. 'Consumed' was how most of the newcomers saw it, but no, the Mages were still present within the new forms. Bura was shorter and leaner than most of the demon forms Artorian had encountered. Pale in shade, the albino gargoyle sported some interesting owl-like features, but was otherwise made of stone.

A-gust-ist was the head-turner of the two. That the eyes of this one glowed as balls of light was small chickens compared to the entire body being a humanoid-shaped greenish-gray mist. Outstanding features were the large baker-like gloves for hands, and that Artorian could see through the demon without any special sight tricks.

"You're being too kind to them." Richard's tone was flat and unamused when Artorian didn't do or say anything to make their demon lives more difficult. His hands were crackling with so much energy that Richard needed to pocket them. The urge to smite was powerful. "We could be doing far more—"

"Patience, my like-minded friend. Patience." Artorian said with more breath than words. "First, parlay. Then, diplomacy."

The Father grumbled, momentarily calmed by a hand on his upper arm by Decorum the stately. The disguised Liger winked, far too amused with the plan in progress to want to muck it up. Richard's words were just more complaints. "Easy for you to keep calm. Your part happens early. I have to wait 'til the end."

Gomez flashed his teeth, then waggled his eyebrows. His voice was rather amused when he caught Artorian's innocent hand-motion from the corner of his eye. "My time is now, in fact! Bon voyage!"

Richard ground his teeth together as the stately man bounded out from the formation, fist-bumped Snowball like the ancient friends they were, and twisted into a frankly oversized beast mid-leap. As planned, a significant part of the right flank demons chased him down when Gomez zipped away. Richard kept his face tight in a faux-grimace, doing his abyss-best not to let a single hint of satisfaction peek through his annoyed facade.

The Father then mumbled under his breath when the demons laughed at them for splitting up their forces and weakening their war host. "All according to keikaku."

CHAPTER THIRTY-EIGHT

During the entire circular trip up Mount Olympus, it was difficult not to notice demons routing them solely through the 'nice' parts of their society. Extra walls had even been erected purely in an attempt to block vision to some slums, and how poorly the place was kept together.

It failed, of course, but the attempt was noted.

The Olympians, for the most part, appeared to be in agreement with their demon... other halves... when it came to most topics, though not everything. One such topic was whether to chase, or to not chase all the members and sections of troops that kept breaking off from the line doing the climb.

Amaterasu had gone straight up, but no demons wanted to follow that one skywards. The rest of the war host had split up and moved to the cardinal directions, and that was of greater demon debate. Raile and his troops went south, Snowball and his cats north, Manny and the goblin division east, while Gomez and Surtur both ended up with Halcyon's secret troops in the west.

McShane and Kellen Shadowbeard were thus offered plenty of distraction to move around the province's perimeter unabated. Their mission was the truly important one. Everyone else served as a distraction. Like Hans had said, people tend to not see what they're not looking for, and the Dwarven Marines were camouflaged with more than just some reeds and peonies.

Moving unseen, like dark objects in the shade, McShane and Shadowbeard fulfilled their mission. They stopped at roughly the planned points after having split up, then pulled out their synchronized compasses. Where the distractions teams stopped in cardinal directions, the Marines worked in the ordinal ones.

McShane, voice stereotypically deep for a dwarf that spat profanity at the same rate he downed his brandy, muttered into the compass while pressing in a button at the top. The object was hidden from view as it shone a soft blue. "Ordinal direction northeast, McShane in position."

Releasing the knob, the glow faded before a red light appeared on the side, a different dwarven voice mumbling through. "WD-Forty, ordinal direction southeast, in position."

The red light faded, a yellow one at the bottom replacing it. "Ordinal direction southwest, Shadowbeard in position."

When the yellow light faded, a green one clicked on. "Ordinal direction northwest, Rota in position. Stones are primed. Be advised, stragglers have picked up presents. Repeat, stragglers have picked up presents."

When the light faded, McShane replied with his blue button. "Copy that, Otter, demons have found explosive dice. To all squads, tavern's going to get rowdy. Set the stage."

With each squad where they were supposed to be, McShane released the blue knob, then pushed the orange button a single time rather than hold it, notifying the Administrator that this stage of the plan was complete, and the totem obelisks were being erected and primed.

In the waiting room of Zeus's fancy gilded box on a hill, Artorian's chest-pocket silently buzzed. He repressed a smile, then looked over his shoulder towards Halcyon with a meaningful expression. Halcyon caught the glint, nodded, and got up from the masterwork bench. She then pointed at some of the Olympians in the room and smirked out a challenge before leaping from the window and twisting into her Orca form. "Pathetic."

Several demons in the room couldn't brook that insult, and leaped out after her, quickly sprouting wings to chase the graceful golden wake patterns Halcyon left behind as she began to circle the mountaintop structure. The palatial castle really did look nigh-identical to what Odin had put up in Eternia's Asgard, down to the ostentatious pathways and tacky wall art.

This left Richard and Artorian alone in the waiting room, everyone else already in position as a mere handful of Olympians and demons remained with them. Richard was keeping his poise, but the spirit of the man was celestial-near vibrating through the wall in order to do so. His scrunched up face, on the other hand, was most amusing to the Administrator. Like the Father badly needed to solve some pent up constipation issues. Or perhaps that shade of red on the man's face was all his anger trying to stay in the bottle? Hard to tell.

"Enter!" Odin's voice boomed from the other side of the gilded doors that could have easily accommodated Halcyon.

The doors did not creak when parting. Instead, large French horns resounded from above as the gates swung wide. The interior of the room was revealed to be a… procession room? A throne room? Odin was sitting his laurel-resting under-dressed butt on a large carved-stone seat at the end, draped in soft fineries, but aside from a nice red carpet leading up to that throne, the rest of the room didn't match the aesthetic. The space looked like a church hall had been converted? Most of the seats were pews.

"I see you've implemented some changes." Artorian cozily shuffled inside, still flanked by demons on all sides as Richard's left eyebrow gained a case of the twitches. He motioned towards an empty table that appeared to have been set aside, with a particularly poor-quality chair behind it. Artorian took note of the Father's motion, and spoke as if to the enthroned one. "I take it that spot is for me? I'll go put my ink down then."

Odin was slumped sideways in his chair, like a ruler who'd had a long day of meeting over-and-self-indulgent petitioners. With his spare hand, he wrist-waved away the mention. "Just get to it. I want this parlay to be as short as possible. In fact, make it easy for me and provide me with your unconditional, total surrender."

"You offer me your unconditional, total surrender?" Artorian quipped. "Very well, I accept. I will lay out my terms."

From his throne, Zeus merely released a tremendous, tiresome groan. "Neither the names Loki nor Hephaestus do you justice, Administrator. I need something far worse for you. The amount of pain in my behind you have caused solely by yourself outstrips any meetings I have with my greedy subjects."

"I'll take that compliment." Artorian hummed, already spreading some fresh vellum on the table as he unpacked his goods, clearly ready and prepared for a very, very long discussion. He was even taking the spare time to lay out his quills with a defined exactness to the spacing. "Luckily for all parties, the parlay is short. I take it you're aware of the stakes?"

Odin growled. "Cal is awake. Has full control of all energy. Can snuff us out like a candle at a whim. That's the short summation. However, he must return us to the land of the living due to an oath of his own. We can't properly die, but we can't properly live either. We have his enmity, and worse, *you*, stuck on our case. I speak for both all Olympians and all Abyssalites, as I embody the most powerful components of both. Even without Ghreziz, I am joined with the next most powerful option. So don't get any funny ideas."

"Oh come now. I'm nothing but funny ideas." Artorian giggled. "It sounds like you understand the waves your boat is bobbing along in. My end of the parlay is simple. We want to build up, and the factions you've chosen to represent currently have no room to interfere, lest it all go to the squeakers. Again. So my offer on the table is this: agree to have every demon turned into a book, and be shelved in a library. When Cal's chains break, you will be freed and returned to your plane of origin. No more being stuck in an endless loop. Not *here*, anyway. You will get to live pseudo-lives as the books in Eternia once it's up and running."

Insulted laughter broke out from all demons in attendance. Odin kept placid on his throne, not moving an inch from his slump. The large man exhaled his words, his tone languished. "No. That offers no benefit to us whatsoever. That's merely imprisonment with flavor, leading to more imprisonment. I reject all of this, and counter-offer that any non-Olympian becomes a subject to us. We will grow the society and everyone else can step back and get out of our way."

"I see we're at an impasse." Artorian calmly placed a hand on his beard. "That likely ends parlay. Shall we move onto diplomacy, then?"

Odin quirked a bushy eyebrow, his tiny moustache doing a wiggle. "What's the difference?"

A vile smile crossed the scholar's features, his hand reaching to his chest pocket. He pretended to scratch, but in reality he clicked one of the knobs on the tucked-away compass. "Well, parlay is talking. Diplomacy is… *convincing*."

Zeus balked with laughter. "Convincing? With what leverage? None of us can die. We'll all just be brought back. You're not strong enough to detain us by force, and that pittance of a war host you brought doesn't have the clout to do more than provide amusement! A cheap tussle for my Olympians with a home-turf advantage. You have nothing. You cannot project force. You entered on the same stalemate we both began with ever since Cal awoke, and refused to interfere himself. Otherwise we would already have been squished."

"Cal has larger concerns." Artorian spoke, then looked at Richard as the lighting outside of Odin's castle took on a distinctly more red and orange sheen, the gradient mimicking a sunset. The Father flexed his hands in anticipation, leaning to the wall so he could peer out the window and observe the exact moment when the sheen touched ground, connecting to the ordinal points where flashes of light pinged their readiness.

A short buzz occurred inside both Artorian and Richard's chest pockets, allowing the Father to release a sigh of utmost relief. "Finally. *My turn.*"

Odin stared the Administrator down for an explanation, but he had stepped away from his table in order to bounce on his metallic tip-toes, tiny *tink-tink* noises sounding each time he touched the ground while he held some simple-looking silver wooden stick in his right hand. "Almost correct, old supervisor! You see, there is *one* factor of leverage. One that I am willing to apply and really shove my stick into, to mess with the wheel spokes."

Zeus chuckled in disbelief, one of his legs shuffling across the other as he adjusted his rich toga so it more properly put his pristine beefcake of a chest on view. "What might that be? You can't beat us in combat. You can't stop us from coming back even if you could. It would be an endless standoff with no victor. Our bodies are eternal."

Artorian grinned wide, his stance primed to release a serious Aura wave. "Correct. Your *bodies* are eternal. Unfortunately, your *spirit* is not. So tell me, old colleague now standing on the wrong side of the line, how many times can you *die* before you just can't take it anymore?"

Odin blinked. "Wait… *what?*"

"Richard, Hallelujah!" Artorian deployed his Sun Aura at full burst, signaling everyone who could see the mountaintop that it was time. He was the signal, and the signal had been served like a solar flare being set off in a confined space. Titania had referred to a signal so large and intense to not be along the lines of casting magic, but committing magic. Like war crimes. Except that, via technicality, all the factions were currently at peace.

Peace crimes? That didn't roll off the tongue as well. They'd find a term when it was time for the history books. Currently, it was time to make that history; the event commencing with one flash, one bang, and one unleashed Father Richard.

All demons in the room instantly screamed as the purifying field permeated both mass and matter, gradually erasing them right out of existence should they remain in the scribe's radiance for too long. With Ghreziz gone, hiding away inside of a Mage also no longer afforded any protections, slimming their options down to fleeing in a hurry or assaulting the offender.

Half fled the scene, but the other half charged at both the living lamp and equally unpleasant sensation that Richard was streaming out. Those who picked Artorian as their target never made it within five feet of the man, their particles consigned to oblivion. The Father packed on a personal Regeneration Aura, then howled in excitement, glad it was finally time for *diplomacy*. "Praise be! Vengeance against the philistine. Manifest to me, *Constantine!*"

Odin roared out in pain as well as the searing light radiated through him, but he was not up from his throne in time for Richard to already be in his face with a meaty right hook, exorcising and punching the host demon literally right out of him. Odin barely moved save for his jaw budging, but the possessing demon smashed right into the wall, directly exposed to Artorian's radiance.

Odin no longer felt any pain after the possession parted from him. The Administrator's Aura instead felt rather nice, which rattled him just enough for Richard to round on him and heave his soul item—blessed brass knuckles named Constantine—into his other cheek with enough force to break the ex-supervisor clean through his own throne and wall.

Debris rained down on the scene as part of the ostentatious mountain castle came toppling down, the construction more visual looks than actual quality. Richard Demonbane howled over his shoulder at Artorian, hungry for more as the demons came at them. "These are mine! Fiat iustitia, et pereat mundus!"

From a geometrically-shaped light source—part of the gnomish B.F.G. division—metal guitar music broke out in the confined chamber when the Gnome dropped its obfuscation effect. As to the allied forces, Richard's booming call automatically translated to: "Let justice be done, though the world perish."

"They're all yours, brother! The only thing they fear is you!" Artorian's own form exploded through the fresh exit in the wall that Richard had provided him. He and Odin had old business to tie up into a neat bow. The era of these dark souls needed to come to an end, an end tested by will, and the strength not to go hollow. "Let's find out whose goals and purpose burn brightest. Time for us to come to an Accord, *Spud.*"

CHAPTER THIRTY-NINE

Lazuli, the demon who'd been inhabiting Odin, gasped in torched relief when the searing affliction from the Sun Aura trickled down in sensation. He hadn't died from exposure, and that was a big plus. However, there was a stark difference between having your face vigorously scrubbed over a cheese grater, and pinpricks annoying the legs after a run. Being laid bare to the prior effect was anything but pleasant. That those feelings were full-body experiences changed the math slightly, but not enough to be worth discussion. The source had left, and more preferable events were afoot.

After all, there was a firefight!

As an earth-based demon with dampening powers, Lazuli was particularly well-geared to guide electricity, and resist intruding Auric effects. Thus why he'd both survived, and worked well with Odin, who was a wind-based cultivator regardless of his channel strengths and Magehood peculiarities.

Lazuli looked like a set of conjoined rocks that had gotten up in the morning with a bad attitude and persistent hangover. Increasing his personal density, his Aura amplified an effect that sought to suppress other Auric effects active in the room. His stony claws then coated in a gravelly brown broil, a petrification effect that dripped like acid from his claws, affecting the ground it touched and turning the previously soft carpet into stony protrusions.

The entire display looked very menacing, and would have done significant damage to anything it touched, had Lazuli's rock for a head not suddenly turned into motes of puffy dust when Richard's knuckleduster pulverized it with a straight lunge.

Lazuli's form went still, then collapsed in a pile of dead rocks, sprawling onto the floor before all his mass was forcibly whisked away to a memory Core. The Core then underwent automated procedures, and deposited Lazuli outside of the ostentatious palatial mountain castle. He and several other demons reappeared in the main courtyard with small pops of sound and flashes of black light.

He looked at his claws in abject confusion, then snapped his head towards the throne room where sounds of combat were clearly ongoing. Sprouting stony thrusters from numerous rocks, Lazuli launched himself as a plume of buckshot and smoke right towards the wall. He broke through the gilded construction with a mighty crash, just in time for Richard to clear a spot in the schedule for Lazuli and back-hand him back to the automatic spawn point.

The hit was so intense, it made Lazuli delirious. Hearing the ding of a bell, and some announcer shouting: *"Mike Tyson's Punch-Out!!"*

Celestial Mana-infused fists *huyt*. Especially against their opposite, even if the abyss was not the same place as the infernal. The infernal just happened to be the best piggyback spot for those from the abyss to sneak through. This hurt Lazuli extra, as the celestial place *was* opposite to the infernal plane. This reality was just something he'd need to die with.

Repeatedly.

This time when he was reconstituted... Lazuli didn't feel so good. Sure, his body was tip-top—hard not to be as a sapient pile of demon-tethered Mana rock. However, there was a definite sensation of 'death' and 'loss' that lingered at that back of his mind. He shook it off. He was a demon! To live, then die, then live again, in many different eras, was how they worked!

Able to stuff the minor feeling away in mental recesses, he took off towards the throne room again, where Richard was cackling in tune to the metallic music that thumped through the entire, ever-less-cohesive space. Soon there would no longer be walls left to keep the roof up.

The man of faith was having the time of his life. Constantine sure wasn't complaining either. It was one thing to demolish a demon physically and send it packing, back to the depths from whence it came. But to fight their very will to live? That was a new feeling to relish entirely. Demons always had the chance to come back, but what about demons so defeated they chose to surrender and give up? To bend the knee and drop their chin?

Richard was burning for the sight, aflame to see if it was possible. A true, redeemer's end to an otherwise voracious, endless set of demon incursions. To fight their very volition, to defeat the spirit which let them stand. This was the fight of the ages, and Father Richard Demonbane hungered for the buffet that came his way ceaselessly. His entire body sheathed itself in angelic light, the full lessons of Cardinal Kere Nolsen brought to bear as all the colors in his vicinity were reduced to clearly distinguishable shades. Richard couldn't contain himself, yelling as he pulled out his big crossbows right away. "Vae victis!"

The phrase translated to 'woe to the vanquished,' or 'woe to the conquered.' Something the nearby demons had freely translated for them without understanding why. The message, unfortunately for them, was clear. Especially when a true to the above celestial appeared behind Richard for a moment. Adam touched his shoulder with a whisper before vanishing as a mote of light.

Whatever was said spread Richard's smile ear to ear. His words were thick and deep. "Pray for penance in the house of the heavens, for if you beg forgiveness, I shall give you *none*."

He punched an open space in the wall. When Lazuli flew into the gap, Richard's fist beamed with blinding light, his punch sent forwards in a line of Mana-infused force that allowed the concept inherent within Constantine to pulverize Lazuli's entire form back into a state of fine gravel and powder. The entire attack launched and culminated with the sound of a piston firing, complete with the dull thud and hot 'pop' of air as Richard swerved to occupy the exact middle of the room.

This was no longer anything resembling a fair fight. It never needed to be. This was a cleanup, and he, as anointed janitor, was now playing whack-a-mole. Demon edition.

A different face appeared in a wall-hole behind him, and

Richard's backhand *vwummed* in that direction. His crackling, shining fist of celestial force sent a beaming shockwave shaped as his fist through the opening. The demon in the way? Reduced to a pile of powdered ice as the cold creature didn't even have the chance to formulate an audible response. At least not during that moment of death.

Vatn, a demon with a body of swirling water who turned the edges of his raging river to ice in order to shred his victims, did exactly so on the trip back from the courtyard to the throne room. Having the clever, sneaky thought to come up from the floor, his entrance was met with Richard's glowing foot, who stomped him out like a mere bug.

Vatn didn't think twice about reappearing in the courtyard. He just sped off to try again, only to blink when he reappeared in the courtyard a third time. Didn't he just do this? He could swear he just did this, then Vatn hurried towards the prey again. He remembered getting to an open window, and feeling like all the blue had been slapped out of him as if beaten so hard across the cheek that his world gained a natural degree of vertigo.

When he stared at the courtyard ground, the blue that had been slapped out of his form still missing, he looked up and needed to address the issue. Vatn's voice was a mixture of anger, confusion, and the beginning of concerned resignation. "What is happening?"

"Oh, don't worry about it. Just tell us when you give up," said the nonchalant angel wearing a long pale robe and matching oversized hood hovering overhead. Holding an equally oversized, strongly glowing white scythe with golden-blue tassels hanging from the shaft that leaned against his shoulder, the celestial appeared exceedingly comfortable.

Adam then hoisted the reaping tool and, with a lazy swing, took off the heads of a dozen, stunned, standing demons like they were wheat to be chaffed. During which Adam whistled a humble farming ditty, like he was mowing tall bluegrass. "It's not a concept weapon, but this is very satisfying. Who knew a grass-mowing simulator would provide me such strong feelings of satisfaction?"

The whistling picked back up, and the demons who slipped through the motions of the floating harvester fled for their lives. One tried to attack Adam, but the celestial grabbed the approaching threat by the presented face with an outstretched hand and merely... squeezed. Then Adam continued his merry ditty when the falling body didn't even hit the ground. Instead reappearing right in time forrrr... *Zwing*.

The demons had a very different perspective. Sure, they came back. Not always in time to do anything but stand there and fear the reaper, but sometimes they remembered to duck, tuck, and roll. Vatn managed to yell between deaths. "Stop spawn camping!"

"No." The angel timed his words for the moment Vatn was actually there between respawns. "Just let me know when you give up. I'll be here." *Zwinggg*.

When Vatn and Lazuli did escape the lazy reaping swings, and didn't attempt to engage Adam, they were at a partial loss. Did they ascend the mountain and storm the palace? The giggling Father in there was specifically geared to be super effective against them. Another attempt, and the man killed them with a pencil! A quill to be specific, nicked from a table covered in the unreasonably deadly scribe's tools. They'd been killed with an abyssal *quill*.

New plan. Did they flee? Actually, they hadn't tried that yet, and perhaps could find easier prey in all of this fray, and then work from outwards, to inside, to win?

A good idea, to be sure.

Lazuli and Vatn picked up the demons Jahwar, Zoko, and Dorian during their mad dash to escape. Jahwar was a gemstone demon, having a body composed mostly of diamond with dark striations running within his form. He blocked a rampant light-beam attack by moving in front of it, the beam refracting and diffusing into blacklight. Jahwar spat out black spittle with his words. "*Urgh*. Specified defenses, and that still hurts."

Dorian scoffed, finding it difficult to keep being negative about the undue save. Though even he knew that they were either getting out of this together, or not at all. The decomposition demon made entirely of frozen mercury waved a sword of matching material at his temporary compatriot. "We live longer from this. We must use it, lest it be wasted."

Dorian's Decomposition Aura flared to life when a goblin spear entered its range, turning the weapon to rust before it crumbled into particles. The screaming goblin that followed tried its best to swing at the separated group, but suffered the same fate as his tossed spear before ever getting close enough to nick them.

Seconds later, that very same goblin came for them again, only to suffer the fate twice and finally learn from his death.

The goblin did not come a third time.

Zoko the gargoyle hid behind the bunch, not being very useful when not on the ground due to being a depth-charge demon. Traveling through ground and stone at incredible speeds was great for his variety of sneaking and unseen attacks, but up here amongst the clouds he was a sitting duck. "We're found. Why don't we flee and regroup for later? This place is lost. No matter where I look, the situation appears grim."

The other four didn't want to admit that Zoko was right, until the gargoyle took off towards the sunset horizon. They spat at the spectacle beneath them, then rushed off after Zoko, until the gargoyle smashed face-first into the orange-red coloration that had been erected before the start of the fight. Which ended up being far more than a meager little shading effect.

On contact, the demon completely vaporized with a sizzling hiss.

The other demons skidded to an aerial halt, though an uncouth move 'accidentally' had Lazuli nudge Vatn into the field. A tiny touch with the barrier was enough for Vatn to screech and be burned out of existence as Incarnate-ranked energy devoured him whole with self-propagating fire. Demanding flames that consumed Vatn's matter so fast, it mimicked a disintegration.

Abyss, might as well just call it one.

"Well, abyss *that*." Lazuli spat, already down two demons from their little group of five. Turning on a copper, he looked around at the Olympus region, realizing the entire area had been completely domed in by this instant-frazzlation effect. "Wait, we're trapped?"

"Wouldn't this be such a kindness if you were merely trapped, little demon?" The burning voice of Amaterasu spoke from the portion of the field where Vatn had perished. Two corona-fueled supernova eyes wreathed themselves in flame against the field, peering directly at the stragglers. "Trapped? No. You are *hunted*."

A flaming claw reached out at a speed Lazuli could not react to. His eyes shot wide for the moment before the claw squeezed down, but the crushing motion didn't have time to count the kill as the consuming fire ate through Lazuli far before the flaming claw could even completely close.

The remaining demons swiftly turned tail to flee, but were met by a thousand spears of liquid flame staring them down like a wall of arrows that could blot out the sun. If only those spears didn't look like they were carved from one. The spears lunged, and the remaining demons died with the time to feel horror, but not the time to scream.

Lazuli, Vatn, Jahwar, Zoko, and Dorian opened their eyes in the courtyard. Metaphorical cold sweat ran down their brows as fear began to find a foothold in their blackened hearts. They trembled as the memory Cores spat them back out in the designated courtyard area, and before one could say a word to the other, their chance to speak was cut short by a lazy *zwinggg*.

CHAPTER FORTY

Pencil, Hanekawa, and Moo did not like what they were seeing. Many demons had guessed that the rainbow totems spilling out both Mana and enemy reinforcements was what glued together the orange and red sunset globe keeping them boxed in. The action being in cardinal directions had left leave for secret plans to be devised and activated in ordinal directions.

They did not like being duped by cheap distractions.

Pencil clicked his mousy tongue. "So much for several of our static defenses and contingencies. They don't even realize how many of our protections they have thwarted. We were ready for a fight, but not *this* fight."

Hanekawa sighed, already too tired for this. "Many are trying to attack the totems instead of being drawn to the cardinal kill zones. Unfortunately, if we don't keep the palace besieged and occupied, that holy madlad in there is going to come looking for us. What madness of a reverse siege is this, where we have to dedicate resources in order not to get hammered to flat nails in our own territory?"

Moo, the Hel-cow, replied in assent, her oversized bardiche vigorously shaken above her head, while her udders undulated in displeasure. "Moooooooo!"

"You tell 'em, Moo," Pencil replied, a sudden pain stabbing his forehead as he didn't remember changing Mu's name, even though for some reason that was now… the right thing to say? Also, her? Since when was Mu a her? No… who was Mu? He didn't know a 'Mu.' He knew a Moo, though. Yes, he'd always known Moo, the female, bovine, Hel-cow. Pencil grunted, one eye forced shut. "I think it happened again. Check for black cats or anything else that can cause déjà vu. The dungeon *changed* something."

Explosions the size of small mountains rocked the northwest quadrant. Every skyborne combatant was buffeted, smacked around, and unless they had a good grip on the current Mana around them, were tossed straight into Ammy's Skyspear shield. Not much was left of them after that until they reappeared at pre-designated locations.

The event also knocked the socks right off Pencil and the other two, their chance of déjà vu source spotting obliterated. If they even remembered to register the mental push. Which they did not.

Bura and A-gust-ist survived the spawn-point gauntlet and made it to the trio. Bura rumbled out his words, both his hands occupied with a large executioner's blade that whistled as it moved due to a diamond-shaped hole at the end. Pencil snapped his vision towards them. "Ah, informants. Good, give me your repo—"

Pencil did not finish, rapidly ducking as Halcyon's tail said hello like a freighter breaching through the waves. Her *Super Smash Bros.* Ring Out Slam collided with force extreme enough to cause a golden-hued thunderclap, one pitched to the sound of a sharp metal twang, as everyone—save for Pencil—turned into bright stars and took an express trip from pound-town through disinte-gration-ville. Destination: *zwingg*.

Halcyon didn't stick around, already hunting for her next target to play orbital patty-cake with, her tail a wake-creating monstrosity that played severe havoc with anyone trying to follow. You could make a Major General out of those waves alone!

Pencil fled, was punched in the nose by an over-enthused goblin in his flight path, and got shivved by a second one wielding a rusty Mana dagger. The Savant turned those goblins into blue goop, and kept going. The demon-banishing rune on the dagger stabbed into his kidney then activated, and popped him back to the respawn point a moment later.

Pencil's only thoughts were to move, move, move!

Getting caught by the hunter whale was just as bad as being snagged by a rampant light beam, tripping over haphazard hovering dice-mines, or hiding too close to already-occupied shadows and finding a Dwarven combat knife where your eyes were supposed to be.

Pencil looked for Odin, and found their supposed leader standing on solid air high above the crumbling palace. The lightning deity looked like an irritated chatterbox as he gabbed with the pillow man like they were a pair of old women annoyed at one another, and couldn't be bothered to deal with the fact that their lawn was on fire.

Bura and A-gust-ist were back with Pencil in short order even as the mouse-shaped demon fled, his Olympian fully subsumed and squeezed down to size. Pencil chittered furiously. "Situation report!"

Bura formed an air whip to swat away a Cloud Cat, the impact collapsing into a sonic boom to send it packing. He coated the sustained effect in poison, causing the whip to emit a constant low-pitch scream as more of flying buggers bore down on them. Making walls of air to buy time, even Bura's patented Air-Thorn-Armor Aura wasn't helping him much when cat claws found their toys. Bura's Tornado Fortress proved to be a much more useful technique for keeping attackers at bay, but only until Pencil and A-gust-ist were properly out of reach of the clowder ball. Then Bura was overwhelmed the moment his gusts died down.

A-gust-ist quickly filled Pencil in. "Our intel is bust! We are *not* stronger than them. We're out-matched *and* outnumbered, in fact, as their numbers, much like ours, replenish the instant they are lost. We are suffering some kind of mental damage each time we kick it, while they are having some abyss-blessed competition! I got close to one of the totems, and the swamp-muck-caked Dwarves holding it down kept telling the creatures pouring out some kind of number. I've heard them tell multiple Goblins that 'a winner is you' or some such, spurring those Goblin Mages on to cause greater... Abyss!"

A-gust-ist took a swarm of said Goblins to the face, his howling wind-form dragged down to the ground. He pulled out his two-handed fan serving as a soul item, but that helped little when the Goblin Mages dive-bombed him into a collection of primed, hovering Otter dice. In unison, the Goblins screeched out some kind of warcry honoring a great hero. "For Splaaaat!"

The wind demon kicked up a sandstorm to whisk the explosives away, summoned twin tornadoes around his hands to buffet the fall, but ended up exploding with a thunder clap as the celestial-cursed dice homed in on him. Tiny demon-banishing runes coated each otherwise numbered surface, and the moment one touched A-gust-ist, they all went up in a grouped cascade, sending out spheres of demon-banishing explosions that made a nasty mess of the sky!

As the banishing rune wasn't good enough to kick the demons out of Cal, A-gust-ist released an almighty yodel upon respawning, shoving everything near him away in a desperate attempt to prev —*zwinggg*!

Pencil cursed up and down that he didn't sign up for this. Not that he had a lot of choice in the matter. Summoned by Barry? No problem. Sudden freedom and a lack of being forcibly evicted at his summoner's downfall? Outstanding. Having to deal with *these* celestial feces? Appalling!

He needed an out. He needed one yesterday. If he had gone with the tormentor squads, he would be feasting on the inhabitants of the New Fringe by now! Except… Why was he seeing most of the demons that had been sent out from Olympus? Even some of the deep-sleeper cells were here, when they completely shouldn't be. How demons on the other end of Caltopia made their way here… That didn't make any sense? Unless…

Pencil peeped. "Unless the bind point for *all* demons is that courtyard, and the places we were poised to sneakily attack all had defenses that rebuked us outright. But how? How?! Some of those areas barely had a B-ranked cultivator amongst them, according to the informants! The big-ear bat-tribe and tiger triumvirate will suffer for this if they've double crossed me! That third one too if I ever catch their snively little webs."

Pencil checked his options.

South? Armored rabbits were running down demons like bouncy bowling balls against crushable pins, with one particularly big one smack in the middle of the fray that seemed to be able to accelerate in place and then release his speed all in one go. He faintly made out the words 'blue hedgehog acceleration' when the rolling tank yelled out his attack name. "That must be Colonel Raile."

Now that he looked, direction appeared to matter little. If there was ground, there was a basher. *Waiting.* Looking like easy prey to pounce until all the prowling cats came into view. The northeast respawn point spat them back out whole clowders at a time, but the cats returned with a vengeance. Worse for him, the A-team of C'towl had spotted his hide, and the winged freaks were bee-lining towards him. Was one of those dark cats decked out in golden chains and a mohawk, loudly complaining about hating flying, and wearing rings on every claw? Must be an optical illusion, because that grayer, middle C'towl couldn't be puffing on a stick of wood right now either, the monster clearly smiling, looking like a plan was coming together.

Pencil almost fled east, but the Goblin swarm was so beehive thick and pervasive that he reconsidered instantly and took the seemingly safer option of the western quadrant. The direction took him away from the raging Manticore, clever clawed murder-cloud, rolling wrecking ball, and towards some unimposing stately man with a fencing blade, and a lamia with a hot glaive. "Much better!"

Gomez and Surtur yelled their kill-counts at one another. Looking like the juicy targets were getting them easy, big numbers! Though, the S.E.P. field-coated stingrays flooding the area sure helped. Surtur giggled when she proudly stated a count of three-hundred. "Do you think they've figured it out yet?"

Gomez laughed at her callout, responding after stabbing an imp through the brain. "Doubtful! Otherwise they would stop coming. *Ha-ha*! En garde, you sycophants! You face Mr. Adamz! Also, three-hundred and one!"

"What?!" Surtur boomed in heated retort, decapitating two low-hanging fruits of demons who thought they were being sneaky. "Three-oh-two!"

"Three-oh-three!" Gomez jovially sang back. "C'est la vie!"

"Don't you use your fake language on me!" Surtur snarled, her breath exhaled in a gout of liquid flame so tight the water-pressure of it alone cut through Mage-flesh with ease. She caught wind of Pencil's scent when he veered close enough, her nose picking him up. He was a bigshot! Bigshots were worth ten points! "That mouse is mine!"

Pencil did not like the sudden turn of events.

Then again, Pencil did not like the sudden turn of many recent events.

This one was particularly annoying as he dodged creatures he could both see, and not see. He only saw the stingrays when he observed them straight on, but then forgot about them entirely once the stingrays were even slightly out of sight. He thought it was promising when the chasing Lamia stopped and groaned, stabbing her weapon into the now-cooked ground.

Safe! She had given up the chase!

He felt less safe when he realized there was a massive spike stabbing him through the sternum, and the Lamia was complaining about it. "My Dreamer be burned, Irwin, you sneak! Gomez, game's up. Irwin got 'em!"

Pencil blinked, faced the stingray, and didn't believe his ears. "Crickey! Look what we've got over 'ere! A bona-fide demon! They're dangerous everywhere you find 'em. Downright deadly to the touch! They'll rip your soul right out of your body at nine-hundred yards. I'ma gonna poke 'em with a stick!"

Pencil died not from being stabbed through the chest, but probably by the stick poke that followed as his reactive flailing made the stingray release a 'Crickey, he's angry!' then flee and drop Pencil. On second thought, the sudden hole in his chest was what got him. That or the poison. Possibly a combination of the three as he—

Zwinggg.

Another moment of blacking out, and when Pencil reappeared, he quickly compressed down to mouse form. "That abyss-cracked celestial reaper is just—"

"Alpha Beams."

Pencil hustled from his standing position when the celestial spoke, darting away from the celestine-colored laser-line eye-beams that bore out of Adam's face from beneath his pale hood. The beams bent and twisted at odd, sharp angles, chasing him down and evaporating any other demon that came into contact with them after the light-lines seared into space, emplacing themselves like permanent, deadly fixtures for about four seconds.

Pencil did not escape. The Alpha Beams got him, and he puffed into an exploded bag of mill-flour. Appearing in the court-yard again with hundreds of others, he barely ducked in time to dodge the *zwinggg*.

Fleeing the scene with his heart pounding, tunnel vision was starting to kick in hard. "I don't want this, I don't want this!"

Turning a corner, his heart sank deeper. Someone had

forgotten to keep Father Richard busy, and now the man was *here*, at the respawn point. "*Ah...* butt-end erasers on a leaden stick with cheap wooden housing."

Richard knuckledustered Pencil right out of his Olympic host, along with most of the host's teeth. The Mage was sent flying into Ammy's barrier while Pencil rolled over the ground, physically coming apart like a broken mirror as his face decomposed. The broken pieces of which became particulates when separating fully from his form and shattering on the ground. Without a host, Pencil bulked in size, becoming the same final-boss monstrosity that Artorian had to contend with, during his first algorithmic Eternia foray.

Pencil the great monstrosity roared, signaling the beginning of a legendary match.

Above them, the roadies of the show pulled their weight. An awesome fight should have equally awesome accompaniments! A different musical regular octahedron floated into the scene, joining in with its counterpart.

The geometric Stratovarius Gnome played Speed of Light in heavy metal, as Father Richard began and ended the boss fight in quick succession. Leaping to the air, Richard hurled himself forward with the holy light that he used to send punches out. Blurring forwards, he caved the Savant's skull in with a falling knee smash. Followed up with another knee smash, and then a third as he mimicked the captain of the falcons and called out the successive strikes. "The knee! The knee! The knee!"

Savant Pencil perished once more. When he opened his eyes, the gargoyle demon next to him was screaming. "He killed me with a hoe! A farming tool! A blasted sheep-herding hoe! A—"

Zwinggg!

CHAPTER FORTY-ONE

While the geometric Stratovarius and B.F.G. division Gnomes swapped out with their Blue Oyster Cult brothers, purely for a song about 'Don't Fear the Reaper,' the situation at Dale's farmstead was starting to look downright rosy.

Possibly because when the Gargoyle troupe had shown up, Rose had been the first to see them. Rather than calling for help, she'd extended an arm, and invoked a command word Ammy had given her. A harmless sounding one to the tune of *"Damocles!"*

The Spirit-quality burning bow formed in her hands, a massive hole blown in the flying demons' formation after the first sword-shaped, cylindrical-space-destroying, devastation-arrow was loosed upon the invading crowd. With more sword-arrows forming at a whim between her fingers, the invading force saw lots of good reason to get out of the sky. After all, someone was shooting swords at them!

Play was for the boys. Rose was here to clean the house! The first Gargoyle to land was devoured by the very green grass his clawed feet touched. The second to land was suddenly missing his head as Brianna divided his problems and doubled his number of friends.

The third was more apprehensive, and turned his attention to the farmer stomping out of a seriously overgrown barn that looked like it had been re-grown multiple times in the last few days. The simple-looking fellow was holding a stick that looked cobbled together out of driftwood: the top a sheep herding cane while the bottom chunk was clearly meant to be a hoe. The Gargoyle charged him, then was plowed into a ditch by an A-nine ranked Dale using part of the earth-shattering technique. The farmer gave the demon a kick for good measure, popping the creature's remains out of his precious topsoil. "Oh, good! I was so worried that ugly thing was going to tarnish my begonias."

Dale then flipped his soul item around and fished an old demon-banishing arrowhead out of his pocket that he'd found in Minya's goods. Granted, he'd needed to dig around for a few hours in search of it, but hey, he found it! He placed the arrowhead onto the upturned hoe, and merged the two by spending an overabundance of Mana and stealing his mentor's invocation ways. Expensive? Yes! Need to know what you were doing? Nope! "That'll make this so much easier."

"Fore!" Dale golf-clubbed the next demon out of existence, then reconsidered the balancing on his haphazard hybrid herding hoe. "Heck, I like it! I'm keeping it this way. The top could have been a crook, but we already have Hans."

"That soul item looks dumb, Dale." Hans was armed with sharp-cheddar and blue-cheese-stuffed bunny-cut baguettes in his hands. The man clearly spoke from very recent personal experience on the topic of silliness, and the ministry of funny walks, as Hans had not managed to breach into Magehood. "They are not ready for *le pain*! My sodden strikes of sliced bread, sharp and cutting with cheddar! My baking methods used hops as yeast starters for these bad boys. Rising for any occasion, the enemy need only be ready for a gluten of pain! If they can't stomach it, and knead some help, we will give them a short rest in order to get a rise out of them. They'll be toast in no time! Then I will say: Gluten Tag!"

A groan erupted from the background from all the women in unison. "Staaaahp."

"If you mess with us, you'll end up bread, trust me. My wife's bow? That's the yeast of your problems. She's a crack shot! If they miss? Dough!" Hans continued, some of the weapons changing who they were being pointed at. "Rose, you could throw a female deer at them as that's a doe! A—"

"Shut. Up!" Hans dodged out of the way of a flaming sword-arrow as Rose was done with his banana-bread baking abyss. "I'm going to punish you for those puns!"

A moment of silence fell to process what Rose had said. Plenty of time for Hans to look really pleased, and Rose to groan and drop her face into her hands when she realized what she'd done. "Now you're rubbing off on me!"

"Well, I've been doing *that* for years." The smirking assassin fell prone onto the grass, another sword-arrow whistling overheard to the exasperated tune of 'Hans!'

A wayward demon trying to be clever was eaten by the hay bale barn at Chandra's direction, while those not smart enough to run and hide were taken apart like swine at the butcher's table. The demon cells had come this way to kill them.

Brianna made them regret their decisions.

Minya tossed up a handful of Rota's Rollers, then caught them between her fingers before hurling them at a few rapidly descending gargoyles. In addition to the homing mines, Rose was doing an excellent job of keeping the sky anything but safe. The demon-banishing kaboom removed the entire lot of them, Minya's clear view of the clouds no longer obstructed as she commented with approval. "Better. I think that's all of them."

Rose snapped open her hand, the Damocles bow fizzling out with a puff of hot smoke. "I don't hear or see any more. Grandma?"

Chandra stepped out of a tree trunk from her left while Brianna unmerged with the shadows from the right. They both glanced around, then nodded sharply at the statement. No demons were left to be seen or found at the farmstead. They looked at the boys, but Hans and Dale were dueling with their... questionable weaponry. Making *hi-ha-hiyaaa* noises.

"Know what? I'ma let 'em play." Minya shrugged before pulling out a round messenger orb from her spatial ring. She punched in the button and turned it blue. "Dev, the farmstead is clear. Any news or emergencies elsewhere?"

The orb crackled before the Gnome's voice came through clean as polished crystal. "Only news, no emergencies. I feel exceptionally bad for all the ones who chose to go to the moon. They interrupted a Crown Game between Valkyries and Family Heads. Poor sods. After how Sunny provoked them last time, there's nothing left of the invaders. The threat was taken seriously right from the get-go. The crabs were particularly crabby about the ordeal, resulting in a snapping victory. Also the squirrels cracked a few nuts, to the amused shoutcasting of Rocky and Bullwinkle."

The women gathered around the messenger ball, a giggle leaving their lips. Minya nodded in approval. "What about the other places? No issues in Nidavellir or Fringy?"

"Not really. I'll pull up a feed shortly and show you." Dev attempted to be helpful. "Aiden actually got the worst of it with hidden sleeper cells waking up very literally under his feet. From the local chatter and sound of battle still ongoing, the demon attack only spurred that entire werewolf nation on? They're all committed to one big hunt. So there will be casualties, but Poseidon already has their scent. The end is a matter of time."

Minya mulled that over, her hand pressing into her hip. "How is the main force and their diplomacy?"

Deverash laughed through the connection. "Proceeding like well-oiled sprockets! Richard is having a *blast*. Artorian is giving Odin a headache, and Adam is working on his whistling and mowing skills. All the old mobs from Cal's dungeon are so well geared to Artorian's infinite respawn war tactic that the few advantages we knew the demons had have become a veritable joke. Richard is punching them right out of their hosts, and the Olympians are all being successfully mass-segregated to the Mist Caverns."

Dev cleared his throat. "Sadly, they do not have a lot of spirit left in them after even a few meager deaths. That, or being surrounded by a few hundred of Brianna's Dark Elves riding on the back of the larger arachnid variants from Zelia's multi-million strong spawn took the fight out of them. I'll admit that seeing an endless field, plus wall-to-wall covered caverns of mandible-clicking arachnids, is rather intimidating. Old Guild or not, they don't feel too good about all those spiders looking at them and making 'tasty' sounds. Not with their respawn point being tethered to those caverns."

The women paused, let the squirm pass over them, then shook it off. That mental vision really was pretty terrible, allied or otherwise. Brianna commented. "There are worse ways to go... but maybe not many."

Deverash spoke through the orb. "The scenes in Nidavellir and N.F. are best seen, rather than explained. Or rather, the scene *near*

Nidavellir is what's interesting to see. Any abyss-boys that ended up in the Dwarven capital were pulled apart in a builder's frenzy. If you think the spiders are bad, try getting in between a Dwarven clan and their construction project. If those demons hadn't become particles, they'd be part of a wall right now. Unless they were lucky enough to set foot on the specific patch of land altered by Sunny, as the Dwarves can't affect that area. No amount of convincing the ground is going to work when it loves someone else more."

Brianna sourly commented again. "My mention was *not* an open invitation to provide an example of a worse way to die, Deverash."

"Sorry." Their Gnome said through the orb. "Force of habit. I'll get back on topic."

"Thank you." All the women replied in unison, making it very clear to the dapper Gnome that it would be best if he didn't bring it back up again.

Dev controlled himself, and spoke while letting the communication orb start filtering through moving diagrams. "First, let me get you a visual of the Nidavellir border. Tom has been *handling* it. I'll rewind a good chunk of time so you can see it all from the beginning, otherwise a few things won't make sense. Ah, here we go."

The diagram burst to life with color, showcasing the scene of Rose's dear old friend and party member, Tom. Though, the man did not appear to be alone. To his left, seated in a delicate pose, sat a Chinese porcelain doll of a woman. To his right, a man with more muscle than the barbarian himself had sat cross-legged. Eyes on the prize for dots approaching against the horizon.

"Who's that?" Chandra asked, not recognizing either of the forms aside from Tom. "Haven't seen them before."

"I suppose we're about to find out?" Rose was equally as interested. "Let's watch!"

CHAPTER FORTY-TWO

Tom enjoyed the flowing, spicy breeze provided by the Coast of Rica. The smells brought him home, in a way. Even if home made little sense these days. A frozen fortress ruled over by an infernal dungeon? A mountain of dales with friends galore? A guild in another world, smiling faces fraught with laughter? A small farm tucked away in a glade?

No.

These were no homes for Tom. These were temporary refuges, pleasant corners for a warm meal and warmer nap. Not hard lands to put roots down, especially when his roots kept being pulled by the clamor and sounds of action craved by the heart.

Tom wasn't like his friends. He could be around them, and be social. But his spirit yearned for the sound of hammer hitting anvil, hammer striking bone, hammer crushing foes. Like a steady, repeated beat that chased an ever dipping sunset.

No matter where he went, that urge and feeling followed him, just like his bloodlust had. Yet, his bloodlust and fire-Essence side effects? Those he'd gotten under control. This? This yearning? This calling was something else entirely. It was not an effect to shield himself from by throwing up his arms, standing his ground, and centering himself. This pull on his soul was a direction of life, and his feet refused not to follow.

He was Tom, the jovial. Tom, the barbarian. Tom, the guild

master. Tom, wielder of the great hammer. Yet to Tom, all those titles felt hollow. None of those descriptions were more than a convenient fit for something to give a society. The words didn't fit his needs, the puzzle piece wrong for the corner frame of his heart and soul.

Tom saw the black dots in the distance grow larger, and then without warning, there they were once more. The sound pounding in his ears that dug their way up from the back of his mind. The *drums*. Could nobody else hear them? Nobody else ever seemed to. His friends instead told him of strange words that didn't make sense, whispered from a wind that didn't waft. A breeze that didn't blow.

Tom only knew of the drums.

What *was* a djembe drum circle?

How did he know the notes, having never played or studied any music? Those sounds and thudding of hands striking the instruments played at the forefront of his thoughts, and with a single note that hit the side of the drum instead of the top, Tom stood.

A silent question breathed across his eyes, the sight one of an empty camp, bonfire still flickering with one last flame. Tom scoffed at the notion, speaking to nobody that could be seen. "A hall is best filled with clamor. A fire best surrounded by brothers. A battle best when broached by brethren. Stop whispering images, and come stand with me, brother of the drum. I know you are there. I welcome you to my hot heart, burning with fresh flame. I was part of the ancient north, but that path is nothing but cold snow under my feet. Come, drum-brother. Come! Share this feast here! You will find no empty camp with me!"

Tom reached out to empty space. The porcelain woman and man of boundless muscle became effigies of flame as he did, their forms solid no longer. Merging together in a twister, they formed Thud in his hand, the mighty warhammer brimming with life and power.

With Thud fully formed, Tom turned his head and planted the weapon maul-first into the ground, both his hands resting on the back of the hilt. He was looking to his left where, rather than the porcelain girl, a new figure formed like heat drawn from a forge.

A red inferno crackled around the figure, forcing Tom to back up several paces as the energy twisted to create the outline of a man. The man gained his outer layers first, clothing forming over his being before the dark skin color settled into place. A fashionable dashiki and matching headwrap became prominent features, until the man moved as if getting accustomed to the body that his mind filtered into. When the figure got a handle on his being, he looked himself over. Then he smiled, and turned to Tom. "I am Shaka, when the walls fell. I am the manifestation of **Fire**. I thank you, fire-heart of old cold, for inviting me. I would give you a boon for this gracious gift. How may I do so?"

Tom stepped back into position, his hands wringing around the bottom of his hammer. It was a strange question to be asked, but the truth of his answer slid right into Tom's thoughts. There had been something bothering him lately, something he was ill-suited to tackle. He silently looked at Shaka, and could feel in his soul that the man *knew*. This man understood him. Down to what moved his feet, and kept his heart beating.

Where most would ask this being of obvious power for something selfish, or self-serving, Tom was merely honest, and humble. The canvas of Tom's soul, always striving to be better for those around him, was one that several celestials would behold, and nod at with approval.

Tom heaved Thud towards Shaka. "I need... I need help. They need a name, and nothing I can think of does them justice. Thud is where they began, but they have moved so far past Thud. Please. I think you hear the drums as well? Do you know of anything which I could give them that would do them both proud?"

Shaka's bright white teeth shone as he smiled at Tom, his dark hand laying on the offered weapon, Tom's actual, closest family. The manifestation of **Fire** spoke softly, though his accent bled through. "I see the names of you both. Dey are written in countless pyres."

The dark man flashed with Spirit energy, a wave of silver fractals rolling over both Thud and Tom at the same time. The control was exquisite, refined beyond immortal means. Shaka spoke with proud fondness. "Your hamma'? Dey is named *Erraverunt*. A proud name. A strong name. One driven by passion, and the heart. Your name? You, my friend that I have long been eager to meet and see with my own eyes, you are *Fiyah*! Were you a Mage, I would be personally be greetin' you on the bottom of da first stairway step. Yet as you are

297

not, let me ask you, one wild roamer to another. Do you wish to be of **Fire**? I welcome you with all my heart, and all my flame."

Tom didn't understand why his face was scrunched, or why he was crying. His upper lip stiff, but lower lip curled. His grip on the hammer wavered, but gravity could not take what Erraverunt did not offer. The hammer remained in space, hanging like it was nailed to the very air until Tom gripped the haft once more, his fingers comforted by the familiar squeeze. "Will it ease the yearning?"

Shaka was honest, his spare hand's motion causing the notes of a xylophone to play, matching the tune of the drums Tom could not unhear. "No, my brother. It *is* de yearning. There are people who belong to the wilds, and the wilds belong to them. You may be barbarian, berserker, mighty hammerer, and leader of a people who laugh as you do, and drink as you would."

Shaka broadly motioned at the distance. "Yet I see into you, my strong little flame. You see the horizon, and your feet call for you. Your arms beg to reach. Your hand wishes to grab. Against this yearning, there is no escape."

His voice spoke strong, ending in a whisper. "Yet rejoice, my brotha, for it is not an escape, but a *direction*."

Shaka then pointed straight up at the sky. "There will always be people who reach for the unknown, all the way to the ends of all the earths, and deep through da stars. You are da wild, and da wild is with you. You are no house on a prairie, but a camp in the densest woods, the coldest snows, and driest deserts. Where you put down your hamma', those who follow will find you. You are Seeker, for the highest of dangers. You crave to wrestle the unknown, and the unknown calls to you. You are meant for each other, and I would go on this journey with you. For I know for certain, that you are a Keeper of da flame."

Tom solemnly stood, his wet eyes meeting with Shaka's. "You feel the yearning?"

Shaka's arm pressed around Tom's back. "My brotha, I was one of the *first* to feel the yearning, and I feel it still. Like fire well fed, the heat does not go away. For creatures like us, comfort is complacent, and secondary. But the fresh smell of a new breeze? The crunchy feel of new sand beneath our toes? The taste of a new leaf as it steeps to flavor our hot wata'? This is *home*. This home, nobody can take from us. No matter how often the unknown tries."

Tom wiped his face with the back of his arm, gaze resolute. "That... that sounds nice. I like that. I have not introduced myself, but I feel you already know me better than a name. I am Tom. Well met, Shaka."

The men shook wrists, and hot energy roiled through Tom's arm, coursing to fill his body with new strength. Tom locked gazes with the manifestation of flame again, then grit his teeth. "And I would be honored to be of **Fire**."

A flash of impossible heat blazed, and Tom the C-ranker was replaced by a burning man. Tom, the B-rank zero Mage of **Fire**, bearing the blessing of Shaka, stood firm; his honor worn on his sleeve and his excellent character visible right on his face. Now dressed in a black and red dashiki with silvery trim, fractal patterns detailed in the cloth.

A good man and soul, truly worthy of high praise.

The manifestation smiled as he spoke. "Cal did well with your body, but I can do betta! I improved your mortal form before the change. You will find that tasks previously difficult for you will come easy. As to da normal difficulties of da Mage ranks? Throw those thoughts out of the straw hut. *Go all out.* Do not hold back. Swing with all your force. Step with all your might. Shout with all your vigor. You are Fiyah! There is a feast to be had! Show da unknown da meaning of **Heat**! Brandish your hammer, for the unknown comes to claim your home! When it comes knocking at your door, speaking falsehoods, saying you have lost, claiming victory, and that you can never hope to match it, then you tell da void—"

Tom aimed his hammer at the incoming demons, finishing Shaka's sentence. "Who decided that?!"

Shaka vanished like smoke carried by jungle wind as Tom exploded off his hill. The manifestation was needed no further, and Shaka could sustain his presence for no longer than he'd done. At Shaka's campfire, the tents warmed. A surge of flame flaring from the bottom of the pile of embers that had a massive, charred broadsword stabbed right through its center. A broadsword whose shape morphed, turning into that of a mighty warhammer as the flames grew to become a roar.

The cycle would turn again. Tom's addition kept the light strong.

The man of living flame roared as Shaka's campfire did, surprising the demon host when he appeared in their midst like an erupting volcano. Erraverunt broke through the lead Gargoyle with a mixture of melting heat and crushing precision, the bisected halves of the stone monstrosity goopy on the insides while crumbling in all other segments. The rest of the demon's frame was reduced to shrapnel via a loud smash and *bang*.

Demons with the power of density attempted to catch and stop the roaring swings, but Erraverunt was no mere hammer under the influence of an effect. Erraverunt the undaunted was a rhinoceros of the stretched plains, a lion of the burning savannah, an elephant of curving hills, and a bear of the frozen mountains all rolled into one. Erraverunt was living history carved into stone, a journey through multiple worlds, and first-hand accounts of a thousand battles. The delicacy of the swings were dictated by gentle porcelain touch, while the force of the blow carried through as if Tom counted for two men of his quality and caliber.

Tom felt the yearning, and leaned into it.

Grasping a Gargoyle attempting to spear him with a pitchfork covered in purple fog, Tom's other hand collided with the weapon straight on. He howled heat to the sky, and converged the Gargoyle into his own weapon while the flames wreathing him burned the fog and toxic effects away. When the crumbled demon remains were dropped to the ground below, Tom reached out and snatched Erraverunt from its prone position in the sky, cracking the maul's head down onto the chest of another foe that rushed to be in melee range.

Erraverunt shifted into the form of a Lucerne hammer to lay the next enemy low, returning to that of a two-handed warhammer immediately afterwards for a follow up.

Tom relished the fight, his smile wide, and laughter full of force. This was part of the true, good life. He would crush these enemies. He would seek the horizon. He would be dauntless, and treasure all that was new and could be found in the wilds! The great, boundless unknown. Tom's fire surged around him, approaching attackers shrieking as they began to melt from sheer proximity before the threat of his hammer could reach.

Their claws turned into molten slag as Tom released his cry, his very Aura becoming a fire that surged outwards with new purpose. "I am Tom, of **Fire**! I am Seeker! I am Keeper! I am the hammer that falls. I *am* the camp on the border of what is known. I am the warmth in the night. I am what gives darkness fright! Come, foes of stone. Come! For good ol' Tom is *not* alone. I am home, brothers!"

He grit his jaw, his enemies falling in defeated piles around him as his feet lowered and touched the ground. Erraverunt became a full person, merely to squeeze a muscled arm around the burning man's shoulders. Tom's eyes were wet with flame, the lines staining his cheeks as the depth of the sensation truly and properly hit him, the yearning worn like a cape. "I am *home*."

CHAPTER FORTY-THREE

Rose exhaled deeply, her puffy cheeks bloated as her crossed arms and raised eyebrows didn't do her feelings on the sight justice. "Well, that was... *wow.*"

Deverash broke the trance everyone was in, reminding them he existed when his voice crackled through the communication orb. "Told you rewinding to the start was necessary!"

Rose needed a minute, her hand kneading her forehead. "I'm out. I can't handle more. Is N.F. fine?"

"Sure is, those diagrams are up next." Dev said from the orb. "Take a breather, the battle Jiivra leads is intense, but decently one-sided with how the populace chose to handle it."

That was enough for Rose, who'd had enough excitement for today. She needed to lay down. Maybe eat some pickles and ice-cream. Preferably together? Those cravings were back. Rose commanded the men's attention. "Hans! Dale! I need you."

The boys both popped their heads up from the coffee fields, completely coated in face-paint with reeds sticking out of their hair. The reason why didn't make a lot of sense until Hans Jr. and mini-Minya poked their heads out from over their fathers, like some makeshift totem pole. The kids were equally as fronded-up! Embroiled in some incomprehensible, complicated game where the rules were made up and only the journey mattered.

She scurried off with them while Brianna, Chandra, and

Minya kept posted. They were going to keep up with the flow of events, since it would not be surprising if there was a meeting later. Or a quiz.

Dev loaded up the new diagrams. The initial sight of the shaky, flickering images caused confusion to all three onlookers. They stared in silence before Minya braved the first words. "I think they're singing?"

"Doesn't explain the glow." Chandra leaned in for a closer look. "Or how a bunch of C-rankers and below are making Gargoyles flee. I can understand they'd have the upper hand over anything not at the B-ranks, but even *those* are scuttling around."

"Looks like a formation?" Brianna figured while watching the display. "This reminds me of something the old Church faction would do. I don't know the details, but it's hard not to assume that the specific pattern and pathway in which the entire town is standing has something to do with their potency."

"Wasn't Jiivra part of the Choir?" Minya sussed out. "Could be one of her tricks. Though I've never seen a battle chant applied on such a massive scale. What I'm wondering is... where's Blanket? There's no way he wouldn't be in the middle of this, and I haven't seen him flash across any of the diagrams even once."

The women studied what Dev showed them. Brianna held her chin and turned to a nearby shadow cast by a fat tree. "Gomei. Take some Counts and get me a firsthand account."

The Moon Elf elite of the Dark Elves hiding in the shadows released a sharp *huhn*! of confirmation, then left, the space feeling oddly empty while remaining visually the same. Brianna then turned back to the messenger orb. "We will get our information, Dev. You are a tiny plump patch of sweetness for indulging us. Do come visit, you peach. Your cheek looks better with my lips against it."

The orb turned pinkish red, then puffed out a gout of steam as all the images frazzled and fizzled out one by one. Minya slapped her forehead, and Chandra smirked while turning to Brianna for a comment. "That was *one* time, must you continue to tease the poor engineer? You know they get flustered easily."

Brianna smiled, then shrugged. "It's just so cute."

The messenger orb, still a shade of embarrassed hot pink, cleared its metal throat before speaking in an attempt to regain a sense of composure. "Personally, I think Jiba-Su-Wong might suit your tastes more, Madame Brianna."

"Well he's not here to tease right now, and I'm feeling bratty." Brianna winked at the orb, which crackled, popped, and then snapped in half. Dev wasn't built for this kind of flirtatious talk, and fled back to his comforting, cold machinations and prized two-dimensional art pieces. Brianna purred, pretending to sound responsible. "Oops, I broke another one."

The three women all broke down laughing after that, after which Minya and Chandra hooked Brianna's arms, and dragged her off to Tyrian's corner with scheming expressions plastered on their faces. Chandra could not stop herself from indulging. "So who are you shipping out with? Or do the rest of us keep huskily trading whispers and making a guessing game out of the harbor?"

Brianna balked out with amusement. "Ha! Play with your harbor. I have yet to find someone I truly desire in such a fashion. I am content to be myself, with myself. Or perhaps…"

Chandra and Minya devolved into full chitter and gossip mode with Brianna leading them on by the nose instead of giving them any answers, but that was part of the fun. Brianna's mind unfortunately refused to release the prior thought. She was burning to know what Gomei would find. Chant Formations were prized Choir secrets, and she wanted them all.

Gomei wasn't going to disappoint in that category, as he found goodies layered like a fat triple-milk cake served in spades. When he and the Counts arrived at the New Fringe in short order, the fight was still firmly ongoing. Though calling it a battle was generous.

The grumpy Moon Elf grumbled. "This is no *battle*. This is a party with casualties."

He sneered at all the humans he saw, but tucked that feeling away deep into his double-stitched velvet chest pocket. "Pale Moon squad. I want a visual account of the energies running through this Choir conduit, from every angle, with sketches."

The shadows around him split, vanishing away to good vantage points to fulfill their appointed tasks. Gomei himself went sneakily to sit on the roof of an A-frame home smack in the middle of it all so he had optimal information to work with. A smile crept into the sharp corners of his mouth when all the people in the Choir Formation began to jump at the same time. *"Well, well, well.* What have we here?"

Astrea raised the roof. "Three, two, one, *bounce!"*

Gomei was glad to be holding onto something solid when both Astrea's voice and effect coursed through the conduit made by the pattern of everyone's synchronized movements, and location in the village. Her call resounded through the air and up to the clouds, only to be drowned out by a dirty bass drop and heavy wub. Gomei rocked from the sensation that he had been thrown down a steep hill covered in particularly spiteful rocks.

His world felt like it had been turned sideways, and had convinced gravity to do the same. He had been prepared for physical assault, with a heavy focus to stealthily remove interlopers. His body and Aura were attuned to that function and purpose, so the mental push that exploded out from the formation hit him like a ton of Nidavellir bricks.

The ground was moving to his senses, even if he knew that he was standing otherwise perfectly still on the home's roof, as little more than vibrations were coursing over his physical form. The ground *felt* like it was moving, but wasn't actually moving. Centering himself was an effort lost to the booming thud and drop of more sound that rippled out of the Choir Formation. It dropped demons out of the sky just as easily as it unsettled his footing. Impressive, to be able to affect even an A-ranker! His curiosity piqued, Gomei began his work.

Several factors were complicating this mission.

Operating overhead, the local Wisps had been let in on the fun, and had their *own* Choir Formation going. Save that instead of being a conduit for sound, each Wisp acted as a beacon for individual strobing laser lights. Colors chosen at whim? Which was a boon of a sort, as it was dusk and evening when he'd arrived. The added bright beams flashing across the darkly hued violet and black backdrop of the sky was... Alright, even *he* liked art of this caliber. The fleeting nature spoke to him. Plus the Wisps weren't human, so that was an instant improvement.

Gomei watched as a Gargoyle dipped and dove between the assaulting beams of color, his acid-coated claws reaching out to slash at a random member of the formation. The demon cackled as he felt an impact, but Wux cackled louder as a barrier of sound thick as solid static rebuked the hit.

Wux the Miller broke from the verbal sounds he'd been making, even if words did not apply. Gomei was going to call this... beatboxing? Sounds all made with the mouth and throat. Wux spoke normally, his voice heard with surprising clarity over the chorus of sound like it traveled along an undercurrent. "Tag, I'm it! I vote for... Megheara!"

Megheara whooped from her own spot in the formation when Gomei got a buzz in his ear. He pressed a hand to the side of his head and grumbled as the Air Mana reached him. "Report."

"Master, the Choir Formation on the ground forms an ancient letter in a language we thought the Church had abandoned. The symbol, when taken and viewed in its entirety from above, forms to mean the word 'sound.'" Gomei thought that good news, and grunted for his Count to continue. "The symbol in the air, when viewed in its entirety, is the one for 'light.'"

That stacked up logically and tracked, according to Gomei. "Well done. Continue monitoring."

The Mana near his ears faded, observations continued. Within the formation, the 'focus' of the energy visually shifted. All the force congealed and concentrated around Jiivra who, now that Gomei focused on her, was making entirely different motions than the rest of the formation. "She is *directing* the unified mix of Essence and Mana? Across the bodies of mostly non-cultivators, every rank of the rainbow, *and* esteemed Mages?"

Gomei's Cheshire smile spread from ear to ear, his eyes sparkling. "Magnificent. Music is truly the medium that brings the disparate together."

"Conflux!" Jiivra inhaled the words rather than speaking them out, a skill afforded to purely the most gifted of singers. When she spoke, the energy-conflux swirling around her hands was sent through the conduit of the Choir Formation, the Mana swirling around Megheara. "Meg! Ivaldi's performance of The Four Seasons; Summer!"

"What the abyss is a conflux?" Lunella asked mid-bounce.

Craig had her answer. "It's another term for confluence. In geography, a confluence occurs where two or more flowing bodies of water join together to form a single channel. So in this case, a bunch of energy coming together. Think of it like rounding up your children so you can lecture them all at once."

Lunella adored Craig for his easy answers. She both laughed, and had been given a non-cultivator version of an otherwise complicated topic. Excellent.

Megheara grinned when she felt her personal Essence connect to the conflux, all that delicious, dripping power at the control of her fingertips. Her eyes sharpened and blazed with a mixture of Air and Infernal, her irises bursting with a deep violet glow. Seeing the flow of music, she pulled free a humming billy club.

Meg tapped it against the static-stuffed air, a chime sounding that was both the chord of a piano and the extended *ting* of a triangle. Inhaling the power so it roiled in her voice box, she waited for the exact, proper moment before the beat, then unleashed her vocal attack before the big bass drop. "Vibrato!"

Gomei clung to the roof of the house again as the mind-altering effect slammed into him. He methodically shifted his Aura, but didn't have the right Essence types to defend against anything Infernal-based. Not naturally. He succeeded in using Mana to clog the gaps, but it was imprecise and slap-dash. Luckily, slap-dash was good enough for him to no longer be affected by the dissonance.

Just in time too, as Megheara's old weakness had become her new specialty. Vibrational frequencies shattered stone Gargoyles anywhere close to the ground-based formation. When the sound-wave hit them, tinnitus rang through their ears, and the mental became physical. The violent, violet rippling caused visible rock-bending shockwaves that liberally shook the stone beings to pieces as the Mana-fueled attack broke the demons apart from the inside out. Rock became rubble, rubble trembled to gravel, and gravel crushed away to dust.

As the attack faded, the ground-based singers harmonized, re-engaging and strengthening the conduit. Each member was haloed by celestial effects as the mainstay of energy re-focused on Jiivra, who had spotted even more incoming hostiles.

The new demons arriving did not have the luxury of retreat. According to Olympus Intelligence, the New Fringe had been a priority target with poor defenses. They had to take it, or die trying.

Irene cackled through her dance moves, as the set-up to provide all that misinformation had been most glorious. When the next wave of Gargoyles found what they thought was prey, half were strobe-lanced right out of the sky when the Wisps unloaded on them. Multi-elemental beams cutting, crushing, and piercing right through the opposition with strobing precision. One Gargoyle in particular slipped through the entire defensive net, and nearly clawed Jiivra in the face.

Jiivra instead bit the stone monster's hand off, then whooped after spitting it out because it was now her turn! "Yes! I'm it! Blanket, I choose you! Go, Blanket's Angry Tooth!"

From her hip, she detached a chakram with a fluffy white handle.

The item hovered in place, shook itself much like a particularly ornery crown had in Eternia, then hummed, aglow with power before spinning in place and building up a seriously impressive cutting edge of sharpened celestial Mana.

A trick that Blanket had learned from Raile. His head-smashy friend!

Blanket, currently practicing being a chakram, connected to the Choir Formation with ease. When the conflux of energy transferred, the weapon glittered before zipping through the space so fast that only the after-images were noticeable. To make the enemy's already burdened dodging lifestyle difficult, Blanket's Angry Tooth moved at purely sharp angles each time a turn needed to be made.

The very specific frequency of the cutting spin put out by the chakram quickly gained a name when a few more Gargoyles landed and tried to flee on foot instead of choosing to contend with the strobe lights. The sound was identified as either E and F, or F and F sharp from a brass tuba. The chakram had sliced into the very ground, then chased them like a landshark as the pitched approach of its cutting blade put the fear into many a stony heart. Because no matter how fast they ran, Blanket was faster. Thinking there was more than one of these monstrosities, and that they were in dire need of a bigger boat, the Gargoyles named these terrible ground-rippling beings 'Jaws.'

Blanket was just having fun, and the extra sound was him being noisy. Plus, it was so much more fun to chase toys that ran! When the spinning chakram killed the last demon in the last wave, the weapon cut skywards.

Pausing mid-flight to *poof* into a large tapestry of fluff and happy screeches, Blanket declared victory. Jiivra laughed at the sight of the oversized sugar glider looping around the Wisp formation, mucking with their conduit as he attempted to gather them all up so he could hug and lick each and every one like they were an oven-fresh cookie. When the fluff-ball got down to Jiivra, she had collected and condensed all the conflux energy into a pellet the size of a marble.

Blanket used it as a jawbreaker and snacked on the energetic candy, indisposed for the next several hours with his treat.

It then hit Jiivra how smoothly this test had gone. "That formation worked great! I've never gotten to use the Umbral Choir technique! Holy smokes, does it work well with Mana involved. No wonder nobody wanted us to use this when we only had Essences available. The whole thing would have exploded if anything else had mixed with the celestial!"

Megheara quipped back now that the party was over. Since the majority of the village had changed from mass-beatboxing to actual singing and proper celebrations. "That must be why Occultatum named that scroll 'the biggest drop.' Also, did they have to look so old and dingy? I've picked cleaner cloth out of an elder's lint box."

Gomei did not stay for the following festivities. Information in his pocket, he reconvened with his Counts and set out on the next mission. "Find me more of these 'Elder Scrolls.' Go."

Jiivra laughed, looking upwards at the complaining bundle of Wisps that weren't fighting back nearly enough to *really* be complaining when Blanket decided he wanted to cuddle and chew on his snack at the same time. She commented on Blanket's good work as she let the formation fade, watching him chew on a Wisp in addition to the jawbreaker. The fight was won. "Blanket protecc, Blanket attacc, but more importantly, Blanket never skip snacc."

CHAPTER FORTY-FOUR

Alexandria held her clipboard tight to the chest, eyes narrow and focused on the horizon. Razor and Ali kept her steady while she stood upon the edge at the very top of the spire, mere inches from tumbling doom, and preventing her from leaning forwards too far. "I still do not see them."

Behind her, Snookem Bookem was giggling about some puffy pink cloud he was laying on; leafing through a green scroll detailing Oak's Wood Elven techniques. He glanced at the edge himself. "They're there! Give it a few minutes, you'll see the living statues soon."

"Gargoyles, Mr. Bookem. The designation for the type of demonic body you are describing is Gargoyles. Non-host-bound demons revert to the forms that their natural essence channels lean them towards." Alexandria corrected him, once again pulled back from the edge by Ali as the crunching of floor gravel nearby signaled that another had joined them.

Emilia Nerys had finished the stairway trek. "The Lady Librarian is correct, Air Dean."

"Water Dean! You made it! How was your tour of the big tall rock?" Snookem joked as he rolled over onto his other side to face them, spare hand scratching that difficult to reach spot on his spine. "Find anything interesting, mossy, or otherwise of note in all those empty rooms at this Academy?"

"No." Nerys remained curt. "Vacant rooms in a vacant building leave only vacant spots for fresh dreams. I intend to claim one, where I will teach my ways. My **Law**'s Exemplar track demands that I offer the path to others, should they be suitable."

A rustling of tumbled rags behind them turned all heads.

Alhambra and Jin, both red faced and out of breath, looking disheveled as wet rats, burst through one of the open doors. They looked around and saw only dead ends. With pleading eyes, they whimpered and looked to Alexandria, who took the situation apart like it was a mechanical puzzle box to reassemble. She quietly snapped a finger towards one of the open windows nearby, causing Alhambra and Jin to flee towards it and throw themselves through.

Unfortunately, not in time for the literal horde of children on their tails to not have seen where the duo had gone. Ian, Exem, Ra, Bastet, Hathor, Osiris, Set, Anubis, Ptah, Isis, and Ma'at all spilled from the doorway that 'large children' one and two had fled through. Ra, being Lunella's oldest, pointed at Jin's disappearing feet as he vanished through the hole in the wall. "There they are! Get 'em!"

A screeching warcry of tiny voices called out with a *reeeeeeee* before the children horde frightened Ali and Razor by ignoring surface orientation. Some clung to the walls and others speed-crawled across the ceiling in order for them all to fit through the open window with any sort of directed haste. All while making that high-pitched sound as they chased down their current caretakers.

Ra's voice howled. "For the cookies!"

The cultivators on the mountaintop blinked as the voices receded. From the doorway all the hubbub had occurred, Amber strolled through calm as a fiddle, holding a basket of Lunella's cookies. One of which she was currently munching on, and clearly taking her time to enjoy. With a mouth full of crumbs, she leaned her head down the window of fleeing noise and chuckled. "Easiest. Heist. Ever."

Taking a fresh bite of the ill-gotten gains, she shuffled over towards the rest of them. Her mouth still half-full of food, she swallowed and remembered her candor. "They here yet?"

Alexandria took that question as an opportune moment to whip around and cut the horizon with her eyes. Snookem glanced and shook his head no, instead motioning at Nerys. "Not yet. Say, you're on the Exemplar track? Now that I've had that explained to

311

me, I feel like… I might be stuck on that one as well when I get there. Anything to worry about?"

"With the track? Probably not." Nerys formed a ball of **Blood** Mana above each fingertip, but both Snookem and Amber locked eyes with the energy and began having questions. Emilia chuckled. "Noticed? Good. It seems I will be able to teach everyone something after all."

Snookem rolled up his scroll and sat up on his pink cloud, providing a rare moment of full attention. His brow furrowed as he took in the sight of the multiple orbs, not all of them red. "I can tell all of those are **Blood** Mana. I can also tell that those aren't all on the same *Tier*. Three of those have different Essences as their base formula. That is *not* how **Laws** work. *What?*"

Amber did not scarf down the next cookie. "I'm… I'm with Mr. Bookem. I am tied to the **Portal Law**. One node, on Tier four, with one *set* combination of Essence types, and one *set* ratio within those Essence types. Not whatever's going on… in *that*. Could you explain?"

Emilia smiled like a blood drinker provided an invitation to enter. "Of course. My **Law** requires it of me. Blood Essence is… a lie? A convenient lie, perhaps. Many creatures require blood to live, but not all creatures have the same blood. Nor kind, nor type, nor details within. Some blood is blue, some blood is red. Some have no color at all, and could even be toxic to the prior two. Yet all these differences are lumped in under the same word. **Blood**."

Nerys rolled the orbs of differing colors across her hand to swirl them on her palm. She did not quite have the skill to do tricks, but this was a beginning. "In the old world, it was thought that celestial, fire, water, and 'something else' made blood Essence. The 'something else' is earth Essence. But only if the person had the four affinities to match, and the inclination."

Vanishing all but one ball, Nerys held up the globe of celestial and water Essence. "In addition, the old world rarely had cultivators of more than two types. Yet the Church had oodles of blood cultivators. If the true formula requires four Essences, but the availability of those with the inclination is two or less, how did they have so many?"

The orb shimmered red and rose above her palm to form a falling teardrop that shuddered in place. Never reaching her palm, never fully finishing a descent. "Human blood by itself has multiple types, and if one was going from mundane to mundane, then one would need to transfer either the exact type... Say 'Type A' to 'Type A,' or one special type that can give to all. Let's call that one... 'Type O.' After that one dungeon from the Lion Kingdom."

Creating a second orb, she shifted her Mana to allow for earth Essence to be part of the mixture. "Due to there being so many different and problematic combinations of blood when the mundane scales up to cultivator and Cored Beast, it appears that the Tower applied its own solution. One that is confusing, unless the Wood Elves have been explained prior."

All of the orbs returned as falling teardrops above her extended fingertips. "The **Blood Law** is not a primary, front-and-center concept in any node. It *is*, however, secondary or tertiary in *many* nodes. Instead of a single **Law** of blood, there are many nodes of blood, each connected together into a single consciousness that forms the Heavenly of **Blood**. Many minds, as one. Like the Wood Elves, they form a gestalt consciousness."

Emilia then made a point to single out the second teardrop she had created, the one with the earth Essence mixed in. "With normal Essence, the earth to water ratio affects fluidity, thickness, and iron count."

Her finger motioned to the third teardrop over. "Fire parts in differing amounts determine blood type. The type with zero fire Essence parts is our precious O-type. While the ones with too many parts become poisonous. Earth increases toxicity. Water affects venomousness."

She then formed a new teardrop, this one a mixture of dark browns and violets. "This toxic blood? I severely overdid it on the earth and fire Essences. Yet still, there's an old-world creature that used this blood type to live, and therefore it counts as a valid combination. It bit me in the leg once; I had corruption in my techniques for years until I learned how to use venom as a cultivation aid."

She dismissed all her teardrops. "As a Mage, I suffered toxic burnout from using a combination of **Blood** Mana that I didn't have the base Essences for. I could do it due to Mana allowing all types, but it was not without cost."

Snookem partially complained. "Hey, I was studying those!"

Emilia chuckled, her arm extending towards the spire's ridge.

"My personal specialties lie in taking from my enemies, and providing for my allies. *New* blood just entered my effective range, which should be the same range as—"

"I see them!" Alexandria proudly proclaimed. "They... Those are not Gargoyles. Those are just people. Olympians, based on the tiny moustache and toga-type clothing."

Nerys grinned. "Correct, Alexandria. Now observe further. This is how one makes Mage jerky. First, the power invested in your attack must breach the Aura of your opponent. You cannot affect their body with a special effect unless you do. The only alternative being that you can get through by default if they didn't have the correct defenses up at all. Second, they must believe that they have blood, and given the bodies in use, they certainly do. Third..."

"Third?" Alexandria's eyes were still firmly on the prize.

Nerys flashed a vampiric crimson, her attire aglow with brimming power as her scarves shifted around her like an ocean wave. Her outstretched hand made a crushing grip, fountains of blood exploding in the distance as she crunched all the Olympians together. "Power Overwhelming."

The extracted plasma and blood then surged towards her, the pooled Mana-rich fluid warbling like an orb affected by soundwaves, as if it was picking up some song and dance routine elsewhere on Caltopia that was heavy on hard-bass drops. The bodies of her... perhaps not defeated, but certainly demoralized foes continued their approach with a significant increase of apprehension, and decrease of speed.

Snookem stretched, got off his cloud, and meandered over to Amber while some furious air collected above his extended pointer finger. "Excuse me, High Mageous? Could you please?"

"Of course. More convenient this way." Amber waved a cookie around in a circle. While only a single small portal formed near her, multiple opened in tandem in the flight-path of the approaching undesirables. "Give or take about forty-two rips? They'll last two more seconds."

Snookem would have to complain about being hurried later. He dropped the finger channeling the furious air towards Amber's mini-portal, and sent it through. One the other side, each of Amber's forty-two portals released an identical dot of furious air into the midst of the enemy formation, which was flying conveniently slow.

The Mana in their vicinity looked at the mass-duplicated furious air-effect, snapped its metaphorical fingers in a Z-formation to proclaim an 'aw abyss no,' then had to decide where all the extra Mana was going to come from in order to pay for the existence-debt of the forty-one *other* furious air dots. All Mana around the Olympians was ripped from both their surroundings and themselves as forty-one effects demanded payment to continue existing, making the space they occupied look like it was being clawed and chewed apart by a horde of comically angry cats meowing in a language made of cavitation bubbles.

This instant drain of all the Olympian's resources dropped them out of the sky, as they no longer had the juice to continue flying. Their demon 'helpers' were of no assistance. Before that was ever a worry, on the other claw, the forty-two dots of furious air, existence-debt paid, unleashed their intended purpose.

From Alexandria's perspective, angry orbs of plasma detonated from forty-two tiny points within the enemy formation. The orb-shaped explosion merged together, rolling out as a light blue shockwave when the extreme pressure differences created by Snookem balanced out. What reached Alexandria was a prickly breeze, a sensation of heat, and some tangy static on the tongue. The leftovers of all the air in a space throwing a hissy fit and flipping some tables.

"Smells *off.*" Alexandria's tone was short. "That's not jerky. That's burnt meat."

Nerys stepped up next to her, the globe of blood hovering nearby as the waves over its surface ceased. The cause must have ended, so she absorbed the blood ball like a light snack. "*Hmm.* Indeed. I am corrected. That is burnt meat, in flake form. The Air Dean's little bombs didn't leave much left for the imagination to play with. So much for our extended plan."

Amber started on another cookie, nodding in agreement. "I did my part."

"Better to have it and not need it." Alexandria turned, her writing utensil wildly scribbling on her pad without the quill ever diverging from between the evenly spaced lines. "Thank you for this demonstration. Can we return to work? We have classrooms to set up, and I expect to have a busy library shortly."

"You had the cookies?" Ra's voice spoke with a mixture of suspicion and accusation.

Everyone turned, finding a horde of children that had snuck up on them while the fight had occurred. The noise of the situation had masked their arrival, and all young eyes were on the basket in Amber's hands. A heaving Alha and Jin were dragged along at the ankles, both boys wheezing in exhaustion before the horde dropped them like potato sacks. Alha opened an eye and saw what the children meant, then mouthed the word 'run' at Amber.

Amber could swear that she heard Ephira Mayev Stonequeen cackle and laugh as clouds drummed with thunder overhead. For some reason the thunder sounded like the words 'just desserts.' Perhaps she imagined it?

The cookie was kept firm in her mouth as she turned to flee, running when the horde charged her with a *reeeeeeee*!

CHAPTER FORTY-FIVE

Odin's face was purple and pruned from the amount of pent up rage he'd accumulated 'talking' with the old man. He kept snapping his fingers at the Administrator, hoping it would erase the annoyance right out of existence in some sandy particle wave. Alas, he had no such luck. He lacked the stones. "Zeus! I said my name is Zeus! I have said this twenty-seven times! How do you continue to get this *one* simple difference wrong?"

"On purpose, of course." The Administrator was calm as a cloud as he practiced standing on the pommel of a floating sword. The Strikers had gotten him up here, but he had not mastered stable hovering with them yet. His stance wobbled on the hilt, clothing fluttering with the breeze, and otherwise didn't seem bothered about the remaining details.

Odin held his forehead and kneaded the Mage-flesh like it was a potato to be crushed and remolded. Perhaps it would help the Mage-quality migraine. He wasn't even going to question where the sword had come from. The object had flown to Artorian, halting under the old man's metal feet right when those replacement sticks had stopped putting out thrust.

He'd never achieved that kind of teamwork with Lazuli, and the thought served as another notch on the irritation stick. "I'm going to kill you, Artorian. I'm going to make it slow. I'm going to make it hurt."

"Oh, we're back to this, are we? Well, come on then, Spud. I've got all day." Artorian exhaled, his eyes on the battlefield down below while the brick-house of potato-meat simmered in front of him. Mentally, he queued a finger-tap onto a strained, weak, but open mental connection. The forum responded to his tap as Anansi's presence made itself felt, telling Artorian he could speak to the arachnid. <Anansi, any updates? The backup forum Pylons seem to be holding for now.>

Anansi replied with a couth attitude and professional demeanor. <Some, sir. I'm afraid they are degrading faster than the webs can hold them. No amount of sticky tape fixes a Core problem. The Core problem in this case being that the Pylons are... well, they're dissolving. Quite literally. Like pouring water over spun sugar, they turn into goop, and the goop evaporates. The Task Manager is painfully skilled and thorough. Our operation was found via a meticulous check, like a box to be checked off from a list. We will lose this service shortly.>

Artorian mentally clicked his tongue. <A shame, but that's how the cookie crumbles. Please send a few spiders to my new office aboard Zephyr? We must prepare to do things the manual way for quite a while.>

<I shall come myself, sir.> Anansi said with a puffed up chest. <When my mother rejoins us, I will *not* regale her with news that inferior methods were implemented. Instead, I shall see to a succinct and smooth handover, as she will undoubtedly step to fill my meager silk shoes. Thus I find it only fitting to prepare the carpet.>

<As you see fit, Anansi.> Artorian heaved a content sigh. <The space is currently empty, please feel free to consult with Gomez, Titania, and Zephyr when this is all wrapped up. Speaking of the wrap, my glances show me that we're walking over them handily in every quadrant. Any issues?>

<None, sir.> The spider was smug. <Yasura had a deal with the four great Quacks, and did not interfere. Or is it five? Never know with Quacks.>

They both chuckled, and Anansi continued. <Odin could not find a replacement as potent as Ghreziz, and we can confirm your suspicions that being **Synergized** to that particular specimen did make his Tier-value numerically weaker, even if the end-result of his demon merging allowed for utility that our consensus agrees

made him, and his forces, stronger overall. In this current instance, having a symbiote host counts as additive power, but nothing more. Odin remains a Tier ninety-eight **Revelry** Mage.>

Artorian made a sound of understanding, but didn't interfere with the report. <Odin's Olympian forces, additive bonuses or not, were simply overrun with a whole gamut of effects specifically geared to be effective towards them. The majority of Olympian forces have surrendered, while the demons are... receiving diplomacy.>

The old man scoffed at the notion. <Glad to hear my word-use being appropriated. I really am surprised we did not encounter more problems with the high-rankers. C and below I can certainly understand when it comes to quick turnover. B and up? I expected more of a fight out of them.>

<The Solar Saintess is likely the cause, Administrator.> Anansi mused. <For people who come from the olden times, I am told power was paramount. Fighting Mage-ranked bunnies, goblins, and cats they may have thought to be somewhat beneath them. Or perhaps they thought that until maybe their fourth death at the claws, shivs, or teeth of one. The sight of the reaper also likely did not help, nor their glorious leader bickering above the palace. Some took one glance at the top of the dome where Amaterasu sat, understood their situation by taking in the carnage around them, and put their hands in the air.>

<A clean sweep, then?> Artorian approved. <Good. I expect Spud to boil over soon enough, he's been stewing. I'm surprised he's held out for this long. Though, from where he keeps looking, I think that he believed he would win this handily if the situation came up. A society of nothing but his *precious* elite? The disappointment is eating him alive. Though, why he thought that his oppressed workers wouldn't rise up given even the smallest chance? That I don't know.>

Anansi chuckled, the connection frazzling before abruptly cutting out. An effect that didn't appear intended. Merely fated.

Artorian looked up from his ground-study musings, watching the expression-ripples traverse across Spud's fuming face, then spoke. "Well, this looks about wrapped up, doesn't it?"

"I haven't agreed to any terms, Administrator." Odin growled, clearly seeing the same outcomes play out on the ground that Artorian did. Yes, his forces were cleaning and clearing through whole platoons at a time when they were higher ranked. However, with the enemy forces of assorted dungeon critters not diminishing by the smallest dent, his strongest were constantly overwhelmed. Unlike his Olympians, the dungeon beasts did not appear to have a mental fatigue limit.

His Mages lasted a good few deaths, but either upon separation from their demon, or a particularly humiliating or horrifying end, they called it quits. Soon enough, his forces were a quarter of what they had been while the dungeon-crew remained in full force, keeping up the same unrelenting attitude and battle strategy. He may have spent two whole centuries practicing to specifically counter Artorian's skillset, but the geezer's clear rank and Tier difference was really biting him in the stew right now.

In the prior fight, this preparation had allowed Odin a clean sweep. Barring the unwelcome interruptions that had roadblocked his win-streak. In the current fight? The variables did not favor him.

Artorian's form, likely due to those mangled metal sticks poking out from the bottom of his robe, kept steady at a surprisingly neat and even A-rank one. Like there was a Core at work keeping the Mana flow balanced. Odin of course spat that idea away. If he couldn't get his hands on even a single Strong-ranked Core, then clearly an old man couldn't either.

The problem was that the nuisance was now a full and proper A-rank seven! How the Administrator had gained an entire rank, he did not know. He blamed Cal either way. Likely some cheapskate method of rank increasing. The reason A-rank seven was an issue was because it meant that the other six ranks were tucked away into that *fortress* of an Aura. The radiance had dialed down to nothing, but any demons that got close stopped existing like they'd rubbed up against the world's largest Cherenkov eraser, leaving little more than a smear behind before that too was wiped away like a stain from a glass table.

Odin really wanted to attack regardless, but a detail pecked at his mind. Never act incautiously when confronted by a little, bald, wrinkly, smiling old man! All the greatest villains were always old white men. He knew better.

So, he employed the very trick he'd picked up from said shriveled little man. Power mathematics. No special tricks? That meant one rank of Tier seven-twenty came out to a score of seven-twenty.

A beefy number for the body measurement. Six ranks of seven-twenty accounting for Aura, came out to four-thousand three-hundred and twenty. That was *more* than a beefy number.

That was straight up a problem.

Because, when Zeus measured himself, seven ranks of **Revelry** at Tier ninety-eight only came out to a score of six-hundred eighty-nine. His demon had bumped that number up to be above Artorian's base of seven-twenty, but Lazuli was currently subject to the courtyard conundrum. Leaving Odin stranded with all his ranks pumped into his body, coming up a whole thirty-one ranks short from not getting his keister whooped by the Administrator's *prosthetics*.

That was bad math to build a foundation on.

This meant victory via alternative means.

Technical skills could net him some victories, but with Artorian being able to take apart his non-physical Mana techniques like a seasoned artificer disassembled a crossbow, that meant he *only* had those technical skills at his disposal. Fancy fighting styles weren't going to net him a win, much less the desired victory.

Then there were the ancillary factors. Artorian might be feuding with the Task Manager right now, but that being and Zeus were on good terms. So when Odin called up Eternia-quality information on the stick in Artorian's hands, he got the full break-down via a very clean prompt.

Creation Code: C.C.A.A.
Item Code: R.4.F.1.K.1.
Name: The Last Straw.
Creation: Purple Heartwood's Instant Bo.
Type: Bo-Staff.
Material: Silverwood.
Rarity: Artifact.
Damage: Wisdom Attribute.
Special Quality: Rafiki.
Description: Imparts Affliction: 'Blunt Force Corrective Trauma'.
Special Effect: Asante sana Squash banana, Wewe nugu mimi hapana.
Description: Struck foes can communicate only in baboon sounds.

Odin did not want to get hit by that if the special effect actually worked. With nothing invested in his Aura, he wouldn't be able to stop it either. The Administrator has clearly come well-armed enough to beat the tar, the pride, and the fight out of him. He was even egging the Master of Olympus on by keeping only a single rank invested in his body. The gall. The *insult*. He wanted to lay his fists into the old man and claim victory, but the relaxed body language of Artorian said: test that assumption at your earliest convenience.

He had to defeat the old man, while at a strength disadvantage, in a don't-get-hit-by-the-stick scenario, with three fourths of his arsenal missing. *Great.* He was going to need to pull out clever trickery for this one, no matter how much he preferred rolling over his opponents like Raile down there seemed to.

This left Odin with… only three major options. None of which he was keen to dip into.

One: he revealed that A-rankers could cultivate directly from concepts, specifically the ones they were bound to, when it came to personal growth. Then direct that more refined energy into a variety of offensive options, rather than personal gain. There was a chance the more conceptual energy type might bypass Artorian's auto-decompiler, but he only had one shot and it was a toss-up. Worse, once that C'towl was out of the bag, Artorian would know it existed. Possibly a far more dangerous thing to occur than using it in the first place.

Two: Night Lily toxins from Asphodel. Sneaking in had proven disastrous, but the expenditure in elites had been worthwhile. Even a little bit of this stuff coated over the spear he was hiding in his back-pocket, and he might have the win.

Three: a vial of the River Lethe. The identity killer. If he used it… Victory was certainly assured, and the battle won. The breath of heat from above on the other hand… told him he'd lose the war, and every other war thereafter. Dawn would do things to him worse than anything Artorian might do if he snagged the win that way, meaning it wasn't a *win* at all. Ending up in the Asphodel Meadows would be a kindness compared to an existence where he had Dawn's ire.

He tossed option three.

Odin's gaze then looked to the old man when Artorian made a strange motion towards the distance, forming a quizzical face. Zeus's tone was hopeful. "Losing somewhere?"

Artorian's response didn't make a lot of sense. "My yard is so swampy I just tried to tap it for one black mana."

"Sounds like nonsense." Odin crossed his muscled arms.

"I'd have agreed with you…" Artorian paused, his upturned palm now holding a blackened square of voidy mass that clearly confused him. "If it hadn't just *worked*."

Artorian didn't know what he was holding, but Odin did. There was no more time. Artorian was figuring out option one all by himself, even if merely the Tier one **Infernal** version. If he did before Zeus got his attack off, then the option would become moot. That black, Tier one **Infernal** energy might not be Artorian's direct concept, but in a way that made what Zeus was realizing even worse. Mana nodes not even directly tied to him directly were responding to the old man. With Artorian's proclivity for sticking his nose into matters and fingers into pies at a whim, this meant that giving the Administrator more time to keep poking would result in an immediate loss.

Zeus vanished from his spot in the sky in a percussive crunch of high explosives. A heartbeat later, the sky rained drunken electric death.

CHAPTER FORTY-SIX

Odin's javelin materialized, became coated in Asphodel toxin, and then became moot. The hand-and-a-half sword Artorian had been pommel-balancing on moved with the guidance from two of the Administrator's digits. Directed from the same hand that held The Final Straw, as his other held the black square. While the blade itself was not impressive in Tier or Rank, the obvious celestine coating along the weapon's edge was anything but harmless.

Striking tip to tip, Artorian's telekinetically directed sword cleaved Thundy's javelin in twain from spearpoint to haft, forcing Zeus to kick the sky and put distance between them as the blade returned grip-first to Artorian's infernal-coated hand.

Artorian's Strikers flared to life, but his attention leaned elsewhere as he limited his ascent to a slow crawl.

The old man frowned at the blade as it muddled together with the void-like energy that he'd been holding. Giving it a good shake, he cleared the weapon of infernal influences as he invested Mana into patching up the sudden damage it had accrued. Raw energy of decomposition did not go well with that which he wanted to keep whole. "Well, that was *unkind.*"

The sky continued to crack with alcoholic brown electricity as a wide-eyed Odin tensed, his breathing heavy. Option two had just gone right down the drain, but at least option one was not on the verge of discovery. A worthy tradeoff, even if he'd hoped to end it quickly. His mind flashed to option three, but cold shock ran through his veins when he felt his pocket to notice the vial was missing.

Instead he pulled out a small piece of paper? He unfurled it in a hurry, reading only two words. 'No.' Signed by 'Cal.' He crumpled it in his hand and burned it with electric flame, eyes furious as they turned to his direct opponent. "Cheater!"

Artorian was sadly far too busy with the damage done to the blade. A motion of the hand vanished his silver stick, before he cradled the sword like a baby and rocked the weapon while whispering to it. "No, no. You'll be alright. I'm here. You'll be alright. That wasn't intentional, but very much my fault. I'm fixing you up. Are you feeling pain anywhere?"

While Odin could only hear half the conversation, it was clear Artorian was talking to the blade. The tone made him think that the weapon was asking for more than a simple restoration, and an apologetic Artorian was abiding, to repay for causing the unintentional harm. "Yes. I can do that if you want, but are you sure? Well, I'll support you if that's your decision, but I don't want to… Alright. No, alright. If you're sure, I'll Artifact you. Name? Oh. Well, aren't you funny. Very well. Shape?"

Artorian paused. "A… strange request, but if that's how you'd like it, I will do so. Alright. No, he's looking right at us, do you want some spectacle with it? Oh certainly! Yes, yes indeed. Cal will help me, I'll be fine. You are most correct, **Pride** does come before the fall. Thank you kindly for the forgiveness. We'll start right now."

Odin conjured another weapon into existence, charging his opponent with a boom of thunder. An opponent declaring that it was going to be distracted, even for a moment, needed to be capitalized on.

Artorian raised the blade and locked eyes with Spuddy before speaking. "Artifacting."

When Odin realized his mistake and kicked away to avoid the changing blade that was now on a rapid descent, he got everything save for his right leg out of the way in time. Losing it directly below the knee as Artorian mocked him. "Polly says hello! Oh, my apologies. New name now."

Twirling the hilt of the sword that evolved into a claymore with a broken blade of maybe a few inches, Artorian grinned proudly.

"Hmm? More spectacle? As you wish, Polly. Oh, sorry, I mean... No? I can still use Polly? Well aren't you sweet. Thank you kindly, give me a moment for a fresh breath and to ham up the drama."

Posing as he flared his Strikers to cause a plume of heat and light, he presented the blade by holding it to his chest. "It is time to put an end to this war. Do you remember the ex-parrot that you wronged? Be reintroduced! To Ex-Calibur!"

Ex-Calibur's oversized grip was squeezed by both of Artorian's hands as they came together. Had the claymore's blade been full and intact, it would have obscured half his face. Instead, from the broken sharp shard, a void-coated hue overlapped the existing nub in full force. The confines of which were filled up with rainbow colors in the textured pattern of a parrot's wings before erupting upwards to create the full claymore's blade. Fully on display in proper glory, the claymore sported a forty-two inch blade and thirteen inch grip, making the total length of the weapon fifty-five inches worth of spectacle and power.

Odin winced while holding his leg.

Cutting the Mana flow, he did not share the Administrator's luxury of the leakage returning to him. Thundy was now on a severe timer, and the clock was running. Without a complete body, several of his static defenses had already failed, and staying in the air was now a strained endeavor. Crackling with energy, he skipped steps in the procedure and called Gungnir to his hand. "*Phah.* I am rather engaged by a true blade than a humiliating stick."

"I will admit, I was looking forward to you making some baboon noises." Artorian flourished and dropped the blade so its scintillating business end pointed at his enemy. "Justice, on the other hand, will taste just as sweet."

Odin counter-flourished and brandished his weapon, charging it with the drunken lightning Mana still pouring freely from his missing leg. He couldn't cut off all of the leakage, but if he could channel the lost power into being useful rather than it sapping away, he would bitterly accept that reality. "Fine. I am Zeus of Olympus. Odin of Asgard. Supervisor of the greatest realms to have ever graced existence! Let this feud be ended by glorious combat! Though, know this! Should you fell me, I will still not assent to your—"

"I know." Artorian cut in, rudely interrupting as he listened to Polly's request, and filled it. Swinging the blade below him to build momentum, he flowed the motion into the upwards arc of a crescent moon. As he did, lambent Mana sang and hummed from his hands to fuel the sword's desires as the visual speed of the upwards swing appeared too slow. Each few inches of the blade's path became a silvery imprint that artfully showcased where Ex-Calibur had been, until the image of a waning crescent remained imprinted on the sky.

Artorian moved as the background altered.

Amaterasu observed the scene, and shifted her barrier from oranges and red to whites and evening blues, mimicking a midnight sky as the image of the moon flashed and compressed, the image embossing itself into Polly's pommel with a sharp silver sheen. Artorian then became obscured by clouds that looked whisked into reality by oversized paintbrushes.

He spoke the words the sword wished him to, the opener of the new technique tree. "Tsukiyomi Series. Excalibur Style. Lakelight Legend."

With the blade held high above his head, Artorian shifted his Auric fortress into a compressed Sword Aura as the image completed, prompting Gnomish musicians to take a cue. Beginning with a chorus of Wisp voices, 'White Light Majesty' began to resound through the space as a constant cone of force erupted from Artorian.

The shivers that crawled over Odin's skin felt sickening. To his eyes, Ex-Calibur's blade grew enormous as the power pooled into the weapon and burst from the hilt, forming a massive silver beam of moonlight in the shape of a sword. The rainbow striations within the weapon momentarily replaced to allow this new luminance to find a home. The realization that Artorian had swung down while appearing to remain immobile delayed his dodge.

Artorian spoke the second set of words requested of him, acting as intermediary for Polly's act of justice. "Ex-Calibur Style. Fallen **Pride**."

Odin's left leg twirled and flew through the air as he cartwheeled out of the way, using some of the new clouds as handholds in order to dodge a sword that was the same length as his mountain's height. Spewing rock through the open space as Sword Aura met opposition, Mt. Olympus was messily bisected, gutted past its base. The swing formed a new gorge that split the landscape in twain and spat out sparks of moonlight flame from the cleft ground.

Odin at first felt lucky that he'd gotten away with merely the ironic cost of a leg. With the lack of both legs, however, he suffered the expected problems of no longer having a complete enough Mage body to uphold his cultivation skills, causing full technique failure. Falling from the sky, Odin hurled Gungnir at Artorian as a last ditch kill effort, howling out his anger. "Curse you!"

Yes, he would hit the ground very hard, but Gungnir never missed!

Artorian looked down on the man falling into the burning canyon with a flat, neutral expression as his grip on the sword twisted to prepare for an upwards follow up. The mountainous blade angled to intersect with the falling spud. "You're fired."

Odin raged mid-freefall, unable to adjust his trajectory enough to avoid being demolished by the moonlight blade as **Pride** cut deep. The swing however, wasn't finished. Continuing upwards, Ex-Calibur also enveloped Gungnir in its strike, destroying the entire weapon outright and preventing that pesky 'always hit' effect. A weapon that didn't exist couldn't fill its function, after all.

Artorian huffed with his chest puffed out, momentarily affected by **Pride**, considering the win 'only right.' He then frowned, looked at the sword as it contracted back to the standard fifty-five inch length as the moonlight effects faded, and shook Polly like a baby's rattle with both his hands. "Stop that."

Ex-Calibur mentally apologized, then sent over the next request. This one put a giant smile on Artorian's face. "Now *there's* a thought! Sure!"

He then looked straight up at Ammy. "Dear! Could you bubble or shield all the allies?"

Intrigued, the Incarnate shifted her attention to make the scene less thematically fitting and more one of pragmatic functions. With the mystical sky effects draining away, the music left as well, as each friendly combatant contained within her disintegration field gained a shiny sheen. Ammy then pointed at the mountaintop below Artorian. Or what was left of it. "All set. His bind point is right there. He will be back in three, two..."

"Ex-Calibur Style." Wasting no time, Artorian one-handed Ex-Calibur, performing a mighty spin while condensing his Sword Aura around the claymore. He then hurled the empowered weapon like a dagger straight at Odin's spawn point. "Mystic Lake!"

Odin woke in a fresh form.

He got as far as a blink before feeling stabbed by the sky itself, his location changing from the top of the split mountain to all the way under it. Breaking through layer after layer of rock with a rainbow sword impaled through his chest.

Ex-Calibur hit with enough force to turn the Olympus region —mountain included—into a dust bowl. All neatly contained within Dawn's field as the blast buffeted those within, causing catastrophic damage to anything and anyone without a shiny sheen.

At the bottom of the devastation, buried under tons of hot, glowing dust, rubble, and molten rock, Odin sputtered and spat out granulated destruction. His upwards movement to stand was enough to throw all those tons of dust from his being. He felt woozy, and strange. "What... What just hit me? Did I die?"

The question was rhetorical. He most certainly had, and had respawned once more at a new bind point, as the previous one no longer existed.

Odin couldn't see past his own hand as he waved it in front of his face, the swirling waves of dust so packed and thick that there wasn't a whole lot of difference between where he was and the filthy hurricane in the exact center of an active volcano. Everything was browns, reds, heat, wind, and spin. Lots of spin.

"You did. Won't be the last time, either." Ex-Calibur was seated nearby on rubble as an androgynous human form dressed in rags. "That's the least of your problems. You ruined my world. I ruined yours. I have no idea what I saw in you, but breaking both you and everything you've built isn't enough to compensate for what you did to me. What you did to so many."

Odin spat. "As if this is my fault? I—"

"Yes," Ex-Calibur coldly retorted. "Your fault. You are to blame."

"Lies!" Odin was given no further chance to speak as a Spirit-infused glass chair bashed him across the face and sent him rolling across the ash and rubble.

Artorian, with said chair in hand, calmly dropped his metal feet to the ground as the thrusters kept steady enough to allow for a soft landing. "We don't want to hear it, Spud. You either have no grounding to understand how horrible you've been, or have chosen to be oblivious to the moral measurement scale. If you can't understand that *you are the problem*, you will simply be dealt with. You are mistaken if you thought I ever came here to *convince* you that the jig was up. I am here to *enforce* it. Or did you forget what I told Brianna about handling supervisors that get uppity? *'If I must.'* You brought this on yourself. You're out."

Odin roared as he shot up, but was bonked on the head by the glass table that accompanied the chair. Artorian had pulled it right out of a brand new storage ring provided by Minya, and smacked Thundy with it a second time for good measure. The table didn't dent, but Spud's face sure did. A third whack, and it was back to respawn for Jasper.

Odin gasped when he opened his eyes a few seconds later, once again bound to a different point that appeared to be some mostly intact, bubbled-in, flat courtyard. This time, he was surrounded by other demons? What a strange—

Zwingggg!

Odin's perspective went topsy turvy as his head was removed with no pause in the celestial reaper's scythe swing. He processed the event barely in time to find himself in the crowd of demons again, but this time hunkered low so the swipe passed over his noggin. Slightly panicked, he looked around and grabbed a nearby demon. Robur, looking hollow and vacant while on his knees, barely seemed to recognize him.

Odin spoke to him in a hurry. "You! You were important. What is—"

"You picked Robar? Well, as good a choice as any, I suppose." Artorian spoke from above as Ammy let him into the bubble, the thrusters vectoring to find Artorian a seat on the celestial reaper's oversized shoulder like a pigeon having found a spot on a statue. When had Adam even become so large?

Artorian didn't provide time for consideration. "Robar! Can you look up at me, kiddo? Are you still with me?"

"No, do not listen to him!" Odin's authority fell on flat ears as the demon looked up without a fight left in him. He was worn, and just wanted this to end. Anything was better than this. Wordlessly, Robar nodded.

"Good!" Artorian had a chipper tone. "Want to become spokesperson for the end of this whole mess? It can all be over right now, if you want. For all involved. I don't think there's many who would begrudge that you made decisions for them. Based on what I can see, you're all about of the same mind."

Odin, of course, wasn't going to take this sitting down, but his words were prevented by a knock on the head. Some silver stick had whacked him! When he opened his mouth to complain, only baboon sounds came out. *Ho-hoo-hoo. Haa-aah-aah*!

Aghast, he gripped his own neck, but it was too late.

Shaking his fist up at the Administrator to complain, the old man let his Aura swoop over the confined space like a broom and dustpan, cleaning up the area in a hefty circular swoop as he drew in with cultivation and directed where he was pulling from. This turned the bubbled-in courtyard, now noticeably floating in mid-air over the giant dust hole that the Olympus region had become, spectacularly clean.

Artorian cocked his head sideways, wondering if he could do that for the whole region while he was at it. He glanced up at Ammy still sitting at the very top of the region-enclosing dome, and made finger motions at her courtyard bubble. His Aura couldn't make it through hers, but when she dropped it away to let him at it, his follow up sweep proved his assumption to be correct.

This resulted in the entire Olympus region becoming a wedged-in cylindrical hole rather than a haphazard impact crater.

The courtyard descended from the sky, slotting into a hewn out spot of the actual ground below them. The demons suffered a hard fall from the drop not having been particularly gentle, but everyone who was bubbled enjoyed harmless bouncy fun as Amaterasu thought it amusing to alter the confined space within her large dome. This also served to suppress anyone else's Aura, including funny ideas from Odin as he, much like all the other vanquished in attendance, were pressed to their knees.

She considered the diplomacy concluded, and the time for verdicts to be at hand.

Inhaling deep, Artorian exhaled with comfort as the excess Mana he was holding onto from converting rock, rubble, and debris to energy, turned to rain. Polly had wanted a lake, after all. Olympus Lake sounded pretty good!

He clapped his hands together, then watched as friendly forces began to cheer while hurtling through the space. Bouncing in their bumper bubbles while attempting to adjust their trajectories, in order to smash into someone else and send them flying. Some Dwarven Marines in particular were making an entire game out of it, with points.

One of them shouted: "Goblins are worth five!"

The battle was won. The fight over.

A few demons were still struggling to hang on to hope, but they acted skittish, cornered, and like they understood the full implication that there was no way out. A cursory glance at their situation dashed the last embers of that hope. They had been meticulously defeated in detail, and now an Incarnate was pressing the issue, having stayed out of it seemingly to prove the point that she had never been necessary for this outcome to come to pass.

She had merely dictated the size of the arena.

Seeing that they had well and truly lost, the demons slumped to the ground, raised their hands, and appeared relieved when the shouting rose. Accepting defeat was a fate less stressful than continuing this Mad Max carousel ride.

Artorian glanced to his left, picking one of the defeated out from the crowd. "Well, Pencil?"

The groaning demon rolled over and away from the speaker while Richard loomed over his monstrous being, ready for round thirty-seven. Pencil adopted his tiny mouse form when Ammy took off some of the Auric pressure keeping them all glued to the ground. She'd made her point.

When Pencil lifted himself to observe why he'd been addressed, the question filtered through slowly, but ended in him shaking his head and dropping it back down to the hard stone floor before putting his hands up. "I yield."

Nodding in approval, Artorian's vision moved a few inches. "Hanekawa?"

Hanekawa's eyes were locked on Halcyon, who was swimming in the sky overhead; looking down on him like a fish to have for breakfast. One that had been tail-slapped into a tender fillet. "I didn't wanna do this in the first place. I yield."

Artorian looked to his right, interrupted by Odin who physically approached him with lumbered steps. Like a bear trying to seem intimidating. A two-fingered swipe from the old man shot an object right into Thundy's forehead, dropping the troublemaker down onto a knee. The injured Mage hooted out in baboon to complain about the bruise on his forehead, but Artorian could tell that Odin had just asked what hit him. So the Administrator smirked and pointed as the weapon above him was turning back into a person.

Odin winced. He'd been hit by, he'd been struck by, a smooth... hilt?

Artorian smugly smiled, indulging the last of Polly's requests. "Finish him."

Ex-Calibur grinned and sat on solid air, stealing one of Odin's hidden tricks. One of Polly's arms partially transformed and became a rainbow claymore blade, the tip rising to apply execution. "You're not rid of me. Did you think you were? You're stuck with me, *Spud*. You are now my cracker."

Odin squinted at the parrot, then concentrated on himself and shattered into a thousand pieces, denying Ex-Calibur either victory or the room to gloat as he escaped to his seed Core, and refused the next pull into another body. As it was Odin's choice, the body then faltered and failed to complete, turning it back into particles. Leaving the grumpy, defeated man to grumble in his seed Core.

Ex-Calibur hovered over to Artorian as the blade arm turned back to normal, then high-fived the Administrator with the old man only needing to move his hand straight up to receive it, smiling as they spoke to confirm the win. "Flawless Victory."

CHAPTER FORTY-SEVEN

Robar felt his senses return to him as the rain ran down his face. The squirrel-shaped demon blinked a few times, sitting up to feel at his neck. His head definitely *felt* attached, but certainty was not affirmed of that fact until a telltale and expected sound did not pass his ears.

No 'zwing' put a lot of health back into his little squirrel heart.

An old, grandfatherly voice hummed from behind the demon. "Welcome back."

Looking behind him by rolling his head back, he saw the Administrator working on some pages while upside down. Rolling to straighten that scene, Robar then sat up on his butt, looking around to get more of a sense of self and current location.

He was in a very deep cylindrical pit in the ground where a mountain had once been. There was a summer shower coming from a bright blue sky, and he was sitting on a glass table that appeared shielded from the rain, while people in bubbles played some kind of physics defying game by throwing themselves at others.

Surrounding this table were multiple chairs, most of them filled.

At twelve o'clock, Scholar D. Kota sat with his dungeon Wisps in front of him, each snuggled on their individual fluffy pillows placed in a miniature gazebo. One pink Wisp, one purple Wisp.

The three of them were talking about logistics, the scholar noting down the good ideas resulting from the discussion.

Robar turned slowly, going around the table.

The one o'clock seat was strangely decorated. Reverently so, as floral garlands had been wrapped about the chair, its edges lined with goblinoid fetishes. The seat was occupied not by a person, but by a finely carved totem of some old goblin that had clearly been loved by every single crafter involved in the project. The ivory skull face paint on the well-detailed head stood out. As if in prayer, the goblin's wooden hands pressed together in thought and thanks. Like death was an old friend he'd shared the table with.

Robar searched for some kind of name, and found a descriptor on a plate that had been ceremonially hung from the goblin effigy's neck. 'Bob. - The best of us.'

The two o'clock seat was also vacant, though this one lacked any fanfare. A small metal plate had been hung across the top lip with the message of who was supposed to occupy it, and why they weren't here: 'Occultatum. Currently in Eternium.'

The three o'clock seat was taken by a person that Robar initially mistook for a tree. When the branches moved and morphed to form more of a bark-clad Dryad, Robar tossed all assumptions of that arbor being another respectful totem, and gained the stern feeling that he was looking at **Nature** personified. Her form was elegant and beautiful, some of the branches lush with vibrant leaves and blooming carnations.

She was handling the paperwork that the pink Wisp handed over, the effigy of **Nature** dutifully double-checking the work, making minor corrections, then sliding it over the table towards the next individual.

When Robar momentarily met eyes with Brianna, the individual present in the four o'clock seat, he felt the deep urge to respectfully inline his head. Offering a small wordless bow, the distinct sensation of a knife removing itself from his kidney made him thankful for his sharp senses. Or sharpening senses? Much of the world remained a dull blur, as while he knew it was raining, the sound hadn't registered yet.

The Dark Elf clad in extremely refined regalia accepted the documentation, then either slid it to the next person with commentary, or remained silent and passed the form behind her. Handing her current missive off to an invisible shape that blurred at the edges during movement, Brianna smiled lightly at knowing that the squirrel had noticed her knife. Robar couldn't be certain, but several hundred unseen servants would not have been an incorrect guestimate of what lurked behind her.

Robar watched as Brianna studied the latest piece of paper. She hadn't handed it off to one of her innumerable invisible attendants yet. Instead, she placed it onto the table and slid the page towards a dapper Gnome, one surrounded by a veritable horde of floating geometric shapes.

Robar... wasn't going to try to make sense of that, listening in to the words instead as Brianna spoke. "This one will be too complex for the basic conversion package. The rank may not be at A-zero, but the makeup and abilities of this B-ranking demon put it above the threshold of Journeyman-quality tomes. This one needs to be in the Master section. Skip the Expert rank entirely. Both Bura's Air-Thorn and Tornado Fortress abilities are vastly above average. These tricks class as 'overpowered' for the tier they are, so up he goes. We don't want any Journeyman players who get ahold of these toys to roll through whole zones."

One of the geometric forms accepted the paper and manipulated it with unseen hands. Robar felt the static push of telekinetic forces at play, but knew better than to comment. The geometric shape beeped and dooted at the Gnome, but the pattern was indecipherable to the demon. The Gnome's response was easier to grasp as he first replied to another geometric shape that appeared slightly upset at what had been dooted.

Deverash kept calm. "No, he's fresh to the clan. He's welcome to ask about what he doesn't understand. Just because you've heard it a hundred times doesn't mean he can't hear it his second time. He used to be a Spotter; asking for clarity is ingrained."

The Gnome flipped over the page and touched his fingers to the empty space, writing up a swift explanation as cobalt ink covered the page with text. "So long as the matter is their choice, there will be no problems. So we must facilitate the transition and measure out which section of the library to place them in. We have so far done this by comparing power to section placement, and we have nicked Tim's quality system for the filing process. If those values get bumped up a rank in Eternia for balancing, that ball is out of our court."

Robar snuck a peek.

Preliminary balancing project: Eldritch Tomes.
Rank Levels to Cultivation comparison table.
Generalized measurements only, supervisor bias included.
Values not indicative of a demon's actual cultivation base.
Novice - F-rank.
Beginner - E-rank.
Apprentice - D-rank.
Student - C-rank.
Journeyman - B-rank.
Expert - A-rank.
Master - S-rank.

Deverash motioned around the table. "Cal compiles who is who, what they have, and what they can do. They are trying to determine an initial book placement. Chandra is in contact with Alexandria, and is adding more specified filing details based on Cal and company's measurements. Brianna then takes those suggestions, and does a personal control check on the demon in question to see if anything was missed; or if some power, ability, or skill should have more weight to it in the determining process. She's very good at sussing out strengths and weaknesses. Some abilities look harmless until you approach them from a different angle. If we're not careful, one will slip through the cracks, and then we suddenly have a red mist that devours everything living on whole landscapes, and keeps self-propagating as it does so. These demons—as Eldritch Tomes—will be able to impart knowledge of their specific skill set, so we want as little to leak as possible. We can't prevent people from reading them, but we can at least try to section away the worse ones under a higher clearance."

He then motioned behind the Dark Elf. "If Lady Brianna finds no errors, the document is added to processing. That demon is taken from the pile, and spell-formed into an Eldritch Tome after being sat down and explained the what and why of the operation. So far, none of them have put up any fight and have been glad for the reprieve. Some of them already have the scheming glint in their eyes back, so we're getting this done while the going is good."

Deverash made a notation on his page, then motioned to himself. "We are the stage where personalized corrections apply. If Brianna finds something, then the automated process isn't going to work. We don't question the reason, and we go through the process manually. The pile of woodland creatures in the middle of the table are the gathered demons that we expect to run into this issue with. Also, hello Robar. I can see you listening in, and yes, you are on this list."

Robar had forgotten entirely that he was present, blinking and then nodding in swift apology as he had completely forgotten not to stare. Dev spoke to the demon while his eyes returned to the paper. "Stay seated. We'll get to you when we can. You're a special case. Artorian and Dawn are working on your file."

The squirrel did not feel the best about being singled out, but nodded politely all the same. He stopped paying attention to the Gnome's explanation for one of the geometric shapes, and turned around fully so he faced the old man flanked by a massive gourd of ink. The Administrator's eyes flicked up, then returned to his work before speaking. "I'm currently processing Pencil, Robar. Do you understand why this is happening?"

Swallowing hard, the squirrel found his voice. "I was expecting… a far worse fate, if the battle was any measure. I have been in many a field where strength and power has determined the day, but having my very will to fight attacked? That… that's *new*. I plead defeat. Please, no more. I would go hollow with even one more death. Tell me what you wish from me. I yield."

Artorian understood and placed his quill down. "I will take that as a no."

He motioned at the Incarnate next to him, Ammy pausing her concentration to wink at the squirrel. Robar didn't have the mind to formulate a response. He was just glad not to be a smear. "That… that is a no. I was a direct summon by Barry the Devourer. His end should have spelled mine, but we are all trapped here. A plan went around that, if we are stuck here anyway, we should rule the place. None countered the thought. Many countered the effort. We are now at the mercy of our captors, but I don't know what is needed of me unless an exposition on taxes is required. I am good at taking and regulating, but not at being fair."

The person in the seventh seat clicked his tongue, Father Richard leaning back with crossed arms. "*Bheh*, another one that is behaving. Eventually, we're going to get an uppity one and then I can do my part. Constantine always leaves an itch on my knuckles after I am forced to stow my dusters."

Ammy chuckled, turning to the other old man of the group. "Richard, you are the one who chose the job! You wanted to be the enforcer, yes? That there is nothing to enforce is positive."

Richard pressed a hand to his chest, bowing slow and deep with utter respect. "My apologies, Saintess. It is as you say. I shall contain myself."

"Always so polite, Richard." Ammy's eyes sparkled with amusement. "Your demeanor always reminds me of the old ways in the old days. If you're not pleased with having nothing to do, could you check on the major town centers? I'm keeping tabs on all matters, but some require an in-person touch from a caring hand. Adam is playing Silverwood tower defense with the Wisps. The Chosen are all catching up with the army, and this round table is going to be a rondelle of paperwork. Little else. Barry is handled, Odin is taking a time out, and the demons are being shelved by choice. When all of that is done, we can move onto the next issue."

Richard held his own hands. "May I... ask what that could entail?"

Ammy nudged her nose at his seat, and the open seat next to him. "Henry and Marie did not come. Too busy with their own little projects. Another kingdom management simulation, which they seem to hold in higher esteem than their actual assigned tasks. I don't know if they're absorbed, or have skewed their sense of responsibility during their time in Eternia. The management seems to be all they can think of. That will need... handling."

The mention earned a grunt from both Brianna and Chandra, but no other commentary was forthcoming. They flashed their gazes at Artorian, passing the male deer of who had to deal with that problem. Artorian closed his eyes and loudly exhaled in response. "Not this book. Next book. This book is wrapped. Speaking of..."

He finalized some notes on his current document, and passed it to Ammy, who gave the page to Minya who occupied seat eleven, before looking down at Robar's blank page. "You're up, Robar. Scoot closer. I will tell you how this ends."

CHAPTER FORTY-EIGHT

Robar sat in front of the document that was going to determine his fate as Richard Demonbane left. He thought of that twist of irony, then scoffed. "All those years controlling others with rules. Look at me now. Set to be spined and shelved as some coverless stack of pages."

"Not quite." Artorian scribed in the basic details of Robar's profile. "I'm required to explain that you still get to live a life. That you have chosen it, by defeat or otherwise, was really the only goal. We need to work on the Soul Space, and unless you can conjure a convincing argument for how you would not be a detriment, I'm certain you are intelligent enough to understand why we must shelve you for a while."

"A while?" Robar's tiny squirrel ears perked up. "That does not mean the same as 'permanent,' and I have done my fair share of fine print ledgering to indeed understand this… isn't what I thought it was. What is going on?"

Artorian gave it a minute before responding, both due to some detailed scribbling that needed to happen, and to let Robar ruminate on the implications. All the Savant-class demons were smart, even if they got knocked down a peg.

"What kind of lives could a book…?" Robar stopped his own words while his eyes were trained on the summer showers drizzling in from above. "We're not living in *this* Soul Space."

"Told you he'd get it." Soni's voice chimed in as he portaled in and dropped on the table. The bat then flashed a toothy grin at his old coworker. "Hey there! Look at us! Standing on the table together in front of another big-shot. Strange how the same things happen under different circumstances. How are you feeling, Ro?"

The squirrel blinked mightily. "Did... you just ask me how I am *feeling*?"

Soni's expression fell. "Really? That's the part that got you? I've been on team self-betterment for a long time now. I might be a demon via makeup, but—"

"Nephilim." Adam hovered down from above, a chorus of down feathers accompanying his descent as his very presence caused a pause in local rainfall that the table's shielding didn't already buffet. "You have become another type of entity entirely. Being from a place does not tie you to it by more than circumstances. As the Great Mew the Second once said: 'I see now that the circumstances of one's birth are irrelevant. It is what you do with the gift of life that determines who you are.' I also enjoyed: 'The world pushes us with no mercy and when some push back, the world points and cries evil.' Both are great food for thought."

Robar paled at the celestial's appearance, regardless of Adam missing the now trademark holy reaper attire and accompanying scythe.

"I don't consider outliers to be the norm." Artorian cut in for a moment, eyes still on his work as there was a lot to fill. "However, I do like that of the demon spectrum, we now have a path that allows them a way out. A name and title does allow for convenient referencing, I will admit. Congratulations, Soni. My apologies for doubting you."

"Please do not." Soni grinned, sheepishly rubbing the back of his bat ear. "Demons are not creatures worthy of a lot of trust. The baseline model and social average still comes out to not surgeon-general recommended for anyone. The more extreme cases are toss ups, but you never know with extremes. I just got lucky. I have been considering jumping on the local 'changing form' bandwagon? That or I'm thinking of adopting some moths."

Robar cut in with a short laugh, sneering. "You as a moth Mage? What a joke. Might as well mothball your Magehood and hang up your hat."

Soni snapped back, doubling down. "I don't need to take that from you, hatless. So you know what? Yes, I *will* be a Moth-er Mageous!"

Artorian lifted his vision at that mention. "Why moths?"

Soni shrugged. "How do I explain? You… ran into a tribe of them at one point. I was told you were looking for a place to civilization-settle, and that the spot you found ended up going to your Dwarven friends instead. Ludere and I have had a large amount of assignments around those parts, and picked up the thread you had to put down. I meet with them on an almost weekly basis, and while there was some significant distrust at first, now I'm extended family. I don't know… I love them?"

That was enough for the Mage of that very topic, who instead of a hug, brushed the bat's head with his whole palm. "I'm proud of you."

Robar pressed both his claws to his chest, looking like he was about to retch. After a fourth failed attempt, he blocked the view of the awful sugary goodness with a paw. Soni's pink cheek blush and claw-fingers daintily pushing together was not something the proper demon could handle. "Stop. I *ugh…* my stomach. I already surrendered. This is worse than death. Just tell me what I have to do."

The celestial and bat snickered, both unfurling scrolls from their carry bags for handover. Artorian took them, laid them out, and nodded. "That's exactly what I was hoping for. This will let us settle all of Barry's direct summons in a much better fashion. Thank you for playing courier, please don't let me keep you."

They both nodded, Adam offering an open palm to the bat. "Nephilim. Do you desire a lift?"

Soni bounced up into Adam's hand without a second thought, taking the stance of a captain on a ship's prow, pointing to the clouds. "Allons-y, Alonso!"

"It's Adam." The celestial playfully scoffed.

"Doesn't sound as good!" Soni shot back. "Let's go!"

When Adam left, the rains returned. Soft summer drizzles that were barely noticeable.

Robar once again watched the sky in abject defeat. "Life as a book means I don't have to be subject to that. At this point, I consider the change an improvement. I'll not pretend, Pillow Man. I have an understanding of what you need and why you need it. Demons in any space means we are… going to do what we do. My

attempts to run Alfheim give me more insight than I'd like in your current predicament. I take it that we will exist in the Eternium world?"

"Correct. Though 'exist' is something you'll do regardless. To 'live,' as the correct operative term, is an event that you will do with Tim. Yes. I don't know what will become of this Soul Space yet, but I'll keep working on it with the others until Cal is happy. Your life in Eternium is going to occur through the gamified system when that's up and running again. Names and places will change, but the contract will remain the same."

Artorian turned the page around and slid it towards Robar, offering the inked quill. "You get to pick several factors. Your own book title. The contents you intend to show to anyone who picks up and reads you. A this and that. If you check any of the boxes related to additional liberties, you must then also check an equal amount of boxes in the 'additional limitations' section. You will be able to converse with any other Eldritch Tome housed in the same library tier as you, but much of your agency will be revoked. I cannot, unfortunately, prevent anyone from picking you up and listening to you. So do keep in mind that we are going to take measures against this event."

Robar squinted his vision. "I do not like that you so casually told me several loopholes and ways I could…"

The squirrel's eyes widened in a hurry. "You are *required* to!"

Artorian nodded as the starry eyed squirrel took the quill and wobbled over to the contract. The Administrator confirmed the guess. "I am indeed required to allow you to live. Life includes not being completely locked into a box, even if you are going to be the size and shape of one. A measure of agency and freedom to act is mandatory. Personally, I would have opted to give you considerably more freedom than what is stipulated here, but my ideals of what constitutes a good life—even for souls who are of the darker persuasion—are more generous than the ones I am required to uphold."

Robar scoffed, carefully reading the start of the contract that read like a straight up Mana-Oath. "You would send me on a one way trip to the abyss given half a chance."

"I would indeed. Yet if Soni can do it, then I cannot hold to the measuring stick that none of you can. If one demon can change, all of them can change. You merely lack the circumstances. Please sign every dotted line, and fill in your book, scroll, or document title at the top."

Robar began to scribble like it was second nature. "Reminds me of the office days."

"Why do demons hold to such a setting?" Artorian softly interjected, somewhat curious.

"Yasura might know." The squirrel shrugged. "At best, I know that some Daemon in the past found it hilarious to subject all his lessers to the dull and dreary. My guess was to make the visceral edge more enticing."

Artorian helped turn the page of a document. "I noticed you said 'Daemon.' Not 'demon.' Particular difference?"

Robar stopped his writing to make an unpleasant expression. "Something about how adding an 'A' was special? If not that, there's an old story that the word was supposed to signify the change from a demon into another creature altogether. A divinity, or supernatural being of a nature far above where we began."

He twirled the quill. "Amusingly enough, Nephilim is a word referenced in that same story. It never occurred to me that the so-called giants might be Risen Demons. Fallen Celestials was easy to understand, and the extreme end of the Daemon was something we all know firsthand. Easy to believe what you can see. A demon who went to the other extreme? Not only has that been unheard of, but seeing it for myself is…"

Robar stopped talking as his insides hurt. Just considering all the 'good' required for that to come about made the Savant physically ill.

"Demons have scholars?" Artorian queried as a distraction, tapping the bottom of the page so the squirrel could focus. "What a twist."

Shaking the awful feeling away, Robar leaned heavily into the offered segue. "Everyone has… members of their kind who are different. Demons have a very direct and cruel way of approaching that kind of personality. We are predisposed to pick on the weak, after all, and anything that you can easily oppress is weak. A demon's rules are very simple."

The quill began to tap the same spot on the document as Robar considered the listed questions. "Relations with other demons? This will go poorly, but I take it I cannot omit sections?"

"No incomplete answers, either," Artorian clarified patiently. "Costs of being the loser of the engagement, I'm afraid."

Robar sighed and began to fill. "No need for pity. I understand. I would have done the same, and much worse. Now why can I not...? I am trying to write a name in the section of who I would like to be placed next to and the quill refuses me."

Artorian leaned over to check. "Someone appears to have called 'Dibs.'"

Robur furiously threw the quill down, shaking both his tiny claws to the sky in obvious anger. "Who dares invoke the most holy of laws upon me! I shall sunder their being and crack them like ornery walnuts!"

"Dibs are important?" Artorian asked with complete amusement.

Robar fumed. "Dibs are one of the great nine Daemon commandments! All demons must respect the Dibs. To invoke it is a great act! One not to be questioned! In their whole existence, a demon may call *one singular* Dib. To call one is an act of the most profound honor, for you only have the one! To expend something you will only ever have *one* of? *Unthinkable.*"

He stomped his foot. "*Whomst?!*"

Giggling, Artorian wiped a clean cloth under his eyes, checking his massive ledger for an answer. "Did you not just say they're not to be questioned? Oh, who am I to not indulge in something so funny? The spot you requested was claimed by a... 'Vh'uzathel the Hundred-Armed, Ninth Principality of the Depths, Consul of Mysteries, and Unholy Divine of the East.' The reason appears to be... to be next to the grill?"

"That spice-allergic Hecatoncheires? He couldn't make a rack of ribs edible with a professional chef hovering over his shoulder!" Robar complained. "That butterless biscuit! He's all hands and words! Big talk. No skill! A hundred arms and not one that can operate a spatula."

Robar scrambled to pull at the pages, returning back to the first. "I am changing my book title!"

Artorian tried to stop further giggling, but it was such a difficult attempt that he kept failing tiny hiccups at a time. Helping the demon flip pages, they got back to the first. He even erased the original entry with a bit of starlight. "What would you like it to be?"

Robar glared death at the open space. "Something that tells anyone who witnesses me that I am respectable. That I am a basis for something truly great. That they can pick me up and sneak me away to create some vast, unfathomable project. Some kind of mechanism for a binding contract so that I can do what I'm good at. Bad rules and worse taxes."

Robar muttered. "Calling *Dibs*... I'll... *razzle-frazzle* show you how to do things without invoking a grand commandment."

He chewed the inside of his cheek, finished with the details. Now he needed a good title. "What's a good word for a document where people have to agree on the things it stipulates? One that isn't a contract. Something fancy? Something starting with an 'A.'"

Artorian replied with a Cheshire grin. "May I interest you in '*The Accords*'?"

ABOUT DENNIS VANDERKERKEN

Hello all! I'm Dennis, but feel free to call me Floof. Credit of the name now being accumulated by the vast and powerfully cultivated viking beard, that grows ever more in potency. I'm now counting my writing experience in years, so let me say it is my great pleasure that you are reading this, and welcome back to the goodness!

I have been the designer, plotter, and writer of Artorian's Archives since its inception, and look forward to gracing your eyes with ever more volumes of the story. Indulging my dear readers in secrets otherwise forever obscure.

If you have any questions, or would like to chat, I live on the Eternium discord server. Feel free to come say hi anytime! I will keep you entertained for years to come!

Connect with Dennis:
Discord.gg/mdp
Patreon.com/FloofWorks

ABOUT DAKOTA KROUT

Associated Press best-selling author, Dakota has been a top 5 bestseller on Amazon, a top 6 bestseller on Audible, and his first book, Dungeon Born, was chosen as one of Audible's top 5 fantasy picks in 2017.

He draws on his experience in the military to create vast terrains and intricate systems, and his history in programming and information technology helps him bring a logical aspect to both his writing and his company while giving him a unique perspective for future challenges.

"Publishing my stories has been an incredible blessing thus far, and I hope to keep you entertained for years to come!" -Dakota

Connect with Dakota:
MountaindalePress.com
Patreon.com/DakotaKrout
Facebook.com/TheDivineDungeon
Twitter.com/DakotaKrout
Discord.gg/mdp

ABOUT MOUNTAINDALE PRESS

Dakota and Danielle Krout, a husband and wife team, strive to create as well as publish excellent fantasy and science fiction novels. Self-publishing *The Divine Dungeon: Dungeon Born* in 2016 transformed their careers from Dakota's military and programming background and Danielle's Ph.D. in pharmacology to President and CEO, respectively, of a small press. Their goal is to share their success with other authors and provide captivating fiction to readers with the purpose of solidifying Mountaindale Press as the place 'Where Fantasy Transforms Reality.'

Connect with Mountaindale Press:
MountaindalePress.com
Facebook.com/MountaindalePress
Twitter.com/_Mountaindale
Instagram.com/MountaindalePress

MOUNTAINDALE PRESS TITLES

GameLit and LitRPG

The Completionist Chronicles,
The Divine Dungeon,
Full Murderhobo, and
Year of the Sword by Dakota Krout

Arcana Unlocked by Gregory Blackburn

A Touch of Power by Jay Boyce

Red Mage and
Farming Livia by Xander Boyce

Space Seasons by Dawn Chapman

Ether Collapse and
Ether Flows by Ryan DeBruyn

Dr. Druid by Maxwell Farmer

Bloodgames by Christian J. Gilliland

Unbound by Nicoli Gonnella

Threads of Fate by Michael Head

Lion's Lineage by Rohan Hublikar and Dakota Krout

Wolfman Warlock by James Hunter and Dakota Krout

Axe Druid,

Mephisto's Magic Online, and
High Table Hijinks by Christopher Johns

Skeleton in Space by Andries Louws

Dragon Core Chronicles by Lars Machmüller

Chronicles of Ethan by John L. Monk

Pixel Dust and
Necrotic Apocalypse by David Petrie

Viceroy's Pride by Cale Plamann

Henchman by Carl Stubblefield

Artorian's Archives by Dennis Vanderkerken and Dakota Krout

Vaudevillain by Alex Wolf

Made in the USA
Coppell, TX
28 October 2023

23532810R00208